I.D. RUSSELL

Sudden Death: River City Hell Book 2

PROLOGUE

"Sir, the lab test results have come back. The initial findings are promising and—"

"Promising? We want more than promising."

The man in the white lab coat swallowed deeply, clearly dreading having to impart bad news, but also well aware of what making false promises could lead to. "The tone, in three rounds of testing, has proven to create the desired subconscious implantation."

"Then what is the problem?"

"Hypnotic suggestion in all three cases was successful, but…"

"But what? A success is a success, is it not?"

Arthur Fritz was already impatient. Firstly, with this interruption, and secondly, because they were still behind schedule after the incident with Simon Karlsson's unit a few months ago. The cover up, the payoffs, the complete lab transportation, an overall loss of progress; all had been overcome, bringing them back to the testing phase, but they were only a few weeks away from the planned rollout and now, he was being told that things were only promising. They were supposed to be assured by now.

"Maybe it's better if you come take a look at the most recent round of subjects."

The man in white pivoted in place, clearly assuming his recommendation was going to be followed. Fritz didn't budge.

Impertinence.

These scientists had such high opinions of their place in the organization. They had to understand that they were simply pawns in a much larger game. Even he was just one head of a hydra. But a head that knew his worth.

Arthur Fritz sighed. He looked at his computer screen full of emails awaiting his attention, at a stack of printouts he still had to read through, and a blinking red light showing messages unchecked on his private phone. So much to do, so little time.

"Sir?" the man said when he realized that he hadn't budged.

"Alright." Arthur Fritz pushed himself up to his feet. "But this had better be worth the delay. I've got much more important matters to attend to."

The man in the lab coat led him through stark white hallways, down a level, to the large one-way window on the south wall of one of the testing rooms. Through the glass he saw what looked like a normal family room: couch, television mounted on the wall, easy chair, bookshelf, poster of Sidney Crosby framed with an autograph scrawled on hastily. They'd done a great job on this at least. And yet, something was very wrong.

The easy chair was tipped over, something had been smeared over a wall in a swirling brown arc, the glass frames from the photographs were spiderwebbed. A shape lay on the couch.

"Sleeping?"

The man in the lab coat shook his head. "Look behind the couch," he said.

Fritz moved closer to the glass, trying to see what the man was referring to. There was only the one shape and—

Something crashed up against the glass, pounding, screaming silently, frantically trying to break through, as if it somehow knew that it wasn't another wall it was striking.

He jerked back.

The creature had once been human, male judging from the jagged thing it held in its hand, painting red along the glass like it was a brush. His clothes were gone, his skin dangling down in loose strips, revealing crimson flesh gouged out in chunks. Something grey was slowly leaking out of a hole in the lower abdomen, swaying as the force of each impact on the wall forced it outwards inch by inch.

But it was the face that was the worst of all. The skin had been peeled away, a hideous sinewy toothy visage, crying out in silence, with patches of hair left on what little of the scalp remained.

"How is it still alive?" Fritz asked the man in the lab coat.

"We wanted you to see it before we dealt with him."

"And the other one?"

"That's who's on the couch," he said.

Straining to look past the horrible, flayed creature, Arthur now realized that the shape on the couch was just as twisted. A broken and dismembered pile of component parts, with the head propped up on the blood-soaked cushion, empty eye sockets locked on the black television.

"I see," he said. "And this was the result in all of the trials?"

"No, sir, just the most recent one. We're not sure why the tones prompted this violent outburst but—"

"Set up another trial, right away."

"But sir—"

"This could be an anomaly."

"It could also be the result of the frequency on a certain brainwave pattern and—"

"Theories are useless to us. We want results. Time is of the essence."

The man in the lab coat looked like he was going to protest further, but he bit his tongue. He pressed a button on a console below the glass, sounding a buzzer somewhere else in the facility. They both turned to watch as a door set into the wall of the false living room swung open. Two men in hazmat suits entered, one carrying an electrical cattle prod. The creature stopped its pounding on the glass and turned to face the intruders. It threw the severed organ at one and rushed forward. The technician tried to bring the prod to bear but the thing was too fast, knocking it aside and tackling the man. Blood smeared all over the white hazmat suit. Intestines fell out in a thick wave as the monster bit down through the protective clothing.

Neither one of them could hear the screams, they could only watch as the thing that shouldn't still live took the life of the clean-up crew.

"Good god," the man in the lab coat said as he frantically pressed the button for more help.

"This is far beyond any god," Arthur Fritz said softly. "But a good first step."

CHAPTER ONE

"We go now to the River City Ice Plex as the hometown Jets gear up for a new season. Hopes are high after last year's disappointing early exit from the playoffs and part of this anticipation is due to the team's newest rookie, local boy Rick Hansen."

The image on screen shifted from a panel host in a collared shirt to players on the ice, skating around pylons, taking slap shots, stopping with tiny clouds of snow to the coach's shrill whistle. The helmeted, visored faces were all unrecognizable to Samantha Abraham; she had only a passing interest in hockey, but one man stood out as he stayed in central focus of the camera shot. The voice of the off-screen host narrated the practice footage.

"Hansen, chosen in the second round, was a surprise pick for the Jets. After going undrafted at eighteen, his phenomenal freshman university season put the hockey world on notice. Most scouts had him going later in the draft, a third or fourth round pick, but the Jets obviously saw something in the nineteen-year-old hometown centre and used their forty-eighth pick to snap him up."

The words of Sportscentre analysts blended together in a montage, a gibberish of terminology and descriptive idioms that meant nothing to Sam.

"—good hockey sense and a playmaker's eye."

"Likes to grind for loose pucks."

"Strong two-way forward with leadership potential."

"Still growing into that frame—"

She'd been hearing this talk all summer, on all the local news reports, in the River City Free Press and Sun papers, on Sportscentre, even in the most recent issue of—

"Sam, why did you buy a copy of *The Hockey News*?"

Avital picked up the heavily dog-eared magazine, from the stack on the coffee table in front of the couch. It stood out among the others: *Cosmo, Maclean's, The Economist, Restaurant Owner's* – most of them were her dad's.

"How do you know it's mine?" Sam asked.

Her best friend, dark curly hair dangling near her chin, looked at her with a raised eyebrow. "Let's look at the evidence, shall we?" She flipped to a dog-eared page, showing a picture of Rick Hansen from his university student ID, smiling, with dark hair and eyes, and smouldering good looks. "Bookmarked page to the hottest guy, check. The exact same guy we're currently watching on TV instead of, oh, I don't know, anything else, check. The same exact guy that you told us you—"

"Okay, okay," Sam said, cutting her off. "I get it. Fine. You found out my secret."

"Secret crush?" Erin asked from the other side of the couch with a smirk.

Her other best friend, with the slightly too loud voice and olive skin sat nursing one of their attempts at making a homemade martini.

"I'm just, you know, thinking of taking up an interest in

hockey," Sam said.

"Sure," Avital chimed in. "And the fact that the Jets just signed a super hot guy has nothing to do with it."

"It doesn't," she lied. "I just want to support the local team is all."

"Hey," Avital said. "If they all look like him, maybe I'll start supporting the local team, too."

"Besides," Sam said, "it's a good way to, uh, boost the local economy."

Lately she'd been digging into the world of professional hockey from every angle, trying to figure out if what she'd seen that night on the television was true or just a figment of her overactive imagination.

The night after the incident downtown with Simon Karlsson and his twisted experiments, where she'd stopped a brainwashing project, and put an end to the nightmare of her first year of university, the hockey draft had been in full swing. Flipping through channels to escape the news coverage, she'd landed on the sports channel, saw the NHL draft night: hundreds of kids nervously awaiting their fate like cattle, with tables for each team, and a parade of analysts discussing every move. It was like watching a documentary on a foreign civilization – a world she knew nothing about. The best junior players offered up for the teams to fight over, dangling the carrots of million-dollar contracts and national idolatry. An entire industry of number crunchers debating which player had the most potential to make it big, which teenager had the untapped skills to help a team make it over that hump to greatness and a shot at the Stanley Cup. Under normal circumstances, Sam wouldn't have paid any attention and kept flipping. She didn't even know they televised the draft, but in trying to get away from the news about Karlsson, she'd caught sight of her old classmate Rick Hansen, namesake of the man in motion, former superstar for the John A. MacDonald Rangers, and her ex-boyfriend, being called up on stage.

They had history.

"Local economy, my ass," Avital said. "There's more to this sudden interest than you're letting on."

"Yeah, Sam," Erin said. "You can't fool us, not after what we've been through."

All the images of what she and Rick had shared flashed through Sam's mind, as fresh as if they'd just happened yesterday. The secret crush, the eventual consummation, the Joshua wedge that had pushed them apart, the shattering of his trust in her.

"Have either of you ever made a mistake that you didn't even realize was a mistake when you were making it? Like, you thought you were making the right decision, but it wasn't the right one and that decision was a mistake, which you only realized after the decision that you made, that you thought was right, blew up in your face so badly that it turned out to be the biggest mistake of all?"

"Holy ramble much, Sam," Erin said.

"Was that even English?"

"You remember the guy I dated for a while in high school, Joshua?"

"The one that died," Erin said.

"Yeah. Well, I was dating him, then he went away, and I started dating Rick. But then Joshua came back, and I thought that it was the right call, so I kind of ditched Rick for Joshua. Then he... died."

She still hadn't explained to them how she'd been the one who ended his life. Not like she'd had a choice. She been forced to free Joshua's soul from its imprisonment in the ruby gemstone that kept him alive as a golem. By breaking the jewel, she'd shattered the weird magic that had created him, killed him, and separated him into his component pieces. He'd never truly been alive in the first place. He was a creation of dark science or magic that she still didn't understand. But his last words to her had shown her that she had also been responsible for his transcending his state into something more... human.

"Holy fucking shit, Sam," Avital said. "That is top tier backstory."

"Why did you keep this a secret from us?" Erin asked.

"Isn't it obvious?" Sam said, eyes never leaving the screen. "Because I treated him like dirt. That was the mistake."

And what a mistake it was. Rick had loved her for who she was inside at a time when everyone else had made her a pariah. High school had been hell for Samantha Abraham, but Rick had briefly changed all that. He didn't care about the prominent mole above her eye, that she wasn't model thin, super rich or blue blooded; he'd loved her and that was enough. But Sam hadn't seen that until it was too late and now he was out of her life, back with Debbie Peterson, her arch enemy from high school.

"So that was why it was so awkward when you bumped into him at the mall when we bought the second band-who-shall-not-be-named's tickets," Erin said.

"You can say Factor 5ive," Avital said. "Sam kicked their asses and put a stop to their freaky bullshit."

"I'd still rather not," Erin said.

Sam barely heard them. She was too caught up in Rick's image on television. It was like something from a dream, a guy she'd known in the most intimate way, there on the sports channel. A panel of experts talking about his skating ability, hockey sense, drive to compete. Another decrying his lack of size, the potential problems that could arise should he be unable to pack on those all-important twenty extra pounds of muscle needed for the big show.

"—definitely a top prospect—"

"—extra year in the juniors did wonders—"

Images from the draft flashed on screen as the men debated Rick's abilities. A man in a suit standing at a podium, speaking mutely into a microphone as the flashes of cameras erupted around him. Rick and his family leaping up in surprise in the audience.

"—kid will be a great fit for the Jets."

"—local boy will bring in more fans—"

More images from the draft: Rick approaching the podium to put on his jersey. Rick posing for pictures with the team general manager and owner. Her jaw dropped in horror again, as it had done that night when she saw the man in the grey suit standing proudly. A ghost; the spitting image of a dead man. The owner of the River City Jets was almost the exact twin of Simon Karlsson, manager of Factor 5ive and Radiant Cyanide: the man in charge of the mind control program that had brainwashed women with subliminal messaging in hit songs.

"—jersey's already a top seller."

"Can he step right in and compete?"

Seeing it again proved that it hadn't been her imagination. That man at the draft was the exact same build and size, even shared the same facial features. Slender and angular, with prominent cheekbones and pointed chin, his brow high with slicked back hair. The only difference was that his hair was dark while Simon's had been light. Otherwise, a clone.

"You know you don't have to keep beating yourself up over what happened," Avital said. "Everyone makes mistakes when they're a teenager."

"Besides," Erin added, "who knows if you'd still be together if you'd not dumped him anyway?"

A chill had run through Sam's spine at the sight of Simon's twin. She'd tried to push away the memories of what Karlsson had done to her.

Keep them buried and they can't hurt you.

She rewound a moment and paused the image on screen to make sure. It was there, as clear as daylight. A bulge under the man's shirt. It could only be one thing, a chain around his neck attached to a heartstone: the controlling apparatus of a golem, just like Simon had, just like Joshua's creator and all of the necromancers in Toronto. She couldn't ignore it. It told her that this man, whatever his name was, was another part of whatever was going on. The freeze frame on his face, the way he was eyeing Rick, the lizard-like smile, it painted a dark vision of her ex-boyfriend's future.

"Earth to Sam," Avital said, waving her hand in front of her face. "You spacing out on us?"

She snapped back to reality and unpaused the action, letting the panel go on about Rick to justify their existence on national television.

"Sorry, I was just... thinking."

"Yeah, about Rick, we can tell," Avital said, tossing the *Hockey News* back to the pile and picking up the *Cosmo*.

"It's not healthy to dwell on exes," Erin said.

"I know, I know. But this is different," Sam insisted.

"He must have been some lay," Avital said jokingly.

"Av…" Erin said.

Neither of them saw it. They didn't see Simon Karlsson's twin. For them, life was back to normal after Sam had ended the Rock 'n' Roll Nightmare. Simon was dead, so was Factor 5ive; the mind-control plot ended in an explosion of blood. But his clone owned the River City Jets. How far did the conspiracy truly go?

"It's okay, Erin. He was sort of my first," Sam said.

"Oh, that makes sense then," Erin said.

Her first human, at least. Did Joshua count when he was never alive?

"My first was nothing special," Avital said. "Talk about wham, bam, thank you, ma'am. The whole thing was done in about twenty seconds."

"LOL," Erin said. "Kurtis, right?"

Avital snorted. "I never boned him."

"But you said—"

"Yeah, I know, but that was BS, okay?"

"Why?"

"I don't know." Avital flipped through the magazine. "Everyone else was doing it and I just… you know."

"Lied."

Lies.

The trigger word brought up all of Sam's own lies. They'd been all over the news, the top story for weeks. Retired Detective Inspector Sargent Frank Malone – "Senile Cop Slaughters Band and Manager." He'd taken all the blame for what she'd done. The headlines, the experts postulating about how a respected cop could lose it after so many years in the trenches. "PTSD, Alzheimer's, an adverse reaction to medications"; talking head after talking head working out a city's confusion over a hero cop's stunning fall.

It made Sam sick. Frank had taken a bullet for her. He was innocent, just a retired cop making a few extra bucks as a security guard. Even if he did have a knack for always being where the action was, he didn't deserve the full glare of the twenty-four-hour news cycle, and he certainly didn't deserve having all the good work of his career suddenly second guessed, old cases reopened and re-tried based on "new evidence that the arresting officer was insane." He was just doing a job and he'd flushed a lifetime of work away. For her.

"Just say that you won't stop fighting..." he'd made her promise before she'd fled the scene of Karlsson's twisted experiments as reporters and police made ready to pounce.

She'd desperately wanted to thank him, tell him that she wouldn't let him down, but he was locked up, declared senile, unfit for any exclusive interview, hidden away from the bawling fans of Factor 5ive who wanted his head on a pike.

Lies.

Nobody would know how sick those five guys were, what they were doing to girls. They were all dead now, the subjects of tribute albums and glowing documentaries, no mention of the exploitation, the abuse, the degradation on the internet for anyone to see.

Endless lies.

"Oh, shit, Sam – look," Avital said, tapping her on the shoulder. "Looks like an interview with the man himself!"

The images on screen of Rick skating faded away. The

location shifted to a locker room. A blonde reporter in a tight red top stood next to a sweaty picture of boyish good looks, dark hair a mess, skin glowing in the lights, shirt soaked through. He was still partially dressed in his equipment.

"She's totally eyeing him up," Avital said.

"Oh, come on," Erin interjected, "she's a reporter. She's just doing her job."

"No way, watch her eyes."

"—here in the locker room with Rick Hansen after a tough practice. Rick, you look great. Great out there on the ice and in here. So, how does it feel to be a Jet?"

"It feels great, Dawn," he said, looking down at her. Sam could have sworn she saw the woman blush. "It's a dream come true for sure."

"Is there something extra special about doing it at home? Playing in the NHL, I mean." The woman stumbled over her words.

"Yeah, of course," Rick said. "It's a thrill to do it in front of all the people who have supported me along the way."

"You like a hometown crowd?"

"I think it makes me perform a little better, you know? You don't want to fall on your ass in front of… whoops, can I say ass on TV?"

"I don't think anyone's going to complain about your ass," she said and immediately blushed again.

Rick laughed. "Good to hear."

"I told you that woman has the hots for him," Avital said. "She's flirting so hard."

"Even I can see that," Erin said.

"I've got to help him," Sam said in a slip.

"Help him?" Avital said, confused. "I don't think he's got

14

anything to worry about being hit on by a reporter. She's a total babe."

"Yeah, Sam," Erin said, laughing. "She could hit on me any day."

They didn't understand. Rick was in danger, and she knew it. Whatever Simon Karlsson had done to Factor 5ive, his twin would try to do to Rick. He'd transform him into a golem. But not made in a lab from component parts like Joshua; rather, this new way of transforming a regular human. Duckie had mentioned the process to her back in his lab before he died, but it seemed that Karlsson's group had perfected it. Was his twin going to transform the whole Jets team?

"I didn't mean it like that," she said.

"Wait," Avital said in sudden realization. "Were you a puck bunny in high school?"

"A puck bunny?"

"You know, a girl who only dates guys on the hockey team."

"No, of course not."

"What did that Joshua play?"

"Defence, but that was—"

"Oh, snap, Sam, you dated TWO guys from the hockey team in high school? And you ditched one for the other? Talk about drama!"

"You are just full of surprises. Just when I think we know everything about you, we find out this," Erin said, smirking.

"It wasn't like that, I swear. It was just a coincidence."

"And now you want to 'help'," Avital said, making air quotes, "Rick. Yeah, help him get into your pants again, am I right?"

"Does this season opener seem extra special?" the reporter asked. "Increased pressure to be playing at the MTS Centre?"

"Oh, for sure, Dawn, but I'm just going to take each game one at a time, do my best to contribute, try to play all sixty minutes of hockey and hope that the bounces go my way so I can put the puck in the net."

"You'd like his puck in your net, eh, Sam?" Avital teased.

"Maybe help him hold his hockey stick?" Erin chimed in.

"Guys," Sam said curtly. "It's not... I don't know how to explain it, okay?"

"Still having feelings for someone isn't anything you have to explain," Avital said. "I get it. I mean, if I'd boned him, I'd probably still think about him, too."

"Av."

"What? It's just us girls here."

"Do you have anything you want to say to the River City fans, Rick?" the reporter said, gently touching him on the shoulder.

"Uh, sure. Just that I appreciate all the support, and I hope to have a great season. See you at the rink."

"Serious question, Sam," Avital said when Rick finished. "Was he as, I don't know, vacant in real life? These guys always sound so boring in interviews."

"Puck in the net, one hundred percent, coach, play sixty minutes," Erin said mockingly.

"No, he was actually really smart and..."

She trailed off as it hit her. Interviews. That was the key. She'd been digging into hockey all summer, watching everything she could, and it was staring at her the whole time. Every player said the same thing, some variation on the theme of contributing, hustle, teamwork, playing all three periods, putting pucks in the net. But it wasn't so much what they said that was the tip off, it was the way that they said it: vacant looks, forced smiles, flat voices speaking into the microphone. Was that a sign they weren't human?

"Thanks a lot for the interview, Rick," the reporter said. "It's been a pleasure talking to you. And good luck this season." She touched him again on the shoulder and he smiled at her. She blushed and turned back to the screen. "This has been Dawn Wilson for TSN Sportscentre, here in River City, Manitoba, with the hottest player, I mean, hot new rookie, er, Rick Hansen. Back to you guys."

She'd hoped she was past all this. Sure, she'd enacted brutal revenge on the men who had violated her and so many others, but there were clearly more of them. She tried to bury the trauma deep inside, but there was still another target. She would love to relax and settle back into a normal life with her friends, enjoy second-year university and burgeoning adulthood, but Rick needed her.

The panel returned. The grey-haired host smiled. "It certainly looks like Hansen has ignited the interest of Dawn and the entire province of Manitoba. I'll bet all of River City is looking forward to what he's going to accomplish."

"We'll just have to take your word on that, Sam – he sounds just like any other jock on TV," Erin said.

"Maybe…"

Just what was going on? Did this conspiracy stretch beyond the confines of River City to the entire National Hockey League? Were all the players and owners a part? And just who was the man who was the spitting image of the dead Simon Karlsson?

"Maybe what, Sam?" Avital asked.

There was only one way to find out the truth. She had to get back together with Rick Hansen.

"Maybe we should get tickets to a Jets game."

CHAPTER TWO

"So then, I says to Bill, I says, Bill, you get down from there right now!"

Frank rolled his eyes as Mrs. Vann droned on and on about her dead husband, Bill. He'd heard this story already, everyone had. In fact, they'd all heard it a hundred times before. Mrs. Vann was pushing ninety and wasn't quite right in the head.

"But you see, Bill doesn't hear me, he's up too high, so when I says that to Bill, he just looks at me all queer like, you see, so I have to yell, I do, but that doesn't help either. On account of his deafness. So, he turns around to try to figure out just what in the heck I'm trying to tell him, he does."

God, he wished this woman would just have a heart attack and end all this suffering.

Mrs. Vann rocked in her chair, shawl draped over a floral print nightgown, eyes firmly locked on the past. "So then, Bill, that's my husband, see, he must've figured that I had something important to say, so he takes a step down that ladder. But Bill wasn't too bright, you see, so he didn't realize that the ladder was on the other side of the roof."

Yes, yes, we all know this part, get it over with.

"So then, Bill goes POOF!" She held up her hands in the

19

air like a prayer at a revival meeting. "One minute he's up there, you see, the next minute, POOF!" she repeats. She then guided her hands down to waist level, smacking them together in a loud clap. "And splat. And my poor, poor Bill, he makes a real sad stain on the concrete, just like that, no goodbyes, no I love yous, no nothing."

He probably wanted to get away from you, you crazy old bat.

"So, I walks over to the stain, and I says, Bill, you dolt, look what you done did, you made yourself all dead." She shook her head. "And that was... ohhh... nineteen sixty-four if memory serves me right. I been alone ever since. The Widow Vann, they call me." Her false teeth chattered in her mouth as she puckered her lips in a wrinkled grin, the grim spectre of death written all over her like a roadmap.

This was the ultimate slap in the face to former Detective Inspector Sergeant Frank Malone, a man who had busted more crime in his almost sixty years on the force than there were cockroaches in a crack house, open sores on a whore, or spots on a leopard. He was more than a cop, he was the law incarnate, delving out hot heaping helpings of justice one fist at a time. Frank smiled when he thought of how many perps he'd sent to the big house and how many dreams of crime he'd crushed beneath his boots.

Drug dealers, pimps, stickup men, bank robbers, vampires, werewolves, demons, ghosts – that was all over now. A career of golden memories tossed away, and for what? So some girl could have a second chance out there in the big bad world? A girl he'd seen something in. A girl who'd killed. Killed what, he had no idea. He still wasn't sure just what in the holy hell had been going on; patchwork men falling apart, detachable johnsons, cloned brains and mind controlling sex maniacs. It was all too much for a simple River City boy like him. He preferred his crime honest and straightforward: theft, murder, extortion, blood sucking, the usual. None of this futuristic science fiction shit for him.

"—can we have some of your delicious Saskatoon berry pie, Widow Vann? they'd ask..." An evil corporate dick using hypnosis to make others get their hands dirty; in that girl's world, you cut that cancer out with extreme prejudice. He had to admire her gumption. Today's kinder, gentler law enforcement would be too worried about rights and 'innocent until proven guilty' to do what had to be done. He smiled when he thought of how she had taken care of business brutally and on the spot, no fear of the consequences, no thought of whether or not the perps had a bad childhood or some kind of brain disorder, she just tore off their dicks and beat them to death with 'em.

She'd make a good cop one day if she wanted. Come to think of it, Frank had no idea what she wanted, they'd never really talked about it – there hadn't been time. He'd spotted someone in trouble and decided to help. He couldn't let her go down for what she'd done, couldn't let a pretty young thing like that get sent to the big house for doing the right thing. Frank Malone did what had to be done and he took the rap for the whole goddamn scene.

"I think it was the summer of fifty-eight when I found it..."

It wasn't hard to fool them – people already assumed he was half crazy. And hell, who was he to doubt them? You had to be crazy to keep doing what he'd been doing for so long. Who wants to stay on the beat for almost sixty godforsaken years anyway? He'd left C.A.N.U.C.K. once, but he never had the desire to leave the RCPD. Or was it sense?

With the girl sent away, he'd ranted and raved for the benefit of the press and the cops called to the scene; told of golems and sex fiends, mind control and turning hippies into normals. All true, of course, but the truth sounds insane to those with their eyes shut. His old partner, Jimmy Hooper, no longer the rookie, had been the one to slap the cuffs on him, saying in his softest and kindest voice, "Come along, Frank, we're going downtown."

Fuck him anyway. And his new partner, the girl. What the hell did they know? They'd been too busy out canoodling while he'd been uncovering the truth.

"The kid should have listened," Frank said.

"What was that? Kids?" Mrs. Vann said. "Sure, I had lots. There was Timmy and—"

It didn't matter what Frank said to Hooper and Tockett, they didn't believe him. He saw their pitying looks when they thought he wasn't paying attention.

"Jimmy saw the patchwork man, he saw that crazy house in the suburbs, he should have believed me."

"Jimmy? No, I said Timmy. Then there was Billy and—"

In the end, despite all they'd gone through together, Jimmy was just like all the rest, blind and living on a river in Egypt, DE-nile.

Statements, interrogations, psychological assessments, a farce of a trial, more tests, then a verdict. Advanced dementia. Finally, a sentence, here, to another circle of hell; the Shady Acres Retirement Home, locked up with the other nuts until death does he part. He'd read about places like this, seen them on *Sixty Minutes*. Personal care homes, where the old are kicked to the curb to die. Where their ungrateful loin spawn drops them off one day to stop worrying about whether Grandma is pissing herself and stealing grapes from the Safeway. A place to forget about the elderly, the greatest generation, the ones who built this damn country from nothing but a bunch of shit and dirt.

"…canning, jams, preserves, the whole range of activities…"

He sat on one of the couches in the so-called lounge. It was firm, high up to allow those with poor mobility to get on and off. He had his legs draped up on the arm rest, kicking it old school. Screw the rules around here. Mrs. Vann was telling her story, dressed like she was ready for a rainstorm, white hair under plastic, umbrella at her side. Her wrinkled face and withered hands told him almost as much as her vacant eyes; cloudy with the memories of a life fading away from her.

"And that marmot, let me tell you, it was a wild one to be sure and—"

They wouldn't let Frank dress like a cop here, no suits and trench coats, wing tips or shoulder holsters. He wasn't even allowed shoes, at least not in the "common room". Here he had to dress "appropriately", and that meant track suits or sweatpants with his name written on the tags in Sharpie. He felt like a goddamn yuppie waiting for his tennis lesson, but he did what he was asked. There was no sense rocking the boat, not yet at least, not until he had discovered a way out of here.

"Mushrooms. That's the secret ingredient, you see. Mushrooms and—"

Dr. Hans talked to him every now and again, asked him questions to see if he was lucid, things that were so obvious, like, "How are you feeling today, Mr. Frank? Do you know

23

what year it is? Do you remember why you were put here?"

Of course I do, you kraut bastard. I'm Frank Malone, not some senile old pants pisser.

He played the game, tossed in curveballs to make sure that they thought he was still a little loopy. Better this than the big house; half the cells there were filled with his busts, so there was no way he'd live through a trip to Stoney Mountain, not without Big Bertha. Frank still felt the phantom weight of his gun, put his hands where it should be, ready to take it out and test fire, only to find nothing. It made him sad to think they had taken her away. That gun had shot a lot of bad guys over the years...

"...I liked most of all was that delightful Knowlton Nash. Now there was a voice!"

He scratched at his leg through his track pants, soft and velour, a deep crimson colour that made him stand out even more than he already did among the rest of the nut jobs. He'd found it way in the back of his closet. Apparently, he'd bought it sometime in the early eighties and forgotten about it. It was one of the only things they'd let him bring from his old apartment.

What a place this Shady Acres locked ward was. It was full of kooks. There was Mrs. Vann, the weaver of the same story a thousand ways, Ben and Jerry, the twins with the Super Mario moustaches, grey and bent, once powerful backs stooped from a lifetime of labour. They shouted at the drop of a hat, got into fights, refused to listen to anyone but each other, controlled the tension like a drill sergeant. But they were good guys if you related to them on their level, and Frank could do that. He nodded as Ben caught his glance, looking away from *The Price is Right* for a second. Then you

24

had the others: Oscar, Enid, Marlena, Felix, Sanchez, Delilah, ahh, who the hell could keep all their names straight, anyway? One wrinkled old face looked like any other. There was no point in remembering who anyone was when they might not wake up tomorrow.

"You call that a motherfucking showcase showdown?" Ben screamed.

"Ahh, shut up. A trip to Florida ain't so bad," Jerry shouted back.

"You thought it was a hellhole in ninety-two."

"Yeah, because they just had a fucking hurricane, dipshit."

"What was the name of that one?"

"What the fuck do I look like, a weatherman?"

"Andrew," someone else shouted back.

Shady Acres was a monotony of routine – Monday: Wii day; Tuesday: movie day; Wednesday: chair aerobics; Thursday: bible study; Friday: line dancing. Breakfast, lunch, and dinner served in the cafeteria; a slop of God only knows what and a side of pills to ease the mind. Frank wanted out in the worst way, but there was something not quite right in all this, he could smell it. His cop's nose still worked, and it smelled shit. And not from anyone's full diaper either.

He couldn't quite put his finger on it, but it was there. A look from Nurse Ironhide here, a strange glance from Dr. Hans there, whispers from the orderlies, strange sounds at night. He didn't know the big picture yet, but he was working on the script.

"Andrew?" Mrs. Vann said. "No, my husband's name was—"

So, each and every day, Frank went about the routine, pretending to be just another resident waiting to die. He slipped his pills into his pocket, keeping his mind free from their poison, looking for that little slip-up that told him what was really going on. It wasn't so bad really, at least no one was trying to kill him in here. As of yet, no one suspected that he was as sane as the Prime Minister. If he kept playing his cards right, no one would catch on to his little ruse either. And that was just the way Frank wanted it – keep 'em off guard, let 'em think you're a loony, then BAM, surprise 'em with a left and a right and a get out of seniors' jail free card.

"He took the ladder and went up to the roof, you see."

The worst part of Shady Acres was that there was no one to talk to, not with their head on straight at least. He couldn't trust people who still thought Nixon was in the White House, let alone count on them for backup should the shit go sour. He was on his own, alone against an army of doctors, nurses, and orderlies that had some secret conspiracy between them. An army of one against the entire health care industry.

"He was so high up, too, but he said he knew what he was doing."

He would crack this case, cut into this apple pie of evil and take a bite of the sweet deliciousness of truth. He was Frank Malone, super cop, he could do anything, even locked up in crazy town with a bunch of walking corpses. He just hoped he lived long enough to find out what in the hell was going on.

Mrs. Vann rocked in her chair, nodding. "So then, I says to Bill, I says..."

Then again, maybe he didn't want to live that long.

CHAPTER THREE

"Cheer up, Sam," Avital said as she slid her blouse over her head. "Not being able to score Jets tickets might seem like a bummer, but if you look at it another way, it's actually a good thing."

"Because all of the games are sold out and the team is as hot as ever?"

"No, because it's been forever since we went out clubbing."

"Totally," Erin said as a techno beat blared from speakers on the dresser. "I heard the Shark Club is pumping."

"Pumping?"

"What Erin means is, word on the street is it's where the Jets players go after the games to party."

"Word on the street?" Sam said, raising an eyebrow. "What are you, like, connected or something?"

"It's all over, okay? Facebook, Twitter, Instagram, everyone in the city is talking about it."

"At least everyone who's looking to hook up with hockey players," Erin said. "Eww, hockey players."

Avital shrugged. "Hey, some of those guys are freaking hot. Right, Sam?"

"If you're trying to get me to say Rick, I plead the fifth."

"We don't have that in Canada, just admit you still get a

little moist for him."

"Av!"

"He's a local celebrity, so it's okay to have a crush. Didn't you used to think Joey Gregorash was cute?"

Erin dropped her eyeliner pencil and shot Avital a dirty look. "Not now! He's a million years old. I only said that the picture of him on my mom's old record was cute!"

"So you wouldn't bone him?"

"Not even if 1971 him time travelled here."

"What if you time travelled to 1971?" Sam asked.

"No way, everyone was gross back then."

"Except Joey Gregorash." Avital snorted.

"Can we move on, please!"

Sam, Avital, and Erin were all crowded inside Sam's bathroom, getting dolled up for a night out at the fancy Shark Club. Connected to the MTS Centre by a walkway, it was the newest "ultra" club in town, whatever ultra club was supposed to mean. The place had put out an advertising blitz, plastering images of the Jets players partying anywhere it could to make the place the most popular club in town.

It was working.

"How do I look?" Avital asked as she finished her lipstick. She wore a slim black skirt and purple silk shirt, her hair and makeup immaculate.

"Like a million bucks as usual," Erin said.

"You could have come to the mall with me, too," Avital said. "I told you there was some good stuff down at Chez Elle."

"Sorry, I chose paying for textbooks this time," Erin said. She wore a more conservative grey dress and white shirt and vest combination, one of her favourite outfits.

The Shark Club had a dress code, so they needed to look a

certain kind of classy to get in. It had been an excuse to go to the mall for new outfits. Not that Avital needed an excuse. Sam had found something tight and black showed more skin than she felt comfortable and that had forced her to dip a little too far into her savings. Again.

You have to spend money to... uhhhh... oh, who am I kidding here?

Every visit chopped away at the bankroll she'd once intended to use to go out of Province for university. Instead, she had a closet full of clothes she'd only worn once and a crippling sense of guilt over each pair of impractical shoes stacked in boxes below.

"I say we look nice," Avital said, admiring their reflections in the mirror. "Not filthy rich nice, but classy."

"Maybe you guys do, I look like a fraud."

"Oh come on Sam, you pull that dress off as well as anyone."

Sam tugged the too-revealing dress up higher over her chest. "I don't know."

"Act like it's you and nobody will notice," Avital said.

"That's what you do?"

"Not telling. But if it was, you didn't notice did you?"

Sam suddenly wondered how much of Avital's persona was all an act. Was she as plagued with self-consciousness as her? And what about Erin? She was still applying eyeliner and hadn't seemed to have noticed the revealing moment between them.

"There shouldn't be trouble getting inside, right?" Erin asked as she replaced the pencil in its cap.

"If there is, maybe Sam can pull some strings with Rick," Avital said, smirking. "Or at least that dress can."

"I keep telling you I was a jerk to him. If anything, he might not want me there at all."

"Oh, come on, he was totally civil at the mall."

"A year ago."

"Haven't you heard the expression time heals all wounds?"

Did it? Sam wondered.

The Shark Club was going to be a major party. It would be a zoo of people desperate to get close to one of the Jets. In just a few weeks, Rick was already a local hero. Tonight might be her best chance to meet up with him, who knew when it might come again? An NHL season was hectic; training, practices, games, travel… it would be next to impossible to track him down on the road. Tonight was the night that she had to reestablish contact, at least try to get his new cell number or find out where he was living. But could she break through the crowd to get a word with him?

"Don't worry," Avital said. "The bouncers will take one look at us three babes and wave us right through. And even if you can't talk to Rick Hansen, I'll bet there'll be tons of other cute guys there."

"And loads of girls lusting after them."

"Puck bunnies," Avital corrected.

"Do they call the gay guys lusting after the players that, too?" Erin asked.

"Now that is a good question," Avital said. "Maybe you could ask Rick that, Sam. You are going to try to talk to him tonight, right?"

"If I can."

"Maybe try to get back together?" Avital grinned.

"What? No, that's the past and—"

"You can't bullshit us, Sam. We saw him on TV. He's smoking hot. And now that he's on the Jets, he'll be making big money. Someone's going to try to reel him in."

"I'm not some gold digger."

"If you don't bag him, maybe I will."

"Av," Erin said.

"Relax," Avital said. "We all know Sam called first dibs."

"Look, I—"

"Ding-dong." Marlon's voice echoed in the entranceway as the sound of the door opening interrupted her train of thought.

"Oh, shit," Erin said in a panic, quickly doing up her shirt.

"What's the matter, girl?" Avital smirked. "Don't want to give the boys a show?"

"I'll go," Sam said and left the bathroom.

She'd left the apartment door unlocked. Marlon and Everett had walked in earlier than expected. The apartment, while technically her dad's, was pretty much their home base now. He was always out of town, so it was just like living alone. So far it had been great.

"Hey, guys." Sam peered around the corner of the hallway to the entranceway. The guys were sporting full suits, dark black, maybe Italian. Everett wore a fedora tilted over one ear.

"Holy shit, you did dress up," she said.

"This thing itches," Marlon said, tugging at his jacket.

"I didn't know you owned anything other than WWE shirts," Sam said.

"Avital said there was a dress code."

"How did you convince him to buy a suit?" she asked Everett.

"Don't get him started," the blond man said as he checked his hat in the mirror.

31

"It's Big Bubba Rogers cosplay," Marlon said proudly. "I can use this for Halloween later."

"Who's—" Sam started but Everett waved her off. "Whatever, it looks classy. We're almost ready. There's beer or whatever in the fridge if you want."

"Sprite zero?" Marlon asked, unconvinced.

"Yes, Marlon, there's Sprite zero."

"Big Bubba Rogers."

"Right. Okay, Bubba. Just help yourselves."

She shook her head and went back to the bathroom. The girls were done. They all looked as good as they were going to look: twenty-year-olds ready for a night on the town. Even though they'd done this plenty of times, she still felt like she was playing dress up and that everyone in the club would instantly know.

Act like it's you and nobody will notice. I can do that.

"Alright," Avital said. "Let's get some pre-gaming on in this bitch."

CHAPTER FOUR

"Relax, Hooper," Veronica said from the passenger seat of the cruiser as they drove downtown. "What could possibly go wrong working at a night club?"

"Besides drunks, fights, drug deals, someone taking a shot at one of the Jets players, or just the usual random shooting? Not much, I guess."

The woman with the dark hair and slightly downturned mouth sighed over-dramatically. "Jimmy, you worry too much. You let your time working with Frank rub off on you."

"I'm just trying to be prepared here. I've done nights like this with…"

"With Frank. You can say his name."

"Right. With him and—"

"You still won't say it? Jimmy, it's been months. He's locked up and it's over and done with."

"I know, it's just that it was a lot to process, okay? I was his partner for almost four years and—"

"And he snapped and went insane. Or maybe he always was."

"Not maybe."

"Exactly, so just forget about him and focus on the future."

She put her hand on his leg. He quickly looked over and saw her smiling at him. He knew what that touch was for, and what it meant. But here on duty, they were supposed to keep their relationship a secret. Even alone in the car, they were never truly alone. All it would take would be one slip up, someone on the street to see what they weren't supposed to, snap a photo, and they'd both be in deep shit with the department. Partners weren't supposed to date.

He frowned and she pulled her hand away. "I know, I know. Not here. But later tonight for sure. Your bed or mine?"

"The kids home?"

"Where else would they be?"

Veronica had a couple of kids from a previous marriage, Carter and Olivia. They were real cute, oblivious to what his presence meant when he stayed over, but no matter how much he tried to convince himself otherwise, there was still something off about dating someone who had so much—

"They're not like luggage I can just leave in a locker, Hooper," she said curtly.

"I didn't say that."

"But you were thinking that."

"No, I swear." He was, but he'd never admit it. "It's just a little weird to be going to town and worrying that a kid's going to walk in asking why mommy is moaning so loudly in the middle of the night. There'd be questions and—"

"And we'd just make up something. Uncle Jimmy's just teaching me Brazilian Jiu Jitsu, honey, the no pants variation."

Jimmy snorted despite himself.

"There we go, now you're loosening up a bit."

"Ha ha. I'm not trying to be a prude or anything, I'm just… adjusting to this whole clandestine love affair thing."

"We could always go public, put in the report with HR."

"And be split up?"

"Might make sense if this is long term."

"And if it isn't?"

He pulled the cruiser into the parking spot they'd been saved behind the Shark Club. A huge no parking sign was plastered to the wall of the alley. The back entrance was further in.

"See?" Veronica said. "There you go worrying about the future. Just go with it."

Jimmy Hooper had been going with it for a long time now. Coming out of the police academy with top scores but drawing the ire of someone high up, he'd been paired with Frank Malone, the oldest cop on the force. They'd gone through a lot over the years. Cannibals, serial killers, that weird bug creature – events he couldn't explain rationally – and yet it was how it all ended that was the craziest of all. Frank, finally retired after his true age was exposed, taking a job as a security guard and losing his mind, killing a record producer and boy band, utterly convinced the concussion research lab he was stationed at was something far worse. It had shaken Jimmy's convictions to the core. That a man he thought was a good cop, if a little old fashioned in his methods, could fall so far in the end... what did that say about life? He'd figured Frank would retire, live on a beach, and enjoy his final few years. But instead, he was locked away in a care home, drifting further into senility by the day if accounts were true.

But life went on. He had a new partner, they were closer than they should be, and he was just trying to chart his way forward with all of the changes going on. So why did he feel so apprehensive about everything?

He shut off the car. "You're right," he said to Veronica. Even saying her name made things a little better. She was something else; down to earth, straightforward, a great partner in more ways than one. "Let's just do this club thing and hope the night brings nothing more than a bunch of drunks dancing to shitty techno music."

"Deal. But if I get the chance, I'm getting that Rick Hansen guy's autograph for Carter."

* * *

Working on a four-shot buzz, Sam and the crew entered the Shark Club to face an epic party.

The club had pulled out all the stops and the place was packed. A DJ spun on a small stage at the far end underneath a massive screen playing a visualization freeform of swirling colours and 3D effects. A throng of people moved on the dance floor, suits and dress shirts pressed up against dresses, skirts and heels.

The music was loud, a thin mist of fog hung in the air from machines next to the DJ, and every table was full of people; everyone young and dressed to the nines. Sam couldn't see Rick or any other Jets through the crowd, but then what was she expecting, a spotlight?

"Fucking A!" Avital shouted in her ear. "This is wild."

Sam nodded.

"I feel underdressed," Erin said in her other ear.

"I'm off," Everett announced. He darted off into the melange of people, presumably after someone wearing something tight.

"Great, now we'll never find him," Marlon said.

"What do we do?" Erin shouted.

"Table?" Sam shouted back.

"Good luck," Marlon said.

The pounding beat throbbed, the floor vibrated, the cymbals and keyboards of the song lifted her on an invisible cushion of air. They hacked their way through a stygian jungle of expensive fabrics, looking for any sign of an empty table. They found nothing, settling on a corner of wall near the bathroom.

"This is as good as we're gonna get," Sam said.

"This is no good." Marlon struggled to find the best way to lean against the raised outcropping that circled the room along the walls. It was the perfect height for a drink, but useless for anything else. Finally, he gave up and stood normally, fidgeting first with his hands in his pockets, then under his arms, then hanging at his sides.

"You sure we can't just leave and go somewhere else?"

"You can," Avital said. "This is great."

A waitress in a barely-there plaid skirt and white shirt was on them like a shark, the chum of their empty hands calling to her.

"Orders?" she shouted.

Sam was about to say something when Avital took over, getting them shots and chasers before anyone else could object.

The server melded back into the throng, quickly invisible amongst the party goers.

"What a place," Erin said. "No wonder the Jets all come here."

Shark Club was swank. Tastefully decorated in understated

colours, divided into sections. The dance floor, the bar, and VIP area were populated by huge leather couches. The room was multi-levelled, with tables a few steps up on all sides, a catwalk area on the second floor that stretched over and looked down on the dancers. The second floor branched off into a room of VLT's and huge televisions showing multiple different sports. But the focus of the main room was the dance floor itself. Lit up in checkered colour patterns, a disco ball twinkled above as people moved over the ever-shifting brightness of the electronic ground.

Everything smelled of booze, sweat, and sex. It was almost impossible to see much of anything through the crowd and fog. It was a maelstrom of activity. Everyone who was anyone had to be here and Sam felt out of her element.

"You see your guy?" Erin asked her.

"Nope," Sam shouted back, unable to spot Rick anywhere.

"Then let's dance." Erin pulled her by the hand into the hurricane of the dance floor. She was surrounded by the rich and wannabe rich, all bouncing to the house beat. Someone's arm rubbed against her back, another's leg touched hers. Erin tossed her hair along to the sounds of the electronic instruments, her smile and the shots brewing inside making the feeling infectious. Avital joined in, the three of them bouncing and screaming in joy, letting loose, finally having the chance to just have a good time and forget about everything else.

"Wait, where's Marlon?" Sam asked.

"Paying for the next round," Avital shouted.

The thought of him standing awkwardly alone near the bathrooms barely crossed Sam's mind as the song drove faster and the three of them hopped and twirled.

Erin grabbed Sam's hands and danced with her, stepping back and in, laughing as they imitated an old-fashioned step amidst all the breakers and hip-hop dancers. Avital grabbed the other hand and the three of them were off in their own world, dancing in an anachronistic style to the odd looks of those around, too hip to try something so oblique.

"We totally needed this!" Avital shouted.

They moved in unison, somehow dancing with the rhythm in a way that all seemed planned. Erin hugged her, Avital spun under a raised arm. The rest of the floor disappeared and only their circle remained. When the song ended, they cheered and hugged, laughing at their goofiness.

"I'm thirsty as F," Avital said, fanning her face with her hand.

"We should get back to Marlon, the poor guy's all alone," Erin shouted.

"And he's got the next round," Sam said.

"I'll join you in a sec." Avital looked off in the direction of something hot and muscular. A Jet? Before Sam could check, Erin pulled her by the hand back to their spot on the wall. Marlon stood sheepishly uncomfortable in their little corner with a row of drinks next to him, ice slowly melting as tiny straws bobbed upwards. He was scanning the crowd, clearly desperately hoping his friends would return. He perked up when he saw Sam and Erin emerge from the morass of dancers.

"'Bout time," he shouted.

"You've got shots!" Erin cried.

She and Sam grabbed a drink and toasted, pounding it back in a quick gulp.

"And martinis!" Sam said.

The chasers were fruity and sweet, just the right thing to

erase the harsh shot.

"You talk to anyone, Marlon, or did you just stand here looking scared shitless?" Erin said, grinning.

"I was guarding the drinks."

"And you did a fine job." Sam patted him gently on the shoulder and sucked back the rest of the martini.

"You find that Rick guy?" Marlon asked.

"I don't even know where to start looking," Sam said. She looked around the room, but it was a sea of suits and ties, gelled hair, and shiny lips. She couldn't make out any features through the fog. She felt her buzz transitioning to drunkenness.

"Fuck that guy," Erin said. "We're having a good time without him, are we not?"

"Of course." Sam smiled. "He's probably not even here anyway."

"Umm, is that him?" Marlon tapped her on the shoulder.

A huge spotlight shone down from the ceiling onto a table in the far corner of the VIP area. The DJ took over the house mic. "Ladies and gentlemen, give it up for the man of the hour, the newest draft pick rookie sensation of your River City Jets, Mr. Rick Hansen!" He let the name roll off his tongue and carry, floating in the air as the crowd cheered. Rick lifted his drink to the audience.

"That's him, alright."

The VIP area had filled up, each table manned by rugged looking guys, their crews, and girls dressed in tight clothes wearing too much makeup. Rick was surrounded by his old teammates from the John A. MacDonald Rangers: Bruce, Chuck, and the others who'd so tormented Sam back in high school.

"He looks even hotter in real life," Avital said, coming back to the table to take her shot and chaser.

It was true. Rick's long hair shone in the light, the disco ball revealing a wave even from this distance. He was fuller than she'd remembered, thicker, with a few extra pounds of muscle packed on over the past year. He'd obviously spent a lot on his clothes. He looked really good in a tight suit and tie. It was quite the change from the team jacket and jeans she'd never known him not to wear.

"Meh," Erin said. "He still looks like a jock."

"Correction. A famous jock," Marlon said.

"There's your chance," Avital said. "Take it before someone else does."

Sam stood up.

"Seriously, Sam?" Erin said. "He's in the VIP section."

"So?" Avital said. "Just walk in like you belong."

"You think that will work?" Sam asked.

"Go for it, tiger."

Sam left the table, not hearing Erin's parting words, but catching the sound of disappointment in her voice.

* * *

"I can't hear myself think," Jimmy said to Veronica.

"What?" she answered back.

"I said, I can't hear—"

His words faded away when the DJ introduced another one of the Jets with the spotlight and an excited cheer. There was no point in trying to carry on a conversation against this noise. Instead, he just watched the crowd, waiting for any signs of trouble. So far, the only thing he'd spotted were overpriced drinks and university students with more cash than sense.

You're sounding like Frank now.

The air was heavy. His throat was parched. He elbowed Veronica in the side.

"Thirsty?" he asked.

"On duty?"

"Water."

"Make it a double."

He started to move away from their spot up against the VIP area when he spotted someone emerging from the mass of dancers, waving her hands at one of the players from the Jets.

"Probably a puck bunny," he mumbled as he headed to the bar.

* * *

Sam walked directly to Rick's side of the VIP area, through the crowd, dodging waitresses as she single-mindedly stalked her prey. It was just him and the guys, drinking beers and laughing. She started waving to get his attention, was almost there, only a few feet away.

"Rick!"

A living Barbie doll stepped in front of her, blocking her. Bleached blonde and stacked, made-up to the nines with a stunning diamond necklace resting in bountiful cleavage pushed up in a tight blue shirt over the top of a short skirt and stilettos. Debbie Peterson. Of course she'd be here. How could Sam have forgotten the ex-cheerleader, volleyball star who'd latched on to Rick and never let go? The woman was as fit as ever and acted like she owned the joint. It only took a look from her for Sam to feel poor and inferior.

"Spot Check. Surprised they let you in here. Especially in that dress."

Spot Check: that horrible nickname the jocks had given her when they'd noticed her tendency to constantly try to keep her hair over the prominent mole over her eyebrow. It was just cruel enough that the pain all came rushing back. She had to stop herself from pulling her hair over it again or tugging on her dress. She wouldn't give Debbie the satisfaction of seeing she could still affect her.

"I waited in line, just like everyone else, Debbie."

"Not the ones on the list. And I don't need to tell you that I'm on the list."

"You don't, but you did anyway. I'm sure that makes you feel like, what, a very important piece of shit?"

Sam tried to wave to Rick again, but he was oblivious. Debbie scowled at her.

"What do you think you're doing?"

"Trying to say hi to Rick," Sam replied, attempting to move past her.

"Hell no, he's done with you," Debbie said, stepping in her path.

"Shove off, Debbie, this is important. I need to talk to him."

"This is the private VIP party area, Spot Check. Rick's table. There's a list. And since I made the list, I know you're not on it. Which means you don't get in." Debbie motioned to the velvet ropes cordoning off the VIP area from the rest of the club.

"I know what a VIP section is, Debbie. I'm not looking to party with him, just talk. It'll only take a second." Sam waved and tried again to push past her, but Debbie held firm.

"Nuh-uh," Debbie said curtly. "Rick's got everything going for him now, so the last thing he needs is for some skank from his past trying to leech off his moment."

"Leech? Debbie, you're a goddamn slug."

"You're only going to rekindle trauma I've helped him work through. The trauma of being cheated on by the school slut."

"You fucking—"

"I will not have you messing up his big break, Sam. Shove off."

Sam wanted to sock her one. The nerve of her, what did she know? She was the queen bitch of the school, had treated Rick like shit, had been the one who'd triggered everything that had gone wrong with Joshua and him. She'd even stolen Joshua's heartstone, spent weeks humiliating him, even trying to force him to violate Sam on camera. But the stones had weird pulls over people. Sam couldn't be sure how much of what Debbie had done was of her own will, or the twisted magic of the ruby.

"Debbie, this is the last time I'm saying this. I just need a minute of his time then I'll let you go back to being a goddamn puck bunny."

"Excuse me? What did you call me?"

"You heard me. A puck bunny. Now, move or I'll make you."

If Debbie could have shot steam out of her ears, she'd be doing it. She clenched her teeth, tightened a fist, looked like she was going to take the first shot. Sam hoped she did.

"You're going to regret that, Spot Check. Regret it so hard."

Sam spotted the rest of the slugs now. They'd joined the table with Rick and the others, carrying fruity drinks and dressed as expensively as Debbie. They were laughing along to other hockey player jokes. The whole evil crew was here: Stacey, Xiu, Nan, Lindy. But they weren't paying attention and were in no place to help her. Sam was pretty confident that if they tried, she could take them all anyway. She was getting better at Hapkido by the week.

"What are you going to do, Debbie?" Sam cracked her knuckles, ready for a fight.

"Simple," Debbie said. She took a step back and shouted, "Security!"

* * *

"Looks like we've finally got a situation, Jimmy," Veronica said, putting down her empty glass of water on the ledge jutting out of the wall.

"Huh?"

She pointed to the VIP area, where a massive brute, more orc than human, gripped the arm of a girl dressed in black. His neck was as wide as her waist. Tattoos lined his bare arms as she struggled against his grip.

"Let them handle it," he said. "We're just here to—"

"Jimmy, that guy is triple her size and she's probably drunk. This could get ugly."

"Right." He put his drink down and the two of them walked over to the scene. The girl was trying to pull her arm away. A blonde was shouting at her. Another group of women joined the fray.

"What's going on here?" Veronica asked.

"This girl is drunk and won't stop bothering us. I'd like her thrown out," the blonde demanded.

"That's not true," the girl in black said.

45

"She's also uttering threats," one of the others chimed in.

"She's been stalking Rick Hansen," the blonde said.

"This true?" Veronica asked.

"She's lying."

"She's not on the list," the bouncer grunted while the girl struggled. The girl in black tried to pull her arm away and the bouncer jerked it behind her back in a hammer lock. She squealed in pain.

"That doesn't mean you have to hurt her," Veronica said, reaching out to stop him.

"Let her go," Jimmy said. "We'll take it from here."

"I just wanted to talk to Rick for a second," the girl in black said. "He knows me. I'm not stalking—"

"You see?" the blonde said. "She admits it. Officer, she's scaring us. Hockey players have to deal with these types all the time and—"

"You lying bitch!"

The woman in black jerked again and the bouncer wrenched her arm up into the shoulder. She cried out in pain.

"Come along, miss, no need for a scene," Jimmy said.

Veronica took her by the shoulder and looked her in the eye. Others in the club had stopped to watch. A few phones were out. She motioned to the crowd and that seemed to calm the girl.

"We good?" Veronica asked her.

"Yeah," the woman said.

"Let her go."

"But—"

"We'll take her outside."

"Alright."

He let her go and Veronica took the woman's shoulder gently, patting her where the bouncer had wrenched up against the joint.

"Did he hurt you?"

"I've had worse."

"Come on. You don't want to be the next viral video."

The situation calmed, as Veronica and Jimmy led the woman away from the VIP section, towards the exit. A few eyes followed, but the woman went along peacefully.

* * *

"Was that really Spot Check?" Nan asked.

"The one and only."

"How the fuck did she get in?"

"The same way she's leaving."

"The cops escorted her?" Nan asked, confused.

"No, I meant by the door."

"Oh."

Debbie smiled to herself as she watched Sam being booted from the club. The scene had gone better than she could have ever hoped.

"What did she want?" Xiu asked.

"What do you think? What all these girls want and what I have."

"The VIP list?"

"No – Rick, you goof."

Another bad influence from Rick's past had been blocked from rearing its ugly head. He was hers now and she was going to protect her investment. Debbie Peterson was attaching herself to his rocket all the way to the top.

"She get nasty?" Xiu asked.

"About to."

"Too bad. I was hoping for round two with that one."

"She won't be back. I'll make sure of it."

Satisfied that Sam was gone, Debbie turned back to the table. Rick sat oblivious to it all, chatting with his old buddies and nursing his one beer he was allowed.

An NHL player. Hers. The pros made the kind of money she had always dreamed of, and there was no way she would let Rick get away. She slid in next to him on the vinyl booth and slung her arm inside his. He turned and smiled, his grin showing her that he appreciated all that she did for him.

"What's up, Debbie?"

"Oh, just had to keep some skank from trying to crash our party."

He leaned in and gave her a quick kiss, then went back to his buddies.

Rick was hers now and there wasn't a damn thing that Samantha Abraham could do about it.

* * *

Sam had been all ready to reverse the bouncer's hold, twist in and lock him up with a behind-the-back armlock, when the two cops had converged on them. There was no way she was going to escalate things then, even if her dress could have handled it. There would be other times, other battles. She let herself be escorted outside, trying to avoid the glares of the other patrons, hoping nobody filming had her face on screen.

"You have someone to drive you home or do you want us

to call a cab for you?" the male cop asked.

"Detective Hooper, I could give her a ride."

"Do you want Detective Tockett to drive you home?"

"No, it's okay," Sam said, taking out her phone. "I'll text my friends inside."

She kept her head down and typed in a message to Erin and Avital, hoping that neither one of the cops realized who she was. She'd blanched when she realized they were the two that had interviewed her after the Factor 5ive incident. Then she'd been a mess, wearing sweats. They probably couldn't place her now, dressed and made up like this. She hoped that held.

"Okay," Detective Tockett said. "But if you want my advice, stay away from that guy for a while. I don't think his girlfriend wants you around."

"Yeah, no kidding."

"That means don't come back inside tonight, you understand?" Detective Hooper said.

"Gotcha," Sam said, nodding.

She kept her head down, texting, until they both left her to return inside the club. She stomped away and kicked a garbage bin, forgetting the heels she wore, feeling the shock through her toes.

"Fucking hell." She limped away.

She'd blown her first real chance at getting to Rick. Spectacularly. Now Debbie would be watching out for her.

"There she is," Erin called out from the club entrance.

"Sam, what happened?" Avital asked, running up to her.

"They booted me," she said.

"For what?"

"Trying to talk to Rick."

49

"Oh snap, he does still hold a grudge," Erin said.

"It wasn't him. It was his girlfriend."

"Someone beat you to him, eh?" Avital said.

"Av."

"I told you, puck bunnies are everywhere."

"There's more to it than that," Sam said. "I'll tell you over pancakes."

"I was over dancing anyway," Erin said, wrapping her arm around Sam's shoulder in comfort.

"Wait, we need Marlon," Avital said. "Where is he?"

Erin turned her phone to show a text message. "He's looking for Everett."

"Shit," Avital said. "We could be here a while."

"Then how about that story, Sam?" Erin said, motioning for her to sit on the curb alongside her.

"What do you guys know about cheerleaders?"

CHAPTER FIVE

"You know, I've been working in this lab for two years and I still don't understand what we're trying to accomplish."

Jensen George turned to his co-worker Janice, who sat behind him typing on a laptop. She didn't look up or answer.

"Everything's so hush-hush. Who do you think we really work for?"

Janice adjusted the glasses inching lower on her nose. "That's above our pay grade," she said curtly.

"You've never wondered who's signing the checks?"

"No."

"I've got a few theories," Jensen said. "One is that this is a military research project."

"But—"

"Hear me out. Secret military project set up through dummy corporation fronts and chopped up piecemeal in parts, so no one knows exactly what's truly going on. It's exactly what they'd do so that nobody knew, right?"

"Maybe you should just focus on the work instead of these wild theories. Don't you want that group bonus?"

Jensen sat watching a couple on the other side of a glass partition. The male subject was sitting on a couch, drinking beer from a glass in front of a television showing hockey, the woman reading a romance novel. It wasn't work that required his total attention.

"Look, I get it," he said to Janice. "The pay is incredible. I couldn't believe the offer sheet, but we're cut off from the outside world. No contact with family, no phone, nothing. You know I had to tell all my friends I'm working in Antarctica doing polar research? Me! Hell, if they only knew I was in River City."

"We're not supposed to discuss our outside lives," Janice said. "That's a part of the agreement."

"Relax, it's just the two of us here."

Janice pushed her glasses up again and shifted in her chair uncomfortably. She motioned with her finger to one of the many cameras mounted along the walls.

"Oh, they're not worried about what we're saying, they're worried about them in there," Jensen said, pointing to the man and woman on the couch.

"Still," Janice said. "I'd rather we—"

"Some days, I think I'm going stir crazy down here. I was even thinking of going to our division head and putting in my resignation."

"But the work here is so—"

"Exciting, I know. And there's the bonus cheque, the staff parties, blah blah blah. I'm just talking out loud here. I can put up with this for the rest of my contract. I've done worse for less money."

She raised an eyebrow in curiosity.

"Then there's the lifetime NDA's. Only a secret military project would insist on that. Shit, what would I say anyway? I still have no idea what to tell people about what we've been

52

doing all this time."

"As much as I enjoy hearing your complaints, it's time to apply the first trigger sound," Janice said.

"Sure, sure. Lose yourself in the job, I get it." Jensen pressed the red button on the console next to the glass. Neither he nor Janice could hear the sound emitted inside the room on the other side, which was for the best, since it could have strange effects on some.

Janice's fingers stopped moving along the keyboard. She froze in place, staring through the glass wall.

"Now the second," she said.

Jensen pressed the blue button. This time, the man on the couch stopped his drinking motion in mid gulp. Beer sloshed over his face, down his shirt, pooling on his crotch and down to the floor.

"Oh great, another mess," Jensen said. "Wow-ee-wow."

"It could be worse. Did you hear what Wallace and the others had to deal with the other day?"

"Oh, come on," Jensen said. "You don't believe that horse-shit, do you? Subjects tearing their own skin off and—"

A thud from the other side of the glass stopped him in mid sentence. He turned to see the woman pressed up against the glass, the man behind her, thrusting repeatedly.

"Holy shit, they're going at it like rabbits," he said.

"That's an interesting response," Janice said as she noted it in a logbook.

The couple's faces were contorted in silent screams of primal fury as they gave their unknown watchers a show right out of a blue movie. Jensen just stared, never having been so close to something like this before.

"Interesting. But what happens if you apply the third trigger sound?" Janice asked.

"Let's find out." Jensen pressed another button.

This time, both subjects stopped, stood erect like the man's penis and marched over to the bookcase. Naked from the waist down, they began to slide the furniture over, rearranging the room's layout.

"Fascinating," Janice said.

"Do they understand what it is they're doing?"

"They're not supposed to. It's a part of the subliminal implantation."

"But why these actions? What do they accomplish?"

"Try another trigger," she suggested.

He pressed the yellow button now. The bookcase toppled over. The woman held her head. The man dropped to his knees and started what appeared to be barking like a dog. A flash of something red sprayed all over the room. It took Jensen a moment to realize that the woman's head had exploded in a shower of blood and brains.

"Holy fucking shit," he said, mashing on more buttons. "We have to stop—"

"Too late," Janice said, pointing.

The man howled to the ceiling, lips outstretched in a silent moan. His eyes began bleeding, his head vibrating. The teeth chattered so hard that they started cracking, shattering into tiny shards of bone, mixing with the blood and beer on the floor.

Hands shot to his oozing eye sockets, dug in deep, pulled outwards, somehow impossibly splitting the man's own head in two, ripping the skull and skin, leaving a brain attached to the spinal cord to flop downward, landing against the stump of a neck before the whole mangled form fell forward and stopped moving.

"How…" Jensen said.

"Also way above our pay grade."

He stared at the gore-splattered room, realizing that it was all the result of his button presses.

"We killed them…" he said.

"This has got to beat Wallace's story for sure," Janice said as she made notes.

CHAPTER SIX

"And this is where I keep my beef jerky." Felix proudly pointed to the top drawer of the small nightstand next to his adjustable bed. He had the bed propped up to an almost ninety degree angle, but was still partially under the covers.

"Any left?" Frank asked.

"Lots," Felix said, grinning.

"Then let's have some, man. I'm getting a little tired of the mush they pass off as grub around here."

Frank reached for the drawer and pulled it open. He peered inside eagerly but instead of finding delicious jerky as promised, he found a mass of elastic bands and plastic combs. He fished around, but came up empty.

"What do you need all these combs for?" Frank asked the old man, brandishing a purple plastic one that looked brand new.

Felix was mostly bald, with more hair jutting out of his ears than on the top of his head. A wheelchair was parked next to the bed, the man's usual source of transportation up and down the halls.

"That one's an antique," Felix said.

"You're an antique, old timer."

"Old? I'm not old."

"Sure you are. Have you looked in a mirror lately?"

Frank reached over to the nightstand and picked up the clamshell alarm clock. He turned it to face Felix so he could see his reflection in the glass.

"Wesley, that's a clock. I already know the time."

"I keep telling you I'm Frank, Felix. Frankie, Malone, Francis, I don't care. Just not Wesley!"

The old man spotted his image now and he rubbed his chin thoughtfully. "Who's that guy?"

"That's you."

"That can't be me. I'm only forty-four years old."

Frank put down the clock and pulled the sheets down lower off Felix's body, revealing his stomach sticking out of a shirt that rode high. "How do you explain the wrinkles and liver spots?"

"Too much sun."

"What year do you think this is, Felix?"

"Year? What a stupid question. It's…"

Frank waited, wondering how long it was going to take the old man's internal computer to process the question. He'd come for a chat because Felix seemed like a man who might have a unique insight into the inner workings of Shady Acres. One of the longest tenants, he was always dragging himself up and down the halls by his slippered feet and hands on the railings. Most of the staff and residents paid him no mind, exactly the kind of person who saw what they didn't think to hide. And yet, poor Felix's brain seemed to have the consistency of the pudding they served here for dessert.

"I need the closet," a woman called out from the door.

Frank turned from his chair to see Enid, a stooped woman

with wild grey hair, walk in. She had a pile of sweaters and shirts, still on plastic hangers, dangling in her arms. She walked over to Felix's closet and pulled it open.

"Oh no, no, no. There's not enough room." She brought her mound of clothes over to Frank and handed them to him. "Here, hold." She went back to the closet and started taking out all of Felix's clothes, bringing them back over to the bed and dropping them on the prone man's legs.

"What are you doing?" Frank asked as she emptied out the closet.

"Are you here for laundry?" Felix asked.

"I've got to hide my things," Enid said. "They're always taking them away from me. I'm putting them in here. You'll keep them safe, won't you?"

"This isn't my room, lady," Frank said. "Ask him."

"Make sure you stay quiet. They'll know if you don't."

She loaded all her things inside the closet and left the room. In a moment, she was back with another armful. Poor Felix was almost buried under his own wardrobe.

"Don't you have your own closet?" Frank asked.

"It's not safe. They want my clothes and my organs."

Out and back again with even more. They couldn't possibly all be hers. Frank spotted men's shirts, too.

"Oh, great," he said and pushed the call button next to Felix's bed. An alarm would sound at the nurses' station down the hall. In a moment, an orderly stood at the doorway.

"What's the matter, Mr. Felix?" the Hispanic man asked.

"It ain't him," Frank said, "it's her." He pointed to the woman stuffing even more clothes into the closet, piling them on the floor in a huge collection.

"Mrs. Enid," the orderly said condescendingly, "you know

that we don't put things in our neighbours' rooms."

"He's one of them," Enid said, pointing to the man in white. "Not like us. He's in on it."

"I don't think those are all hers," Frank said, gesturing to the clothes.

"She's been doing this for a while. We'll have to put them all back. Won't we, Mrs. Enid?"

He grabbed her by the arm and gently tried to pull her to the door. She jerked her arm away in a panic. "No. Keep off. You just want to take my organs. You just—"

"Help!" a woman shouted from the hallway. Frank's cop instinct kicked in. A surge of adrenaline ran through his veins as the orderly tried to calm Enid.

"Help!" the voice called out again. It was coming from down the hall.

"You handle her," Frank said. "I'll deal with the damsel in distress."

He pushed past the two and emerged into the stark hallway, brightly lit, stretching down to the nurses' station at the far end. Rooms with names stencilled on and photographs of the resident mounted in plastic frames lined the railing-ringed hall.

"Help!"

"Maybe I will have something to do around here," he said as he motored to the room which he figured was the source of the cries for assistance.

Inside, another room like the others: bed, dresser, closet, television showing the weather channel. A woman sat in a chair next to the window, pounding on the glass.

"Help!"

"It's okay, ma'am," he said calmly, "Det... Frank is here."

"Help!"

"I'm trying, but you have to tell me what you—"

"Help!"

"That's why I'm—"

"Help!"

"Lady, what's the matter!"

"Help!"

Frank reached out and grabbed her shoulder, wondering if she was deaf. He spun her gently around.

"Just point me in the direction of—"

"Help!"

She became more agitated, rocking in her seat.

"Help, help, help!"

"Lady, I want to but—"

"That's all she ever says," one of the female orderlies said from the doorway.

"Help, help, help. H-E-L-P!"

The woman, seeing the orderly, grew increasingly panicked. She shouted over and over again and tried to get out of her seat, but didn't have the strength.

"What can I do?" Frank asked. "She clearly needs something."

"She's looping, Mr. Malone. It's a symptom of her dementia. She's caught in some kind of traumatic memory, unable to get out. You can't help her."

"That doesn't sound like—"

The orderly held a syringe in her hand and approached the desperate woman. "All we can do is calm her down. She'll snap out of it after a bit of rest. Won't you, Mrs. Halsey?"

The orderly grabbed an arm, pinning it tight, and forced the needle in.

"Help! Help. Help… He…"

The calming medicine kicked in fast. She rocked silently in place.

"There. You see? All better," the woman said and moved past Frank.

"That's it?" Frank said. "You just pump her full of drugs and leave her?"

"There's nothing else that can be done for her, Mr. Malone. She's only going to sink deeper into her own mind."

The woman left, leaving Frank alone. He walked over to the old woman and did his best to crouch down. He looked into her fogged eyes for some sign of life still there. She seemed lost. He sighed and rose. But her hand grabbed his forearm. He saw her snap back to reality.

"It's not what you think," she said.

"What isn't?"

"Everything."

"Everything where?"

"Here. It's not right. It's not…"

But the fog returned and overtook her. Almost comatose, her head slowly sank down her chest. Soon she was snoring peacefully.

Frank watched her for a moment before stepping outside. The orderly had returned to the nurses' station, talking with her co-workers. One of them said something and she turned to look at Frank. A cold stare, with something sinister behind it. She motioned to walk towards him, but he turned the other way and started walking down the hall. When he came to his door, he looked over his shoulder to see that she'd gone back to her conversation.

That was two warnings now. The more he talked to the

others, the more he was being told that his hunch was right. The cop's nose never missed. But was he being fed only the ramblings of the senile, or was there really more going on here than met the eye?

"Time for Frank Malone to do a little undercover work," he said.

CHAPTER SEVEN

"Oh! He's totally doing the Ricky Steamboat twenty elbow drops from the eighty-nine Clash of the Champions," Marlon shouted, fists clenched, a massive smile on his face as they sat in the stands watching live pro-wrestling. One grappler, wearing long white tights and a red headband, was repeatedly dropping an elbow onto the leg of the other, wearing small purple brief-style tights. He held the left leg, dropped down with all his weight, then stood back up to do it over and over again. To Sam, it was all Greek, but Marlon was in his element.

"You see, Steamboat had beaten Flair for the title at the Chi-Town rumble in eighty-nine in a huge upset, so they had a rematch, two out of three falls, and man oh man, what a match. It was, like, an hour long, crazy back and forth action. At one point, he starts dropping elbows down on Flair, and that's nothing special really, but he keeps doing it, over and over again, something like twenty times. The crowd goes crazy, the announcers go crazy, everyone going nuts. Even now, it's freakin' awesome!"

"And that's what this guy is doing? Steamboat? He doesn't look that old," Erin asked, confused.

"No, no, no, no, no. He's doing a tribute to that match.

63

Duplicating the spot. It's post-modern wrestling!"

After so many hours of listening to Marlon go on about pro wrestling, they had all agreed to go with him to a live event. Sam was on the banned list from the Shark Club anyway. The ring was set up in an empty warehouse; bleachers on three sides under spotlights. A couple of guys in blue polo shirts circled the ring with handheld cameras, filming the action, while a larger stationary camera was positioned on the side without the bleachers. The 'hard cam' side, Marlon had told them.

"So, he's doing the same thing as that other match? How does that make sense?"

Marlon shook his head. "You don't get it, this is *meta*!"

"I thought it was supposed to be a pretend fight."

"It is, but this is a comment on that previous match. They're re-enacting it because both guys are cosplaying as Flair and Steamboat. It's supposed to be—"

"You're right," Avital interrupted, "I don't get it."

"Maybe if you saw that match first then you'd—"

"You want us to watch another hour-long match before we can see this one?"

"It provides context," Marlon said.

Avital turned to Sam and Erin. "Remind me again why staying at home wasn't an option?"

"Come on, Av, it's not that bad."

She looked around the room at the crowd, mostly men in black T-shirts with varying levels of facial hair. They all seemed to be having a good time.

"I think we're the only women here," she said.

Sam had realized the same thing when they'd taken their spots in the bleachers. She, Erin, and Avital looked way overdressed.

"Is that normal?" Sam asked Marlon.

"Let's just say that this is one of the only places where the line to the guys' bathroom is always longer than that of the girls'," Everett chimed in from the other side of Marlon. He was scrolling through pictures of girls on his phone, barely paying attention.

"There you go, Av," Erin said. "You pretty much have your pick of 'em here."

"You first," Avital said.

"Does everyone here understand what's going on, you know, with the context?" Sam asked curiously.

"Maybe. But you don't have to get it," Marlon said. "They're doing it for those of us that do! It's like a whole other layer of subtext!"

"Context to the subtext to the two guys in tights fake brawling?"

"Exactly," Marlon said. "It's live action cinema!"

This was Sam's first time seeing professional wrestling live and just like Avital, she quite frankly didn't get it. Two guys in their underwear pretending to fight, dancing around the ring executing moves that were so broad and over the top as to look ridiculous. Most of the time you could clearly see that they weren't hitting each other, let alone hurting each other – it was all acting. But Marlon seemed to love it.

"Yeah!" he shouted and stood up momentarily.

He wasn't alone. Most of the people here seemed in tune with what was going on, cheering and booing the 'faces and heels,' as Marlon told them the good and bad guys were called respectively.

Every so often someone would start a chant and the

audience would pick it up in full force.

"This is awe-some!"

"Fight for-ever!"

"Mongo's gonna kill you."

It was like a game of call and response, the marshalling of others to say what you say. Everyone else seemed to understand the rules.

"So, which one is Flair and which one is Steamboat?" Erin asked.

"I'm not sure," Sam said. They'd announced the names of each wrestler over the PA before the match, but she couldn't remember who was who.

"Neither one is. Those are the original two who had the match that this is a tribute to."

"I'm so lost," Erin said.

The guy in the white tights started twisting around the legs of his opponent on the ground, locking him up in some kind of strange leg lock Sam had never seen before. It looked like it might actually hurt.

"Figure four!" Marlon shouted. "That's Flair's move!"

"He's the one in the white?" Avital asked.

"No," Marlon said in exasperation. "He's the one that Steamboat fought in eighty-nine, the sixteen-time world champ, greatest pro-wrestler of all time. Wheelin' dealin' stylin' profilin' limousine riding..." He looked to the rest of them for some kind of recognition, but they all stared back blankly. "Oh god, guys, WOOOO! You know, Ric Flair? Argh."

Marlon was really into this, desperately trying to get them to share his love for the spectacle. But what was more obvious to Sam's eyes, was that he was desperately trying to get Erin to like it specifically.

That's new.

She'd always assumed that Marlon had a thing for Avital – hell, most guys did, she was gorgeous. But he was turning his attentions to Erin. Had he given up, or was there more going on here that she wasn't aware of?

"See." He motioned for Erin to follow his explanation. "The move puts pressure on the leg. He wants him to give up."

"Is he going to?"

"Just wait!"

The two muscled men in the ring played out some kind of drama, the one in the leg lock swinging his arms in the air, the other shaking his head and yelling, "Nooooooo."

"What's going on now?" Sam asked.

Marlon smiled, happy someone seemed interested. "He's trying to counter the move by flipping over, which puts the pressure on the other guy. It was a classic staple of Flair matches, hell, Ted Dibiase matches, Jack Brisco – really, anyone who used the figure four as a finisher."

Sam made a mental note to try that leg move in class sometime, to see if it actually hurt at all. It certainly looked interesting, but it was hard to tell with the way these two guys were screaming and scrunching up their faces in over-dramatic pain. In her estimation, if they were seriously hurting like that, there was no way they could keep fighting; she knew how real the pain from joint locks was and this was silly and over the top. The guy in the purple reversed the move and the two of them were now on their stomachs, the grappler in white screaming in agony, reaching for the ring ropes, grabbing hold of them. The referee broke it up.

"Saved by the ref!" Marlon shouted. "Boooo!"

The guy in the white pants stood up and grabbed the other man's arms, pulling and throwing him into the opposite ropes. He bounced off and then jumped over him. He kept running and bounced off the opposite ropes to come back again. "Oh, come on, why is he still running?" Avital asked.

"Yeah, why wouldn't he just stop?" Erin asked.

"It's called an Irish whip, it's a move." Marlon rolled his eyes.

"But it makes no sense! Does that mean if the ropes weren't there, he'd keep running forever?"

"He rebounds!" Marlon said.

Avital and Erin laughed at his displeasure. Then their jaws dropped in horror. The two men crisscrossed the ring, narrowly avoiding each other. Purple dropped onto his stomach and white jumped over him. Then purple stood up ready to punch white. White leapt up high, up and over purple, grabbing his legs as he hit the ground, trying to pull him over backwards. Purple refused to go down, so white pulled his short pants down, revealing a bare ass and G-string tan line. Purple desperately tried to keep his tights up as he dragged the other man along the ground wildly, the audience laughing.

"I draw the line at male nudity, I'm going to the bathroom." Avital stood to leave.

"I'm coming, too," Erin said flatly, hypnotized by the sight of the muscle head tearing around with his ass hanging out.

"Sam?"

"I've seen worse." She shrugged.

The two girls left, climbing down the bleachers through the audience to find the bathroom.

"I'm going to go talk to that woman wrestler at the merch

table," Everett said. "She was hot." He got up and left, too.

"I don't think they like this wrestling stuff," Sam said.

"No... I don't think so either."

"But at least they came, right? That has to count for something."

"I guess," Marlon said as he watched Avital and Erin disappear off into the washroom area.

Sam wanted to cheer him up, as he looked like a sad puppy dog with lost eyes. "Don't worry, just because Avital doesn't like this doesn't mean you don't have anything in common."

"Oh, I'm over Avital. I've come to the conclusion that there's no hope in hell for me there. I mean, look at her and look at me." He waved his hand over his large frame.

Despite the sad feeling it gave her to admit it, he was right. There was a massive difference between the two. Avital was a dark-haired beauty, stacked and slim, with thick eyebrows and a slightly prominent nose. She was vivacious, loved to party, and guys fawned over her. She had her pick and kept a few on leashes at all times. She knew what she wanted and wasn't afraid to go for it, or at least that was the image she put forward. She was what Sam had dreamed she could be at one time, but Sam just wasn't that open, couldn't act so carefree. Sam gravitated towards brooding, she was a dreamer, a loner at heart. And that was before her past. There was still a lot of trauma to work through from Rick, Joshua, Scott, and Duckie's death. She knew she'd never find a way out in the party girl lifestyle like Avital.

"Don't sell yourself short," she said, but it was clear Marlon wasn't buying her humouring him.

"Sam, I'm not blind. She's a Jewish princess, and I'm a textbook fat guy."

Brushed back hair, hairy arms, a slight extra chin, glasses, a crooked toothed smile. His skin was on the blotchy side, and he tended to wear only wrestling, band, or video game shirts.

"Textbook? I wouldn't say that."

"I'm great at video games, love pro-wrestling, and have zero luck with the opposite sex."

"Zero?"

"Zero."

"Come to think of it, in all the time I've known you, I don't think I've ever seen you go on an actual date."

"Because I haven't."

"Not one?"

"More like negative one."

"What's that mean?"

"What do you think it feels like to drive around someone you have a thing for only for her to meet and hook up with other guys?"

"Then you freely admit that my theory of you crushing on Avital was right."

He shrugged. "No point in denying it. I've just moved on."

"You don't always have to be the designated driver, you know."

"I don't drink."

"I don't want you to feel like we're using you. We all enjoy your company."

"Don't worry, I don't feel that way. It's honestly fine to just be around three good-looking girls. You see anyone else here rocking that?"

She looked around at the crowd, a few hundred other Marlons, all in groups of guys only. Maybe he was getting something out of all this in the end.

"Look, I just don't want to crush your dreams. Avital might come around. And hey, isn't unrequited love better than no love at all?"

"Sure, if you like raging against windmills."

"Oh, I don't know," Sam stammered. "I wouldn't say it's the impossible dream, Don Quixote."

He held up his hands. "It's okay, you don't have to humour me."

He'd seen through her attempt at flattery with laser-like precision and it made her feel worse. There was no sense in patronizing him anymore. "So, Erin then. You figure that's more realistic?"

Marlon didn't look her way, intent on the action taking place in the ring, but he nodded his head slightly, giving Sam all the answer she needed. "Promise you won't tell her?"

"Cross my heart." She made the motion over her chest.

"I guess it took finally coming to terms with the fact that I had no chance with Avital to see what Erin had to offer all along."

"I can see the appeal."

Erin wasn't a stunning model like Avital. She had a slightly too small chin and an overly loud voice, but she loved to laugh and seemed to take Marlon's strange fascinations with wrestling and video games in stride. Was there a chance for them? Sam honestly had no idea. Erin was great to be around, but Sam had never seen her date anyone either – in fact, she had no idea what kind of man she was even into.

"You think I'm crazy," Marlon said. "I can tell. I have no chance with her either, do I?"

"No, no, no, I don't," Sam stammered. "I have no idea really. I could ask for you if you want."

Now he turned to her, eyes bulging. "Oh god, no, don't do that. Then she'll know and it'll get all awkward."

"So, what do you want me to do?"

"I want you to realize that you can't run away from me." Marlon's voice was all wrong, like it had come from—

"Excuse me?" Sam said, looking over at him. She jerked back. He was gone. She hadn't heard him leave, let alone felt it, but in his place was a ghost.

"Scott."

Her breath came in gasps, her heart pounding. The skin on her arms stood in goose pimples. How had he snuck up on her?

"Hey, babe," he said, flashing a smile. His skin was sallow, and he was missing a few teeth. "Long time, no see."

"Where's Marlon?"

"Who?" another voice said to her right.

She spun to see Scott sitting there as well. Chains dangled around his neck. His loose shirt was open to reveal a chest crisscrossed with scars, still bloody. One oozed dark yellow pus down his abs.

"Jesus Christ," she said, jerking away from him.

"Come on, babe," Scott on the other side said, "don't be like that." He put his arm around her. It elongated like a snake, up and over her shoulder, around the neck, constricting, blocking her airwaves.

She gasped, tried to paw at his face. The other Scott grabbed her arms and wrenched them around her, almost dislocating the joint.

"I know you thought you could just walk away from everything that happened," the gap-toothed Scott said. "But you need to understand that it's not that simple."

"Sc—" she croaked out. The room was growing dark. They were killing her.

"They're coming for you, Sam," chest wound Scott said.

"Who?"

But the light was gone. She was surrounded in darkness, trapped in some kind of negative space. The two Scotts had faded away. She was alone. A spotlight hit her.

"One!"

"Help," she called, trying to orient herself. She was no longer attached to anything, simply a presence floating in the void.

"Two!"

"Who's there?" she shouted.

"Three!"

A bell rang. Someone shook her. The world came back, and she saw Marlon pushing her on the shoulder, back where he was supposed to be.

"Sam? You sort of zoned out there for a minute."

"I did?"

"I get it. This wrestling thing isn't for you either, but I've never seen anyone fall asleep at the finish of a match before."

"Oh, ha ha, sorry. What were we talking about? Erin, right? You want me to start meddling?"

"Don't do anything. If things happen, they happen."

"Alright, suit yourself."

The crowd cheered. The guy in the white trunks held up a gold belt, parading around the ring in victory. The grapplers cleared out and a man in a suit came into the ring, taking up a microphone as the house lights lit up the rest of the warehouse. She spotted Everett leering at the woman wrestler at the merch table as she signed an eight by ten for

73

him. The girls must still be in the bathroom.

"Who's that guy?" Sam asked.

"He runs the company." Marlon squinted. "Not sure why he's in the ring, though."

The man held up his hand, quieting the clamour of the audience. "Ladies and gentlemen," his voice came through the speakers. "I just wanted to thank you for coming tonight and every night these past six years. I've said it before and I'll say it again, the PWF has the best fans in the world." The crowd politely clapped and whistled, cheering the gratuitous praise. "But I have some sad news. This is going to be the last PWF show for a while."

Shocked moans came from the crowd. The man held his hand up again, looking morose. "We hope to be back soon, but for now, we have to close up shop. The building's been bought and the new owner plans on razing it for some kind of condo development."

Now the crowd viciously booed. Evidently, they really disliked neighbourhood gentrification.

"We're evicted. As of tomorrow, actually. So, we're done. I hope this isn't the end, but for now I just wanted to thank you for all the support."

The crowd clapped and started chanting: "Please don't go, please don't go."

"Is this part of the show?" Sam asked.

"I don't think so," Marlon said flatly.

"What'd we miss?" Erin asked as she and Avital returned to their seats. Sam and Marlon shared a conspirator's glance, but she kept her mouth shut.

"Sam fell asleep, and the good guy won," Marlon said.

"LOL, Sam. And who was the good guy?" Erin asked.

"Does it really matter?" Avital said.

Sam looked at Erin as she sat down next to Marlon. They certainly looked like a mismatch, but the idea of them wasn't that insane really. Maybe there could be something there.

People began filing past them to the exit. A line of men in tight pants, with long hair flowing behind them. One looked over his shoulder. Scott. He winked at her with a blood-red eye. She grabbed Erin's forearm.

"Sam? What's the matter?"

"I just…"

Scott was gone. It was just another one of the bearded guys in black. Was she seeing things?

"Want to get out of here as bad as the rest of us?" Avital said.

CHAPTER EIGHT

"We will begin the training... now!" Dr. Franz said. Rick pedalled furiously on the recumbent bike. A tube attached to his mouth measured his breathing. Sensors monitored his heart rate as the team physician kept track of every pant and drop of sweat. He'd been doing these tests for months and he was beginning to question the point. He'd gone through a battery of them before the draft, so by now, the Jets should know whatever they needed to.

"Yes, good work," the man said, watching the readouts.

He usually zoned out in moments like this, emptying his head and just trying to work. But his new life kept popping up.

The hot tub should be delivered first thing tomorrow, installed by Friday, hot tub party Saturday. Debbie'll take care of the details.

The new condo Debbie had helped him pick out was coming along. He was adjusting to the travel schedule, getting used to the hotel rooms, flights, bus rides, afternoon practices.

The life of a pro hockey player. What you always wanted.

Dr. Franz wrote in his clipboard. He wore a white lab coat and tiny wire-rimmed glasses. His slicked back hair was icy blond and his eyes tiny beads of black. He took a tiny dropper from out of his pocket and sucked up some of the sweat above Rick's eyes.

"Excellent coloration," he said as he examined the clear liquid in the plastic tube.

What a weirdo.

Rick shook his head, sweat flying from his long hair, sending the doctor scrambling to catch it all.

His feet pedalled around and around, his mind off again. The lingering sense of jitters of being a rookie, and for his hometown at that, were nearly gone. He just tried to take it shift by shift. His parents were so proud. The pressure was intense. He had to keep perspective. The NHL could break people. There was a long list of players that had flamed out under the glaring lights of the big show.

Thank God for Debbie.

She'd stepped up to help and he couldn't get over the change. The conniving, ruthless, bitch who dominated John A. MacDonald High was gone, replaced by his new right hand. All the history between them: the pact to pretend to be dating, the occasional rolls in the hay that left him feeling used, the controlling vindictiveness, her pathological hatred for Samantha Abraham, the Joshua incident, the jealousy, the lies, the fights. It was as if they'd come from a different person.

"You are slow, Rick," Dr. Franz said. "Please exert with greater vigour."

The guy sure talked strangely. Rick picked up the pace.

He'd be home soon. She'd be waiting.

Their rekindled relationship had been almost as much of a whirlwind as joining the NHL. He'd never seen it coming either. Eighties Thursday at Johnny Q's, the campus bar. His freshman season was going great. He was drinking with the guys when he'd looked over to the entranceway of the bar to see Debbie walking in. He'd noticed right away that there was something different about her. She seemed lighter, breezier, as if she no longer had to control every room.

She'd ended their for-show relationship after prom. She'd received a scholarship for McGill and told him she didn't need a small-time anchor. When he wasn't drafted out of high school, people had written off his chances. Despite the bitterness, he'd been curious why she was at Johnny Q's.

He'd lost sight of her, soon forgotten her presence amidst the pitchers of cheap draught beer. A tap on his shoulder and there she was, smiling sheepishly.

"Hey, Rick, can I sit?"

Asking was unlike her.

"Sure," he'd said tentatively.

She'd worn a tight blue shirt and black pants. They'd chatted casually, nothing too deep until the soulful wails of Chris de Burgh's *Lady in Red* came over the sound system.

"Dance?" she'd asked.

"Sure," he'd said and followed her out to the floor.

That was when he knew that she wasn't the same person. She'd opened up, confessed how awful she felt about how she had behaved back in high school, how she'd taken him for granted, let the power and status go to her head. She'd torn her ACL and MCL in only her second volleyball game, ruined her knee and her career in the sport. The scholarship was revoked, her entire life plan wiped out.

He felt sweat pouring into his eyes, like he was crying. Like she had that night when she told him how losing everything had forced her to reevaluate her life. She'd just wanted a chance to make things right. His libido answered before he did. They started off slow, but now, he knew that he'd made the right decision. She definitely wasn't the same Debbie Peterson.

"Excellent, Mr. Rick, you will please step down from the bicycle apparatus and approach the full body mirror."

He'd drifted so far away that he'd forgotten where he was. He stepped off the recumbent bike and stood in front of the large mirror adjacent to the weight rack.

"Please remove your shirt."

He handed the man the drenched top. It quickly disappeared into a laundry hamper. Franz raised an eyebrow at a couple of bruises on his neck. The man took some measuring tape and checked his chest, neck, and forehead dimensions, writing them down in his pad.

"What's that for?"

"Progress results. For the team uniforms. We must have the correct sizing now, mustn't we?"

He ignored the man as he went about sizing him up from every angle.

"We almost done?"

"But of course."

"I've got someone waiting for me to come home," he said.

"Yes, I can tell."

Debbie had found the upscale three-bedroom condo downtown, had filled it with the best furniture and electronics. She was cooking for him, even offering massages when he came home. At this point, he had no idea what he would do without her. She'd become such an integral part of his life that he was thinking of making it official and popping the question.

"Don't do it, bro," his buddy, Chuck, had said. "Enjoy the pro life for a while. Puck bunnies in every city!"

He debated the question in his head as Dr. Franz began to draw strange lines over his bare chest in dotted patterns.

"Doc?" he asked.

"Oh, Mr. Rick, this is an old-world technique. I am tracing your energy lines, widening the channels. It will give you a new vigour. In this business of hockey, it is every advantage that makes a champion, no?"

"Drawing black lines over my body does all that?"

"Indeed."

He didn't see how this could do anything other than force him to need a deep scrubbing, but he wasn't here to rock the boat.

Franz took a large set of metal tongs and wrapped them around Rick's head, the cold steel sending a shiver down his spine.

"And what's this?"

"You've perhaps heard of phrenology?" Franz said.

"No, what's that?"

Franz burst out laughing. "I jest. A joke that you do not understand. Forgive me. This device is merely to measure your head size, for a new helmet, you see. We must protect that valuable brain inside."

"Oh, right." He already had a helmet, but maybe they were going with a new supplier.

There was a knock on the door to the testing room. A security guard wearing the dark navy jacket of arena staff pushed open the door cautiously. It was Isaiah. Rick knew him right away because he was the only Black man on staff. He'd made it a point to get to know as many of the arena crew's names as he could. His dad had always taught him to treat the regular staff with respect.

"Sorry to interrupt, doctor, but there's a visitor for Rick at the back door. She's pretty insistent that she needs to see him."

"We are presently engaged," Franz snapped back.

Isaiah cringed at the doctor's tone, clearly nervous.

"Did she say what it was about? Or give a name?" Rick asked. Maybe it was Debbie.

The doctor scowled at him.

"It could be an emergency," Rick said off his look.

"Samantha Abraham. Said it was pretty important that she speak to you."

"Sam? She didn't say why she needed to see me?"

Isaiah shook his head. "Only that it was important. Should I let her in?"

Why was she here? And what could she possibly have to say to him now? It had been nearly two years since she had tossed him aside for Joshua. He'd finally moved on from the pain of giving her his heart only to have it crushed. More of Debbie's help.

"I don't know why she'd show up out of the blue like this."

"Is that a no?" Isaiah asked.

The last time he'd seen her at the mall with Debbie, she'd barely had two words to say to him.

"Perhaps it is not my business, Mr. Rick," Dr. Franz said, "but have you heard the expression puck bunny?"

Debbie had warned him that now he was playing in the big leagues, people would be coming out from under the woodwork for a piece of him. He had money coming in, prestige and fame. Leeches would be everywhere. Even exes who'd tossed him aside like trash for a man who'd been created in a laboratory and died.

"No, I have nothing to say to her. Tell her to go."

The doctor smiled.

Isaiah nodded. "Gotcha, Rick." He hesitated before leaving, struggling with something. "Was this okay? Coming here? I wasn't sure I should, but the girl seemed so convinced that you'd want to see her. I don't want to mess this gig up – it's finally something normal, you know?"

"No worries, Isaiah," Rick said. "Sometimes people can put on a good show. I'm glad you told me."

Isaiah waved and turned around, disappearing back the way he'd come, leaving Rick and Dr. Franz alone again.

"A wise decision, Mr. Rick. Now we must continue the processes." Franz licked his lips and Rick tuned out another round of tests.

CHAPTER NINE

"The kids were asking when you were going to be coming over again," Veronica said as she waited for the hotdog vendor to finish cooking her wiener.

"Oh yeah?" Jimmy dumped some onions on his hotdog and lathered it in mustard.

"Carter thought you were funny."

"Kids love fart jokes."

"Here you go, officer." The vendor in the apron handed Veronica her dog.

"Thanks." She moved next to Jimmy to top it. "It wasn't just the fart jokes, Jimmy. You're great with them."

"I wasn't sure how you'd want to handle the whole me meeting your kids thing in the morning. It's sort of, I don't know, a line."

"Well, if it makes you feel any better, you're their new favourite of Mommy's sleepover buddies."

"You've brought home others?" He took a bite of his hotdog.

"Does that bother you?"

"No, I just thought…"

"That I shouldn't have been dating since my ex-husband ran out on me? That was over four years ago. I'm not ready to be celibate."

Jimmy saw the hotdog vendor grinning, checking out Veronica's ass. She seemed to have finished topping her dog, so he led them over to the side of the arena, leaning against the light brown brick of the MTS Centre. They'd parked around the block, stopping in for a hotdog from the vendor who'd staked out the spot in front of the hockey arena. He was the guy Frank had always insisted on going to. He'd said, "He's the only one I trust with my wieners." And he'd been right. The guy made the best dogs in town.

"I get it," he said. "I—"

"No, you don't. You never had a spouse run out on you after having kids."

"True, but—"

"You have to remember that I had a life before you, Hooper. Some could even call it baggage."

"No, it's—"

"If any of this stuff is a problem for you, you should probably say it now."

"It isn't, I swear."

"Because I don't want to see my kids hurt again."

"Ronnie." He put his hand on her arm as she took a bite of her own loaded hotdog. "I promise. You have kids. You're divorced. I get it. You're still you. That's who I'm interested in, okay?"

"You know, you were right about that hotdog cart. These are great."

"Frank was good for something in the end, I guess."

"Too bad we had to park around the block."

"The exercise will do us good."

"Yeah, I don't want this to go right to my ass."

Jimmy tossed his wrapper in a nearby trash receptacle and

waited for her to finish. When she'd balled hers up, they started walking back towards the cruiser, parked in the alley just behind the arena.

* * *

"He didn't want to see me?" Sam said to the security guard standing at the back door to the arena.

"Sorry, miss, he's busy training with the doc."

"But he *is* in there."

"Uh…"

For a brief moment, she considered pushing her way past this Isaiah, as the name tag identified him, and just rushing through the arena looking for Rick. But even if she did, she had no idea where he was inside. She'd been through some of the bowels of the MTS Centre that night at the Factor 5ive concert – that was how she knew to come to the receiving door in the back alley – but the training facilities for the Jets hadn't been a part of that tour.

"Look, you shouldn't be here, and he said no, okay? So how about you just go before you get me in trouble?"

"I'm not here to get anyone in trouble," Sam said. "I'm here to keep Rick from getting into trouble."

"I think he can handle himself, miss. He's a pro hockey player. Those guys fight all the time and—"

"Not like that. It's a different kind of trouble." She could tell by his confused look that he didn't understand and there was no way she could explain it without coming across like a lunatic. "It's just, I think he needs to be aware of some weird things going on and if it came from me, it would probably—"

"Ain't nothing weird in there, miss," Isaiah said. "Trust me.

I'm walking around, looking at security footage, talking to the players. It's as normal as can be. And I've seen weird, so I know."

"Not like me," Sam said.

Isaiah smirked. "Try me."

Sam didn't want to argue with the guy, let alone get into a history lesson. She sighed, realizing that she'd come up empty again.

"There's nothing you can do? Like, maybe escort him here? Get me his phone number?" She patted her pockets. "Maybe get me a pen and paper so I can write him a note? Anything?"

"Sorry. You've got to realize that Rick's big time now. People want a piece. We can't just let in anyone who shows up in the back alley ringing the receiving bell to talk to him. You could be a stalker."

"Stalker? I'm an ex."

"Oh shit, that's even worse."

Sam slumped down. "I just don't know what else to do. I need to warn him he's in trouble, but I can't get to him."

Something in her voice must have reached Isaiah. He looked down each side of the alley nervously. His voice softened. "Look, you promise me you ain't some crazy stalker?"

She looked up. "Yeah. I dumped him."

"Wait here."

He shut the door, disappearing back inside. Sam perked up, wondering if maybe her plight had convinced the guy to try again to get Rick to come. Maybe she would have the opportunity to talk to him, after all. Maybe this whole idea wasn't going to turn out to be a bust in the end.

She watched the door for what felt like an eternity, waiting for Isaiah and Rick. She heard the beeps of the security code being pressed, held her breath, going over what she was going to tell Rick. The door pushed open.

"Rick, I—"

Rick wasn't standing there. Neither was Isaiah. It was five men. With leathery skin, gelled hair, spray tans, leather pants, ethnically diverse.

"Another bitch looking for some action."

The members of Factor 5ive stepped out of the door into the alley. Sam backed away.

"No. It's not possible. You guys are—"

"Live and in colour, baby," Joey, the blond one, said.

But they weren't. Not anymore. The skin was cracked, revealing crimson flesh. Nazim's head was slightly caved in. Anthony's arm dangled awkwardly.

"Ready to get a little freaky?" the muscled Freddy said.

"Oh, you know she's down," Joey said, grinning, revealing a broken smile of missing teeth.

"No." Sam lunged for them. She wasn't going to give them the chance to get her first. She charged, but hit a metal wall, smashing up against the loading dock door and knocking herself to the ground.

Stars danced in her eyes. "Ow."

The door beeped. Isaiah opened it up and saw her lying on the ground holding her head.

"What were you doing?"

"I slipped," she said.

Isaiah paused, as if reconsidering whatever it was he'd come to do. "Shit, maybe this wasn't a good idea."

"Did you bring Rick?" Sam asked hopefully.

He revealed two tickets in his hand. "No. I went and got

you a pair of comp tickets for the next home game. I figure you can't get into anything freaky or dangerous surrounded by fifteen thousand people and maybe you can get Rick's attention with a sign or something. Shit. Maybe this was stupid, I—"

"No, please. That's so amazing. I don't know what to say. I—"

"Don't say a goddamn thing about where you got these, alright? I don't know why I let myself get suckered into helping when I shouldn't. My mother always told me I was too nice for my own—"

"Is everything okay over here?" a woman's voice called from the left. Sam and Isaiah both turned to see two cops standing in the alley, looking at her.

"Officer?" Isaiah asked, confused.

"We saw her run face first into the door and—"

"It's okay, officers," Sam said, snatching the tickets from Isaiah's hand before he could react. "It was a mistake. I was just waiting for my tickets and thought the door was open and… yeah. All good. Thanks for checking in." Sam darted away, hoping that the two cops didn't recognize her. It was becoming way too coincidental that she kept running into them. It felt like they were the only cops in River City.

She didn't notice Isaiah's shrug or pay attention to them walking back to the cruiser parked a few meters away.

CHAPTER TEN

"Sir, we've done it. We've broken the code."

Arthur Fritz looked up from his desk at the man in the lab coat, standing excitedly at the door, holding the clipboard so tightly that he thought he was going to break it.

"The trigger sounds, the hypnotic state, the reactions, all of it. It's working. No complications. At least, not following the metrics that—"

"Layered? Gender specific?"

"After the incident with lab three and the intestines stretched over the florescent bulbs, I was a little concerned, but—"

"Technician. I am aware of all our failures. I only need to know if we have passed them. Can the project be undertaken on the required scale?"

"Absolutely, sir."

"Good. Then go and celebrate with your team. Order pizza."

The man turned before he'd taken two steps, as Fritz stopped him. "No, get Chinese. Someplace nice but not too expensive. And make sure you get an extra order of lemon chicken. I'll be down later. Right now, I have a phone call to make."

"Right away, sir. And thanks." The man pivoted on his heels and started out. "Chinese, sweet!"

When Fritz was confident that the room was empty, he rose from his desk and shut the door. This was incredible news. The work of Simon's team, that of the necromancers, it was all coming to fruition at long last. He stepped around his desk and looked at the photo of his dear departed twin.

"Simon, your death will not be in vain. Your work will live on. The great outcome will be met."

Arthur Fritz picked up the phone and dialed the private number that only he and those in his tier knew. He waited as the line connected through.

"Speak," a voice on the other end said.

"It is time."

CHAPTER ELEVEN

"I'm telling you, Francis, I know that thousand-dollar bill was in my top drawer, I put it there every night for safe keeping."

"In a sock, I hope," Frank said.

"Of course – what better place is there to put your money?"

"Good man."

Dressed in a plaid shirt tucked into pants pulled up to his chest, Oscar sat in the guest chair in Frank's room. He ran his hand over thin hair. His distraught wrinkled face showed each and every year he'd struggled through this world, biting and scratching, only to be left in a prison for his final days. And now, even the tiniest piece of pie he'd fought for had been taken away by the crooks who ran Shady Acres.

"That bill meant the world to me. When I was in my twenties, right when the war broke out, I put everything I had into a GIC. I watched that thing grow from a few dollars into a few hundred, then to the big three zeroes. I cashed it all in to one special bill, to show the world what being smart was all about. I used to show that thing to my kids, then to my grandkids. I'd pull it out to teach 'em what investing and frugality really meant. That thing was like a brother to me, a wife even. 'Specially after my Nancine died. Tell you something, it was the best friend I ever had in the end. It's the only one that came with me here."

"A man and his money have a special bond, Oscar, I know."

Oscar's chin rested nearly on his chest. "Now it's gone, and I know they took it! I'll bet it was the Mexican one. He never looked right. They shouldn't have let them in here. Fucking Mulroney and his Free Trade. Ruined the country, it did. I'll bet he's sending my bill back to his family south of the other border one burrito at a time."

Frank rubbed his chin thoughtfully. "That's a theory I can look into, Oscar. It's clearer than the water down there, that's for sure."

"That means you'll help me?"

"It's what I do."

Frank had overheard Oscar complaining that one of the nurses had stolen his lucky thousand-dollar bill. The staff laughed it off, but not Frank. He'd been around long enough to know when someone was telling the truth. Oscar had the look of the victim. He may have been many things – senile, almost ninety, unable to dress himself – but he was not a liar. His cataract clouded eyes told Frank all he needed to know; there was a crook amidst the staff of Shady Acres.

"So, what's the plan?"

"You leave that to me. I may be locked up in here with the rest of you apple saucers but I'm not fruit salad yet."

Oscar looked at Frank with his head cocked to the side, like a confused puppy.

"I'll set up a surveillance of the most likely suspects, weed out the guilty from the innocent."

Frank tapped the man on the shoulder and rose to his feet. "Don't worry your liver spotted head, old man, I'll find that thousand-dollar bill or I'll eat the shit they call sloppy joes around here next Friday night at dinner."

Frank wandered the halls, making a list of suspects. First was Jesus the probable Mexican. Frank had a long history with that country. If it wasn't the food, it was the weather. Montezuma had gotten his revenge more than once, but for what? Jesus was the possible centre of the scheme, but by no means was he the only possibility.

Trina, the hippie with the strange dreadlocked hair. Her story was that she was on work experience through the university, but Frank didn't buy that for a second either. What kind of reputable institution would take a girl with hair like that? There was a web of secrets hidden in that matted, mashed up mess of a mop, and Frank knew that the more he unraveled, the more dirt would fall out, maybe even one missing thousand-dollar bill.

Next was Paulie, the girl with a guy's name and a build and voice to match. She said she was into bodybuilding, but to him it looked like she'd built up all the wrong parts and built down the best ones.

Ginny was the final suspect, a sweet and quiet little mouse of a girl, with great big glasses and a tiny voice. She seemed lost in the massive halls of Shady Acres, far too nice and comforting to the residents to not have something up her sleeve. Maybe something sticky and in need of a few extra clams.

Frank followed them as they went about their normal day-to-day duties: bedpan cleaning, sponge baths, dressing up and down, mopping, insulin shots, the works. He saw so much that pretty soon he was sure that he could do their damn jobs himself. He knew their routines: where they went on their rounds, when they took their breaks. He made pages of notes, but saw nothing that gave a hint of which one might be criminal scum.

He heard a commotion at the nurses' station, chatter among his suspects. "Mrs. Ween just died."

"When?"

"A few minutes ago. In her sleep."

"Another visit from the Grim Reaper himself," Frank muttered.

Frank walked down the hall and around the corner, to find more orderlies amassed outside Mrs. Ween's door. Some of the residents stood watching at the other end of the hall. The news went around fast when you had nowhere to go.

"She was a good soul."

"Such a pity."

"At least it was peaceful."

Looking into the open door, he saw the woman laying on the bed. Frank had seen death before, bodies riddled with bullets, missing a head or an arm or a leg, some drained of blood, others that had fermented in their own feces for weeks, but this was somehow different. Mrs. Ween was a tiny little thing, no more than a hair's whisper of a person, thin and frail with faint white hair in a bun, a voice like the soft hum of a humidifier, a gentle smile that was warm and inviting. And now she was dead. Her features blanched and white, the warmth of the soul gone forever. She looked peaceful as the orderlies covered her up with a sheet and placed her on the stretcher service wagon.

Here today, gone tomorrow.

That's when he noticed something out of the ordinary: Dr. Hans talking in a low voice with Nurse Ironhide. They were looking over the body.

"Yes, many interesting features on this one," the man said as he pointed to areas on the corpse with a pen. He carried a clipboard in his other hand. Frank couldn't see what was written on it, since the good side was against the man's chest.

"What the heck is so important about the corpse of old Mrs. Ween?" he muttered.

"I trust you have already begun the preservation proceedings?"

"Of course, Dr. Hans."

They were talking about the old woman like she was set to be next week's beef patties.

That was when Nurse Ironhide looked up, noticed him noticing her and reached over, shutting the door, and cutting him off from any more eavesdropping.

"Now what in the world are those two going on about?" Frank said to himself, too loudly.

Something hit him in the leg. He spun around to see Enid in her wheelchair. She harrumphed. "Those two are like vultures," she said, "circling around the dead for a piece of scrap."

Could they be looking for some loose change?

"Would you call them sharks circling the chum?"

"Worse than that," Enid said. "They're on the corpse so fast you'd think they knew before anyone else."

"You don't say?"

"No, I did say. Just right now."

"That's what I'm confirming. That you did say."

"I did."

"Very interesting, ma'am." It looked like Enid might have just given him more than he'd anticipated.

"Real pity about old Mrs. Ween, too," Enid said. "She seemed so healthy and full of life. Why, just yesterday, she beat me at Wii tennis and—"

"Death doesn't always follow the rules."

"Oh, she wasn't cheating, she was just much better than me at that thing and—"

"No, I was talking about the Grim Reaper."

"I wasn't playing him, I was playing Mrs. Ween."

"And now she's dead, we've established that."

"But that's what's so shocking," Enid said. "You'd never have thought she was next. It never seems to be the sick ones that go, always the ones you least expect. Pity."

Frank left Enid in her wheelchair gawking at the shut door. The old woman had given him a lot to think about. Maybe he should expand his surveillance to Nurse Ironhide and Dr. Hans. Could the conspiracy go all the way to the top?

He went back to wandering the halls.

CHAPTER TWELVE

"Ladies and gentlemen, your River City Jets!"

Van Halen's *Jump* blared over the arena speakers. Players streamed out onto the ice from the dressing room. The crowd rose to their feet, voices unified in a massive roar. The sound was deafening. Sam's stomach tingled with nervous anticipation. She'd never been to an NHL game. It felt so much bigger than the John A. MacDonald High School playoffs. The crowd was amped. The team had a lot of buzz going and it was all because of—

"There he is." She nudged Erin.

Through the standing crowd cheering and clapping, she saw Rick, circling the Jets half of the ice. He looked completely at ease, like he was always meant to be in the big leagues. They were already calling him the future of the organization. In a short time, the Jets were the hottest ticket in town, and it was his doing.

"This is insane," Erin yelled in her ear.

"It's so loud," Sam screamed back.

"How much did you have to pay for these seats?"

"Don't worry about it!"

They could barely hear each other despite sitting side by side. The seats were lower bowl, the expensive ones. She could run down the stairs and be right at the glass. It was better than she could have expected for a pair of pity tickets given to her by a well-meaning backstage security guard.

"Let me buy the drinks at least," Erin said.

They watched the warmup. Players took casual shots at the goalie, chatted as they did laps, then a buzzer sounded, and they lined up on their respective blue lines.

"Ladies and gentlemen, please remove your hats and stand if you are able as the Jets' own Stacey Nattress sings our national anthem," an announcer called out over the sound system.

A woman in a blue dress stepped out onto a carpet patch laid on the ice. She belted out a rousing *O Canada* and nearly sixteen thousand fans sang along.

Sam watched the Jets players for any evidence of what she suspected. Were they still human? Golems created by the necromancers revealed the truth in their vacant eyes. Joshua acted the same when under the control of his heartstone. But the guys from Radiant Cyanide and Factor 5ive were different. They'd been human first. If Karlsson's twin owned the Jets then she had to assume that whatever process had been done to Scott, Tommy, and the others, was also intended for the players here.

But was she too late? Was the team standing at attention to the national anthem of Canada already transformed? And if so, what was the endgame? The bands had used music to hypnotize women into performing degrading acts on camera. Would the same thing be true with the players? She doubted it. The reach an NHL player had was completely different to that of a band. There was some piece of the puzzle she was missing. She needed Rick. If he was still human, he had eyes on the inside.

"—we stand on guard for thee!"

The arena erupted into applause as Stacey Nattress finished. The two teams hopped on to their benches. Five players from each one stayed on the ice, lined up to face off. They waited for the ref to drop the puck and start the game.

"This is so exciting," Erin said.

Rick was at centre, leaned down to go for the puck.

"That's Rick, right?" Erin said, pointing.

"Yup."

He was only a few hundred feet away from her.

The puck dropped and the game was on, the players moving around the glistening, fresh ice surface in blurs.

How could she get through to him?

The snapping of sticks, the whack of the puck, bodies hitting the boards, the ping of the post, the crowd rising and falling with every shot and increase in pace. She and Erin were just as caught up in the drama as everyone else. Sam absorbed it all, waiting for the right moment.

"Rick's some kind of heartthrob now," Erin said. "There's so many signs here."

Erin pointed to a dozen women brandishing large poster-board signs, with things like, "Rick I love U," his name surrounded by hearts, or, "Rick – marry me!" written on them.

Primal screams rose as he was shown on the big screen sitting on the bench. Sam thought she saw someone faint. The player next to him elbowed him in the side and pointed up, making Rick realize he was on all four screens of the scoreboard. He waved sheepishly as the other player teased him. The girls screamed even louder.

"Sam, he's gorgeous," Erin said.

His long dark hair, already matted with sweat, glistened in the bright lights. His smile lit up the huge screen. He seemed larger than life. It was so strange that he was the same guy she'd dated and broken up with. How would things be different if she hadn't been so stupid?

"No wonder there's so many screaming girls," Erin said.

"Puck bunnies," Sam said derisively. "People who only want to get close to him to fuck him."

"And it's different with you because you already did," Erin said, snorting.

"It's not like that."

"You still haven't told us why you need to get in touch with him so badly."

Sam couldn't tell them about her suspicions. They'd already been caught up in the Factor 5ive and Radiant Cyanide firestorm. It had been a small miracle none of them had been hurt. She didn't want to risk them getting involved again.

"Can we just leave it at personal reasons?"

"Personal enough to make a big sign like the other scream-ers?"

Sam's hand clenched around the rolled-up paper she'd brought, hoping to use it to draw Rick's eye as he moved around the ice, maybe during a face-off. It had seemed so perfect until she'd seen that there were dozens of other women here with the very same idea. She might have to improvise something else.

"I told you, it's not like that."

The arena rose in anticipation as the Jets rushed in on a two on one. Rick took a pass, people sprang to their feet. He took a shot on net, but the opposing goalie saved it. The crowd "oooohed" in disappointment.

"Whatever the reason, this is fun." Erin hugged Sam. "Thanks for inviting me."

They'd done their make-up, fixed their hair, debated over the best combination of pants and hoodie to wear under their brand-new team jerseys, pre-gamed with some homemade Irish coffee, studied the player numbers so they'd know who was who. But now, Sam wondered if it had all been a giant waste of time.

"You think there'll be a fight tonight?" Erin asked.

"I don't know, maybe?"

"Does Rick fight?"

"He didn't on the John A. Rangers. He was the guy the other team tried to pick on. But the Rangers always had an enforcer to protect him."

"Enforcer?"

"A guy who would fight someone who picked on the star player. Joshua, the other guy I dated, used to get in all kinds of brawls even though he didn't like fighting either."

"I still can't believe you dated two guys on the same hockey team and don't think that makes you one of those puck bunny things."

"It was just a coincidence. What did one of your exes do? Tell me so I can call you a whatever-that-was bunny."

"Okay, okay, I'll lay off. It's just that you have all these interesting stories in your past you never really tell us about."

"I think everyone does, don't they?"

"Fair enough, I guess."

A guy with a massive tray of beers strapped to his chest walked down the aisle. Erin waved in his direction. He stopped at their row, and she looked over the lines of plastic cups with lids, filled with amber liquid.

"It's only beer, right?" she asked. "You can't do, like, mimosas or anything?"

He rolled his eyes. "Not easily. But you can order a few different drinks at one of the bars in the concourse. From me, it's beer one, beer two, beer three. And each one is the same. Molson's."

"Oh, well, I guess two beer twos then." Erin handed him a ten-dollar bill.

He stared at her, waiting. "That'll be fifteen," he said.

"Holy shit," Erin shouted so loud the people in the row in front of them turned to stare. "Fifteen bucks for two beers? Yikes." She handed him a five and then he passed along the drinks.

"These better be the best beers in the world," Erin said as she handed one to Sam.

Sam took a sip. "I've got some bad news for you…"

* * *

"Go Jets go, go Jets go!" The arena was hopping, the home team was up two-one. It was almost the end of the first period. Sam and Erin shouted along with the rest of the fans, swept up in the furor of the moment as the home team skated up ice. Rick had the puck, driving into the offensive zone with his wingers at his side. He made a quick move, sidestepped a defenceman, made a deft no-look pass, the winger took the shot, but it hit the post. A collective "awwww" rang out from thousands of voices.

Sam was on the edge of her seat. Looking over at Erin, she

saw that she was along for the ride as well.

"Sam, I think I love hockey now."

"I know, right!"

The ref blew his whistle, stopping the play. His voice came over the sound system.

"Winnipeg number thirty-four, two minutes for hooking."

The crowd erupted in "booos" and "ref, you suck" catcalls.

"What's hooking?" Erin asked.

"Bullshit, is what it is."

Dance music came over the sound system as the game paused for a television commercial. Sam scanned through the crowd. Nearly everyone was wearing a team jersey, hat, or scarf and it was clear that they were having as great a time as she was. Everywhere she looked, people were loading up on beer, popcorn, and hotdogs.

"Oh, look," Erin said. "Kiss cam."

The scoreboard screens showed couples in the audience. As they realized that they were on screen, they'd lean in and kiss each other to applause.

"Cute."

She watched the images cycle through two more couples kissing. The image shifted to another shot. It was blurry, out of focus, zoomed in. Sam squinted, confused. The music drifted away.

"Hey, did someone mess—"

It wasn't in the arena. It was in a white room, with a poster on the wall of Kurt Cobain in the background. The person on screen looked drunk, her head lolling back. Sam blanched. Her heart raced.

It was the video of her hypnosis state threesome. There on the big screen for everyone to see.

"No."

She turned to Erin. She was looking at her, but her eyes were all wrong. Black holes, empty sockets. The entire row staring at her, no, the whole section. The entire lower bowl. Everyone in the arena. All the players had lined up to look. Sam jerked to her feet.

"No. No. It's not—"

She was pulled back down to her seat hard. The music was back. She saw Erin looking at her. She pointed to the scoreboard.

"Look," Erin said. "Kiss cam!"

"No, I—"

"Sam, it's a part of the experience."

They were in the frame, the kiss cam logo below them, the crowd cheering them on.

"Wait, no, we're not a—"

Erin pulled Sam in and gave her a quick kiss on the lips. The crowd erupted in a huge cheer.

"Hey, why'd you—"

Erin grinned. "Must be all these beers," she said and took the last sip from her cup. "Which reminds me, we're dry."

Sam watched Erin turn her cup over in disappointment. It was then that she realized just how many empties were strewn around them. Together they'd had way more than she realized.

"Holy crap," she said.

"I know. We need more!"

Sam never was much of a beer drinker, but here was evidence to the contrary. She downed the last sip of her own cup. Maybe there was just something about this particular brew, or maybe it was the atmosphere in the place, but she wanted more.

"Where's that guy with the tray?" Erin asked.

"I don't see him."

"Wait, he said we could order from a bar in the concourse."

"To the concourse," Sam replied.

The two of them rose and headed up the arena stairs, passing through curtains and leaving the ice area to the concourse that surrounded the building. Other people waited in lines for food and drinks, a few milled about chatting. Noise from the crowd echoed through the hall.

Sam felt a sudden need to use the washroom. She saw one with a line already a mile long.

"Gotta pee," Sam said.

"Okay," Erin said. "I'll get the beer."

"Oh, and mini donuts."

"One bag or two?"

"Two. But get some for yourself, too," Sam said.

Erin dashed off to join the line of people standing at the bar kiosk.

The thought of sweet, deep-fried mini donuts filled Sam's thoughts as she waited in line. She slowly moved forward, thinking about how much fun she was having. Wondering how much she'd actually had to drink. She found her way inside the navy and white arena restroom. Women dried their hands on paper towels, tossing crumpled balls into a huge pile spilling out of a nearby trash can.

Then it hit her. Erin had kissed her.

No, she wouldn't have done that.

The room emptied. No one followed Sam inside – was she the last in line?

The noise from the game was muffled. She chose the door

furthest from the exit. The toilet inside had recently been the sight of some disagreements with someone's stomach.

"Next."

The adjacent stall was cleaner, but still not ready for a commercial. She laid out a series of toilet paper strips on the seat and sat down.

Did Erin kiss me? Or did I imagine that? She caught the faint aroma of strange lip gloss and gently touched her lips. *Was it on the big screen?*

The room was strangely quiet. After seeing that huge line it felt unlikely that she was really the last person to come in.

Footsteps.

Someone else was here now.

Sam grabbed a line of paper. The feet of the other patron stopped at her stall, boots pointed directly at Sam from under the door. Whoever it was pushed at the locked door.

"Uh, occupied."

The girl was insistent. She pushed harder.

"There's, like, six other stalls."

A pounding now, incessant.

"Okay, okay, just let me flush." Sam stood, pulling her pants up, triggering the auto-flush when the door crashed in, knocking her back onto the seat.

"What the—"

A weight pressed down on her, trying to crush her beneath a wall of hard plastic. The toilet dug into her spine, sending shooting waves of pain up and down her legs as she desperately fought back.

Whoever it was on the other side was strong, too strong.

"—hell do you want?" Sam tried to shout.

The door pushed into her face. She couldn't match strength

from this angle, she had no leverage. She had one chance. She kicked up with her feet. The door swung up and hit her in the face, but the girl's feet were knocked off balance. Sam slid off the toilet seat. Twisting, she let the door slide off her as she got to her feet. The attacker crashed down in the space between the door and the toilet. Sam slid through the stall opening. The assailant scrambled to her feet, pushing the broken door away.

She was a brute of a creature, some kind of female body-builder, massively muscled, with a square jaw, and red and black hair pulled back in a tight ponytail. Her expression was impassive, eyes dead.

"Another golem? But how?"

The girl stepped out of the stall.

A bizarrely squeaky voice said from behind them, "We know you."

Sam spun around, saw the reflection of the woman in the mirror, but at the wrong angle. She was only visible from the shoulders up. Her eyes burned with life.

"We know who you are."

Sam spun back. The woman was right on her and threw a looping punch. Sam sidestepped, her face feeling the faint breeze of the blow as it flew past and hit the wall behind her, leaving a cracked impression of a fist in the mirror, right in the unmoving reflection.

"You can't hide," the woman's image said again, despite the actual creature's lips not moving.

"From who?" Sam said.

Another punch. Sam sidestepped again, this time bringing her arms up in double knife hand blocks on opposite sides of the girl's elbow, a chopping action designed to break the arm

107

if done right. The brute was too big, too muscled and Sam's attempt did nothing.

New plan.

She thrust her elbow into the woman's face, cracking her nose with a sick crunching sound, pushing the cartilage halfway across her face in a disgusting bit of amateur plastic surgery. Blood dripped out of nostrils that aimed towards the ear.

The creature grabbed Sam by the collar of her jersey and hoisted her up in the air, throwing her down to the ground with a double handed sack toss.

Her wind was knocked out as Sam connected with the concrete floor. She groaned in pain and struggled for air. The beast reared back and threw a punch down towards Sam's face. She rolled away and the fist hit the floor. Concrete was stronger than the girl's hand. Her bones shattered in a bursting of flesh and sinew. The monster reared back with a mangled mess of a stump to strike for Sam again, but Sam kicked up, hitting her in the face, knocking her off balance. She slid her foot under her ankle and pushed with her opposite foot on the beast's knee, tripping the thing and sending her flying. Her head hit the sink with a loud *kabong*.

Sam popped up and grabbed the brute by the ponytail. She rammed her head into the wall then down into the sink. The auto tap sprang to life, swirling the dripping blood around and around.

"Tell me who sent you," Sam shouted at the laughing face of the girl in the cracked mirror. "Who?"

The creature, head submerged, went limp. The face disappeared. The body dangled half out of a blood-filled sink. Sam let go and it slunk down to the floor, lifeless.

Had she killed her?

"Shit."

The bathroom was a mess. A broken stall, blood everywhere, the shattered floor. There didn't seem to be any security cameras in here as far as she could tell. Sam quickly dragged the girl into one of the stalls. She washed her hands and straightened herself up as best she could.

She headed for the door. It was locked from the inside. She unlatched it and peered outside. An out of order sign hung on the door handle. Erin stood waiting against the far walls with two beers and two bags of mini donuts in her hands.

Sam slid out, shut the door, and ran over to her.

"What took you so long? Everything okay?"

Sam shrugged. "Someone didn't flush."

* * *

Walking back to her seat, two more beers in hand, the room was starting to spin. She didn't fully remember even getting up for them. Rick had just scored the fourth Jets goal. The home side was up four to three. The collective shouts of orgasmic joy in the stands had lifted her into the air.

Now, they were up five to three. When had that happened?

She was sitting next to Erin. They were both drinking beer. No, wait, there were two more in the coasters attached to the chair backs.

Metallica blared over the PA. She bobbed her head. The bathroom was open again. She took a place in line. It moved quickly. Back inside. The mirror, the floor, the stall door; all fixed. Was this the same one she'd been in last period? She stepped into a stall and was back in her seat next to Erin. Had she even gone to the bathroom?

"Ladies and gentlemen, time for our 50/50 draw," a voice called out.

Sam had a ticket in her hand. *When did I buy this?* The announcer read over a number that didn't match any of hers. She tore up the paper and tossed it in the air. All around her, a sea of confetti from other disappointed patrons floated down like snowfall.

Erin put her arm around her. "Oh well, next time!"

Sam put her arm around Erin. The clock showed a minute left.

She couldn't remember how many beers they'd had. Erin smiled at her. A horn blared. The room erupted.

"Jets goal, his second of the night, scored by number twenty-three, Rick Hansen!"

Rick?

They leapt to their feet, beer flying from their cups, jumping in joy, hugging each other close. Sam could smell the beer on Erin's breath. She kissed her happily.

"Whoooo!" they cheered along with the rest of the crowd.

Wait a minute, had they just kissed?

"Excuse me, miss?"

A hand patted her on the shoulder. Sam turned to see a security guard and a cop standing at the edge of their seats.

"Yeah?" she said, slurring.

"I think it's time to leave," the lady cop said to her.

"What, why?" Sam asked.

The cop pointed to the people sitting below them, covered in beer. They held out dripping hands and looked frustrated.

"Oh, shit," Sam said. They must have spilled their drinks when they were cheering.

Glares from all around her, accusing looks, judgement from a jury of her peers. Conviction; banishment.

"Come along."

"Okay."

She and Erin rose and were led up the aisle in shame. A few people filmed them with cameras, whispering among themselves. She never saw the rolled-up poster fall between the rows of seats.

CHAPTER THIRTEEN

"You hear the news?" Teddy said to no one in particular. "Linseman's coming back."

"Linseman?" Jaxxon said. "I thought he was holding out this year."

"He is," Jonesy said. "The kid's agent told him not to sign, thinks he's worth more on the open market with free agency."

"Something changed his mind then," Teddy said. "I heard Coach on the phone."

"Probably heard about all the pussy that's coming out for me and Rick and wanted the run-off," Jaxxon chimed in.

"If you've touched it, nobody wants it," Jonesy said dismissively.

"Not all of us got soft cocks, old man," Jaxxon said.

"Rookie, shut the fuck up."

The locker room, after another practice. Coach Chapman had them doing break-out drills and two on one rushes for over an hour. Said they'd embarrassed themselves the other night by blowing so many of them in front of the hometown crowd. Even though they'd won the game, there was always something to work on.

Rick leaned back in his spot, his skates unlaced, shoulder pads on the floor in front of him. The large, circular room, with individual seats and alcoves for each player, all numbered, was full of tired and sweaty men in various states of undress. He and Jaxxon, the two newest members of the team, were side by side, in the rookie spots, furthest out from the door.

"Hey, man," Jaxxon said. "Not my problem the chicks are digging me and Rick. Right, Rick?" Jaxxon elbowed him in the arm.

"Whatever you say, Jaxxon," Rick said.

Jaxxon was the other great white hope of the Jets this year. He was a full year younger, drafted a round higher at eighteen years old. The kid was good, he never had to play university hockey just to prove his worth. From Minnesota, he was a natural goal scorer, but he was struggling so far. While Rick had all the attention, Jaxxon was confronting the reality that he wasn't just going to skate around and do whatever he wanted with the puck. He also never shut up.

"Come on, Rick," Jaxxon said. "You're such a stick in the mud. This is the big time. Fuck some bunnies, buy a fast car, wear a fucking Rolex or new shoes, anything. Just don't sit there and be all serious Mr. Hockey motherfucker."

"I—" Rick started but Jonesy cut him off.

"You should be more like Rick, Jaxxon. He's the one having the plus season, after all."

"My time's coming," Jaxxon insisted. "Just getting used to these off-brand skates."

He kicked his unlaced skates into the centre of the room, right on the Jets logo painted into the carpet.

"Don't be a slob," Jonesy said. "Your mom ain't here to pick up after you."

"No, that's what the equipment boys are for."

While Jaxxon was a good-looking teenager with a baby face, deep green eyes, and carefully styled hair, Jonesy was the elder statesman of the team. He was the longest serving Jet with grey hairs at the sides of his nearly forty-year-old head. Jonesy was what Rick hoped he could be in the future: a well-respected captain, leading his team, still contributing. A leader, making a difference in the community; the kind of guy who had his number retired at the end of his career and went on to a lucrative job in the front office, maybe an assistant coach gig. Someone who could parlay his time in the league to a lifelong position, who would always be around the game.

"Not for rookie slobs," Jonesy said. Lines on his forehead, crow's feet, tanned skin revealed the truth of his advanced age if you looked long enough.

The old man stared down the rookie. Jaxxon made no move to do anything. Jonesy turned to Dave, the thick-headed man of few words with even thicker hands, covered in scars and calluses. Dave was the enforcer of the team, the man who let his fists do the talking when someone dared to take advantage of one of his brothers.

Dave, vacant-eyed, began to stand up. The implied threat was enough to make Jaxxon move to grab his skates and bring them back to his alcove.

Rick tried to avoid the kind of trouble Jaxxon was already a master at getting himself into. He knew he had to prove himself with his game and just wanted to fit in. He kept quiet in the locker room unless he was addressed specifically.

Across from him, he watched Igor, their odd-ball goalie from Czechia, taking a toothbrush to puck marks on his leg pads, scrubbing frantically to try to clean them off. The man was full of more superstitions than a fortune-teller. His scraggly beard was uneven and dripping with residual sweat.

Rick had been with the team for a few months now and still didn't know everyone all that well. Some of the guys kept pretty quiet, but a few never seemed to stop talking. Despite all of that, Rick was beginning to feel like a real NHL player.

"Alright, boys," Coach Chapman said as he came marching into the locker room. "I've got good news and bad news. What's the vote on good first?"

Teddy, his shaved head under a towel, snorted audibly. "Coach, you always tell us no news is good news, so wouldn't that make actual news bad?"

"Did you take a puck to the helmet out there I didn't see?"

"No, sir," Teddy said.

"Better send you in for concussion protocol anyway."

Teddy looked around the room, confused. "Was that the good or bad news?"

"That was a joke, Teddy," Coach Chapman said. "If you had trouble figuring that out, maybe you're further gone than I thought."

"But—"

"Patrick's coming back," the coach interrupted. "I'm sure you've heard the rumours already on account of Teddy Brain Damage here spilling it, but it's true. Now if anyone has any shit to say about him, we deal with it now, right here. In the open. I don't want any festering resentment fucking up our season. We're on a solid roll right now and I, for one, think Linseman's one-timer can only help."

"He sign, or he just coming back to try to pump up his value?" Gord asked.

"There," Coach said, pointing. "That's the kind of snark I'm talking about."

Gord, a thirty-two-year-old third line grinder with one mangled ear from an errant stick five years ago looked as if he wasn't sure if he was being praised or not.

"He's signed a year-long extension, so it's a bit of both. I don't give a shit about next year, I want to win now." Coach scanned the room. "Anyone else?"

"Who's cut to make room?" Petr called out.

"To be determined. But if you're on the first two lines, I wouldn't worry."

Nobody else spoke up. Rick had never met Patrick Linseman, but he knew his reputation. A former Jets top pick, amazingly skilled, but lacking a certain mental toughness, he could score seemingly at a whim, but would rather stay in and play video games than work on his game. The press and he had an antagonistic relationship at best.

Igor raised his hand. "Mister Coach, is Patty coming back the good news or bad news?"

"I thought that was obvious. That's the good news."

The room's reaction didn't necessarily agree with him. He let the silence linger a while, but nobody spoke up.

"Then what is bad news?"

"They fucked up our flight to St. Louis so we're leaving in two hours instead of tomorrow morning."

Now the room groaned, and voices rose in complaint.

* * *

Jimmy, sitting in the idling car at the end of an alley off of Waterfront, watched Veronica talking to the man in the hood standing partially obscured by a dumpster. He couldn't see

116

the guy's face. He wore sunglasses and had a beard. She handed him an envelope. He shoved it inside his hoodie and pointed towards the river.

She'd insisted they stop to meet one of her street contacts. They'd been going through a slow patch, with nothing more serious than a few break-ins to deal with. She said that her connections could give them some tips on anything happening in the underground.

The man said something to her, and she looked back to Jimmy, stone-faced. The man said something else and then walked away. She turned in the opposite direction and came back towards the waiting car. She slid into the passenger seat and checked herself in the mirror.

"So?"

"There's not much going on out there. At least as much as he's heard."

"And how much did that information cost?"

"Don't worry, I'll make sure I file it all appropriately in the paperwork later."

"Usually payoffs give us something."

"Call this continuing to foster a long-term relationship. And besides, he promised to let us know the second he hears something."

Jimmy looked at her as she brushed an errant hair back behind her ears. Getting nothing from an informant added to the nothing they had going on, leaving them with double nothing. It was times like this that he almost found himself missing Frank's ability to uncover situations, whether real or not.

"Great, so I guess we just go back to patrol then."

Veronica saw something in the mirror and looked over her

shoulder. She leaned her head out the window, then opened the door and left.

"Hey, wait," he said and shut the car off to follow her.

By the time he was outside, she was jogging across the street. She followed a woman walking, tapped her on the shoulder to no effect, then stepped in front of her and put her hand up.

"Hey, miss," she said. "Are you in need of any assistance?"

Jimmy caught up, joined Veronica and almost let the surprise show on his face when he saw the poor girl they'd stopped. While she was built like a pro-wrestler, her face was mangled. Her nose was pushed halfway across her face and dried blood had crusted over her cheeks and down to her shirt.

"Jesus," he said. "What happened?"

The woman said nothing, simply stared at them.

"Ma'am?"

"I think she's in shock," Veronica said. "We should get her to a hospital. That nose needs to be, uh, reset."

"It needs a hell of a lot more than that," Jimmy said.

Veronica took the woman's arm and started to lead her towards the cruiser. She followed along, but stayed mute.

"Ma'am, can you tell us what happened?" she asked. "Did someone do this to you?"

"Maybe she doesn't speak English." The woman's hair, half red and half black, was disheveled, her clothes torn. It certainly looked like she'd been in some kind of situation.

"Hold her so I can check for some ID."

Jimmy took the woman's arm while Veronica patted her down. "Nothing that I can find."

"Maybe the system has some record," he said. "You call it

in."

Together they helped the woman to the cruiser and loaded her in the back. Jimmy looked at the poor battered thing, sitting oblivious in the backseat, as if she had no idea where she was, and pulled out onto Waterfront, heading to the closest emergency room.

CHAPTER FOURTEEN

S
am awoke to the soft light of the sun shining in through her bedroom window. The warmth on her bare skin, the thin sheets barely covering her, she slowly came to realize that she was naked. Her head pounded, like someone was stabbing her with sharpened pencils through the skull. The roof of her mouth felt like sandpaper.

Hangover.

"I need a shower, some coffee, maybe a total blood transfusion."

Fleeting images of the night before. Rick scoring, the crowd going wild, she and Erin having a great time.

Then what?

Arm in arm walking home, singing something at the top of their lungs. The crowd leaving the arena jazzed at another home victory. Pizza at the late-night place on the corner. She and Erin laughing over some joke about—

Sam rolled out of bed and slid on an extra long shirt. She looked at her dishevelled face in the mirror of her dresser.

"You look like you've been asleep for a week."

Her hair was a mess. There was a pimple on her chin. She was pale, more so than usual, but the mole remained unchanged.

Flickering images of streetlights, Erin taking her hand, the footbridge over the river. Staring up at the stars. Tossing a wadded-up napkin into the water to watch it float away.

A kiss.

She remembered a kiss. Erin kissing her. Or did she kiss Erin? On the bridge? At the game? Somewhere else? The picture was cloudy in her mind. She was seeing it jump through different backgrounds as if in a fog.

The quiet night, her eyes, the soft press of lips against lips. It had felt… great.

Sam's head swam and she almost fainted. She braced herself on the edge of the dresser.

"Did we kiss?"

It was so fleeting that she didn't know if it was real and had actually happened or if it was the afterimage of a dream she'd been having before she woke up.

Naked.

She didn't usually sleep naked. The apartment was weirdly cold at night. But—

"Morning," a voice came from next to her on the bed.

It was Erin. They were still in bed.

Sam pulled the blanket up to cover her nakedness.

"What the…" she said, trying to understand how she'd gone from standing up and looking in the mirror to right back where she'd woken up.

"Bad dream?"

Erin wore one of Sam's old ratty, torn and faded t-shirts. She was rubbing her eyes. "How's your head?"

"Ugh, pounding headache," Sam stammered.

What was the dream here?

"Me, too." Erin lifted herself from the pillow, swung her legs off the bed and stretched. She walked over to the mirror on the nightstand to check out her own reflection.

"God, I look like death. And there's a pimple on my chin, great."

Sam saw herself standing there. Erin's reflection gone, in its place, Sam, examining her mole with the usual disappointment.

"Coffee, a shower, maybe a complete blood transfusion," Erin said.

Sam could only watch in confusion as Erin slid on a t-shirt over her naked body. Long, past the waist, with John A. MacDonald High written on the back. No, that's not possible. She'd been dressed when she woke up.

"I'll go make some coffee," Erin said. "You see if you can hook me up with fresh blood."

Erin walked out of the room.

Sam rubbed her eyes, digging out some residual sleep in the corner.

Her face in the mirror. She was staring at her reflection. A pimple on her chin, messed-up hair, old Simpsons t-shirt.

She spun around to look at the bed. Empty. Had Erin been there? Or here? Anywhere?

She turned back to the mirror and used a sock from the dresser to wipe some dust off. Erin stared back at her. Sam rubbed the spot again and Erin was gone.

She rubbed a third time. The fog of the mirror cleared. She was looking inside the shower. Erin was lathering herself with body wash. Her olive skin glistened with the sheen of moisture. Erin looked over at her, catching her staring.

"Oh, hey, sorry, I—"

"Room for two?"

The stream of hot water pelted Sam's back. She felt the lather sliding down her skin. The shower door was partway open. Erin stepped inside, dropping the towel on the floor as she came.

"Whoa, I—" Wasn't she just outside looking in?

A finger on her lips. Water pouring down Sam's face. She kept blinking, wondering if this was all real when Erin moved in and kissed her. Her hands gently held her by the chin, then moved down over her shoulders. Sam tingled, shutting her eyes as Erin kissed her neck.

Wow, this is intense.

Her hand reached up to touch Erin but pawed at empty space.

The refrigerator door was a foot away. How had she missed it?

Milk. Cream. Eggs. Orange juice. A carton of leftover Chinese food.

Erin passed Sam a shrimp held securely in chopsticks. She bit in and savoured the sweetness.

The coffee machine gargled as it poured out a cup of black roast. Sam reached for it but was holding an ice cream cone. The sun above shone on her face as she waited outside Sargeant Sundae. It was the last week before the place usually closed for the winter months and they'd both agreed to—

"Go Jets go!" Erin shouted.

The full arena. Fifteen thousand screams deafening. Another goal. The buzzer sounded.

"River City Jets goal, scored by number twenty-six—"

"You hungry?" Erin asked. "I could make something."

Sam rolled over on the bed, seeing her friend laying there

on the other side. They both wore old shirts.

"I need a shower, coffee, and maybe a total blood transfusion first."

"I hear that," Erin said. "How much did we drink?"

The steam clouded the shower doors. It was so warm in here. Sam kissed back, meeting Erin with equal intensity under the falling water.

"God, this line is so slow," Erin said, standing and waiting for mini donuts.

"That's because mini donuts are so awesome!"

Erin handed Sam a mug of coffee.

She took a sip. "Thanks, I need this."

She looked at her new pimple in the mirror, touched it carefully, realized that she wasn't wearing any pants and slid on a pair of sweats.

Erin turned away from the mirror and walked out. "Shower first—"

Sam opened her eyes, saw the sun shining on her naked body. She pulled the sheets up and—

Erin stepped out of the shower, wrapping the fallen towel around her body. She stepped behind Sam at the mirror and looked over her shoulder.

Sam stood at the stove, playing with a frying pan full of scrambled eggs.

"Coffee second—"

"God, my head is killing me," Erin said, walking inside the apartment. She tossed her jacket to the couch. "You got any Tylenol?"

Sam rolled over off the bed, slid her feet into some fluffy rabbit slippers Avital had given her last year as a gift and walked to the mirror on her dresser. Her hair was a mess, a pimple forming on her chin. The ratty old John A. Mac-Donald shirt dangled just over her waist. She pulled out a ticket stub for a Jets game placed in the crack between the mirror and the frame. She'd marked a score in. Five to four Jets. She replaced it below one of the others. Others? Her head throbbed.

"—then a total blood transfusion," she said, sitting up in bed.

The bed was empty. She slid off and pulled up the sheets quickly. She put on a shirt, left the room, and went into the kitchen. She poured herself a glass of orange juice, then went to the bathroom. She pulled open the shower door and turned on the water. She waited a moment before stepping out of her clothes and inside.

CHAPTER FIFTEEN

"The glitch in the system won't be a problem anymore, sir."

Arthur Fritz looked up from his screen to see Dr. Januz standing in the doorway of his office.

"Oh? I was told the attempt to bring her in was a failure."

"It was. But the new process wasn't. A rousing success. Complete and secure."

"Simon felt the same way, you know. And look what happened to him."

"This is different, Mr. Fritz. This time the manipulation is not only stronger, but subtler. She won't—"

"She'd better not, Januz. We don't need any more problems. This rollout has to go smoothly. The board is getting impatient."

"The board? They're watching this?" The man fixed his lab coat collar, as if his appearance now made any difference.

"Indeed," Fritz said. "They are extremely interested in our success. They have big plans for additional uses of a more refined technique. National plans."

Januz grinned. "We will be ready, sir. We're monitoring every metric. There's been increases across the board."

"Don't get ahead of yourself. Overconfidence has ruined

greater men."

"I assure you, you have nothing to worry about. Everything is running as it should."

"Let's hope it continues to do so."

"With the girl out of the way, it will."

Fritz rubbed his chin in thought. He was put in his position because of his ability to prepare for all contingencies. He didn't think this was as open and shut as Januz did.

"Make arrangements just in case."

"Another assassin?"

Fritz nodded. "From the same pool. Nobody will miss another one."

"Right away, sir."

Januz stood at the door, waiting for something else. Fritz waved his hand dismissively. "I mean now, Januz."

CHAPTER SIXTEEN

"Mr. Malone, I understand that you've been making quite a nuisance of yourself around the facility." Nurse Ironhide folded her hands, locking her fingers. She looked at Frank over the dark black graphite desk in her office. The room was spartan; nursing degree, calendar marked with the different theme days of the month, the desk, and a quietly humming computer were the only decorations. Her hair, perfectly pulled back in a bun, seemed to shine with silver under the harsh lighting. Her eyes were as cold as steel, and she folded her mouth into a curt frown that could break even the hardiest truant child.

"I have no idea what you mean, lady." Frank leaned back in his chair. He'd dealt with people like her before. The stick-up-their-asses, backs bent all out of shape. They expect you to follow the rules like it'll kill you. They're the no fun, schoolmarms from hell. He'd broken his grade one teacher way back when and he'd break Nurse Ironhide, too.

"I think you do, Mr. Malone. I'm hearing reports of you sneaking around at night, hiding in people's rooms, talking to the dementia cases, sneaking extra pudding cups."

The woman knew more than she let on. How had she found out about Frank's little racket of trading pudding for information? Maybe he hadn't been as careful as he thought he'd been. He'd have to watch it from now on.

"One, I tend to sleepwalk. Two, Oscar likes to play hide and seek. Three, even the senile need someone to talk to once in a while, and four, is it a crime to get some seconds on chocolate pudding? Hell, we're all staring down the end of a candle in this joint, so can't we at least go down with guts full of Jello?"

She looked over the open folder on her desk. Frank couldn't see what was inside, but he assumed it was a laundry list of what he'd been doing in here. That meant she had eyes, maybe even a few stoolies. He'd have to flush out those turncoats.

"Always with the retorts, Malone. I see we're going to have our hands full with you here."

"You're not the first woman who told me I was a handful."

She almost flinched. The side of her lip quivered, but the stone mask of Nurse Ironhide held. "Mr. Malone, the Shady Acres Retirement Home is a calm, quiet, and dignified establishment. We cater to the needs of those in their declining years with care and efficiency. We look after those who have become a burden to their families, or in your case, society itself. We are here to make their remaining time as pleasant as possible. But you insist on making things very difficult."

Frank put his feet up on her desk. At the sight of his blue slippers, her eyes grew three sizes. She pulled open a drawer from her desk and took out a rubber glove, slid it on her hand, and then brusquely pushed Frank's feet back to the ground.

"Do you take pleasure in being a problem case? Have you gone through your entire life living like an animal?"

"Hey, I was doing just fine before they locked me up in here, lady," Frank said.

"Yes." The nurse shut the folder and looked him in the eye with the chilling manner of something not quite human. "Yes, you were at that. Brutally gunning down an important member of upper society, a shining light of the business community, and then what you did to those boys in the band. It was inhuman. Did you enjoy dismembering them? Smearing their blood all over the walls of Mr. Karlsson's office? Damaging brains being used for important scientific research? Did those desecrations scratch some twisted itch deep in your soul?"

Frank shrugged. "Way I hear it, those folksingers couldn't keep it in their pants. I think I did the world a favour." Even now, Frank wouldn't betray the girl by letting her secret slip. It was locked safe and would stay that way until he died. Even if he did squeal, they'd just think it another sign of his dementia. He had to take comfort knowing she was still out there fighting.

"The reason we agreed to take you in after the trial was to help you, a clearly deranged and sick man, go gently into that good night. We specialize in easing the suffering of those with severe mental deterioration. Our locked ward is the finest in River City, but had we known what kind of trouble you'd cause, well... there were other options presented to the courts."

"I'm too big for the big house, big momma."

She refused to let him get to her. He'd have to get needling.

"In here the world runs by my rule and my rule is law. You will straighten up, you will follow the program. You will go gently."

"Like hell I will."

"There are patients in here much further gone than you. Some who believe we are living in a world secretly ruled by alien shapeshifters, who can't recognize their own children's faces, people who can't go to the bathroom without a team of help, who need machines to breathe, to operate as their kidneys, people taking more medication than Elvis. Even they follow the rules."

"What can I say? It's a talent, I guess."

She stood up abruptly, slammed her hands down on the desk. It was the first sign of emotion he'd seen in her. Maybe she was human, after all. "If you don't start playing straight, I will shoot you full of more morphine than Bela Lugosi. I will have you restrained and drugged into a stupor so deep you won't even notice time passing until it all goes dark. And rest assured, Malone, that day is coming, maybe sooner than you think."

"There's a list a mile long of people who want a piece of me. You can take a number. I'll give you cuts in front of the Grim Reaper."

"This was a warning, Malone. I know the game you're playing. You might think you have everybody fooled, but not me. I don't know what you hoped to accomplish coming here, but you know the consequences should you fly left. Now get out of my office and go and join the others downstairs. I hear they're playing Boggle."

Frank stood up. He opened the door, but before he left the office, he took one last look in at Nurse Ironhide, in all her buttoned-down repression. "My game has always been Scrabble. Eleven letter word, starts with an A. Arrivederci." He waved and left.

CHAPTER SEVENTEEN

"Holy crap, Sam, does the bag owe you money or something?"

She reared back and kicked again, as hard as she could, trying to will her foot through the black leather free-standing training bag. Each kick knocked the target of her ire further off balance. Jan was falling behind, unable to match her ferocity.

She swung again, even harder.

They were supposed to be drilling roundhouse kicks, alternating kicker and side, two people per bag, but Sam barely noticed Jan's presence. She focused all her power on taking that inanimate heavy bag down.

Tuesday night Hapkido class, a way for her to try to sweat the nightmares away. She seemed to be living in some kind of fog. She'd wake up for class, blink and be coming back home. She'd be sitting listening to the professor talk about an upcoming quiz, then find herself writing the answer down on a paper in front of her. Jumbled moments and faces, merging together in a blur. The details fleeting, but always the feeling like something was coming for her.

THWACK!

She kicked the bag again, not even waiting for Jan's return

kick. *THWACK*! Again. Again, again. The thing on edge, finally fell over. Jan moved out of the way and just let it crash down, raising an eyebrow at her as she panted in exerted fury.

"Everything alright, Sam?"

She turned to look at him, sucked in a breath.

"Sam?"

* * *

She was in the apartment again, her father on the couch watching the Jets game. The intricate skating patterns drew her attention away from him.

"I said, how was school, Sam?" her dad asked.

"Uh, you mean university?" She tossed her bag to the floor and sat in front of the television.

"I assume that's where you were," he said. "Unless you're just pretending to pay thousands of dollars for an education."

"No," she said, watching the players.

"Sorry for interrupting the much more interesting game," he said.

"Huh?"

He grabbed the remote and clicked off the television. Sam felt as if a weight was lifted from her shoulders. She let out a relaxed breath, stared at the black screen in silence.

"Earth to Sam."

She'd forgotten her dad on the couch and jerked in surprise. "What are you doing here, Dad?" He was usually away on business so much that him being here was off-putting.

"Doing here? I live here! This is my TV, my couch, my flowerpot. What do you mean, doing here? Is that some way to talk to your dad? Also your roommate? Or do you have something to tell me on that regard? Something about some items I found in the bathroom and—"

"Dad," she said, rolling her eyes. "What do you want to talk about?" He was so transparent.

"Alright, alright, I get it. You're a busy girl, you have things to do. No time to spend chatting with old dad, right? Mind my own business. Fine. I'll just tell you my news and if you want to tell me yours, you can."

What is he going on about?

He ran his hand through his salt and pepper hair, searching for the right words. "You may have read in the papers that the restaurant downtown has been having some problems."

* * *

"You look like you've got a problem on your mind. Is everything okay? Sam?"

Outside. In the parking lot after class. She was at her car, opening the door. Jan stood holding his gym bag over his shoulder, his hair slicked with sweat.

Class?

She couldn't remember a thing. The still night. Stars above, suburban houses dark on the other side of the large wooden fence that surrounded the Tae Ryong Park Academy; she certainly knew where she was, but not how she'd gotten here.

"Sam? You alright?" Jan asked again.

"I don't know," she said.

"Do you want to go someplace and talk about it? Maybe get a drink?"

Jan wore a loose-fitting tank top. The sweat still shone on the muscled skin of his bare shoulders. He wasn't unattractive, but they were classmates. That seemed like a dangerous line to cross. And besides, hadn't he asked her this before?

"I'd better not, I made a promise that I'd come right home."

A promise? To who?

Jan looked unsure how to take that. "I'm always here if you need to talk to someone."

* * *

"—all that I've done for them that they went and formed a union."

"A union?"

Her dad paced in front of the television. "I can't be dealing with unions. Not in the restaurant business. No one does. They'd kill my margins. Ruin me. It's a domino effect. Like that whole Vietnam situation. So, I made the tough decision to close the whole place down."

"You did what?" Her head throbbed. She barely remembered sitting down here.

"Not permanently, just until the heat dies down, and this nonsense blows over. We'll come back, do a few renos here and there, re-open with a big party and lots of press, it'll be great."

She felt a lap behind in the story. "Okay, Dad, but how does this affect me?"

He hadn't shaved in a while, looked more dishevelled than she remembered, like he'd been under some stress. "Right, I get it. You kids with your short attention span. No need to remember what I said two minutes ago. Sure. Well, like I said, without the downtown location, I really have no reason to keep a condo downtown, do I? I'm always travelling. I figure I'll just get a room at the Fairmont and write it off. If I need a home base, I'll get something on the west coast. We're expanding huge in the lower mainland and—"

"You're selling the condo? What the heck am I supposed to do?"

"Sure. I can see how that news might have been so big that it wiped out your memory of everything I said immediately thereafter. But I'm not selling the condo, Sam."

"But you said—"

"I said, I sold the condo this morning. You have until the end of the month."

"To do what?"

He put on his salesman mode, the one she recognized from years of his explaining to her how he'd make up his missing some event with something big later on. "You've got a couple of options. I could hook you up with my finance guy and you could get a downpayment together, go out and buy your own place."

"I can't afford that. I'm in university."

"Exactly, so you could do what most people your age do and just look in the papers for an apartment to rent. Oh, right, you don't read the paper, so maybe check the internet listings then. They have those, right? I just use Gino for everything."

* * *

"Class, white and yellow belts punching drills, Jan and Miss Abraham, demo practice," Master Park called out.

The other people broke off into pairs and began strapping on small leather gloves they used for pad work. She and

Jan adjourned over to the soft blue mat area to practice the demonstration routine that they'd been working on for the past year. Master Park had asked them to do some public performances: at schools, shopping malls, the local international culture festival.

No. He was asking them to do demonstrations in the near future. They were still working out the routine, weren't they?

She remembered her first night on stage, being so nervous that she had actually clocked Jan in the head instead of pulling her punch. But had that actually happened? Why was it all a blur?

"Sam?" Jan said, standing in the middle of the mat. "Are you ready to do this?"

"Oh, uh, yeah."

She was standing next to the portable stereo near the mats. She didn't know why, but she pressed play. The familiar first few notes of the theme from *Mortal Kombat* played. She pressed stop.

"Are we really using this?" she asked.

"Every martial arts demo has to use that song, it's some kind of law."

The door chime rang. A man in a suit walked inside, letting the sound of traffic flow in from the street. He didn't look like a prospective student – his face was stern, and he carried a briefcase in his hand. There was nothing unusual about someone coming inside during a class, people often stopped in to check out the gym to see if it was somewhere they might like to join, but there was something odd about this man. His face didn't say curiosity, but power. He didn't take off his shoes at the door, despite the large sign that told visitors to do so. For some reason, people never seemed to understand that taking off your shoes wasn't just for the sake of inconvenience, it was a sign of respect to not bring outside dirt into one's home or gym. He walked towards the office at the back of the dojang where Master Park was working on some paperwork.

"You know that guy or something?" Jan asked.

"No," Sam said. "He just looks off."

"Well, Master Park's going to be coming out here any second if you don't hit that button and get on the mats."

"Right." She pressed play again and *Mortal Kombat* blared.

* * *

"Dad, how could you do this to me?"

He held up his hands. "I'm sorry, but it's a seller's market. Gino had the whole thing cleared faster than I could find a pen to sign the paperwork. The man's a market wizard, I'm telling you. You sure you don't want him to help you put together a package to—"

"No! I want to stay here. In this condo. I like it here. It's been a year and I'm settled. It's close to school and clubs and—"

"Wherever you met she-who-shall-not-be-named."

"What?"

"No judgement. I'm a modern guy. Have to stay current being in the restaurant biz and—"

"Dad, I'm not in the mood."

He sighed. "Okay. Look, if you need help, I can give you some cash to put your stuff in storage until you can find your own place. How about a few weeks at the Fairmont? I can get a rate and claim you as a consultant."

"Holy shit, I can't believe I'm hearing this."

"What? Sam, playing the system is a valuable skill to learn. It's how people like us were able to live like we did for so long. Now, Gino could really—"

"I don't want to hear anything else about fucking Gino. I want to know where I'm going to live."

"You could always move back in with your mother in the house. I'm sure she'd—"

"No!"

"—probably like that. Reconnect and— oh? No? Well, that might break her heart. She misses you, Sam."

Sam was finally at a loss for words. Her dad had completely floored her and upended everything she had going. The future was suddenly scary.

"Call her. She'd love to hear from you."

He turned the television back on.

"Oh, just make sure you're all packed up and out of here before the end of the month. Sooner if possible so I can get the cleaning crews in."

The game sounds returned. She found herself staring at the figures moving onscreen.

"Damn, this Hansen kid is having some season," her dad said as he turned to her with a smile on his face.

* * *

Moves and counter moves. Kicks, punches, knife defences and blocks at three quarter speed, every move and sequence now muscle memory. At times Sam didn't even realize she was a part of it.

Test your might!

Crowds liked seeing a girl beat up a guy. Sam mimed

beating the hell out of Jan, standing tall over his prone body. She flipped herself through the air off Jan's wrist twist, crashing to the ground in a perfect break-fall. He swung around and locked her wrist, posing to the invisible audience.

She was up. He threw a kick, she caught it, spun into him and swept out his planted leg. He crashed to the ground, and she locked his ankle in an outward twist, then punched down at his groin. He put his hands over the area, making a high-pitched hoot that always brought laughs. Then, she twisted his legs around, dropped herself into a figure four leg lock. She'd seen that move before, somehow knew the motions despite being unable to remember being shown them. Jan slammed the mat in submission, and she let go, rolling backwards to her knees. Jan rose back to his feet. The home stretch now.

How do I know that?

Sweat dripped down Jan's brow from his matted blond hair. He blinked as it fell into his brown eyes. Lost in the sequence she didn't seem to have to think about to fit into, Sam almost missed the man in the suit leaving Master Park's office. He'd left the door open. She saw Park looking over a sheet of white paper. The Korean flag hung behind him on one wall, a full trophy case on the other. Something was wrong. The distraction cost her.

Jan threw a punch. She was supposed to react. He realized too late she wasn't going to, tried to pull up, lost his balance, staggered, tripped, fell forward. His foot careened into Sam's temple, knocking her out in one blow.

* * *

140

She came to, saw the sun shining in from the bedroom window. She lay there, on her side, trying to figure out how many days she had left before this was all going to be taken away from her. The condo was silent. Her dad must have left in the evening. She stayed under the covers, refusing to move, somehow knowing that to be wrapped up in these blankets, she'd be protected from all the shit that was coming.

* * *

"That was quite a blow," Master Park said, pulling away an ice pack from Sam's head.

She blinked, trying to figure out how she'd gotten here when she was just in bed.

"It was?"

"I didn't see it, but I heard it. Jan said it was his heel."

He handed Sam back the ice pack. Her head throbbed. She pressed the cold pack and felt momentary relief.

"Do you remember what day it is, Miss Abraham?"

"Uhhh… the day I come to class?"

"That's certainly an answer. How about this? Do you remember what belt you are in what martial art?"

"Sure. Hapkido. It's going well, I think. It might be the one aspect of my life that is."

Park nodded.

"Black stripe, a red belt with a piece of black electrical tape on the tips, which is two tests away from black belt. I'm so close, I can almost taste it. That all sound right?"

"Wordier than usual from you, Miss Abraham, but I'll accept it as proof you don't have a serious concussion."

She kept the ice attached to her head, trying to piece

141

together what had happened. How much of her mind jumble was from Jan's errant kick. She saw him looking nervously towards her from the mats as he worked with a white belt. She gave him a thumbs up.

Despite the head injury, being here felt good. The higher she rose, the more intricate moves she learned. The more she learned, the more she was trusted to show new people the ropes and lead some classes. The more she did that, the more confidence she had in her own skills. Looking back on where she had started from all those years ago back in high school, to where she was now, was like watching the movie of someone else's life. She'd walked through those doors because she'd been tired of being pushed around and wanted to be able to stand up for herself in the face of her bullies. Now, she had done so much more, even taken on monsters, and emerged covered in their blood.

Golems.

The word was back in her mind again. Joshua. The Professor. Toronto. Scott. Factor 5ive. Everything back in waves like she hadn't thought about them for months. Hadn't she? Had she somehow forgotten? Or had she just finally moved on?

She spotted the strange white paper on Master Park's desk.

"I saw a guy in a suit not take off his shoes and come in here. Was there anything wrong?" She couldn't quite remember when she'd seen that. It had been before the kick, right?

"Well." Master Park rose from his chair and walked over to shut the door. If there was one thing Sam had learned about Koreans from her years studying Hapkido, it was that they tended not to talk about their problems with just anyone. "It's not ideal news."

"Not ideal as in bad?"

"The Geld Corporation has some big plans for this area. They've bought the other buildings out and want this one. Big condo development. I'm the last holdout. There's an offer on the place, ninety days to decide. Twenty-two years. As much as I like the location, I don't know if I can turn this down."

"You can't?"

"That's certainly the implication," he said.

"Can they do that?"

"As long as it stays legal."

"If it doesn't?"

"Then it's about who has a better team of lawyers. My team is my brother, so I give them the advantage."

"What are you gonna do?"

"I guess I start looking. Even if I've been here for twenty-two years, it's still just a building," he said.

Her forehead throbbed. She was at a loss for words. Should she comfort him? Should she ask her dad if that Gino guy he knew could help? Park's expression was a mask of calm.

"Maybe if everyone else hadn't already sold out, I would be able to fight this. But as the only one left, I think it's hopeless."

"Are you going to tell the class?"

He shook his head. "Not yet. So please keep this between us for now."

She pressed the cold pack against her head and stood up. Park opened the door for her and motioned to sit out for a while. She dropped into the hard pews they had lining one side of the gym for spectators.

Another bombshell. Her home and now her escape. Hapkido class was like family. The core group that had stuck around over the years; that she'd hit and been hit by, choked and been choked by, locked in painful joint locks and been locked in painful joint locks by. There was a special camaraderie between people who fought each other night in and night out that went beyond words.

She watched the class for a moment, felt her head throb, replaced the ice pack.

* * *

"What a move!"

On the couch with her dad watching a game. The condo. Still? Wasn't she just—

"Did you see that, Sam?"

"Dad?"

"This guy Rick Hansen is having some season."

"Rick?"

* * *

In her car the soft voice of Emily Haines blaring from the stereo asking her if she'd rather be the Beatles or the Rolling Stones.

"Rick?"

"Sam? Are you sure you're alright?" Jan asked.

"I have no idea," she said with her hand on the open door of her car.

"You maybe want to go talk about it over drinks?"

Jan stood with his gym bag over bare shoulders still glistening with sweat. He'd tried this before, hadn't he? Once? Twice? More. Hadn't she told him politely that—

"I can't. I've just got too much drama in my life to add more."

Jan looked confused. "Okay, well, I'm always around if you want to talk."

* * *

"Come on, Sam. Rick Hansen, the guy you went to high school with? He's a sensation this season." Her dad was practically vibrating in his seat. "I've given you my company tickets five times already. You said it was to see him!"

"See Rick?"

"Yeah. You had to notice him out there. Pretty sure in one game he scored a hat-trick, didn't he?"

"See Rick Hansen. I wanted to see Rick Hansen."

* * *

Sam jerked up from the bed, the covers falling away from her naked skin. The sun beat down on her as it all came rushing back, like a dam had burst. The laughing faces of Radiant Cyanide, Simon Karlsson, Factor 5ive, that sick German website. She remembered it all. She'd been hypnotized. Simon had a brother. He owned the River City Jets.

"I was trying to warn Rick Hansen."

"I thought we'd moved past all that, Sam," a groggy voice said from the other side of the bed. Sam suddenly realized that laying next to her, also naked, was Erin.

CHAPTER EIGHTEEN

"Hey, Jimmy, do you remember that woman we found wandering the streets?" Veronica asked as she approached their desks carrying a cup of coffee.

"The battered case, yeah. The one with arms bigger than mine."

"Right. Turns out there's a reason for that."

Veronica sat in Frank's old spot and spun her chair around once. She was smiling. He wondered if she was giving them away. He was sure some of the guys in the precinct stared at the way they interacted. He looked over his shoulder, convinced they were all looking at them, but the others were caught up in their work. Tapping away on keyboards, filling out forms, talking amongst themselves. Nobody seemed to care about what he and Veronica were doing.

"Yeah, she was probably into lifting weights, big surprise," he said.

"No. You need to use your imagination a little more here."

"Steroids? Because that still fits with—"

"No, that woman, one Madeline Henry, has an alter ego."

"Is she even more built? Because that would be scary."

Veronica rolled her eyes. "Cute. No. Madeline's alter ego is one Margery Slamkowitz."

"That some kind of super-villain name?"

"Yeah. In pro wrestling."

Jimmy leaned back in his chair and looked at Veronica for some sign that she was joking. "Are you serious? She's a pro wrestler?"

"Yup. Or she was. I went over my notes from our interview with her, at the hospital. I know you thought she was unreliable and doped up, but she'd mentioned Bruce Park, so I did a little digging around. Turned out Bruce Park Community Centre used to run pro wrestling matches up until about a month or so ago. I found an old event page, saw her picture listed with the name Margery Slamkowitz. That sent me on another round of searches until I figured out her real name."

"That's great. Now we can scratch off Jane Doe and fill in, uh, Margery Slamkowitz…"

She snorted at the fact that he'd forgotten the name she'd just told him. That was the kind of mistake he shouldn't be making.

"Madeline Henry, Jimmy. We'll put her real name."

"Right."

She spun in her chair again, a full circle, and came back to face him. "You know what, I think we should go visit her at the hospital. See if telling her the name helps her remember anything about what happened. It's been a few days, so she could be finally starting to piece it all together."

Jimmy looked at the partially filled in report, then to his watch, and realized that they really had nothing else more pressing to do. It would also get them out of the office and away from prying eyes.

"Alright. Can we swing by the bagel place on the way? I—"

"I'll drive," she said, cutting him off.

* * *

"What do you mean, the patient is gone?" Veronica asked the nurse.

"I mean she's not here. Left. Departed. Gone somewhere else. Freed up a bed. Should I keep going?"

"But she was almost comatose," Veronica said.

While she spoke with the duty nurse, Jimmy looked up and down the busy hallways of the third floor of the River City Downtown Hospital. People everywhere. Orderlies pushing beds to and from elevators, doctors making rounds, patients holding IV stands sitting in the halls looking bored, visitors carrying flowers, kids, the elderly, cleaning staff, nervous men pacing; the place was a jumbled mess of a thousand stories. It made him feel glad he'd chosen police work instead of medicine.

"She was fine enough to go," the nurse said. "Someone checked her out and that was that."

"Someone? Who?"

"I'm sorry, officer, but I can't just give you that information. We have confidentiality protocols, even to the police. Unless you have a court order, of course."

"Not yet. I didn't know we'd need one. Can you tell me anything about this guy? Was he family? A husband? A—"

"I can tell you he was a man in appearance and that there was no coercion or distress in her leaving. She was completely calm. Didn't say a word, just followed him obediently."

"That almost sounds worse," Veronica said.

"I don't know. At least it wasn't a kidnapping, right?" Jimmy said jokingly.

"We don't know that. Could be Stockholm syndrome."

"Look, officer, if you don't need me, we're understaffed today and I'm in the second part of a double. I've got a metric shit tonne of things to do."

"This guy leave any contact information?"

"Only to save you the time for a court order, no. He had her identification and said he was her father. We're so desperate for beds here, honestly, we were just happy to free up the space."

Veronica nodded and the nurse took that as her cue to dash off to take care of other work. Jimmy leaned on the desk, peering over the sides at the stacks of logbooks and hospital forms.

"I know what you're thinking, but I don't know if we'd find anything worth the time snooping for it," Veronica said. "Besides, we know her name. Maybe we can track her down on our own."

They rode the elevator down to the main floor. As they were walking towards the exit, the stretcher service was wheeling in a body covered by a black bag.

"Looks like a DOA," Jimmy said.

"That's Kelly and Max," Veronica said.

She waved to them as they pushed their cargo down the hall. "Hey, guys, what's under the bag?"

"Someone fell from the roof of a condo downtown," Kelly, the woman with red hair and freckles, said. "Some jacked-up bodybuilder moron hanging from a balcony, they think. Probably drunk doing chin-ups."

"They already do the investigation of the scene?" Jimmy asked.

Max, the man with the shaved head, nodded. "Yeah, I think it was Carlos in charge. All I know is we were given the all-clear to bring the stiff here. No identification, nothing."

"Really?" Veronica asked, interested.

"Ronnie, he said Carlos was on it."

"Yeah, but I'm curious, okay? Our Jane Doe was a jacked-up bodybuilder, too."

"Well, if you want to look at the stiff, go ahead," Max said.

Veronica reached for the zipper, but Jimmy stopped her hand. "I don't think he meant here in the middle of the hallway. How about we go to the morgue first?"

They accompanied the stretcher team to the basement morgue. A massive wall of drawers of corpses lined one wall. More encased in plastic rested on stretchers in the middle of the room as the team worked under the strain.

"Oh god, not another one," the head doctor said as they came inside. "Just put them in the queue with the others."

The body was wheeled over to the far corner. Max and Kelly moved to take their paperwork to the doctor.

"You sure you want to look?" Jimmy asked Veronica as she reached for the zipper.

"Call it a hunch."

She pulled the zipper down enough to expose the man's face. Nearly purple, his features were battered, but it was clear he was a behemoth.

"So? He someone you know?"

"Of course not. But he does look like one of the wrestlers on that poster where I found Madeline's name."

"You think this guy was a pro wrestler, too?"

"Possibly. But I'd need outside confirmation." She snapped a photo of his face with her phone and zipped him back up.

She walked over to the head doctor and handed him a card. "Doctor, I'd appreciate a call if you get any information about the deceased. If someone claims the body, that sort of thing."

He motioned for her to drop her card on the paperwork. Jimmy saw Carlos's card already there.

"If we have time, officer."

They left the morgue and rode the elevator back upstairs. Moving through the hospital entrance, Jimmy saw an elderly man struggling with a vending machine, shouting as he pounded his fist against the side. He wore a hospital gown, open at the back, and leaned on a walker.

"God damn thing won't give me a Snickers!"

"Hang on," he said to Veronica and walked over. "Sir, can I help with anything?"

"Yeah, this thing won't give me a Snickers bar and I'm hungry."

"It ate your money?"

"Money? I don't have any money, I'm in the hospital. I just want a Snickers."

Jimmy laughed and dug out some change. He slid it in the slot and pressed the buttons for the bar. He pulled it out and gave it to the man. "Here you go, enjoy."

"How about a Twix, too?"

A few dollars poorer, he rejoined Veronica outside as she waited in the parking lot.

"You know that old man?" she asked.

"No, he just sort of reminded me of someone."

"Frank, I'm assuming."

"Yeah. I guess I feel guilty that I haven't checked in on him since he got locked up. Maybe I should see how he's doing."

"Maybe. But first I think we need to research local pro

wrestling promoters."

CHAPTER NINETEEN

Sam sat on the couch, head in her hands, trying to figure out what in the hell was going on. Waking up in bed with one of her best friends, not having any memory of how they'd ended up there, let alone of how many times it may have happened in the past. She stood up to look at the calendar on the wall near the refrigerator, marked with exam times, and realized that she'd somehow misplaced almost two months of her life. The jumble of images and moments trickled through as if held back by a strainer, but they were there, if she focused hard enough. "What happened?" she muttered.

The sounds of the shower emerged from behind the closed bathroom door. Erin was inside. She'd given Sam a peck on the cheek and told her she needed "a shower, some coffee, and maybe a total blood transfusion."

That expression had frozen her in place.

"I know I've heard that before."

The instances came back in a blur. Different clothes, hair messed up, mornings after nights out. Just how long had this all been going on?

Sam flipped the calendar back to September. She found that first Jets game written down and circled with stars around the bubble.

"I know we went to that game. We had a good time. I—"

Another game the week after that. "Jets versus Devils. I don't remember that one."

More games written down. The stars became hearts. She flipped through October and November. Saw six more dates. The handwriting was hers. She'd written them down.

"I don't remember any of this."

"Of course you do," a voice said from the other door of the refrigerator. She turned to see a picture of a River City Jet, Jaxxon Downie, taped up near the ice dispenser. Divided in two, one part of the photo showed Jaxxon in an action pose, the other a portrait of the admittedly good-looking man smiling in his jersey. His wavy brown hair seemed to be moving.

"When did I put this here?"

She reached for the picture when the man's face turned to look at her. "The night you fucked your best friend," he said.

"I didn't—"

"Oh, you did," he said. "You've been doing it a lot. Just ask her."

She turned towards the bathroom, convinced that Erin would be standing there watching her talk to a picture on the fridge, but only the sounds of the shower met her.

"Where's the hypnosis this time?" she asked the picture, pulling it from the fridge. "Some new video by 5ive? They implant it in another RC song?"

The image of Jaxxon Downie smirked. "There's no song, Samantha. This is you acting out your deepest desires and—"

She started to tear the photo at the top. Downie stopped in mid breath, looking up at the edge of the frame. "That won't change reality. You've finally been living your truth. It just took some prompting."

"If it's not a song, then what is it? What did I do differently?"

The action pose side of Jaxxon Downie began skating, the background matching his movements, showing him blazing around the ice surface of the MTS Centre downtown. Other Jets stood talking to each other as he breezed past. The fluidity of his legs, the glare of the ice, the sound of the blades.

She started to zone out for a moment.

Then it hit her. She ripped the centre of Jaxxon's photo. Tearing off the action, crumpling it up and throwing it in the corner behind the television.

"It's the fucking game of hockey itself," she said.

"Clever," Jaxxon Downie's portrait said. "But you're not going to be able to do anything about it."

"Not alone. But I'll get help. Inside help."

Something heavy hit the patio doors. She jerked up to see a man standing on their porch, watching her through the large glass. He was heavily muscled, wearing a too tiny tank-top, with traps the size of some people's heads. His head was shaved into two parallel blond mohawks. He said nothing, simply stared at her with dead eyes. A look she knew too well.

Golem.

"You really will need help," Jaxxon Downie said mockingly.

She ripped his picture up into tiny pieces and threw them into the air. The man reached for the handle of the patio doors. Locked, he started tugging on them. Sam looked around the room for something to use as a weapon. Magazine, remote control, umbrella, pair of sweatpants; nothing dangerous.

The man tugged harder. That tiny lock wouldn't hold up very long against something that huge. She ran into the kitchen and was met with two options: rolling pin and frying pan. She grabbed both.

She walked back into the sitting room.

"Sam?" Erin called out as the shower shut off.

"Hey, just a second, I'm, uh, not ready."

Sam threw the rolling pin on the couch and took the frying pan in both hands. She flicked the lock on the door. The monstrous behemoth slid it open and stared at her.

"Okay, you're here," she said. "How'd you manage it? We're fifteen floors up."

She knew the guy probably wouldn't respond. She noticed the calluses on his hands, the bloody fingernails, scratched palms. He must have climbed down from a higher floor, or up from a lower one.

"Jesus," she said.

He lunged for her. She swung hard with the frying pan, crashing it down on his head. The loud *kabong* noise echoed in the condo.

"Sam?" Erin called out.

"Nothing to worry about," she said. "Just, uh, dropped something. Stay in there."

The beast staggered a few feet and Sam swung again. This time he punched out. His fist connected with the descending pan with a sick crunch. His hand bent the steel, but his bones didn't withstand the impact. One mangled and useless broken hand dangled at his side as he lifted the other to strike. She knew she was faster than this guy. His mountains of muscle slowed his movements down too much. She swung the pan again. It clanged on his skull, but the handle broke and her swing spun her off balance in surprise.

He grabbed her by the hair and pulled back, dropping her hard to the floor near the couch.

"Sam?"

"It's all good," she said, cringing against the pain jerking her neck back. "Just stay in—"

He clubbed her with his useless stump of a hand. The blow hurt, but not as much as it may have had he been whole. She reached back, found the rolling pin, stabbed it forward into the grimacing man's throat. His eyes bugged out as the blow knocked him back. Staggering, holding his throat, she took the chance and popped to her feet. Holding the rolling pin like a spear, she charged him, hitting him in the chest, pushing him back against the edge of the balcony, then over the side. She hit the concrete barrier, stopped herself, saw him career over, through the air. His legs hit on the other balconies as he fell, sending him spinning like a top to the ground below. She dropped to the floor, not wanting to see the landing.

Breathing heavily, she tried to catch her breath.

"Sam?"

Erin stood in the sitting room, towel wrapped around her body, staring at Sam with a raised eyebrow. She spotted the broken frying pan and picked up the handle.

"You have some trouble cooking?"

"You could say that," she said.

Erin joined her outside and went to look over the balcony. Realizing that someone might be looking up after that fall, Sam pulled her arm to bring her down to the ground with her.

"Hey, I just showered."

"Erin, I think we need to talk about some things."

"Oh, don't tell me you're reconsidering moving in together now."

"Wait, what?"

"Sam, we move in three days, you're just getting cold feet."

Another thing she had no recollection of.

"We went over this. Two bedrooms, splitting rent, just a few blocks away. It won't be much different than this place. Maybe not so modern, but a first apartment isn't always a glitzy newbuild condo high rise financed by your dad."

"Yeah," Sam said, trying to find that memory fragment amidst all the other jumbled moments.

Erin wrapped her arm around Sam's shoulder. "It'll be fun. A new adventure, right?"

Sam, lost for words, tried to understand how hockey, watching hockey, had scrambled her brain so much. Ever since that kick to the head, time had seemed to pass normally, and yet even seeing that brief snippet of action had started to work whatever twisted effect it held. She would have to be more careful. Would ear plugs help as they did with the subliminally implanted songs?

"You ever wonder how sometimes we have these relationships that might seem to go in one direction, but then there's, like, a twist or a turn or a different path that opens up and suddenly we're someplace we always wanted to be, knew we were going to be, had to be, but not by the route we thought?"

Sam looked at Erin, sitting on the cold concrete next to her in only a towel, and more images flashed through her mind; sharing a giant pretzel, showing each other the foam art in their lattes, holding hands walking under gently falling snow; a rush of feelings bombarding her with a truth that had been happening while she was under the hypnotic effect.

She and Erin had been dating and from all accounts it had been... wonderful.

"I think I understand now," Sam said.

"Who knew, right? It was right there in front of us the whole time. We were just on the wrong side of the road."

Wrong side. Suddenly it made sense and Sam realized that she'd been going about this all wrong, before the setback. She'd been trying to get in touch with Rick in the most obvious way. But there was an entire angle she'd never considered. If she couldn't get through to him directly, then she could go a different way. If the front door was locked, try the back. The wrong side of the street all along. God, why hadn't she thought of this sooner? All she had to do was get close to someone else on the Jets.

"You're so right, Erin," she said. "About everything."

Erin leaned in and kissed her on the lips. "I'm glad you feel that way, too."

CHAPTER TWENTY

"Hey, Wallace, did you hear the crazy news out of section four?"

"No," the balding man with the round glasses said. "What happened?"

"Seems like their team lost another specimen."

"What do you mean, lost?"

Jensen, sitting at the long table in the lunchroom, took a bite of his bland, white bread sandwich and chewed, letting the moment linger to get Wallace more interested. It wasn't often he had news for the guy, so he was going to enjoy it.

"Like that one a few months ago. Sent it out on a test run. I don't know what for, nobody seems to, but the thing was mangled up pretty badly. They had to send out a recovery team."

"I thought the specimens were supposed to be almost indestructible."

"Key word is almost, I guess."

Wallace rose from his chair across the table and moved to sit next to Jensen. He looked around the room to make sure no one else was listening. They were the only ones in the room.

"I heard that section five's specimens are being designed

for… let's just say, more illicit means."

"Whoa, really? Why do they get all the fun?"

"Luck of the draw, I guess."

"You hear anything about this problem section two is dealing with? Janice tells me it's some kind of major glitch. Something the old Karlsson team discovered but never fixed."

Wallace leaned forward and covered his mouth, to ensure that if anyone was watching, they would be cut off from reading his lips. "The glitch is real. It's serious enough that I think they're starting to worry. They might be bringing in more people to work on it. Other than that, I have no clue what it is, or what they're doing about it. Just that it's real."

"Who's your source, Wallace?"

"Top secret, Jensen. Same as yours, right?"

"Right."

They ate their bland food together in silence for a few moments, each wondering just how much the other knew that he wasn't telling. Working here bred curiosity into what the other sections were up to, but also secrecy in keeping your own projects from slipping out. Finally, Jensen had enough of only the ticking clock and Wallace's chewing as accompaniment to the sound of the refrigerator.

"You think they'd let me put in a transfer for section five?"

"You'll have to wait in line. I've already put in mine."

CHAPTER TWENTY-ONE

J esus was cleaning out the common room, Trina helping Marlena with her pills, Paulie setting up a DVD copy of *Cocoon: The Return* for them all to watch for the five hundredth time. Ginny was the lone holdout.

Where are you, girl?

Frank combed the halls, past sleepers and creepers, shufflers and vegetables, marching through Shady Acres like it was his beat.

It is my beat.

This, for better or worse, was his home now and while he still wasn't ready to accept it, he was going to deal with it.

My home will not be compromised.

Deaths, thefts, missing slippers, bland food. Some things he could solve, others he'd put on a list. For now, his focus was not letting poor Oscar's lucky thousand-dollar bill go to bed with a shifty good-for-nothing thief.

He turned the corner to Oscar's room and knocked softly.

"Hey, Oscar, just wanted to ask you a few more questions about that bankroll."

The room was empty. The old man had gone down to watch Don Ameche and Wilfred Brimley ham it up.

"Let's see what clues a cop can find."

Maybe someone's sticky fingers left a print. Frank clutched a container of talcum powder in his housecoat pocket. Crude, but it was all he had.

The room was quiet, white and stark. It looked like the staff had already been in here covering their tracks. The bed was in the far corner near the drapes, hospital clean and filled with about as much personality as a bowl of raisins from anywhere but California. Folded up tight, he fished his hands under the blanket.

"Bone dry. Good man, Oscar."

The small dresser was next. He looked inside, found it full of Oscar's loose-fitting clothes, bland and uniform, like the food here. A couple of family photos sat on the top. Smiling kids and grandkids taunting the man with their freedom.

"Seems a little cruel," Frank muttered.

The closet sat opposite the bed, full of housecoats and jackets, sweaters, and vests. He started fishing through the hanging attire, but there wasn't much more here than the outerwear of a man confined to the inside for the rest of his days.

Frank was all set to start blowing powder when he got an itch, an old cop cue that something was amiss. He ducked inside the closet, hid behind a red and green sweater and waited to see what his instincts would bring him. Sure enough, in came Ginny, her beady little eyes as shifty as ever as she checked to make sure the room was clear. She shut the door and went over to the dresser, pulling open a drawer and fishing through the shirts inside. She pulled out a wallet and carefully removed a twenty-dollar bill, stuffing it in her shirt.

So, they were taking old Oscar's money. Not on his watch. "AHA!" Frank shouted as he hopped out of the closet.

Ginny jumped a mile in the air, screaming as she saw her captor hop out of a tangle of sweaters and pants and rush over to her with a scowl on his face.

"Got you red-handed." He grabbed her by the arm. "You've got a date with Johnny law."

"Put me down, Mr. Malone, you don't understand."

"No, you don't understand, lady, Frank Malone doesn't abide thieves."

"Security," Ginny shouted. "Help!" She mashed the signal buzzer next to the bed.

"That's right, bring 'em in here. They'll bust you back to bed pans faster than you can say cocoa puffs."

Frank beamed as he held on fast to the squirming Ginny. The other orderlies rushed in, Jesus and Paulie, with Nurse Ironhide in tow. "What's the meaning of this?" the big bad nurse demanded.

"Caught a real fast one here," Frank said. "Sticky fingers and greasy palms."

"Ginny, what is he going on about?"

"I don't know, Nurse Ironhide. He was hiding in the closet, and he rushed out and grabbed me by the arm – he's hurting me!"

"Alright, Mr. Malone, let go of her please." Jesus held up his hands to calm him down. "Let us know what you think you saw."

Three on one. And Frank didn't have a gun. He had to play it cool here. He let the thief go. She rubbed her arm where he had held her. "I saw her digging through Oscar's things and taking money from his wallet. I think if you search her, you'll find out that she's the one who pinched his thousand-dollar bill, too."

"Ginny, is this true?"

"Of course not. I was straightening up in here, putting clothes away, when he just jumped out and assaulted me."

"Lies," Frank interrupted, "from the mouth of a criminal. How does her silver tongue explain this!" Frank reached over and shoved his hand in her shirt pocket, looking for that twenty. It had to be there, but all he felt was boob and bra. Ginny screamed. The two orderlies rushed over and pulled Frank away from her.

"Mr. Malone, we need to keep our hands to ourselves." Paulie spoke to him like he was a child.

"It's in there, I swear. I saw. She's a dirty, stinking crook!"

"Take Mr. Malone to his room and give him a shot of Demerol to calm him down, he's clearly agitated."

"I'm not agitated, damn you! I know what I saw, and I saw what I know. Thieving, criminal scum. Arrest her!" Frank felt his blood pressure rising, his adrenaline shooting through the roof. "Let me fish around in her shirt – I know that little mouse is a snake." He lunged for Ginny, but Jesus grabbed Frank by the arm, stopping him. "Come along, Mr. Malone, we're getting a little too excited."

"Would you stop talking to me like a goddamn baby? I've taken shits with more brains than you," he said, pointing to Jesus. "And I've got socks that're older than you," he said, pointing to Paulie. "I know what I saw!"

He felt a prick in his arm. Paulie shot him full of something clear. The syringe emptied and a warmth flowed through his arm. Suddenly he wasn't so mad anymore, the fact that Ginny was a... what was she... a nurse, right? Her glasses reflected the lights of Oscar's room.

"Okay now, Mr. Malone?" Nurse Ironhide asked.

Frank nodded. He did feel okay, actually. Better than okay. Like he'd just had some Jack with the boys and—

"Take him away." She waved them off.

Just before he left the room, he caught Ginny looking at him strangely. Like she knew that he knew something and was going to watch him from now on. But what did he know? He couldn't remember. Then he was in his bed, covered in the sheets, drifting off to sleep. In a moment he was under the boardwalk in Lakeshore, with Bacon, staring through the wooden planks at the women walking overhead.

CHAPTER TWENTY-TWO

"Shoot the puck, man, shoot it!"

"I am, I am, shut up!"

Rick's condo was hopping. Half of the team was here with their wives and girlfriends. An open bar, NHL on the PlayStation, DJ, roving plates of hors d'oeuvres – they'd spared no expense.

Petr and Teddy argued as they played their virtual selves online against a couple of guys from the Wings.

"You're making us lose again," Petr shouted.

"It's not me, they fucked up my stats." Teddy swore at his virtual avatar. "No way I'm a seventy-two!"

Music thumped over hidden speakers, the room was crowded with suits and cocktail dresses. Debbie had wanted magic; professionally catered and bartended. Rick marvelled at all the work. She'd kept the details out of his hair. With a vodka paralyzer in hand, he made the rounds. Italian leather couches, clear chairs in ultra modern shapes, huge canvas art; the place barely felt like it could be his, yet it was.

"Asparagus pate, Mr. Rick?" A well-coiffed Filipino man in a red vest and bowtie held out a tray of appetizers.

"Sure." He took one and tossed it in his mouth. "Debbie said these are all local produce and meats?"

"Absolutely."

"I'll bet it was expensive, too, right?"

The man grinned and leaned in conspiratorially. "You probably don't want to know."

He took another. "Then I'd better enjoy 'em, right?"

More staff circulated the room with trays of food and drinks. Everyone looked happy. And why shouldn't they be? The team was having a great season. He was averaging more than a point a game. His confidence was growing with each shift. Face-off wins, dekes, penalty kills, pats on the back from the coaches; he felt like all the years of sacrifice had finally paid off. Now this: a lavish party in his fancy condo in the heart of downtown River City.

"I want those trays in the dining room and those ones on the table in the sitting room." Debbie led a woman in dark slacks and suit jacket through the house – someone from the catering company, he guessed. She was moving a mile a minute.

"Hey, babe."

Without even breaking her stride she kissed him on the cheek and kept walking.

"Get some more champagne on ice…"

She was in boss mode again, making sure the party ran efficiently. She seemed more nervous about the party than he did, bouncing from one situation to the next, somehow still finding time to schmooze with the other wives and girlfriends.

He didn't know what to do, so he just moved through the crowd, smiling.

"Liking the grub?" he asked Dave as the man munched away on a chicken wing from a plate piled high with bones.

Dave grunted.

"Jonesy, nice to see you." Rick waved to the captain of the team.

"Great place, Hansen," he said.

"Patrick, glad you could make it."

"Excellent party, rookie," someone shouted and slapped Rick on the back.

"Jaxxon, what's happening?"

Jaxxon, with two blondes on his arm, stood in a doorway. The girls looked like models; one was giving Rick a real eye fucking.

"Having a good time, bro," he responded, "but, uh, hey." Jaxxon leaned in. "Mind if we use your bedroom for a few minutes?"

"Debbie would kill you if you messed up the Egyptian sheets," Rick said. "The guest room should be okay."

"Thanks, dude." Jaxxon smiled. "Come on, girls, let's kick this party into gear."

Jaxxon led the girls away.

"That boy better be careful, or he's going to crash and burn," Jonesy said, stepping up beside Rick.

"It's a party," Rick said.

"And he's another Derek Sanderson."

Rick knew the name, but before he could argue, Igor called out, "Hello, Mister Rick! Am glad to be inviting to party house!"

Rick and Jonesy turned around to shake the goalie's hand. Rick nearly dropped his drink. Hanging from Igor's arm was Samantha Abraham.

"Uh, hi, Igor, glad you could make it."

"Am not missing this for world, Mister Rick."

"Igor." Jonesy clapped the man on the shoulder.

"Perhaps you are liking to meet my date?"

"Evening, ma'am," Jonesy said, offering his hand to Sam.

They couldn't have been a more mismatched couple. Igor wore a red flannel vest overtop a brown denim shirt and stained white pants while Sam was dressed better than Rick had ever seen her. She wore something more suitable for a night at the opera; black, sparkly, tight, expensive looking.

"Uh, sure, Igor," Rick said.

"Hello, Rick," she said, holding out her hand.

"Nice to see you," he replied coldly.

"This little one is minx, Mister Rick. A girl of dark majesty with many skills."

Sam scowled at Igor's words but mouthed to Rick, "We need to talk." Rick just shook his head, not wanting to hear whatever she had to say.

"You are not believing me, Mister Rick? Perhaps you do not think Igor has met such a girl, eh? Not in Canada, at least."

"How about a drink, Iggy?" Jonesy said.

"Excellent plan. Would you be liking one, babushka?" he asked Sam.

"Thanks," she said, eyes never leaving Rick. He wondered why the hell she was here.

"Yes, yes. I will fetching this. Where is vodka, Mister Rick?"

"Bartender can set you up, Igor, right over there." Rick pointed and Igor walked to the other side of the room, in the exact opposite direction.

"I'd better give him a hand," Jonesy said. "Or who knows what he's going to come back with?" The greying veteran left Sam and Rick momentarily alone.

"Sam, I—"

"It's not what you think, Rick – I had to see you."

"It doesn't matter what I think. Dating Igor?"

"We've only gone on two dates."

"Do you know what that guy does before a game?"

"I can only imagine. But it's not like that. I'm not sleeping with him, or even touching him."

"Doesn't sound like that from his side."

"I needed a way to get close to you, Rick."

He scoffed. "So, you're just fucking him to get to me? That's puck bunny shit, Sam." Rick was shocked those words came out of him; they sounded like something Debbie would have said.

"Two dates, Rick. So far, he's only asked me to shove a loaf of warm bread over his bare feet. I'm not sure how much longer I can play hard to get before he loses interest. So let me just—"

"Look, I don't want to hear about your love life. Why all the subterfuge? What's so important?"

"Not here. Somewhere more private?"

"The girl that dropped me like the plague two years ago suddenly shows up looking like a cover girl and wants to talk in private? Sam, what am I supposed to think here?"

"Believe me, in this room I feel like I'm wearing Value Village. But I'm here about what happened two years ago, actually. It's—"

"Do you think I'm holding a grudge against you for how we broke up? Please, I've moved on." He waved his hands as if displaying everything around him as proof enough. "Or did you not notice?"

"Please, it's about Joshua and—"

"Debbie warned me there'd be people showing up out of the blue now that I'm successful, Sam, I just never thought it would be you." Rick turned and walked away. He didn't mean to be so curt, but seeing Sam here had thrown him for a loop. They'd barely spoken in two years. Over his shoulder he saw Igor sneak up behind her and lick the nape of her neck. She jumped in fright.

What an odd couple.

Rick went looking for Debbie, found her in the kitchen, on the phone. She spotted him, said something to the person on the other end, and hung up before he could hear what she was saying.

"Problem?" he asked.

"Nothing I can't handle."

He slipped a hand around her waist and kissed her on the mouth. It caught her off guard. She pushed away and looked at him oddly. "What was that for?"

"No reason." He turned and left the kitchen, feeling her confused look on his back the whole time.

Rick grabbed another glass off a tray as it passed by on the arms of a waiter. Wine. He pounded back the whole thing in one sip; he needed something to get him through Sam being here... with Igor.

She had no idea what she was in for. This was a guy who would only use a freshly cleaned toilet bowl, who had to have his sticks taped using exactly three feet of white tape after each period, who would tap each goal post exactly seventeen times at each whistle, who plucked his ear and noise hairs out with his fingers and stored them in a small baggie in his equipment locker. Even for a goalie, he was considered odd. If she really was trying to get through to him, she was taking the worst possible route. Maybe he should hear her out and put an end to it all before it got worse.

"Igor, where's your date?" he asked as he scanned the room but didn't see her anywhere. Igor was alone on the couch with two glasses of straight vodka, watching as Petr and Teddy had their ass handed to them in the video game.

"Unsure, Mister Rick. She is saying she has business. Maybe she went to bathroom or maybe she has left?"

That's probably for the best.

He headed to the bathroom, opening the door to see Jaxxon getting a blowjob from one of his models while the other sucked on his nipple.

"Oh, Jesus, sorry." Rick averted his eyes.

"No worries, man." Jaxxon snorted. "Hey, you want a piece? Shelly here thinks you're hot."

The girl on her knees took Jaxxon's dick out of her mouth and turned to look at Rick. "I'm almost done here, if you want to wait."

Rick held up his hands in surrender. "No, no, no. That's all right, I'll just use the other bathroom."

"Suit yourself, bro." Jaxxon pushed Shelly's head back down.

Rick shut the door, desperate to get that image out of his head. He headed up the stairs to the second bathroom in the master bedroom. He turned on the lights, shut the door and unzipped his pants.

"Finally! I didn't know how long I could hide here for."

He nearly jumped out of his boots to see Sam standing in the shower. He quickly zipped back up. "You scared the shit out of me."

"I'm sorry, but this is important."

"It'd better be. Hurry up before Debbie starts to wonder where I am."

She exited the shower. "I have reason to believe that Arthur Fritz is connected to some kind of hypnosis ring and that he may be creating more golems."

"What the hell? That's insane."

"You remember the Factor 5ive incident last year?"

"Of course! It was national news. Dead bodies, some senile old cop gone mental, ranting about mind control."

"He took the fall for it, Rick, but I'm the one who did it."

Rick backed away, suddenly scared of Sam. Here she was confessing to multiple murders now. Had she gone mental? Did he have anything to defend himself with? An electric razor sat charging on its station near the towel rack. Would that be enough?

"They weren't human. They were golems and Karlsson was using them to coerce young girls. He controlled them with a stone just like the one that controlled Joshua."

"That doesn't make any sense, Factor 5ive had been around forever. You told me golems broke down after a few years."

"I don't think they were always golems. I think they were turned into them. Before he died, Duckie told me he was going to do that to me, too. I think Karlsson, or whoever he worked for, was using the same process."

"This all sounds insane, Sam." He crossed his arms over his chest. Despite looking like a million bucks, she seemed to have lost her mind.

"I know. Sometimes I wonder if I haven't lost my mind, but it happened... I have proof."

"What could you possibly have that would prove all that?"

"First off, you need to understand that the manager of

Factor 5ive, Simon Karlsson, was the identical twin of the guy who owns the Jets, Arthur—"

"Fritz, yeah, I've met him."

"And?"

"And what? He's some foreign billionaire who owns the team and probably uses it as a tax write-off. Seemed a little strange, but that could just be a cultural thing."

Sam turned her phone around to show Rick a photograph. It was a little blurry, but showed a man who, while blond, did look just like Arthur Fritz. "Fucking twins, right down to the beady eyes. Now here's the reason I need you. See, I have a theory he's turning players on your team into these new kinds of golems. Or if not that yet, then planning it."

"Now I know you've lost it… golem hockey players?" Rick reached for the door, ready to walk out on Sam forever, but she held it shut.

"Joshua played hockey, right?"

"Okay, fair point. But he never said a word, and there's nobody on the team like that. Except maybe Dave."

He sat down on the closed toilet, trying to think if he'd ever heard Dave say a thing before.

"The guys from Radiant Cyanide and Factor 5ive weren't like Joshua either. They seemed completely normal until Karlsson used the heartstone. That was the trigger."

Rick looked up at her. She leaned on the wall near the towel rack, next to the photo of he and Debbie. She seemed totally convinced of what she was saying, but what she was saying was impossible.

"Look, Sam, I'm with these guys all the time. Yeah, some are a little weird, Igor being example prime, but transformed golems? What am I supposed to do with that? And why would they want to mess with million-dollar NHL players to begin with?"

"I don't know, that's the thing. With the bands it was about sexual coercion, but here I'm drawing blanks. No wait," she said, as if just coming to a shock realization. "That's it. Drawing blanks."

"Uh, you've lost me."

"I went to a game. I had a few beers and had a great time."

"Wow, some evil plot."

"No, that's just it. I don't give a shit about hockey, I never really did, I was just there for you. But going to the game, being there, it did something to me. I wake up with jumbled memories two months later and find that I've been to almost ten games already, and that I might be in a bisexual relationship with my best friend and—"

"Holy shit, Sam, are you on something?"

"No! I'm better now. I don't know how, maybe it was the blow to the head at Hapkido, but the fog is gone. I'm starting to realize things and—"

"Sam," Rick said. "I don't know what the fuck is going on with your life and from the sounds of it, you've got a really vivid imagination, maybe a severe drug and alcohol problem. But this is all way too out there. I'm going back to the party, and I hope that you leave Igor alone. The last thing we need is a goalie convinced that everyone on his team has been replaced with golem duplicates in order to turn girls into bisexual hockey fans." He reached for the door and pulled it open, but Sam pushed it shut and stepped in the way.

"You can be the eyes on the inside, you can find out the truth. But you need to be careful – they might already be trying to turn you. Or they might do it if they think you're on to them. Fuck, I'm totally aware this all sounds insane, but it's real, I promise you that. You I can trust, Igor…"

"You want me to go snooping to see if my hockey team is secretly being replaced by golems?"

"Just keep your eyes open. Call me if you discover anything and we'll take it from there."

She opened her cell phone and turned it around again to show him her contact info.

"I don't even know what to say to this, Sam." He knew he shouldn't let himself get sucked back into her drama, but there was just something about her belief in what she was saying. He'd seen weird things in her orbit in high school. Could this be true? What did it hurt to take her number? He didn't ever have to use it.

He pulled out his phone and copied her digits in, using "S from JA" as her contact name. Not the most subtle cover, but it wouldn't flag up to Debbie were she to snoop through his contacts.

"I'm not saying I believe you."

"Just be careful, Rick."

Rick never believed in the concept that there was a type of or even an individual woman out there who could make you do anything she wanted, who was your personal kryptonite, and yet, Sam was the proof. There was something about her dark hair and dark eyes, figure, honesty, oblique personality. He wanted to tell her to fuck off forever, but he couldn't. All those feelings he thought he was over, had come knocking back on the door.

Suddenly there was an actual knock on the door.

"Rick, you in there?"

"Debbie," he muttered. "She must have been looking for

me."

There wasn't an excuse in the world that would explain why he was alone in a bathroom with Samantha Abraham.

"Just a second," he called out. He turned on the sink and flushed the toilet.

"You need to get out before she sees you, Sam."

"Just promise me you'll stay alert." She ducked back into the shower, sliding the curtain closed.

Rick took a deep breath and opened the door.

"Problems?" Debbie asked as he pushed past her to enter the bedroom.

"Nope," Rick said, pecking her on the cheek. "Just flushing away something you don't want to see."

"You're so weird sometimes, Rick," Debbie said. She peered inside the bathroom. Rick froze, thinking that she'd seen Sam, but Debbie took his arm and led him back to the party.

* * *

Sam watched Rick and Debbie leave arm in arm, trying to listen for the sounds of their footsteps going down the stairs. The music from the main floor echoed even up here. She waited a few minutes before daring to step out of the shower.

A photo of Rick and Debbie hung on the wall above the towel rack. It had been taken recently. He had the long hair. Seeing him up close again was like a jolt to her system. He was, if it was even possible, more handsome. He'd filled out, gained confidence, was looking more like a man than the teenager she'd known.

"This condo is incredible," she muttered, marvelling at the shining fixtures and lights in the huge ensuite. It was like something from a movie, impossibly expensive.

She left the bathroom and stepped into the bedroom. It was immense, classy, with soft carpeting, a king size bed of dark wood with a plush duvet on top. Another picture of Rick and Debbie rested on the nightstand next to the bed. She sat down on the edge, nearly sinking a foot into the soft mattress.

"She really wants to make sure he remembers they're a couple," Sam said.

In the photo, Debbie looked like the impossibly beautiful woman someone like Rick deserved, way beyond Sam. They smiled like the former prom king and queen they were. Their lives had seemed blessed from the beginning, earmarked for success early and now Rick, at least, was rich and famous.

"Jealous much, Sam…"

She'd had her chance with Rick and had blown it. Had this been her life with him now, maybe she'd be the one stressing about hors d'oeuvres and champagne instead of trying to uncover a twisted conspiracy. Or maybe she'd be a different kind of victim, never knowing the truth. She put the picture back down on the nightstand. All she could really do now was wait and hope that Rick trusted her.

She sat up, saw a man standing in the doorway. One of the catering staff, holding a tray and staring at her.

"Oh, none for me, thanks."

He put the tray down on the dresser. It was stacked high with shrimp on tiny skewers. He held a kitchen knife in his hand. It must have been hidden under the tray. He stayed silent, brandished the weapon, and stepped into the room, shutting the door behind him.

"Really? Here?" Sam said.

He marched towards her, lunged with the knife. The demonstration defence flashed through her mind. She spun away from the blade, grabbed his wrist with her right hand, then stepped back in, flipping him over as he was flung against the pressure on his joint. She rammed her knee into his elbow, pulling back on the wrist, snapping the arm with a sick crunch. He dropped the knife to the carpet.

The man kicked out, knocking her onto the bed. He jumped on top of her, choking her with his working arm as the other one dangled against her head. She was sinking down into the plush sheets, losing air. She jabbed with her thumbs into his eyes, pressing against the soft flesh. His grip relaxed enough for her to push him off with her knees, knocking him to the floor next to the bed.

She landed and kneed him in the face as he staggered to his feet. He went backpedalling towards the door just as it opened to reveal Igor carrying two glasses of vodka. The off-balance man went right past him, falling down the stairs.

"There is little babushka!" Igor said, not even noticing. He looked around the room and smiled. "I'm seeing you have saving me shrimp. Excellent idea."

He started grabbing them by the skewer, taking them two at a time in huge chomps.

"Not now, Iggy, okay?" Sam said, pushing past him, looking for the man. There was no sign of him. She spun back around. The knife was gone from the carpet as well.

"You are needing vodka, this I am understanding!"

He handed her a glass as he continued to eat, looking at her through his thick brows with a twisted grin. He reached into the front pocket of his vest and took out a chicken wing. "I am bringing some snacks of my own if you like."

The bed was ruffled, but apart from that and the serving tray, there was no sign of the guy ever having been here. She fixed her dress and hair in the mirror on the dresser.

Igor nodded in approval.

"Is very nice dress, babushka. Perhaps you would like to be taking off now and using this bed?"

"Uh, not now, Igor," she said. "I just ate shrimp."

She quickly took one from the tray and ate it.

"I can get more if you are still hungry."

He licked a stick clean, sending a shudder through Sam's body. One thing was clear, she needed Rick. She wasn't sure how much more of Igor she could take.

CHAPTER TWENTY-THREE

"Knock knock?"

Jimmy gently knocked on the door of Frank's room. He held a potted plant and a copy of the TV guide. He had no idea what you were supposed to bring when you visited someone at an old folk's home. Were you even supposed to bring a gift?

"How ya been, old man?"

Frank just sat in his chair, staring off into space like a zombie.

In an effort to stop the nagging voice in his head that kept saying he owed the old man better, Jimmy had decided to come on his day off. Veronica was busy with the kids; he had no excuse.

"I know I should have come sooner to check in on you, but work has just been too busy. You know how it is, always something to do in the life of a River City cop."

No response. Not even a blink.

"Frank?"

The old man didn't look right; his eyes were sunken and void, his hair combed too flat. He wore a ratty old tracksuit. His back was stooped as he sat staring off into space. The lights were on but there was nobody home.

"Is he always like this?" Jimmy asked the orderly who had shown him in.

"We had some problems with him acting out, but Dr. Hans put him on some stronger medication and now he's much calmer. Isn't that right, Mr. Malone?"

Frank said nothing, just sat there, slowly sinking into himself like a Popple.

"Acting out?"

"Oh, you know how these dementia cases are. They're never sure what's real and what's not."

"What did he do?"

"Minor groping, nothing serious – don't you worry, officer. Unless you need me, I'll leave you to your visit," the orderly said and left the room.

Jimmy turned back to the old man, not sure what to say or do. He sat down in the chair opposite Frank.

"What do I do here? I'm no good with the elderly," he said.

When his own grandfather had gone into a home, he'd been too scared to visit much. The sight of the man slowly wasting away to nothing ignited some kind of primal fear within him. It had almost been a relief the old man had a stroke and was put out of his misery. It was only later, as Jimmy grew older, that he came to regret that inaction, the lack of communication with his own roots. He knew practically nothing of his grandpa, there was so much he should have asked. What was the war like? What were things like before TV? They could have had hours of interesting conversations. He might have given him a glimpse into a forgotten time. He wouldn't make that mistake again. He would keep visiting Frank for as long as he could, until the end mercifully came.

He looked into those lost eyes for some glimmer of life,

but only saw clouds of confusion. "They treating you okay, Frank? Good food? Lots to do?"

He clutched the potted plant awkwardly.

"Shady Acres Personal Care Home, eh? The locked ward seems nice enough." He looked around the barren room. "You been to the other side? No, I guess you wouldn't be allowed there, would you?"

He hadn't seen Frank since the trials and the media circus that had arisen after the brutal killing of that boy band and their manager. He knew forced retirement hadn't been kind to Frank – the few times he'd bumped into him after that last day on the job showed him a man slipping further and further from the razor's edge of sanity that he had tenuously staked out for himself. But part-time security work and doing private detective gigs for widows seemed harmless really. It kept Frank busy and gave him a sense of purpose.

"I heard some of the guys talking about you the other day," he said. "Some of your old case files read like horror novels, they said."

Things had gotten a little weird at times being Frank's partner. He wasn't even sure that some of their cases had happened in the first place; haunted houses, cannibals, walking corpses, things that defied description, and yet he'd been there and seen them all. So why had life calmed down so much without him around?

"You remember our first case? That sicko collecting dead body parts? What about those worm things? You ever think about what Morty's old assistant Patricia is doing now?"

Still no response.

"You know, I never did get your full side of the story about that lab studying the effects of concussions on the brains of dead football players. I could see how a wall of brains in jars, strange equipment, massive computers, and people in lab coats behind security doors could seem suspicious."

Jimmy had testified on Frank's behalf, one of many paraded in front of the judge and jury to tell how the old man had a great service record, had to be suffering from dementia and belonged in a home where he could be properly taken care of in his further declining years. No one wanted to see Frank tossed behind bars at his age and to Jimmy's relief, he was at least spared that indignity. But then ending up like this wasn't very dignified either.

"You getting exercise? Reading much?" he asked. "I brought you a plant." He waved the potted fern to the old man, but it was no use. Frank was truly gone. Jimmy stood up to leave, feeling that he'd missed yet another chance to learn from an elder, when he heard a cough and a gravelly voice mumble behind him.

"What was that?" he asked.

"Gimme the bush and shut the door, kid," Frank coughed out.

Jimmy closed the door to the room and turned back to see Frank standing up out of the chair, stretching his arms wide, bones creaking with the effort.

"Frank?"

He snatched the potted plant away and put it on the nightstand next to the bed. "What's the matter, Jimmy, forgot what a man older than spit who could kick your ass looks like?"

"But you—"

"I'm undercover."

"What?"

"This place isn't what it seems, kid, the people here are not on the level. If I'm not careful, they'll get me, too."

Jimmy sat back down in the chair as Frank went into his closet and pulled out a small folder hidden in one of the suits. He brought it over to the bed and spread the contents out all over the sheets. Newspaper clippings, obituaries, notes written in a chicken scratch illegible to anyone else.

"What is all this?" he asked.

"Baby steps, rookie. I'm just starting to crack this case wide open, a criminal conspiracy bigger than anything I've ever seen. This decade at least."

Oh no, he was just as bad as before. Jimmy's heart dropped.

"It all started with Oscar's missing thousand-dollar bill. That got me on the trail, but it was just the tip of the iceberg. There's a hell of a lot more going on here than anyone realizes."

"Like what?" Jimmy tried to get a sense of what the notes added up to, but all he could see were the ravings of a man over the edge.

"Body snatching, harvesting, whatever you call it these days. Someone here is farming the elderly that come in, taking their organs and selling them to the highest bidder. And to make matters worse, they steal from us, too. Theft and murder, it's biblical, rookie, right out of the old testament."

"Frank, this is crazy. You can't believe all this."

"Believe nothing, kid, I've seen it. When someone runs out of things to steal, they're a goner. Wake up dead the next morning. Always something sudden – stroke, heart attack, aneurysm, things that aren't questioned. The old just die sometimes, they say. Bullshit."

"But Frank—"

"No buts, kid, look at all the obituaries of the former tenants here. Not a single one died of something that wasn't quick and dirty. No cancer, no comas, no long-drawn-out suffering. These were inside jobs. Done for spare parts. I can smell it. The nose knows." He tapped his nose with his finger in exclamation.

"What about this one?" Jimmy asked, pointing to an article with the headline: "Kiss cam girls become arena faves."

"Keep on topic, Jimmy."

Jimmy scanned the various death notices and sure enough, what Frank was saying was true. Not a single one mentioned anything about "after a long illness" or "with family at his/her side" – they were all "peacefully in his/her sleep" or "the lord suddenly called" etcetera.

"This doesn't really prove anything. This is an old folks' home, people come here to die!"

"Don't you see? It all fits," Frank said as Jimmy read over his clues.

"What about your medication, Frank? They told me they upped your dose."

"More mind control. Never trust a brain pill. They tried to drug me, but I outsmarted them. I hide the things under my tongue and spit them out when no one's looking." Frank flashed a childlike grin. "Frank Malone won't go gently into that good night, not in a hive of scum and villainy like this."

This was all too much, but he seemed so sure of himself. "What do you plan on doing, Frank?"

"Catch them in the act, blow the thing wide open, bring down the whole ring in flames, if you catch my meaning."

"Oh god, Frank, don't burn the place down, there are innocent people here!"

187

Frank scowled. "What are you, mental? Maybe you belong in here, not me. I'm not going to burn the place down… although, now that you mention it…" He seemed to ponder that.

"No!"

"Just fucking with you, kid. I've got a plan, but I need access to the outside world. They don't let me use the phone anymore. I need something small. A camera, to catalogue and save the dirty little secrets of this place while I still can."

Jimmy knew right away that he'd regret this, but guilt was overpowering his judgement. "Here." He handed Frank his cellphone. "You can use this, but for the love of God, keep it hidden."

Frank took the tiny cellphone from his old partner and turned it over in his weathered hands.

"Just don't go over my minutes! I don't want to find a bill for five hundred dollars in my mailbox this month."

"All I need is a few more weeks and I'll have enough to bring these body snatchers down. I just have to know that I can count on you to be here when the shit hits the fan."

"Sure thing, old man, just call my home number, it's in there as home."

"What if you're not home?"

"Then call the office."

"What if you're not there? What if it's your day off?"

"Call the cell."

"How can I call it when I have it?"

"I'll get a new one and text you the number."

"Put it in a Western Union, Jimmy. Encoded. I don't trust these little hand computers," Frank said, looking at the phone with derision.

"A telegram? Jesus, do they even have those anymore?"

"If only he knows, then why are you asking me?"

Jimmy shook his head. "Don't worry, I'll get you my number some way. Just don't go making any scenes, okay?"

"You know something, kid? I always liked you. From that first day they dropped you in my lap after that whole demon business, I knew that you could be moulded into something great. Oh sure, maybe you weren't Playdough, you were more like a thick Texas mud, but in the end, it all worked out." Frank patted him on the shoulder. "And now look at us. Together again! The best duo this city has ever seen. Frank Malone and Jimmy Hooper. Riding high in the saddle, taking a bite of crime bigger than McRuff ever could. Sticking a great big fist of justice into the—"

"I get it, Frank."

He seemed disappointed he didn't get to spew any more metaphors. "They tried to split us up, but heroes always find a way. Partners again, just like we belong."

"Sure thing, Frank, whatever you say." Seeing him this animated was comforting. The old man was almost back to normal – well, as normal as Frank could be. He wasn't some cloudy-brained vegetable wasting away, he was as full of life as ever.

Frank looked up at the clock. "Visiting time's over, kid. You better skedaddle before they come looking for you."

"Right, take care, Frank."

"I will."

He sat back down in his chair, slumping over. He stared off into space, exactly like he had been doing before. Had Jimmy not known any better, he would have thought that he had just imagined their whole conversation. There was a knock on the door, and it opened a crack. It was the orderly. "All done, officer? We have nap time coming up, so…"

"I'm good, thanks."

"He say anything weird?" the man asked as he escorted Jimmy to the exit from the locked ward.

Jimmy thought about telling the orderly about the phone; he'd always heard of the elderly complaining of thievery and wrongdoings in the homes they were stuck in. Was Frank just living out that fantasy, like all the others?

"Not really," Jimmy said. "He just sort of sat there the whole time."

"Yeah, it's the drugs. Keeps him out of trouble."

There was something in Frank's eyes that Jimmy trusted, even if the whole body-snatching story sounded like bad science fiction. What harm would it do letting him use his cellphone for a while? Even if the staff found it, he could just say he dropped it. Or worst-case scenario and Frank starts calling Japan, he could just cancel the contract.

"Everyone here on them?" Jimmy asked as the man punched in an exit code.

"Only the ones that cause trouble," the man said.

Jesus, the name tag told him. The guy seemed normal enough.

"You get a lot of trouble on this side?"

"Nothing we can't handle, officer."

Jimmy took one more look at the locked ward, the wheelchair bound slowly dragging themselves towards the door, others sitting almost comatose in front of a communal television. He doubted that much could be going on here.

"Help me," the elderly woman in the chair called out. "Help me, help me!"

"Officer, can you step out, please? I have to keep her from getting any more agitated."

"Right, sorry," Jimmy said.

He stepped into the regular ward and Jesus closed the auto-locking glass door behind him. He watched the man turn the old woman's wheelchair around and push her down the hall. She looked over her shoulder and reached out for Jimmy.

He shuddered, but turned to leave.

"They know what they're doing," he said.

Somewhere deep inside him, he was curious to see how this would play out. Now that Frank had a phone, just what in the heck would the old man find? Would he hear from him again? Who knew? He'd let the chips fall where they may. Besides, what was the harm in letting the old man have one last adventure?

CHAPTER TWENTY-FOUR

"We put the couch against that wall, the TV opposite that and it should all fit."

"The cable jack is in the opposite corner," Marlon said.

"Oh, I guess we have to switch everything around," Sam said, frowning.

Marlon sighed dramatically and started dragging the couch away from the corner where he'd just pushed it. When it was in place, he leaned back and wiped sweat from his brow.

"Hey, M, I need you," Erin called out from the doorway.

Marlon's feet creaked on the hardwood floors as he walked across the room to where Erin struggled with a new IKEA bookcase, still in the box.

Moving day. It had finally come. Leaving the condo had been tough, but there was no way they could afford anything as nice on their meagre university student incomes. Erin had a part-time job, Sam was living off savings and the money her parents had put away for her education. Neither one made enough to live on their own. Sam had a vague memory of telling the gang about her needing to move and meeting a joyful Erin's reaction: "Ohmygod, we can totally get a place, split rent down the middle, be roomies!"

Or at least that was how she pictured it in her head.

Apparently, it hadn't been that hard to find a place downtown. She didn't remember looking, but this one, in an older building, was within walking distance to university and on a bus route. The signed lease was held to the old refrigerator with a magnet. A U-Haul truck was parked out front and here they were, transplanting their lives.

"Who's going to build this thing?" Marlon asked as he and Erin dragged the box to the wall near the window.

"I'm sure it can't be that hard," Erin said.

"As long as you don't expect me to."

"Don't worry, Marlon," Sam said. "We know it's WWE Raw night."

He shot Sam a death glare. He'd been doing that a lot lately. She wasn't sure why. Had she said something shitty to him during her lost time? She needed to get him alone to find out.

"Can you bring me some of those boxes marked books?" Erin asked.

"These?" Marlon asked, pointing to a stack Everett had left in the middle of the floor.

"They say books on them, right?"

Marlon obediently grabbed the topmost one, finding it heavier than he expected, carrying it over to where she was tearing open the IKEA shelf box.

"Here?"

"Yeah, I'm going to put them on the shelf."

"But it's not built yet."

"Uh, yeah, but I'm working on that." Erin laid out the tiny plastic baggies of dowels and screws.

The new apartment was a modest two-bedroom, second

floor suite in an old building with iron radiators that clicked and hissed as they heated the room, a creaky hardwood floor that echoed every step and appliances that may have been scheduled to come over on the Titanic. None of that mattered much – it was affordable and theirs for a year.

Sam picked up a box marked 'kitchen' and carried it to the stovetop. She popped the top and started filling the drawers with all the stuff she'd swiped from the condo: spatulas, strainers, garlic press, anything her dad didn't care about that was now hers.

"At least our utensils are from this millennium," she said.

She hadn't heard anything from Rick yet. She'd warned him, so hopefully he was watching out and would call, but there was nothing else she could do until that happened. If she got desperate enough, she still had Igor.

Everyone was helping them move; Everett and Avital were downstairs with the U-Haul while Sam and Erin tried to get organized. Marlon was playing gopher, moving all the heavy things.

"What's keeping Everett with the mattress?" Erin asked.

"I'll check," Marlon said and started to head out.

"No, you take over with this shelf, Mr. Expert," she said. "I'll go see."

Marlon stared at the ripped open baggies, loose screws, and pieces of shelf leaning against the wall. "Sure," he said in defeat, wiping sweat from his brow.

This was her chance. Sam left the box of dishes and stepped into the sitting room. Marlon examined the manual and scratched his head.

"Hey, Marlon, can we talk for a second?"

"I'm kind of busy, Sam." He didn't even turn around.

"Look, I'm sensing some hostility here. What did I do? If I said something, I'm sorry, I didn't mean—"

He spun around. "What did you do? Sam, what the fuck? You know exactly what you did."

"No, I—"

"I told you how I felt about Erin. I spilled my guts and then you go and fucking hook up with her!"

"Oh, Jesus," Sam said.

"I trusted you and you go and stab me in the back."

"It's not like that."

"It's not like that? Sam, we've all seen you two. Now you're getting a love nest together?"

"Marlon, what would you say if I told you that I'm not completely clear on everything that's happened the past few months? That I think I may have been under some kind of outside influence and—"

"I'd think you were treating me like an idiot."

"Remember the band, the song and the videos?"

"That only worked on women, right? You dealt with that. Those fuckers are dead."

"I know, but… it's complicated, okay? It's been great, but I think that this whole relationship with Erin might have started with—"

"We come bearing a bed," Everett said.

"This thing's heavy," Avital complained.

"To you everything is heavy."

"Not true," she huffed, "just heavy stuff."

"It goes in my bedroom," Erin said behind them.

She grinned at Sam. Marlon scowled. Sam went back into the kitchen. It didn't take long for the apartment to fill up with more boxes and furniture, bags of clothes, and random

195

junk. With five of them working together, the U-Haul was stripped, and they were eating pizza and drinking beer in front of the television in no time.

"Holy shit, Marlon, how sweaty are you?" Avital asked as she sipped on a beer.

He lifted the armpits of his shirt to reveal dark circles. "Apparently, very."

"I had no idea how shitty moving really was," Everett said. "I'm not sold on this whole pizza and beer as payment just yet."

"I'm just glad it's over," Erin said, leaning back on the couch. She put her feet up on Sam's legs. She caught Marlon frowning.

"Yeah, me too," Sam said, wiping grease off on her pants. "Remind me not to move again for a while."

"You're Miss Expert," Avital said. "Twenty years old and already on your second apartment."

"The first one was a condo, so I don't know if that counts."

"You didn't have to pay rent," Marlon chimed in, "so it obviously doesn't."

"Aren't you missing wrestling?" Avital said.

"Oh, shit." He put his pizza down on a paper plate and moved to the television. He flicked it on but there was no picture. "What gives?"

"They don't have cable hooked up yet, you goof," Everett said.

"Shit, I gotta get home. I didn't record it. I thought we'd be watching it tonight."

"You can miss it once, dude," Everett said. "Doesn't free pizza trump it anyway?"

Marlon looked as if he was trying to do the internal math

on that equation and couldn't come up with an answer.

"Just eat," Avital said.

The apartment door buzzer sounded, a loud shrill bleating from the bowels of the wall.

"God, that's awful," Sam said.

"I guess we should have listened to it when we toured the place," Erin said.

"You won't sleep through that thing," Everett added.

"But who could it be?" Avital said. "We're all here."

"I'll get it," Sam said, sliding Erin's legs off her and getting up. She walked over to the panel near the door and pressed the call button. "Hello?"

"Babushka!"

Oh, fuck.

How in the world had Igor ended up here? She'd never told him she was moving, let alone where to.

"Uh, hello? Sorry? I—"

"Coming in!"

"Who is it, Sam?" Avital asked.

"It's just—"

She had to cut him off before he could find the suite. She ran to the front door, pulling it open to run out when he walked right in. He wore a furry vest over a blue jean shirt. His hair was slicked down, his beard full of crumbs. He carried a potted plant.

"Hello, is Igor time!"

Sam caught the looks of her confused friends.

"I am bringing present for babushka's new apartment."

He spun and presented Sam with the plant. It was a cactus, starting to droop.

"Thanks…"

"Is nice place," he said. "And coming with refreshments!"

He reached for a beer and bit the cap off with his teeth, spitting it under the couch.

"These are your friends?"

"Who are you?"

"Oh yes, I am forgetting my manners. I am Igor Illyanovich, the boyfriend of Miss Samantha."

All eyes turned to Sam. Some shocked, some furious.

"Igor, how did you find me?"

"Is not hard."

"Why did you come here?"

"To give present before we go on road trip."

She grabbed him by the arm and pulled him over to the door. "Igor, I'm sorry, but you can't just show up at my apartment."

He grinned sheepishly. "I thought maybe you wanted to give me going away present to remember you on the cold road trip nights?"

"Not tonight, Igor, I have company."

"What about me giving you housewarming present then? To remember me by on your lonely first night in apartment."

He moved in to kiss her and she held him back.

"I just ate anchovies."

"I am loving anchovies. It will make the kissing taste like home."

She forced him out the door, pushing him into the hallway, leading him to the stairs and the apartment entrance.

"What is the matter, babushka? Are you not happy to see me?"

"No, I'm not, Igor."

"Why not?"

"Because you're about to go on a road trip. You need to

have your head in the game, right? Make a lot of saves to win the games?"

"Is true."

"Right, so you can't be worrying about me. Or thinking about me, okay? You have to focus."

"Hmm…" he said thoughtfully. "Maybe you are truth with this."

"I know I am. So go home, get a good night's sleep, and get on that plane or bus or train or—"

"Aeroplane. We are taking aeroplane. To St. Louis first."

"Right, just worry about that. For me."

"For you, I do anything, babushka."

She held the door open for him. He stepped halfway out into the night when she hesitated for a moment. Maybe she could still use him. "Igor, what do you know about golems?"

He chortled. "Golems? Is wizard magic. You do not want to try that."

"But you do know about them?"

"Of course. Many golems where I am from."

Before she could react, he leaned in and kissed her, right on the lips. It tasted like fish. She recoiled in horror.

"I will call you when I am returned," he said. He waved and walked off into the night.

Sam shut the door behind him and turned to go back upstairs. She stopped, seeing Erin sitting on the bottom step.

"Holy fuck, Sam, you are a puck bunny."

"No!"

Erin turned and stormed upstairs. Sam ran after her. They passed through the open door of the apartment. The others were putting on their coats, making ready to leave.

"Erin, wait."

She went right into her room and shut the door. Sam knocked. "Erin, it's not what you think at all. Trust me."

"We'll see you later, Sam," Avital said.

"Nice place," Everett said. "And thanks for the pizza."

Marlon just stared at her silently. He took two slices for the road and left with the others.

CHAPTER TWENTY-FIVE

"Okay, boys," Coach Chapman said, popping a new stick of gum in his mouth. "The game's not over. It all comes down to the next twenty minutes. Just take it one shift at a time, go out there and hustle. The bounces will come our way. I want to see hard battles for every puck."

Down four to two, they sat in the dressing room, rehydrating, catching their breath, resting before the all-important third period.

"Hey, Hansen," Jaxxon said. "You heard anything more about Linseman's deal?"

"I don't worry about that stuff, Jaxxon. Let the agents handle it."

"No way, man, I saw it on Sportscentre. They got him to agree to a three-year extension. On his original deal. How the fuck did they pull that off? The guy was in line for a huge raise. Why would he fuck all that up?"

Rick looked at Patrick Linseman, sitting calmly in his spot, apparently doing deep breathing exercises. He'd heard so much about Patrick from the other guys, about how he was a prick, didn't have any work ethic, thought he was hot shit, but ever since he'd been back, the guy had been a model player.

Never spoke up, worked hard, was contributing well.

"I don't know – maybe he thinks we can go all the way this year or next?"

"Fuck that. This league is about money. Who knows how long we could be here? You got to get paid as much as you can while you can."

"Is that why you're blowing through so much of yours?" Rick asked.

"Dude, I got a plan. Rookie year is for partying, sophomore for scoring, then contract years for blowing it all wide open. Then you get a big five-to-seven-year deal, drop that shit into investments, and the rest is gravy."

"If you say so, Jaxxon."

"Boys, we're four points back in the wildcard race, every divisional game's key. Let's set March up on our terms."

Rick could hear the echo of Led Zeppelin over the sound system in the arena. JJ was massaging Jonesy's knee. He had the sock stripped down and a bag of ice laying across the thigh. The old man was falling apart, but he was toughing it out every game. This would probably be his last year, but he wasn't going to go down without a fight.

"Coach is right," the old man said. "Trust me."

"Put that last period behind us," Coach Chapman said. "So they popped a few, no big deal. We're not out of it yet."

"Humble apologies, coach," Igor said from the floor where he was laying with his legs over his arms. "Something is not clicking tonight. I think someone has replaced the laces in my skates."

"Any of you motherfuckers switching Igor's skate laces?" Jonesy asked.

"Maybe he's too busy thinking about his chick back home

instead of focusing on the puck," Jaxxon chimed in.

"Cram it, Jaxxon," Jonesy said. "Let the dude have his pussy."

"Is not cat," Igor said. "Is real human girl."

"I don't give a shit what Iggy is fucking," Coach Chapman interrupted. "I just want you all to go out there and play the puck, watch your zones, and for fuck's sake, don't take any more stupid penalties."

The team grumbled an affirmative and went back to their own private rituals. Dave cracked his knuckles unblinking, like a zombie. Petr laughed blandly to a private joke from Teddy. Igor started digging in his nose for hairs as he stretched. Gord seemed asleep; only Jaxxon, sitting next to him, seemed to not be in some kind of trance state.

"Hey, Hansen," he said, elbowing him in the ribs. "I've got a couple of twins lined up for later at the hotel room, you want in on that action?" He was scrolling on his phone, one of Coach Chapman's no-no's during game time.

"Is that two sets of twins, meaning four women, or just one set of twins, meaning two?"

"Dude, twins are sisters, like identical. As in, they look the same. Shit, four broads? I don't know if I'm ready for that noise just yet. But anyway, you in or not? I've been messaging them all day and they are primed up."

"I'm alright, Jaxxon," Rick said. "I promised Debbie I'd Skype her after the game."

"Your loss." Jaxxon got up to go over to talk to Teddy.

Rick had noticed a change in the dressing room these past few weeks. Maybe it was just the mid-season blues, or the long road trip they'd been on, but everyone seemed off. Quieter, more focused. Except for Jaxxon, of course.

This was his first season. Maybe this was all normal,

but ever since he'd seen Sam, he'd found himself watching everyone a little closer, looking for some kind of subtle clues that what she'd told him was true. It sounded so crazy, players being turned into golems. Why? To what end? He looked at Patrick Linseman, so not what he'd expected, and wondered.

He rose and walked over to Jonesy. JJ, the trainer, pulled the ice away and helped him bend a few times.

"Feel better?"

"Yeah, I can walk on it."

"But can you skate?"

"Let me worry about that."

JJ rose. "Okay, but I want to run through some exercises after the game."

"Yes, sir, slave driver, sir."

Rick took the empty seat next to Jonesy. Gord was up taking a leak.

"Hey, Jonesy, can I talk to you?"

"What's up, Hansen? We only have four minutes to go."

"I was just wondering if you thought the team was, I don't know... gelling? Like, everyone seems so quiet and focused. I don't think Teddy's told a dirty joke in weeks and—"

"Look, rookie, you worry about scoring. I'm the captain."

"It's just, everyone seems more subdued. Tired."

"Hansen, the hockey life means every night's a repeat of the night before, only in a different arena. Eight months, more if we're lucky, travelling around the country, crossing the border here, home or away, it barely matters. The fans either scream for us or against us, the white jersey or the blue, the same music in every arena. I swear, sometimes I think if I have to hear 2 Unlimited one more time, I'm going to lose it. We're surrounded by drunks, 50/50 draws, the same four local commercials, kids scrimmaging in the intermission, slap shot for dollars competitions, Zambonis and shovel girls, the stink of hotdogs and mini-donuts and popcorn, women waiting outside. It's a record on endless repeat. But that's what we signed up for. That's hockey. If you can't look past the bullshit for the beauty, then you're in the wrong business."

"So this is normal for the guys?"

"The guys are the guys," Jonesy said. "Dave'll pick the fights, Teddy'll take the cheap shots, Petr will grind in the corners, Patrick'll make the plays. Focus on what you do."

Gord stood silently staring at him, waiting for his spot. Rick looked around the room. At least ten sets of eyes watching him. It was a little unnerving.

"Eighty-two games, Hansen. Practices, travelling, hotels, luggage, airplanes, buses. Things only make sense when the puck's dropped. We're just puppets dancing from a string."

Rick blanched at the metaphor. Was Jonesy just making fun of him or had he exposed the conspiracy Sam had warned him about?

Gord mutely moved to sit, regardless of Rick's presence. He tried to get out of the way, but the big man flattened him.

"You don't take a man's seat," Jonesy said.

"Hey." Rick squirmed. Gord pressed down hard. There was barely any space between the half walls that separated the spots. He was starting to lose oxygen.

"Okay, Gord," Coach Chapman said. "He's learned his lesson."

Gord stood up slowly. Didn't even turn around. Rick slipped free and went back to his spot. Gord stared at him calmly with vacant eyes. Was he in some kind of trance?

Fucking hell, Sam. Why'd you have to mess with my head

like that?

She had him looking for things that weren't there, taking his focus away from what he was here for – to play. He hadn't netted a point in four games. This was his first real slump. He had to put her words out of his mind.

"Okay," Coach Chapman said. "Two minutes. Let's go."

Rick frantically put his shoulder pads back on as the team stood up, almost in unison, to line up and head back to the ice. They stood holding their sticks, waiting. He joined the back of the queue, behind Patrick Linseman.

"Hey, Patrick," he said. "I heard they signed you to an extension."

The man said nothing, like he didn't even hear him.

"Focus on the game, Hansen," Jaxxon said, taking up the rear. "Don't get distracted by bullshit. Isn't that what *you* said?"

"Yeah, yeah."

The coach walked up the line, inspecting everyone. He clapped Patrick on the shoulder but stopped at Rick and Jaxxon, glaring at them.

"Let's pop one early, boys. Make 'em pay every time they touch a puck."

"Sir, yes, sir."

Everything was just a little too perfect, the discipline so ingrained that Rick grew suspicious. It felt like the life was slowly ebbing out of the dressing room.

Damn you anyway, Sam.

"Shots on the net. Get those lucky bounces."

The locker room door opened, and everyone moved silently down the tunnel to the ice, tapping Igor's stick as he stood vigil at the gate.

"I know I'm getting some lucky bounces tonight," Jaxxon said to Rick. "I'm talking titties."

No one laughed or told him to shut up – they were all in the zone.

On the ice, the sounds of the Black-Eyed Peas blared overhead. He momentarily forgot what city they were in. The game resumed. He lost himself in the sound of blades on ice, cheering fans, pucks on sticks, referee's whistles, PA announcements, the snippets of rock songs before a face off, the smell of sweat, the tug of the uniform, the feeling of being a part of something bigger than he was. Before he knew it, he was back in the hotel room. The high started wearing off, his body ached. He looked up at the ceiling and wondered just what in the hell was going on.

CHAPTER TWENTY-SIX

"Sir, we've received word that one of the rookies has been asking questions."

"What kind of questions?"

"It may be nothing, but he seems to be suffering a malaise that could be due to outside influence."

"How is this possible?"

"The glitch. She was at a communal event. They had contact."

"You think she compromised him?"

"It's certainly a workable theory."

Arthur Fritz sighed and rubbed his temples. This glitch, as they were calling her, was becoming a real problem. Perhaps they needed to step up their efforts to deal with her.

"Move his transformation up in the queue."

"But sir, he's not shown any other—"

"It was going to happen anyway. We're simply adjusting timelines."

The man in the lab coat nodded. "I'll make the necessary preparations."

Fritz assumed the man was done, but he remained standing in the doorway of his office as if he had more to say.

"Yes? Something else?"

"Sir, the other rookie is causing problems. He's become a liability in his current state, and we feel that—"

"Put him next on the list then, too. Do them both at the same time. Two fewer problems, right?"

"Of course, sir. If you feel that we can support a double transformation."

"If we can't, then make it so we can. We are in the middle of a highly sensitive operation. We cannot afford any more glitches. Am I clear?"

"Absolutely, sir. I will get a team working on them both right away."

"Good. We both know what happens if we fail like Karlsson."

"We won't, sir."

"See that you don't. Otherwise, you'll be broken down into your component parts and used to further our goals in ways you can't fathom."

The man swallowed hard. The threat was clear and he knew it. He spun on his heels and left.

CHAPTER TWENTY-SEVEN

This whole not using your legs thing is great.

Frank, sitting in the wheelchair they'd plopped him in after drugging him halfway to Woodstock, pulled himself along the floor, hand on the hall railings, like he'd seen others do. The orderlies ignored him now that they thought he'd forgotten how to walk.

Suckers. I'm just playing possum. But this rodent has claws and you're the ones who'll get rabies.

He could get up at any time, but he chose not to. In the chair, he was enfeebled, beyond worry. So he played their game and went back to work. He pulled himself into Oscar's room and rolled up to the bed where the old man lay asleep and drooling.

"Oscar," he said, poking the man in the guts.

He jerked awake. "Huh? How long you been there?" Oscar looked under his sheet at his crotch. "You see if I was sporting wood?"

"I wasn't looking at your junk, old man, I'm looking for your junk."

"I didn't lose it, it's right here." Oscar pointed under the sheet.

"Not that junk, your thousand-dollar bill."

"My what?"

"Your bankroll. The one you said the Mexican stole."

"You sure you were talking to me?"

That's when Frank spotted the pills on Oscar's desk. He reached for them. The lid was screwed on, child-proof tight, thwarting him, but through the orange bottle, he saw little blue lozenges. Just like the ones they'd been trying to pump him full of. The ones that turned you into a cabbage.

"You been taking these things, Oscar?" Frank asked.

"I don't know. They give me so many now I can't keep track anymore."

Frank put the bottle back onto the dresser. "Next time they offer you these, spit 'em in the sink. For your own good."

Frank wheeled himself back to the doorway. Oscar was looking into the pill bottle intently. He left the jumbled man and returned to his hall wandering.

Next was Felix's room. The man was watching television, something in black and white with Dick Powell in a fedora.

"Wesley, you come to watch the movie?"

"No, Felix, I came to see if you found your copy of Shogun you said was stolen."

"Shogun? I don't follow, Wesley."

"It's Frank, I've told you a thousand times. And Shogun was the book you were reading until it went missing. Something about Japan, you said. It was just getting to the good bits when someone walked off with it. I've been looking for you but have come up emptier than Oscar's head."

"Wesley, this is a real good movie. You want to watch?" He pointed to the television helpfully.

Frank spotted the blue pills on his end table.

"They got you, too, eh, Felix?"

He dug into his pants and pulled out his phone. He snapped a picture of the pill bottle, getting the name in frame as evidence.

"Don't take these, Felix," he said. "They're not good for your health."

Back to the halls, into old Mrs. Halsey's room. She was gone, but sure enough, on her table, more of those pills. He lapped around to the door out of the locked ward, pulled on it just to check, found it locked as usual, then dragged himself back to his room.

He swiped through the photos he had so far. The orderlies, the desk log, the lunchroom, pill bottles, the faces of the residents. Nothing added up to enough just yet. He needed that one big piece of the pie.

"I know your secret," a voice said from the window.

He suddenly realized Mrs. Halsey was in his room, on her own wheelchair, looking at him.

"What secret is that?"

"You're not like the others."

"Neither are you."

She nodded.

"What brings you in here?" he asked.

"To warn you. They're watching you. Don't let them find out you know."

"If I know they know, then they'll never know I know they know."

She nodded again.

"Please don't let them get me," she said. "I've seen what they do."

"Care to make a statement on video?"

He switched the phone on and held it up. "Spill it, Mrs.

Halsey."

"They want what's inside us. What makes us tick. They take it. I saw them do it to old Mrs. Ween. A needle when she was asleep, then she was dead."

"And then what?"

Suddenly, a change came over her, like a switch was flicked behind her eyes. They grew three sizes, and she started shaking. "Help! Help. Help!" she cried.

"Hey, hey, quiet down. They'll come."

"Help!"

He stuffed the phone into his pants. He heard the sounds of footsteps on the tiled floor in the hall.

"Mrs. Halsey, are you in the wrong room again?" came the sickly-sweet voice of Ginny. "You know you don't belong in the other residents' bedrooms."

She took the handles of the wheelchair and started to turn Mrs. Halsey around.

"Help!"

The old woman looked at Frank, mouthed, "They want our brains" as she passed by.

Frank did his best to stay slouched and unfocused. Jesus peered in. "Everything okay in here, Ginny?"

"Help!"

"Mrs. Halsey got confused again."

"She bothering you, Mr. Malone?"

Frank said nothing, just stared at the window.

"You want me to put on your TV for you?"

Jesus switched on the set, put it to the same channel Felix had been watching. Dick Powell was still wearing that hat.

"There you go. Something old to watch. It's almost dinner time, so you make sure you're ready to eat some delicious

Salisbury steak and mashed potatoes."

The condescension was as thick as his hide. Frank pretended to be distracted by the movie. Jesus left. Frank had one more piece in the puzzle filled in now. He was so close.

CHAPTER TWENTY-EIGHT

"Sam, what the hell are you doing?"

The coffee shop was quiet, only two tables occupied apart from theirs. Sam, examining the foam art in her latte, knew that Avital had called her here for a reason, but thought they might have danced around the subject first.

"Having coffee with my best friend?" she said, looking up sheepishly

Avital's grim visage showed that she wasn't in the mood to play it this way.

"You know what I'm talking about. You and Erin were a thing, now it's you and some gross Russian goalie?"

"I think he's from Czechia actually."

"Who cares? Why are you hooking up with him on the side?"

"It's not like that, okay?"

"So you're not cheating on my best friend? Because it sure looks that way. And she sure thinks you are."

"I'm trying to explain, but she won't talk to me. I try in the morning before class, but she just takes her food in her room."

"Can you blame her?"

"You have to tell her that I'm not hooking up with Igor."

"His name is fucking Igor? That's some Frankenstein movie shit."

Avital took a sip of her own drink and stared daggers at Sam.

"I'm just using him to get to Rick. I had to get a message through to him. About how I think the Jets are pulling something similar to Simon Karlsson, replacing people with... copies. He's on the inside and he's seen what I've seen. Together, maybe we can expose whatever it is that's going on."

"Oh, so you're only cheating on Erin with Igor so you can cheat on her with Rick Hansen. That's so much better."

"Av, what would you say if I told you that I don't remember ever starting to date Erin? I think it's been great, maybe just what I needed after having no luck with guys, but the past few months are all jumbled and—"

"You idiot, that's love. You guys are so perfect for each other. I was so happy to see Erin finally letting herself be who she's always been. You, I figured, were just exploring another side after being so abused by he-who-shall-not-be-named from the band-that-shall-not-be-named. I never pictured you for bi, but you two, you're just good together. Even you have to see it. We all sure did."

"Even Everett?"

"You're just lucky he didn't ask to watch."

"I don't think Marlon's too happy about it."

"Marlon has a problem with only liking women he can't have, then beating himself up for never making a move. I've known him for so long, I've seen it a hundred times. You don't want to know how many wrestling chicks he's subscribed to on OnlyFans. He's got masochist issues and gets a crush on any girl that talks to him. You know he liked you for a while? Before the whole band incident at least."

"He did? That's… shocking."

"Not really. I know he's been jerking it to me for years. Everett told me."

"And you were never interested?"

"He's a nice guy, but about as far from my type as possible."

Sam stirred away the fading foam art and took a small sip. The latte was finally cool enough to drink.

"I've known Erin since kindergarten and I won't put up with you messing her around, or using her as a phase. She's in a fragile state right now. If this whole coming out thing backfires, it could set her back years. If you're not going to be there for her, you need to break it off, gently, so that she's not embarrassed."

"The last thing I want to do is hurt her, but what about me, though? I'm confused about all of this, too. And there's still the matter of the Jets and—"

"Sam, the last time we got caught up in your, uh, drama, we were all tied up and almost assaulted. We watched you beat the shit out of a bunch of perverts who then ended up dead. I don't think it's me speaking out of turn to tell you that we're not your tag team partners on this one. God, I'm using wrestling terms now – Marlon's obsession has rotted my brain."

"But I might need you guys. I do need you guys. More than you know."

"Then the first thing you have to do is fix it with Erin. Because if you break her, I will break you."

* * *

Erin was sitting on the couch, watching TV, when Sam walked in. The whole walk back, she'd been going over what she was going to say, how she could let her friend down gently, how she could avoid telling her that she had no idea why they were together in the first place.

"Erin," Sam said, slipping off her shoes.

"I'm going to bed." Erin stood up without looking at Sam and headed off to her room.

"Can we talk first?"

A slamming door was the only answer.

God, I have fucked this up completely. No, not me, whatever happened to me at that game.

Sam poured herself a glass of water and went to her own room.

Her head was jumbled with thoughts and emotions as she took off her clothes and slid on a long t-shirt, tossing everything into a pile on the floor. She collapsed on the mattress and shut her eyes.

"Why would seeing that game mess me up so badly? Why would they want people living in a blur? Was it only me? Does Erin have the same confusion? Were we acting out our desires or someone else's? Or was Av right and I was just blissfully happy?"

The room was dark, and she was drifting away as she tried to piece together what was going on. She could hear the sounds of Erin watching something on her phone coming through from the other side of the wall. She needed to know if this was real, but how could she fix things if Erin wouldn't talk to her?

The vastness of space seemed to consume her. She thought she heard the door open. Trapped in that moment between sleeping and waking, she felt someone slide on the bed beside her. Warmth. A body pushing up against her.

"Erin?" she mumbled, unsure if the words were real.

Hands slid under her shirt. A gentle touch, a warm breath on her neck. Was this a dream? Things seemed to happen outside of time.

"Sam…"

It had to be a dream. She lost herself in the moment, her body moved outside her control. No one spoke, she lost all concept of time as desire overtook her. Images were fleeting. She realized she'd been here before. Unsure where here was. Intense heat, soft skin, floating above her own body. A ball of bare skin and heavy breathing. She couldn't be sure what had just happened had even happened, but it had felt more than right.

What a dream. The darkness returned.

She woke up slowly. The sun shone in on her. She rubbed her eyes, tried to remember the intensity of that dream when she heard stirring next to her. A man with dishevelled dark hair stood by the bed and leaned over her. He stared at her from empty eye sockets. A centipede crawled out of his mouth and darted inside the left hole.

"Morning, Sam."

The man was gone. Sam rolled over to see Erin laying beside her, grinning sheepishly.

"Erin? I thought I was dreaming."

"Is that a compliment?" She had… she did. They had. They did. And it was amazing.

Erin gently touched her arm. "Sam, I'm sorry. I overreacted without letting you tell your side of the story. I was sitting in bed, watching the highlights of the Jets game and I realized

219

that. This is something I don't understand. But I want to."

"Understand what?"

"This. Us. Whatever it is we're doing. I've never, you know. Been with a girl before and—"

"Erin, I—"

"I guess I thought, since it was you, it would be safer somehow. Easier than with a stranger or someone I swiped on. I don't know. I never stopped to think what you were getting out of this and—"

"Wait, I—"

She put her finger on her lips to stop her.

"I get you're maybe still processing this. Unsure about who you are, still getting over your trauma from Scott and... I just sort of thought that... well, it's been pretty intense, you know. And that that would be enough for you? But when I found out it wasn't, it hurt. I was super pissed off. Were these past weeks a lie?"

"I wanted to talk to you about all of this."

"Let me finish first, okay? This isn't easy. This is new for me, too. So I wanted to know how you felt, how this felt. Now I know. This is me. This is who I am. But I need to know if this is you. Because I'm not just a side piece, okay? I won't be treated like that. If you're just experimenting, then I want to know. Because I'm not. I don't want to just be looked at as a phase or a way to avoid dealing with shit from your ex. I think I might love you, but that can't be one-sided. So, last night. That was... yeah. But was it for you? Is there an us? Are we a thing? Because if it's not, I can't take it any further. You have to decide. Are you all in?"

"Erin, I'm so confused right now. You're my best friend. You and Avital. Hanging with you has changed my life in so many ways. I—"

"Are we just roommates, or are we… lovers?"

"Jesus…" Sam's head spun, her world getting all confused. There was so much going on right now. And now this ultimatum? What was she supposed to do about it?

"Sam?" Erin asked again, tears starting to form in her eyes.

"Erin, I… I just don't know what's happening. I feel lost and confused, rethinking these past few months, wondering about who I am and what I want… I need to clear my head, sort through so many things, especially about us. I'm just so… confused."

"I think I hear you. But I'm finally not. Maybe for the first time in my life. And it's because of you. And this. And—"

Sam's phone beeped. She reached for it, but Erin grabbed her hand.

"Sam, don't."

"It could be Rick. I have to—"

Erin slid out of bed and stormed out of the room.

"No Erin, please. It's not like that either. I-"

She heard Erin's door slam. She'd really done it this time. But the phone beeped again. She looked at the screen and saw a message from Rick, finally. "Something weird going on."

CHAPTER TWENTY-NINE

Coach Chapman waited for him with a clipboard in hand and a whistle around his neck as Rick walked down the hall to the dressing room for another practice. Jaxxon stood at coach's side, looking dressed to kill in a ten-thousand-dollar suit. The dress code in the NHL was meant to project an air of professionalism and Rick suddenly felt inadequate with his off the rack number. Even for practices, you were not allowed to wear sweatpants and hoodies in public.

"Hansen," Coach Chapman called out as he arrived. The man managed to always look like a gangster with his fedora and dark suit.

"Coach?"

"All-star break, this weekend. You and Jaxxon are being sent for additional seasoning. You guys are slumping at the worst time."

"Coach," Jaxxon said. "I've got two goals in the last four games."

"You should have four. Hansen, you were on a streak, now you're stinking up the joint. They had you earmarked as a Calder candidate. You know I heard them call you a disappointment of the month on Sportscentre?"

"Sorry, Coach," Rick said. "There's just been a lot on my mind."

"Which is exactly why you both need some special training. There's a team waiting for you. They'll run tests, put you through exercises. Linseman was sent before he came back and the man's like a whole new player."

Rick wondered about that.

"The brass wants you guys in top shape, focused, firing on all cylinders. We're going to push for the playoffs. We've got a shot to sneak in. But you two need to step up."

"Coach, I—"

"You nothing, Jaxxon," he said, cutting him off. "This organization wants to make sure their investments are going to pay off." He checked something off on his clipboard.

"So, where we going, Coach?" Rick asked.

"It's a little resort about four hours outside of town. Remote, free of distractions." He looked at Jaxxon who was already on his cellphone, tapping away a text, Rick presumed to a date he'd lined up and now had to cancel.

"When do we leave?"

"Now. Get on the bus, the two of you."

"Just us? What about the rest of the guys?"

"The rest of the guys aren't the ones shitting the bed right now, rookie," Coach Chapman said. "The orders came right from the top. The man who signs your cheques."

Arthur Fritz? This was odd.

"Can I call my girlfriend first?" Rick asked.

"You have two minutes."

Coach Chapman led Jaxxon down the hall as Rick whipped out his cellphone. He called Debbie, who answered on the second ring.

223

"What's going on, Rick?"

"They're sending me to some kind of overnight training camp. Jaxxon, too. I won't be home tonight."

"I heard from the other wives that they do wonders there."

"You have?"

"Sure. Betty told me that Thomas came back a changed man. They used to fight all the time and now he helps out around the house, picks up after himself, doesn't touch beer and—"

"Who else?"

"Well, Halsey said Petr went and he stopped leaving the toilet seat up. Kelly said Teddy started calling her every night at exactly ten o'clock. Tammy said Chris has been so much more attentive to her needs. Julie said—"

"Okay, I get it. But did they say what went on in this special camp?"

"I never thought to ask. They were all so much happier now that I assumed it must be like an etiquette and discipline thing."

"Hansen," Coach Chapman called out. "Time to go."

Rick nodded. "Okay, Debbie. I've got to go. I'll see you when I get back."

"Love you, honey."

He clicked off before he could respond. He followed Coach down the hall to a door that led to the loading docks. Isaiah, the security guard, stood watch as he found Jaxxon outside a waiting charter bus with the team colours painted on the sides.

"Finally, Hansen," Jaxxon said and boarded.

A mute man took Rick's bag. He saw their equipment already tossed underneath in the bins.

"Hey, what about clothes and toiletries and—"

"Hansen, get on the bus. The team's got all that taken care of."

Coach Chapman stared at him. The bus idled, the rumble dimmed in the cavernous loading dock. Isaiah waved at him from the door. He suddenly had a strange feeling about this whole trip.

"Hansen, we're burning fumes here."

"Right."

Rick climbed the stairs. The driver nodded as he boarded. He looked for a seat with leg room and a good view of the driver. Dark blue plush fabric, televisions in the back of each chair, lights in the floor showing the way to the bathroom at the back; it was exactly like the regular team bus, and yet, some things were off. It smelled antiseptic. None of the graffiti on the walls from the guys. He took a seat and Jaxxon slid into one opposite him, spreading out, hands behind his head, a big smile on his face. He obviously wasn't having any concerns about this trip.

"You think there'll be bitches there, Hansen?"

"I doubt it," Rick said. "This is supposed to be a training weekend."

"There's got to be someone there, a desk clerk, a cook, a maid… someone I can fuck."

"Is that all you worry about?"

"Come on, Hansen, I got needs." He took out a small metal tube from his inside shirt pocket and unscrewed the lid. Rick couldn't see exactly what it was, but saw white powder inside. Jaxxon took a quick sniff and shook his head. "You want a pick me up?"

"No, that's all right."

Jaxxon held up the small cylinder to Rick. "Check it out, this snuff holder – dude sold it to me online had a letter that said it used to belong to Al Capone, how about that!"

"Was it expensive?"

"You know it!" Jaxxon put the cylinder back into his shirt pocket.

"You'd better keep that thing hidden this weekend," Rick said. He leaned back, watching out the window as the bus slowly pulled out of the loading dock and joined the traffic of River City's downtown.

CHAPTER THIRTY

"That makes three now," Veronica said as they walked away from the small bungalow surrounded by shrubs.

"You heard her, the whole wrestling company went under."

"Yeah, and the ex-wrestlers are all missing."

"Well, three—"

"Four if we count the woman with the two-tone hair who seems to have walked out of the hospital and off the face of the planet."

Jimmy reached the cruiser first and took the driver's side. Lately, they'd been alternating stop by stop. "Right, but we have no reason to believe that she's in any distress."

"Nor do we have any reason to think she isn't."

They climbed inside the car, buckling their seatbelts. Jimmy turned the key and let it idle. "So, where next?"

"We've almost gone through the whole list that promoter gave us of his former wrestlers. At least the local ones. I don't think we can get away with driving to Calgary to look for the ones he brought in."

"Let the local police handle those."

"That's if they're even aware of the situation," she said.

Jimmy pulled out and merged into traffic. "Put in a call if

you're so concerned."

"It just makes no sense. Why would all the wrestlers from that one local promotion suddenly disappear?"

"The promotor said they might be working in Mexico, or down south. Just because we can't get hold of them, and their families haven't heard from them in weeks doesn't mean there's something sinister going on."

"Jimmy, this is our job. Why are you looking for excuses?"

"I'm trying to play devil's advocate here. We haven't received missing persons reports about any of these people. This is all just your hunch."

"I think it's more than a hunch."

"And I've learned from years of working with Frank to let hunches play out. That's why I'm with you on this one."

They drove in silence for a few moments before Veronica turned to him. "You staying over tonight?"

"Depends."

"On what?"

"Do I get to spend the whole weekend with you?"

"That all depends on how you do pancakes in the morning."

* * *

"Some guy left this forwarding address. Said to send the last month's rent there and they'd make sure it was paid."

The landlord of the slum building leaned on the door scrawled with swears. He wore a stained undershirt and torn sweatpants. The room behind him was a disaster, with food wrappers, plates, and clothes everywhere. Jimmy and Veronica were in the hall doing their questioning.

"Was it Kirk Angelico? Sorry, Kurtis Biggs?"

"Nah, some guy in a suit. Never seen him before. He said Kurt was working for them now up north somewhere. Said there was no cell service. I told the guy, there's bills, you know. Just because Kurt scored some new job, doesn't mean he can just break his lease and walk out. Besides, all his stuff is still in there."

"In the apartment?"

"Yeah, he just left it all. Took off in the middle of the night, I guess. I dunno, he must have got a pretty sweet job offer to just disappear like that so sudden like."

"So you never saw him leave?" Veronica asked.

"Nope. I just, uh, was doing an inspection of the suite and found that he'd been gone a while. Then this guy shows up and tells me he's taking care of the room. Ain't cleaned nothing out yet. I, uh, checked when I was doing another routine inspection."

Jimmy could tell right away that this disgusting, balding, greasy guy with the thin moustache was snooping around the empty suite looking for something he could steal, but they weren't here to protect Kurtis Biggs's stuff, they were looking for him – the last wrestler on the list of local talent they'd been given.

"And this man, did he give a name?"

"Nope, just a card with the forwarding address."

He handed it over and Veronica copied the information down in her notebook.

"How about the room, any changes?"

"Nope."

"Can you let us take a look?"

"Oh, I dunno. That's not really kosher with the Residential Tenets Act and all."

"Neither is looting him when he's gone, so what do you want us to report first?" Jimmy asked.

The man swallowed hard and walked into his disaster of a room, grabbing a set of keys. He waved for them to follow him, leading them up a floor to room 221.

"Okay, this is Kurt's room. But I didn't let you two in here."

He unlocked the door and stepped back.

"An open door? Better go inside and make sure everyone's okay, right, Detective Tockett?"

"Good idea, Detective Hooper."

They both entered the room. It was small, with posters of wrestling events tacked to the wall, a ratty green couch and old tube television. The kitchen was attached directly to the sitting area, with only a change of flooring delineating the two spaces. Jimmy found the sink full of dirty pots and pans, the mouldy food congealing into a mass that fused them all into one large piece of metal.

"The guy did leave in a hurry," he said, holding up a pot stuck to a frying pan.

Veronica slid into a chair at a small computer desk. A laptop lay open. She tapped the keys and it sprang to life.

"No password. Lucky."

Jimmy inspected the kitchen, the bathroom, the bedroom. Each room seemed to be exactly as if someone had simply left for the day, intending to come back. They certainly didn't seem like they'd been picked through for supplies.

"Toothbrush, comb, razor, all still here," he called out to Veronica.

"Jimmy, I think I found something."

He left the bathroom and joined her at the desk. She had his email open. She pointed to a message with the title: "No experience necessary. Immediate help required."

"Looks like he got a job offer."

"Where?" Jimmy asked.

"Says hospitality. There's only a phone number here."

"Call it."

Veronica took out her cellphone and dialed the number. It took a few rings before someone picked up.

"Ah yes, hi. I was calling about a job offer and—"

Whoever it was cut her off.

"I have this email and—"

She was cut off again.

"Ex pro wrestler."

The person said something Jimmy couldn't hear. Then Veronica scrunched up her face and clicked off the phone.

"Well?" Jimmy asked.

"They didn't believe me."

"Who didn't?"

"The Geld Resort and Conference Centre."

"Geld? Where is that?"

She flipped back to the laptop and found an open Google window with a map screen. Surrounded by green, she scrolled back to see that the resort was a few hours north of River City, right in the middle of the bush.

"Here, apparently," she said.

"You think Kurtis Biggs went to work there?"

"It certainly looks that way."

"Okay, then we know where he is," Jimmy said. "That's one at least who's not missing."

"I don't know. They sounded super weird on the phone. As if they didn't expect anyone to be calling that number."

"Maybe it's not a busy resort."

She had a look on her face that told him that she was getting a hunch again.

"Or maybe we should head out to this little resort and do some digging around."

CHAPTER THIRTY-ONE

"This is it?" Jaxxon said upon disembarking from the bus.

The Geld Resort and Conference Centre was a log cabin style resort out in the middle of nowhere. Rick had tried to follow the route, but he'd gotten disoriented when they'd turned up some back country road, deep into the woods.

"Looks like a hunting and fishing lodge," Rick said.

The place was seeped in mist, surrounded by trees and covered in snow. The air was fresh and clean. The driver lifted the bus bins. They grabbed their bags and headed inside. The lobby was deserted. Rick and Jaxxon seemed to be the only guests here.

Jaxxon elbowed him and pointed to the front desk. Two women stood waiting patiently. "Hey, Hansen, what about that blonde? What a body, eh?"

"Dude, we're not here for—"

"Oh shit, check out that Asian chick, she looks like some kind of anime babe. Maybe this place won't be a total waste."

Rick did his best to ignore Jaxxon. A man in a white lab coat emerged from a door next to the front desk.

"Good evening, gentlemen, I am Dr. Hans, sports psychologist. I also have a PhD in biology. I have been tasked with ensuring that the two of you become super elite, tier double one players. I will show you the difference between wanting to win and knowing how to win. After this weekend, you will have the secret and will be among the best in the league."

"So let me get this straight," Jaxxon said. "All-star weekend. Everyone else gets time off to fuck around and relax but we have to do extra credit work?"

"Look, Jaxxon, I'd much rather be sitting in a hot tub with my girl, too, but this is a part of being a pro. Coach expects us to be here and do our best."

"You are such a dork, Hansen."

"Indeed," Dr. Hans said, raising an eyebrow at Jaxxon. "The staff will show you each to your rooms, on opposite sides of the two wings, I'm afraid."

He handed them a folded over schedule. Rick opened it up to see a detailed list of events: training, physical evaluations, film studies, nutrition, skills development, mental evaluation, more testing, more training, more testing, more training. There was almost no time for any break or rest. It was clear that this was going to be a long weekend.

"Hey, doc," Jaxxon said. "When's downtime here?" He looked to the girls and winked.

"Leisure is for the weak. Here, we will make you strong."

The blonde left the desk and motioned for Rick to follow. The Asian did the same for Jaxxon. The man looked over his shoulder and made a dick sucking motion, bursting out laughing. Rick saw Dr. Hans frowning before he was led to his room.

* * *

Sitting alone in the apartment, waiting for another text from Rick, Sam could only scroll through her phone impatiently. None of her friends would answer her. Everett, Marlon, Avital, Erin; they were all ghosting her texts. She was losing her mind over how badly she'd messed things up with all of them, especially Erin. She had to get out.

They would all be working. If they wouldn't respond to her, then maybe she could go and force them to talk to her in person. She grabbed her coat and car keys and headed to the door.

* * *

Measured, poked, prodded, told to breathe in here, squeeze this, pull that, drink this, eat that, run on this machine, sit on that one, Rick was left disoriented before finding himself in a dark room watching old game footage.

"Gretzky has Murphy with him on a two on one, to Lemieux, in on goal, he shoots, he scores! Mario Lemieux with one twenty-six remaining!"

The noise of the crowd on screen was unreal, the image panning over jubilant fans jumping and hugging, a nation going crazy for a game that meant everything back then.

"Positional hockey, passing, being in the right place, Mario Lemieux following the scouting reports and going high glove side."

Rick stared at the footage in the dark as Dr. Hans talked. It took watching the same clip from Canada Cup '87 for the twentieth time before he had finally begun to relax. The projector hummed away as he and Jaxxon watched an endless stream of highlight reel moments from great games, the all-time best players doing their thing, dissected by attitude coaching.

"There's more to this game than just talent," the man said, looking back at them through the darkness. "True greats have heart, skill, and the mindset of a team player working within a defined role."

It was the kind of thing that Rick had heard a thousand times before from a hundred different people.

"Dude, this is boring as F," Jaxxon whispered.

Rick shrugged. "I've been coming to these things my whole life."

He felt at ease now, understanding what this was all about. Sam's warnings had faded away as he came to see this as just another one of the endless development camps he'd been attending since he first laced up skates.

But he was also exhausted. This was the first chance he'd had to sit down since they'd arrived. Dr. Hans watched them as the film rolled, writing down notes in his book.

"Mr. Downie, are you not finding this footage valuable?"

Jaxxon rolled his eyes. "Doc, as much as I like watching Sportscentre, I was kind of hoping to have a chance to catch some Z's, you know? I've not been sleeping all that great lately and we've been going all day."

Cocaine's a hell of a drug, Rick thought to himself.

"Of course, Jaxxon. There will be time for respite shortly. But we must further first study the excellent career of Mario Lemieux."

Jaxxon fidgeted in his seat. The doc wrote more in his ledger. Rick pulled out his cellphone, tapped a note to Sam. His last one, "Something weird going on," showed 'read' but they'd lost service and he had no idea what she thought of it.

No sense in worrying her. He tapped out a new one: "false alarm" and went back to watching one of the true greats.

* * *

"You're the only one who's still talking to me," Sam said to Everett outside the corner Tim Hortons where he'd agreed to come for a quick break. "I don't know who else to turn to."

"Gee, thanks," the blond man said as he pulled the lid off his coffee cup and dropped in another packet of sugar.

"Erin's pissed, Avital's pissed, Marlon's hurt, what do I do here?"

"Seems obvious to me," Everett said. "Stop ditching your girlfriend for hockey players."

"Nobody seems to understand that Rick's in real fucking danger. I'm trying to help him."

"I think he can take care of himself."

"Then why do I get this weird text?" she said, turning her phone to show Everett as he replaced the lid. "Then no replies to all of my follow ups?"

"Maybe it wasn't supposed to be for you?"

"'Something weird going on.' That sure sounds like it was for me."

"Look, Sam, maybe you need to stop worrying about some millionaire who doesn't give a shit about you and start worrying about the people who do."

* * *

Three a.m. Rick awoke, sweating bullets, throat parched, in

237

desperate need of a drink. He rose from the bed and headed into the bathroom. The tap puttered and puffed, but no water came out. He went out into the hallway, wearing only boxer shorts.

There has to be a drink machine somewhere.

He walked the halls. His bare feet on the carpeting, the dead silence of the still night, dim lights, but no telltale hum of an ice machine, no red glow from a coke dispenser.

"What is with this place?"

He walked down the other wing to Jaxxon's room and knocked on the door. Shuffling from the other side. The door swung open. Jaxxon stared at him with dead eyes. Was he sleepwalking?

"Hey, Jaxxon, your sink work? I need a drink and mine's busted."

Jaxxon shut the door. After a moment, he returned with a perfectly balanced glass of water, handing it to Rick without a sound.

"Thanks, man." He drank the whole thing in one gulp. "How'd you make out with those hotel workers?"

Jaxxon just shut the door.

That's strange, dude never misses a chance to brag about his conquests.

Rick turned to go back to his room when he froze. There, at the far end of the hall, was a woman watching him. He hadn't seen her around before. Thickly muscled, with red and black hair pulled back in a ponytail, she simply stood silently. He waved sheepishly. He started to walk towards her, back to the lobby. She stepped forward towards him, matching his pace. He froze. She froze, too, her eyes never leaving his. He backstepped. She stayed put.

238

"Uh, hello?" he said.

She said nothing. He took a step forward, she matched him. He backstepped again, she remained put.

Do I not go that way?

He watched her as she watched him. She seemed to not want him to go back the way he'd come. He turned and began walking in the opposite direction, to make a circuit of the building and come back to his room from the other side. He heard her footsteps following. He froze and turned around.

She'd followed, but stopped.

"Seriously, what?"

She took a step forward and he suddenly panicked. He turned and bolted, ran the halls, his feet pounding on the carpet. Over his shoulder, he saw her moving in a power walk after him.

He didn't know why he needed to be back in his room, but it was clear he had to be. Sweating, mostly naked, he fumbled in his boxer's pocket for the keycard. His hand shook as he inserted it. She was getting closer, eyes locked on his.

"Come on, come on," he said to the door, waiting for the tiny red light to turn green.

CLICK.

He yanked the keycard out, pushed open the door and slammed it shut behind him, locking the deadbolt.

Breathing heavily, he stood watching the door. The footsteps slowed. Her shadow oozed under the door frame. The door handle began to turn slowly. He latched on the deadbolt. Slid the luggage rack in front of the door, waiting for her to burst through. The handle turned back. The shadow moved. He heard footsteps. He looked through the peephole, saw only empty hallway.

He grabbed a towel from the bathroom and wiped his face down. Why had he panicked like that? And why was that girl so weird?

He slid the dresser in front of the connecting room door and returned to his bed, waiting for his adrenaline to die down. He grabbed his phone and tapped another message to Sam. "Maybe not" appeared below "false alarm." Neither one had been sent; his phone was still searching for a signal.

* * *

"Marlon, come on. Please just let me apologize for what happened. I promise you I didn't try to—"

"Sam, you can say this stuff all you want, but it's not going to change what you did."

He pushed another shopping cart into the line, hooking the chain over the handle and taking out the loonie left inside.

The wind howled through the Safeway parking lot. Sam held her arms around her body, trying to keep the heat from escaping. Marlon, wearing a reflective vest and huge fur hat, moved through the snow to the next abandoned shopping cart.

"I never meant to hurt anyone. Things just got out of control."

"Drama, Sam. It's just more drama."

"Look, have you stopped to consider that if Erin is gay, then you had no chance with her anyway? So why should us dating be such a betrayal?"

He stopped and stared at her wide eyed. His cheeks were red from the cold. He worked part time at the grocery store, pushing carts, bringing out stock, mopping up spills in aisle six. They'd occasionally come to bug him in between trips to the mall or for coffee, but now Sam was here trying to repair all that she'd wrecked.

"Sam, have you considered that I liked living in my illusions? And that you rubbing my face in the fact that you were hooking up with Erin is what hurt more?"

"I never thought of it that way."

"Exactly. You didn't think. It seems like you've been doing that a lot lately. So maybe you should take some time to, you know, actually think about how that's affected the rest of us."

"Marlon, I'm sorry for what happened. Being bi sort of snuck up on me, too."

"I can get over it. I've gotten over a lot in my time. But if you really want to fix this friend group, it's not the guys you should be starting with."

"You're the only ones who'll talk to me."

"I don't have a lot of choice right now. You interrupted me at work."

"Can you at least try to forgive me?"

"If you don't undo the shit you've done, I'm not so sure any of us will."

* * *

A fitful sleep. He woke up feeling exhausted. The luggage rack and dresser were back in their place. Rick slid out of bed with a start, wondering how that could be possible. The locks were latched. He pulled open the connecting door and the other side was locked as well.

"Fuck..."

He dressed and headed downstairs. Jaxxon was nowhere

to be found. His phone still had no signal, but at least he had a charge. It had snowed overnight. The drive in looked covered. Amidst an oppressive silence, Rick did his morning workout in the gym, eyes never leaving the door. He went to the commissary and found a breakfast buffet waiting. Coffee, rolls, cereal, protein shakes, eggs and bacon under heated covers.

He ate alone. Every crunch of the bacon felt like an alarm going off. The schedule showed another session in the conference room. He didn't know what else to do, so he went.

Dr. Hans and Jaxxon were already there, neither speaking.

"Ahhh, Mr. Rick, so good of you to join us."

He slid in next to Jaxxon. "Dude, did you not eat?"

Jaxxon said nothing.

There was something off about him. He sat with perfect posture, never once even looking at Rick. He was dressed in a suit, his hair perfectly coiffed, his face precisely shaved. His skin was almost glowing and looked firmer than it had the night before. There was a Band-Aid on the back of his neck, with a bit of blood seeping through.

"You cut yourself shaving?"

The man still said nothing.

"Today, we study the teamwork of the Soviet Red Army national team from the period 1954-1991," Dr. Hans said as the screen flashed to life. "You will see what dedication to a team game, lack of selfish play, and total discipline even in a so-called rigid style, can accomplish."

The lights in the room dimmed, footage rolled on the white screen. Rick watched Jaxxon. The man was completely focused, he wasn't fidgeting, looking at his phone, the clock, or the door. Had they slipped him some Ritalin?

"Jaxxon, you okay?"

"Is there a problem, Mr. Rick?" Dr. Hans asked, pausing the footage.

"Oh no, sorry. I just thought…"

"That you were here to focus, correct?"

"Right."

* * *

"Sam," Avital said. "I'm not talking to you right now."

"Please, Av, I'm trying to fix this."

L'Elle: an upscale women's clothing store, Avital's part time job at the mall. A place they shopped at so often that it just made sense to start working there. "If only for the discount," she'd told them when she'd been hired.

Avital placed another pile of carefully folded sweaters on the shelf. A small pushcart, with four opened boxes of more, was parked next to the display.

"I don't know if you can."

"I tried to talk to her, I tried to explain what had happened, but—"

"Then you got a text from one of your hockey crushes and blew the whole thing."

"She wouldn't even hear me out. Rick is in danger. He's—"

"He's not important, Sam. Erin is. Her feelings. You keep walking all over them and you don't even realize it."

Sam leaned her head on her arm, against the smooth, tan marble walls of the expensive store. "I'm not trying to, I swear. Shit is just hitting the fan."

"You've been trying to make this right with all of us, but

you still haven't tried with the most important person."

"Avital, can we get some help at the till? There's a line." A co-worker, wearing a black dress cinched at the waist with a gold cord, stole Avital's focus as they spoke.

"Absolutely, Yasmine," she said and put the sweaters down on the cart.

"Av…"

"We're done, Sam. Go make things right."

* * *

Rick grabbed Jaxxon by the shoulder as they made their way to the gym for more work. "Hey, Jaxxon, wait up," He felt rock hard, twenty pounds thicker, all muscle. "You feeling okay, man?"

Jaxxon's eyes were distant, uncomprehending. Then he blinked a few times and seemed to finally notice Rick, like he was waking from a trance. "Huh, oh, hey, Rick."

"You were gone there for a second."

"Just tired. This weekend has been a lot."

"You get up to anything last night?" Rick said, pointing to the bandage. "Maybe with that Asian chick you were gaga over?"

"Rick, we're here to improve our skills. This isn't a party."

Rick's mouth dropped in shock. Was he being put on? "Come on, you can tell me. She get a little too scratchy?" He touched the bandage. "I'm not gonna squeal."

"Hansen, grow up." Jaxxon walked away.

Now he knew something was definitely wrong with Jaxxon; he'd never be so coy. Something had happened last night. The hair on the back of Rick's neck stood on end as he followed the man to the gym.

The next hour was even more shocking. Jaxxon had jumped to another level. Every physical test, every metric, every result was off the scale.

"Flawless performance, Mr. Downie," Dr. Hans said proudly.

Rick was unable to keep up with the guy. He felt like a kid competing against a man. When the session was done, he was drenched in sweat, Jaxxon looked ready to go for another two hours.

"Dude, what's your secret?"

"Hard work and dedication, Hansen."

"That's a crock. All year I've been the one in the gym doing extra work outs while you've been out partying. I've been studying game film, staying late at practice, working with the trainers, not you. Why the sudden change? You on something?"

"Must be the grub here."

Jaxxon went straight to the commissary. Rick chased after him. One of the tables was already set with a buffet serving on the counter near the open kitchen. Two glasses, full of something brown and thick, waited for them. Jaxxon immediately began to down his.

"What is that?" Rick asked.

"Mr. Hansen," Dr. Hans said, exiting the kitchen. "Your teammate has taken a liking to a protein shake of our own design. The team has been working on this for over a year, something to help put us over the top. It will remain off market. Our special secret. Mr. Downie sampled it last night and has clearly reaped the benefits."

Rick stared at the brown liquid in the tall glass. It looked innocuous enough and Jaxxon sure was sucking it back.

"What's in it?"

"Nutrients, proteins, enzymes, vitamins; a proprietary formula. I can promise that you will find your energy levels increasing, your skills on the ice growing, perhaps even your prowess in the bedroom."

Jaxxon grinned, with a brown moustache over his top lip. He licked it off.

"You'll feel like a new man, Hansen."

Hans picked up the glass and held it in front of Rick. Rick's internal danger alarm buzzed.

"You had this last night?" he asked Jaxxon.

"Midnight snack," he said.

Yesterday, Jaxxon had been his normal boasting self, now he was some kind of superman. Was this drink the catalyst? Was this how they got you? Set you up for the change? Was the change that bad? Last night Jaxxon was a sex-crazed cokehead, today he was a physical machine.

"Every team needs an edge, Mr. Hansen," Dr. Hans said. "This is ours."

"Steroids? Some kind of drug?"

"Our secret weapon."

"You won't regret it, Hansen," Jaxxon said.

Cold eyes. Both of them staring at him. There was something in the reptilian look on Dr. Hans's face that unnerved him.

The drink. That's how they get you.

He looked into the cloudy glass, seeing shapes dancing in the thick liquid, his mind playing tricks on him. Sam told him to watch out, and now here was the sign. It was too late for Jaxxon, but maybe he could still save himself.

"Say, doc, I gotta take a leak, I'll be right back."

"A drink first," Hans said. "For urethral health and—"

"Upset stomach. Maybe bad eggs this morning. Be right back."

Rick backed away, turned and ran out of the room. He could feel the eyes of Dr. Hans and Jaxxon following him. He pushed open the swinging door of the commissary and ran to the stairs. He had to get the hell out of here and fast. He pulled out his cell phone, still no service, and tapped in another message to Sam. 'It's in the drink.'

He slid his keycard in his room door, rushed to the hotel phone next to the bed. No ring tone.

"They wouldn't be that dumb."

He looked out the window. It was snowing. The drive had been plowed, but who knew about the road in? The bus was gone. There were no other cars parked in the lot. There was no way around it, he was going to have to make a run for it. He grabbed his coat, gloves, and hat. A Manitoba winter could kill you if you weren't careful, but he had no choice. Maybe he could flag someone down on the highway. Bundling up, he rushed to the door, pulling it open, and jerked back to see Jaxxon standing staring at him with dead eyes in the hallway.

"Shit, man, you scared me."

Jaxxon didn't move.

"I'm, uh, just going for a walk. I still feel nauseous. It'll clear my head, you know, make me feel better."

Jaxxon held firm, blocking the exit.

"Come on, man, just move, okay?"

Rick tried to squeeze through, but Jaxxon grabbed him on the shoulder with a vice-like grip of impossible strength.

* * *

As soon as the chime sounded when she pushed open the door to Pinky's Bakery, Sam saw Erin look up, a cloud pass over her face, then turn and start to head to the back.

"No, please wait," Sam said.

It was a small strip mall bakery, with a counter and two display cases partially full of cookies, cupcakes, macaroons, tarts, and other homemade pastries. Another stop to try to salvage her life, another in-person attempt when text messages went unanswered.

"Why'd you come?" Erin said icily, pausing at the swinging door to the back.

"You have to know."

"All I know is that Av warned me, but somehow I didn't think you'd have the guts."

"You know me, full of guts," Sam said sheepishly.

The place was empty of customers in the final few moments before close. Erin had been doing clean up.

"Erin, this whole us thing, it's been…" She struggled to articulate her feelings, searched for the words that would explain them properly. "What I mean is, I think I've learned a few things about myself and who I am and you've been a huge part of that."

Erin seemed to relax, seemed to be listening to what she had to say, which was a good start.

"You said it before, about paths and twisting, thinking you were on the right one, never considering that it might not be, then coming to the realization that maybe you were, are different. That you need different things and mistakes led you somewhere you never saw coming. A little scary, sure, but then you realized there's nothing scary about any of it, you'd just been unaware. You'd lost a lot of time on that wrong path."

Erin looked at her mutely. Sam felt a rush of desire to just kiss her. "Is any of this making sense?"

"I think so."

"You. Me. This thing between us. I'm not sure exactly what triggered it but…" Giving in, she hugged Erin tight. Surprised, Erin started to pull away but then relented. Feeling tears welling up, Sam leaned back, looking into Erin's eyes, and saw that this wasn't so strange a place to be, Erin understood her, cared for her, it didn't matter what label it had. Sam kissed her. Erin returned the kiss, and they stayed locked together for a long time, neither one wanting to pull away. But eventually, Erin detached. They were both flushed, but the smile on Erin's face told Sam all she needed to know about whether or not her speech had worked and the feeling inside her gut told her she was glad for that.

"Sam," Erin said, grinning, "you can be so infuriating. You go hot then cold, all mysterious, like a different person sometimes. But that's you, I guess, and I'm *into* you. So yeah, I'm almost done here, okay? I've got things to do in the back then we can go."

"I can help."

"Uh, no, you can't. My boss would flip. You can wait outside."

"What about waiting on one of these tables? It's cold out there."

Erin looked at the clock on the wall, then back to Sam, still grinning stupidly. "Sit tight while I go finish in back but please don't make a mess, I just cleaned the floors."

Sam sat on a stool and lifted her legs, hugging her knees tightly. "My feet won't touch the tiles."

Erin snorted. "They already did, smart ass. I'll just be a few minutes."

She disappeared in the back. Through the circular window to the cooking area, Sam saw her putting away bags of flour, rapidly wiping down countertops, and filling out some kind of logbook. She hadn't kicked her out at first sight, she'd listened to her. Maybe a flood of text messages had primed her to hear Sam out. Maybe her spilling her guts had just fixed this.

She pulled out her phone, checking for anything new from Rick. Still just that first message followed by all of her unanswered replies: 'What? Where are you? Need help? I'll come help. What's going on?'

She almost didn't look up when the door chime rang, announcing an extremely last-minute customer. Erin hadn't locked the door.

"Babushka, is that you?"

Oh no.

She looked up to see Igor standing smiling in front of her, with a giant fur hat and coat, arms open wide as if he wanted a hug.

"What the hell are you doing here?"

"I come to buy cupcakes. I was going to eat alone while watching teammates in all-star game, but now that you are here, you can accompany me back to my place and we can make sweet love after the cupcakes."

"No, Igor, no."

"You prefer to make sweet love before eating cupcakes? Yes, this is making sense. To work up the appetite."

He turned towards the counter and put his hands on the glass, leaning in close, his breath fogging the glass all over as he panted.

"These are looking quite delicious, babushka. Is there one that calls to you more than others?"

"Igor, you have to get out of here, I'm trying to—" She pulled on his arm, trying to force him to the door. He mistook the movement and leaned in, trying to kiss her.

"Oh my god, I can't even…"

Sam froze as Erin stood in the doorway. Igor had his chance, pushed his face into Sam's. His breath smelled like vodka. She pushed him away.

"He just showed up here, I swear."

"Out, out, out, out, out."

"But I am wanting the cupcakes?" Igor said. "Babushka, too."

"Out, out, out, out. Fucking get out."

"Erin—"

"GET OUT."

Sam knew it was hopeless now. She turned and started to walk out. When it looked like Igor wasn't going to follow, she pulled his collar and dragged him.

"No cupcakes? Okay then."

As soon as they were through the door, Erin slammed it shut, locked it, turned over the open sign to closed and hit all the lights. Sam saw her collapse to the ground and felt like the light had just gone out of her life.

"Your place or mine, babushka?"

* * *

251

"Shit, Jaxxon, that hurts," Rick said, pulling at the man's hand on his shoulder. He couldn't break the grip. "Let go."

The man said nothing.

"Don't say I didn't warn you." Rick said a silent apology to wherever the real Jaxxon was and threw a punch, right at the man's head. A staggering pain shot through his hand as it connected. It was like hitting steel.

"Fucking hell," he said, trying to shake out the blow.

Jaxxon didn't budge.

Rick stomped down on his toes with his boots, again and again, but Jaxxon was a statue who showed no pain.

"Alright." Rick held up his hands in surrender. "You got me." Jaxxon let go. Rick started backing into the room, feigning defeat. Jaxxon slowly stepped inside as well.

Rick backed up to one side of the bed. Jaxxon followed. That was his chance. He dove over the bed, bouncing to his feet and dashed for the open door, stepping around the lunging brute's arms out into the hall. He tore down the carpeted hallway towards the stairs.

A crash sounded behind him. Over his shoulder he saw Jaxxon walk right through the wall, skipping the door, knocking plaster and bits of wallpaper everywhere.

"Ho-ly shit."

Rick bolted into the stairwell, taking steps three at a time to the main floor. Another crash above him. He looked up to meet the stone-dead gaze of his teammate. Eye to eye, locked in place. It was clear now that there was nothing left of the man he knew, he was something else entirely, inhuman.

Rick took off, rushing to the front entrance like a bat out of hell. The desk clerk picked up the phone calmly as he ran by. He could see figures coming from the commissary, the woman with the two-tone hair, a huge man who barely fit in his shirt. Jaxxon emerged onto the landing.

Rick kicked through the great wooden doors into the cold night air and a deserted parking lot. He hadn't expected the team bus to suddenly appear, but he'd hoped maybe someone else might have checked in.

"Fucking hell."

He had no idea how far they were from the highway, but it was his only chance. He ran, boots crunching through the snow, past impassive evergreens that towered over him. He looked over his shoulder, saw Jaxxon crash through the front door, not wearing a jacket, marching after him like the Terminator, the woman and man in white a few feet behind.

"Shit, shit, shit, shit, shit."

His breath fogged. He ran down the twisting route of the lodge drive. The trio followed, walking with methodical purpose. He'd tire eventually. He had a feeling they wouldn't.

* * *

"Igor, where's Rick?" she asked the man as he sat in the passenger side of her car. He'd asked her for a ride home. She'd seen no reason why she should make him walk when the snow was picking up and night falling. It wasn't like a ride would ruin her life any more.

"Hansen? I'm not sure. He and I are not, how you say, best pals."

"But you do have his number, right? You could text him?"

"Yes, but what would I say? You are thinking he would also like to make sweet love and then eat cupcakes?"

"No, just see if he answers. He's been MIA for a day and a

half now."

Igor pulled out his phone and played with it, trying to swipe with gloves on, before giving up and taking them off so he could use his hands. He tapped away a message.

"Is no answer. Perhaps he is already making sweet love with his girlfriend Debbie?"

Sam stopped at a red light, silently wondering why she'd agreed to drive Igor home when her phone pinged. She checked for any police cars around, then dug it out.

Maybe it's Erin. Or Rick.

She'd tapped out a long paragraph of text to Erin, trying to explain that Igor had shown up unannounced, that they weren't an item, that she just needed to talk. There was a response. Erin had typed: "I'll be at the apartment. Last chance."

As Sam typed in, "Coming right there," another ping came from her phone. This time, a message from Rick.

"Help. Police."

A third ping. "Hey, Mister Rick has replied to me," Igor said. "He is under arrest?"

* * *

Rick could hear the faint sound of cars in the distance.

"The highway!"

He pushed on, his legs cramping from the uncomfortable boots. His hands were starting to freeze. As he rounded the next bend, he could see the lights of the Trans-Canada Highway. Cars moved past, driving to or from River City on either side of the twinned roadway.

Stepping out of the drive, he ran alongside the cleared

highway, waving his arms, dashing down the side of the road, hoping a car would see him and stop. A few dashed by, no one made any effort to slow down for the panicked man in the dark.

Jaxxon marched after him, unrelentingly, the two cooks in white just behind him. Rick crossed four lanes of highway. Jaxxon followed, but didn't look first. He didn't seem to see the semi, didn't hear the horn.

"Jaxxon!" Rick shouted.

One second the man was there, the next he was gone. The semi couldn't stop, its brakes squealed, tires locked up as it jackknifed on the cold winter road. The cab flipped, dragged along the ground, heading right for the two others in white. They were knocked hard, launched into the snow.

"Oh God."

Rick could only watch in shock at the accident, the semi scraping the highway, sparks flying. The red stain that used to be Jaxxon hung on the front, dripping gore along the road.

He held his head in shock, realizing what had just happened.

A car pulled over to the shoulder where he stood. A window rolled down and a voice called to him, "Are you okay? What happened?"

He looked down, shell-shocked, to see two police officers in a cruiser. A man with a shaved head, a woman with long dark hair.

"Hey, aren't you Rick Hansen?" the woman said.

He pulled open the door and got in the back.

"I'm calling in the accident," the male cop said, reaching for the radio.

"Did you see it?" the woman asked. "Was it a moose? A drunk driver?"

"It was Jaxxon," he said. "He's dead."

"Who's Jaxxon?" the woman asked.

"I don't know," Rick said.

"Do you need us to call someone?" the woman asked.

Rick's phone began pinging as it found a signal. Text messages coming in fast and furious. He took it out, saw Sam's texts and one from Igor. He tapped one in reply.

"I think he's in shock," the woman said.

"Jaxxon's dead. So's that big woman and that musclehead guy. The semi just clocked them all."

"Big woman?" the male cop asked.

The woman raised her eyebrow. "She didn't by any chance look like a pro wrestler, did she?"

CHAPTER THIRTY-TWO

"Sir, we received word that one of the two sent for the transformation escaped."

"Escaped? How is that possible?"

"It seems that he was warned beforehand. He got spooked and ran."

"All the way back to River City?"

"Well, no, to the highway, where he was picked up."

"There's nowhere he can hide. We'll find him. I'll put in a few calls and—"

"Sir, I meant picked up by two police officers. We think it was a complete coincidence that they were there."

"Then I presume that you've activated our connections on the force?"

"Of course. Anything the man says will be dismissed as a psychotic break. The team will have a member of the medical staff there to get him out. His girlfriend will sign the necessary paperwork."

"Good. Then it sounds like you've got this all under control."

"There was an additional complication."

Fritz leaned back in his chair, knowing that he was going to have to step in again and fix something before it got out of hand.

"Well?"

"The other transformation was successful."

"So then, what's the complication?"

"He was obliterated."

"What the hell do you mean, obliterated?"

"He was hit by an eighteen-wheeler at full speed. There's not enough left for us to fit into a shoebox, let alone for reconstruction."

The man revealed that behind his back, he held a shoebox. Nike by label. It was stained and warped.

"If you want to verify, sir." He lifted the lid and showed Fritz a puddle of bloody mush with a lone eyeball on top.

"I didn't need the visual confirmation, you idiot."

"But sir, our team spent a half hour scooping up what they could and—"

"Dispose of it. The man is obviously of no use to us now."

"Full coverup?"

"I'll put it in motion. You just work on securing the escapee. We're too far along now to have someone like that throw another wrench in our plans."

"We'll get him, sir. But, uh, one more thing."

"What is it now?" Fritz had the phone half raised, ready to start implementing a complete coverup of the story.

"The, uh, glitch. She may have been the one to warn the escapee. It appears that they have a history together and—"

"Then eliminate her, once and for all. No, better yet, let's bring her into the fold."

"Unwillingly?"

"That is the best way, isn't it?"

CHAPTER THIRTY-THREE

"So, tell us again what you think happened," Veronica told the dishevelled man sitting across the table from her and Jimmy. He was nervously sipping from a Styrofoam cup of coffee, eyes darting from the door to them, to the glass window that allowed others to watch the interview.

"How safe is this place?" he asked.

"Mr. Hansen, I'm sure you've seen a million cop shows, but it's just us here right now. This isn't a formal interrogation. We're just trying to get a sense of what led you to be standing on the side of the highway after an accident with a long-haul truck, demanding to be brought back home," Jimmy said in his best calming voice.

"I told you. They're trying to change me."

"Who is?"

"The team. The Jets. I don't know what the hell is going on. He drinks a protein shake and turns into a... a what, a golem? It made Jaxxon... normal. Instead of a partying cokehead, he was all business; a model player, I'd guess. Is that what they want? To turn us all like that? Patrick Linseman. He came back different. They told me so. Some of the others, too. I can see it now. Straightlaced. That's it. In some twisted way, they want to straighten us out. Jaxxon was a wild man, Linseman was holding out for a new contract. But why me? I've been playing by the rules. First guy on the ice, last guy to leave. Why do they want to mess with my head? Why do they want to… change me?"

Veronica looked to Jimmy, who'd written down as much as he could from the poor, disoriented man's ranting.

"Let me get this straight," Jimmy said. "They, the team—"

"The River City Jets, yeah."

"Right. They want to make you drink a protein shake to—"

"Drug me, mind control me to be like the others. I smelled a rat, so I ran. Shit, I know this is out there. You probably think it's just some cocaine nightmare, maybe bad borscht or something."

"Rick, we're just trying to understand," Veronica said. "You claimed there were two huge people after you, that your teammate, Jaxxon Downie, was hit by that truck and—"

"Mashed like a potato. Smeared all over the pavement."

"Now the report from the driver was that he hit a deer. We made a call to the team, and they said Jaxxon Downie was at a night club, The Shark Tank, with some other members of the Jets, that he—"

"Lying. They're lying. We were both at that resort for… seasoning. But it was more than just old Canada Cup footage. It was, I don't know… a transformation?"

"You're saying the team is involved with this 'conspiracy,'" Veronica said, making air quotes, "to make you a better hockey player?"

"Evidence," Rick said. "That's what you want, right? Hard evidence. Bodies. Lists. Dr. Hans. He's the one. Maybe he's acting on his own? Maybe they've already converted the whole team. Sam said Fritz was involved. He owns the team. So then how high does this really go? Everything leads back to the same questions, and I don't know the answers."

It was clear now that Rick was suffering some kind of mental break. Maybe from the pressure of playing in the NHL. He was making no sense. Veronica looked to Jimmy, who just shook his head sadly.

"Rick, there were no other bodies found at the scene. The RCMP told us that the truck did hit a deer. They found antlers and—"

"The Jets paid them off. I know what I saw."

"Hear me out for a minute, Rick," Veronica said. "You're Rick Hansen, star centre, rookie sensation for the River City Jets. You're slumping. You're stressed. Maybe you took something you shouldn't have. You're dealing with so much pressure and—"

"You think I'm crazy."

"No, no, no. It's just, what you're saying is a lot. And—"

There was a knock on the door. It opened to reveal Officer Grounder, a heavyset man with thinning hair. "Hooper, Tockett, there's someone here to pick him up."

Rick suddenly clenched the table, looking frantic. "See, they're here for me."

"Who is it?" she asked Grounder.

"A Deborah Peterson. She says she's his fiancée."

"Debbie?" Rick said.

"Come on, Rick," Jimmy said. "We've got your statement. Let's get you home. Maybe a good night's sleep will clear your head."

He helped Rick to his feet. At first, he didn't seem like he wanted to, but something must have given up inside. He let himself be led out of the room, back through the precinct, to where a blonde in a black coat that looked like it cost more than Veronica made in a year, stood waiting, looking concerned, by a chair in the front lobby.

"Oh, Rick." The woman rushed over to him and wrapped her arms around his neck.

"Debbie?"

"I was so worried. You sent the weirdest texts and…" She collapsed into him, hugging him tightly.

"You'll take him home then?" Veronica asked. "He's quite distressed and—"

"It's okay, officer," Debbie said. "I'll look after him. He's been under a lot of strain lately. You know, with the press obsessing over his slump and…"

"We understand," Jimmy said. "I played high school hockey, I know a bit of what it's like."

"With all due respect, officer, you don't. The NHL is something else. Especially when people were calling you a hometown hero just a few weeks ago. It's not the kind of thing most people have to deal with."

Jimmy stayed silent. Veronica watched this Debbie wrap her arm around Rick's. He seemed to calm a little, but his eyes were still darting back and forth, and she wondered for a moment if he wasn't going to make a run for it.

"Come on, Rick. Let's get you home and into a nice warm bath."

"Hot tub?"

"Sure. We can do that, too." Debbie led him to the door, stopping for a moment to look over her shoulder. "Thanks for finding him, officers. I was so worried. I'll take over. He'll be okay. He just needs rest."

And with that, they were out the door and gone.

"Well? You think that's it then?" Jimmy asked. "You think he's just freaking out over a bunch of reporters calling him a bust? Took something that made him paranoid?"

"It does explain a lot. But I still think it's too big of a coincidence that the place we were heading out to check over, where our missing wrestler is supposed to be working, is the exact same place that this Rick is running away from. And he claimed to be chased by people that could be wrestlers, too."

"Which the RCMP found no evidence of," Jimmy said. "The conference centre said Rick checked in as part of a team retreat for a few of the guys. The team corroborates that. Him taking some kind of drug that caused a psychotic break certainly fits all the facts so far."

"Yeah," Veronica said. "It does. You're probably right."

As they started to head back to their desks, the door opened and a woman with dark hair and a prominent mole over her eyebrow rushed in, right to the clerk.

"Hey, I'm looking for someone brought here recently. He may have been acting strangely. Rick Hansen. I'm here to pick him up. I'm, uh... his girlfriend and—"

Veronica recognized the girl now, the one they'd kicked out of the Shark Tank months ago. It was the mole, that was the kind of thing that stayed in your head. That was when she realized that she was the same girl they'd spoken to almost a year ago after the incident with the attempted rape at the recording studio. She wanted to kick herself for missing that earlier.

"Jimmy." She nudged him. "She look familiar to you?"

He scrutinized the woman at the desk. "Yeah, we've dealt

with her before. Trying to get close to Rick, right? The night club and—"

"And now she's here trying to find him. I just heard her claim to be his girlfriend."

"But his girlfriend just picked him up."

"Exactly."

"You think he's bouncing two girls at the same time?"

"No," she said. "I think this one might be stalking him. How else would she know he was here?"

"Maybe he told her?"

"Maybe," Veronica said. "But that Debbie told us in the club she was a stalker."

She walked over to the front desk, where the girl was pleading with the clerk for help.

"I'll take over here, Officer Smith," she said.

When the girl turned and saw Veronica, her eyes betrayed her. She recognized her, too, tried to brush her hair over her mole.

"You're Rick Hansen's girlfriend?" Veronica said.

"Uhh, yeah…" the girl stammered.

"I wonder if the woman who just picked him up a few minutes ago knows that."

"Do you know where she took him? It's important that I talk to him."

"I'm not so sure it is," Veronica said.

"Look, he sent me text messages." The girl dug out her phone and turned it to show to Veronica. She saw a name at the top of the screen that said 'Rick Hansen', a list of messages, most from the girl, but a final one that said, 'help police.'

"What is this supposed to prove?" Veronica asked.

"He needed help and I ca—"

"Ma'am. Are you sure you're not the one who needs help? We've seen a lot of each other over the years now, haven't we?" Jimmy said. "The shooting in the house, the mall fight, the attempted rape, now a series of incidents with you and Mr. Hansen."

"So you do remember me."

"I'd never forget that—" Jimmy was about to say mole, but Veronica elbowed him to shut him up.

"What my partner means is that you seem to be caught up in your own drama. Is it possible that you think there's more going on with Mr. Hansen than there actually is?"

"Oh god, you think I'm some crazy stalker. A puck bunny who can't face the fact that he's not interested. I promise you, this is something else. Rick is in danger. They're trying to—"

She saw the looks on both of their faces and stopped. "Fine," the woman said. "If you won't help, then I guess I'll have to do it myself." She spun to leave.

"You know," Jimmy said, "this evening was starting to seem a bit like a Frank special for a second."

The girl heard him. Stopped at the door as if she was pondering something, then left.

"Jimmy," Veronica said. "Maybe you're the one who brings all these crazies in, you ever thought of that?"

* * *

Debbie led Rick to her parked car in the lot adjacent to the station. He was sweating, eyes looking in every shadow for someone about to jump out. That woman with the hair, that huge guy, one of the clerks from the resort. They'd try again. He just knew it.

Debbie held the door open for him. "Get in, baby," she said. "You've have a hard couple of days. I'll make it all better."

"Is it safe?" he asked.

"Of course. It's me, honey."

She smiled at him. She seemed genuine. The concern was written all over her. She'd come in what looked like sweats under her coat. She must have run out the door the second the police had called her.

"I—"

"You're worrying me, Rick," she said. "Please, just come home and we can go over it all in the hot tub. I promise you'll feel better. Maybe after a massage. How does that sound?"

"Okay," he said.

He slid into the passenger side door, watching Debbie walking around to the driver's side. As she passed, he caught a glimpse of someone in the backseat through the rearview mirror.

"You!"

Dr. Hans was there, a syringe in hand. He reached forward with a white cloth and held it over Rick's mouth. Rick tried to struggle, but found himself quickly losing energy. His arms felt heavy. Then the prick of a needle. Everything suddenly went hazy.

Debbie slid in and saw the two of them. "Just relax, honey."

"He will go to sleep momentarily," Dr. Hans said.

"It's for your own good," Debbie said as the world went black.

CHAPTER THIRTY-FOUR

Rick woke in what felt like the most comfortable bed he'd ever slept in. Sunlight shone in through the open window, showing the towering downtown skyscrapers of River City against a clear blue sky. He felt refreshed. The sheets were smooth and smelled faintly like lemons. He realized that he wasn't wearing anything and looked around for some sign of his underwear.

"Wakey, wakey, sleepyhead," Debbie's voice came from outside the door.

He pulled the sheet up as she entered the room carrying a tray with what looked like toast, bacon, and orange juice.

"Debbie," he said, running his hand through his hair. "How did I—"

"You had a rough night, honey. It's okay. You're home and safe and I've got some nice breakfast in bed for you."

She dropped the tray down over his legs before he could protest. He saw a second glass now, next to the orange juice, of something brown.

"Bacon, egg white omelette, toast, juice, and a protein shake. I made it all myself," she said, beaming.

His stomach rumbled. He tentatively grabbed a strip of bacon. He couldn't remember when he last ate.

"I'm a little confused about last night," he said as he chewed.

"It's all so horrible," Debbie said. "I just can't believe it happened."

"Jaxxon was hit by the semi," Rick said, jerking back, nearly spilling the tray.

"What? No, Rick, you must have had a dream. That's not what happened at all."

"I don't understand."

Debbie grabbed a remote control from the nightstand and flicked on the TV that hung on the wall opposite the bed. She turned it to CBC Newsworld. The top story 'star Jets player dies in tragic overdose' ran silently. Jaxxon's smiling face was plastered on the screen as shots of a stretcher being wheeled out of his condo ran alongside. A body bag, flashbulbs erupting all around as hundreds of press people pushed in.

"What?" Rick said. "That's not... I saw him get run down by a semi truck. The horrible stain on the road. I—"

"Who's under that blanket then?" Debbie said.

She clicked to another news channel.

"—tragedy whenever someone dies young from drugs, Dean. This has officially been ruled an accidental overdose, but some have suggested suicide as—"

Click.

She changed the channel again.

"—a player who never reached his potential in his short time in the league. An event like this really puts a damper on the all-star weekend festivities."

Click.

This time to TMZ. A woman speaking to the camera wearing way too much makeup. "That's when I took the picture with my phone." On screen, a tiny, blurry snapshot of a man passed out in bed, his privates blurred, his mouth open. "He was fine when we went to bed, but when we woke up…"

Rick squinted at the tiny photo, blurred, shot in poor lighting. The face was unmistakeable. "That's him. That's Jaxxon. But I saw him wiped off the face of the earth by that truck."

"Looks like that hooker was with him when he OD'd," Debbie said. "TMZ's saying it was the result of two days of solid partying and drug use."

"Two days? We were at that lodge for two days."

"Rick, you've been telling me all year that Jaxxon had a drug problem. That he was hooking up with random girls in every city, every night of the week. This is exactly the kind of thing that happens to people like that."

"But I was there. Could this be a cover up?"

"You're still half asleep. How about you eat breakfast? You'll feel better. Then we can take a shower together and I'll make you feel like a million dollars before practice."

"Practice?"

"Don't worry about that now. Just eat. Here." She took the protein shake in hand and held it out to him.

* * *

"Grandpa!" Sam rushed to Frank, who sat hunched over in his chair as the orderly in white stood watching at the door. The room was deathly quiet. No radio, no music, no television, not even the hum of a lamp or an air conditioner. Frank didn't move or even acknowledge her in the slightest.

The orderly raised an eyebrow as if he doubted her story.

"It's me, Grandpa," she said again.

She had to make this believable. She leaned down and hugged the old man as hard as she dared. He looked so frail, like all the power had been drained from him. Had they done something to him here or was this what happened to everyone when they went into an old folks' home?

He was sunken, the light gone from his eyes. She held him by the shoulders and looked into his face, trying to see if he knew who she was, but he just sat there like a vegetable. She was worried now that this was a pointless visit; that he wouldn't be able to offer her any help.

"What's wrong with him?" she asked.

"We had a passing today, so he's probably just upset. Could also be the meds, though."

"Is he always like this?" Sam asked.

"Mr. Malone never mentioned any family," the man said in heavily accented English. "This the first time you visit?"

Sam smiled, trying to seem as natural as possible. "I go to UBC, I'm just here for a vacation."

"You live in BC, and you come to River City for a vacation?" The man looked shocked. "In winter?"

"You miss the snow after a while. And I wanted to see my grandpa."

"Just keep it down, okay? Other patients are sleeping."

"Not a problem."

She waited until the orderly left, then shut the door behind him. She pulled a chair up opposite Frank. The change in him was shocking. He looked like a balloon that someone had let the air out of. His head was in the process of slowly sinking down to his chest, trying to meet his knees. She waved her hands in front of his face, but he seemed zoned out, unaware of his surroundings.

"Frank? Detective Inspector Sargent Malone? Are you in there?"

She'd come all this way for his help only to be faced with a shadow of a man.

"I didn't know where else to turn," she said. "You told me to keep fighting but I'm losing everything. My friends, Rick…" The man didn't even look at her. "I guess I've lost you, too."

She stood up and headed to the door, her hopes dashed.

"The only thing you've lost is your common sense. Any granddaughter of mine wouldn't be caught dead at UBC. As if she'd ever go to that grass smoking, hemp eating, hippie factory on the coast."

She spun around and saw Frank standing up, somehow re-inflating his body, looking almost like his old self again. He straightened his hair, fixed his shirt, and was magically transformed.

"What the—"

"Pick your jaw up off the floor, kid, we've got work to do." He dug around in his drawer for a stack of notes and a cell phone, laying everything out on the bed, waving her over. "Don't just stand there, come and tell me what you think of what old Frank's found out."

* * *

"Stupid kid thought he was invincible."

"I told him to be careful, but he wouldn't listen."

"What a waste of talent."

"He could have been the next Jari Kurri."

"—just another statistic."

His teammates were all discussing what had happened with Jaxxon. How could they not be? It was national news. Journalists were camped outside the arena wanting to get statements from the players. They'd been snuck in the back.

"Sorry to hear about Mr. Downie," Isaiah had said as he walked in.

"Me too, Isaiah."

Rick was starting to feel more clear-headed now. After eating and Debbie's shower shakedown, he was starting to realize that he'd let his imagination get carried away. Hunger, lack of sleep, over-training, stress, maybe he'd even been slipped something by one of the guys as a prank. Whatever he'd thought he'd understood was clearly wrong when he sat here in the locker room, with a room full of guys, all normal, more interested in talking about a dead teammate than him.

"I saw at least four 'drugs in the NHL' think pieces," Teddy said.

"They write those every few years," Jonesy added. "There'll be a hundred more before this thing blows over. I wouldn't be surprised if they started more testing, too."

"I knew the kid had a problem, but not to that extent."

"All it takes is one mistake with that shit."

"What do you think he took?"

"I heard fentanyl."

Everyone was in their usual places, lacing up skates, getting equipment on. Only Jaxxon's spot, next to Rick, was empty. Rick just listened as a dozen conversations happened around him.

"I saw it coming."

"You think that whore he was with did it?"

"Think they'll do a memorial award for him?"

"For a drug overdose?"

"They'll want this under the rug."

"Mister Rick," Igor said, sitting down in the bunk next to him. His leg pads were on, but he carried his shoulder pads in his hand.

"Yeah, Igor?"

Igor slid on the shoulder pads and began going through his routine: doing up and undoing the straps six times, rolling his shoulders exactly four times each. Every time he put them on; practice, game, scrimmage, team photo, didn't matter. If Igor wasn't so gross usually, Rick would have sworn the guy was OCD.

"You have late night?"

"Yeah," Rick said.

Igor grunted in acknowledgement as he went through his personal stations of the cross. With the shoulder pads on, Igor lay on the ground and pulled his leg up to his head in an impossible stretch. He looked over at Rick from beneath his thigh. "Is big news, no? Jaxxon biting bullet."

"Yeah, I never saw it coming."

"No? You were not looking then. Sex and drugs is no way to play hockey."

"I never thought it would turn out like this. I'm surprised Coach never came down harder."

Igor stretched his other leg, "I am wondering how Jaxxon was at home doing drugs when I am hearing that he was with you this weekend."

"What?"

"Maybe I am hearing wrong."

Rick's head started throbbing. "We—"

"My babushka was worried about you, Mister Rick."

273

"Your—"

"Samantha. She was thinking you were in trouble."

"Sam?"

"You were texting us both. Something about the police. And a milkshake?"

A stabbing behind his eyes. "Texts? No, I was…"

"Is probably mistake, yes?"

Grey-haired Jonesy came up to the two of them and dropped the top of his stick on the floor, leaning on the blade as he looked solemn, half dressed in his navy hip pads. "Hansen?"

"Jonesy?"

"Hell of a thing."

"We were just talking about it."

"There'll be a team meeting later. I heard they've brought in a grief counsellor. You know all eyes will be on you now. You're the rookie star. I hope your weekend gave you some new perspective. They do good work at that lodge."

Rick blanched. The lodge. Watching footage, the training, the chase in the snow. It was real. It had happened. It wasn't his imagination.

Rick recovered from his surprise. "Yeah, I sure came away with a new perspective."

Jonesy's greying stubble was thick, like he hadn't shaved in a few days. "Good to hear. I hope we'll see some of that during practice. Coach Chapman is gonna want to see how you perform."

"I'll do my best."

Igor leaned down, stretching, watching Jonesy.

"That's all anyone can ask for, I suppose."

Jonesy left them to finish getting ready. In a moment,

Coach Chapman came in.

"Okay, boys, be ready for hell. We're going to put this distraction behind us. Skating, races, penalty kills, shot blocking, shoot outs, break outs, four on four, power play, skating, more skating, and finally, when you're all too tired to remember your names, we'll do some skating. Hansen, I want to see double time from you."

"Sure thing, Coach."

All eyes were on him as he stood up and joined the queue to head to the ice. Images of Jaxxon being flattened by that semi truck ran through his head, the body bag, the news – what was true here?

His skates hit the ice, and his mind drifted away to think of only the practice.

* * *

Sam couldn't get over what she was seeing. Frank was animated, practically bouncing with energy.

"Kid, this place stinks worse than the bathroom in a Mexican restaurant."

She joined him at the bed and saw a jumble of pages of hastily written notes, scrap paper torn from magazines with single words circled that made no sense to her, crude drawings. He lined them up in some kind of pattern.

"What is this all supposed to mean?"

"Shady Acres isn't just an old folks' home, it's some kind of organ factory. They come in healthy and whole and go out in pieces. Nurse Ironhide, Dr. Hans; they're the ringleaders."

She tried to get a sense of his train of thought, but it was like some kind of secret code that only he could read.

"Oscar, Mrs. Ween, Buster, Harry, Chappie, they stuck 'em with something to make it look like they died – or maybe it did kill them, I didn't check their pulse. Then, they wheeled 'em out into some kind of van."

"You mean an ambulance?"

"I know what I saw. Through the window." He pointed to the one in his room that looked out on to the parking lot and streets beyond.

"What would they want with the organs of old people?" Sam asked. "You'd think they'd want young healthier ones, right?"

"I can't leave here," Frank said. "I don't know where that truck goes with the goods."

"This is..." She waved her hands over the spread on his bed. "What am I supposed to do with all of this?"

"Isn't that why you came? To see what I'd discovered?"

"No, it was to get your advice."

"Well, I'm advising you to help me get the fuck out of here so I can stop this."

"I think the River City Jets are turning hockey players into golems. Just like Simon Karlsson did to Factor 5ive and Radiant Cyanide."

Frank looked at her, confused, as if he didn't recognize the names.

"Those guys you took the blame for killing in the brain lab."

"And? What's your point?"

"My point is, what do I do about it? Rick, my ex, he's in danger. I know the goalie, Igor, but he's... let's just say I don't think he'd be much help. None of my friends will talk to me either."

"Again, what's your point?"

"Haven't you faced something like this before? When you were a cop?"

"Kid, I'll always be a cop. No matter what the rest of the world thinks. And yeah, I've been up against the shit before."

"So? What did you do?"

"I shot people. Usually the bad ones."

"I'm assuming they didn't let you bring in a gun to this place."

"You kidding? They wouldn't even let me have a phone. But I outsmarted them." He held up a cellphone in a scratched black case. "I convinced an old friend to smuggle this in for me and—"

"A guy named Jimmy?"

"What? Who squealed? You have stoolies on the outside or—"

"No, it just says Jimmy's phone on the screen when you turn it on."

Frank looked at the tiny display and saw what she was pointing at. "Huh. So it does. But shouldn't it say Frank?"

"You want me to change it for you?" Sam snatched the phone and moved to the settings page.

"Careful, kid. I took pictures."

"Of what?"

"That's the thing. They keep disappearing."

Sam found the photo folder and opened it up. "You have to look here."

She leaned in and let him watch along as she scrolled through what was there; food, a woman smiling, selfies of Jimmy flexing in the mirror.

"Oh, hell, it's Detective Hooper's phone."

"So?"

277

"I'm not on the best of terms with him right now."

She swiped through more pictures; a dog, house, car, sandy beach, something dark and blurry that may or may not have been a dick pic, then a series of photos obviously taken in the retirement home: hallways, Frank's room, the orderlies, other residents' bedrooms, what looked like people sleeping.

"See? Better than a hundred Zapruders."

Sam squinted, trying to make out what he had shot. "These are blurry. Your hands must be unsteady – everything is out of focus."

"Gimme that." He snatched the phone, holding it up to her as he dictated. "This is Felix, he died last week, only he wasn't sick, see? They drugged him. I watched them take his body away. This is the truck I told you about. Look, no morgue or funeral home stencil anywhere. I know the corpse crew, and this wasn't them. It was a couple of guys in lab coats. They took him, but I don't know where." He pointed to another photo, the backs of two men pushing a stretcher with a body bag, taken from around a corner.

"Hey, this one's actually pretty clear," Sam said. "Look, you can zoom in and see more detail." She swiped in and they saw letters on the lab coats.

"Great Gatsby, how'd you pull that wizardry off?"

"Uh, with my fingers, Frank. But look, it says Geld. Where have I heard that before?" Sam tried to think. "Oh shit, Hapkido!"

"Gesundheit," Frank replied.

"No, Geld were the ones trying to buy the building where I take Hapkido. And shit, I think they also bought the old warehouse where they put on wrestling shows."

"Real estate? What would they want with organs then?"

"Beats me. But this can't all just be a coincidence."

"Then it looks like the pieces are starting to line up, we just don't know the shape of the puzzle."

Sam moved to the window, saw a black truck parked outside.

"Frank, is that the truck you saw?"

He came to join her at the window. "The one and only."

"What's it mean?"

"It means, someone's dying tonight."

She looked up to the clock, saw that it was getting late. "Visiting hours are almost up."

"How about you and me take a little excursion? Say, a truck ride?"

"How are we supposed to do that? This is a locked ward."

"Haven't you ever heard of a jail break?"

* * *

The showers. Twelve steaming hot sprays in sectioned off alcoves with shelves, soap and shampoo dispensers, and drains that swirled as they sucked away the run-off from tired players. The room was silent as Rick joined in, taking his spot at the end of the room. The fog of warmth felt great on his aching muscles. He stood under the nozzle and just let the heat soak him.

What an intense practice.

Coach Chapman had run him hard, but he'd stayed with it. He refused to let the man break him. He grabbed some body wash and scrubbed his sore shoulders. His second shower of the day, but the first had been much more fun.

Everything seemed so normal. The guys were the guys.

The team was the team.

Jaxxon.

The man's endless boasts, his bragging, his attitude. The room felt empty without him.

He couldn't even see who was next to him, let alone the rest of the guys as they stood under their own showers. He could hear the streaming, sense their presence, but no one was laughing or making terrible jokes.

Free from the focus of practice, his mind wandered. Events of the night before flooded back. The old game footage. Dr. Hans. Jaxxon talking about the hot Asian desk clerk. The woman with the two-toned hair.

Rick massaged in shampoo. It burned his eyes. He reached for the shower pole, feeling for the stream of water with his hands, cupping some in his palms to wash his eyes.

He was there. I was there. The truck, the highway. It was all real.

He suddenly realized the room was far too quiet. After practice showers were never—

"Guys?" he called out, but no one answered.

He cleared his eyes. Saw a face through the wall of mist. Jonesy. Stark naked, standing like a statue, blank, expressionless eyes locked on him.

"Jonesy?"

It was like he was under a spell. Jaxxon. He'd been just like this. So had—

Joshua. When he was under the control of that strange ruby.

Sam's words came back: "Golem."

Rick stepped around the silent Jonesy, moving to leave, then saw Dave, Petr, and Teddy, all appearing from the mists

280

like ghosts, with distant, cold, dead eyes staring at him like wax figures.

"Guys?"

No one said a thing. They moved in a circle to surround him. Naked, closing in. The steam and heat in the room were oppressive. He tried to back away, holding his hands up in surrender.

"How about I just leave, okay? I'd like to go home and—"

The circle of stark-naked teammates closed in. Hands reaching out, grabbing him, pressing against his skin, slamming him against the wall. There was no way to fight back. His wet blows struck ineffectually.

"Watch yourself," Sam had told him. But he'd failed. He'd let himself get caught off guard. The last thing he remembered was Dr. Hans in the back seat of Debbie's car as the wall of hands closed around him and shut the world off.

* * *

"You know, this would be a whole lot easier if I had a gun," Frank said as Sam pushed him in his wheelchair down the hallway towards the door out of the locked ward.

"You really think you can pick the lock out?" she asked him quietly.

The orderlies paid them little attention. A few of the other residents moved down the halls in their chairs. Frank nodded to one older woman and she, wide-eyed, nodded back and moved down the hall towards the nurse's station.

"I learned from a woman who could suck the paint off a battleship."

"I'm not sure how that's relevant to lock picking," Sam said, confused.

"She had a diverse skillset, okay?"

"Right, so the big plan that you've thought about for all these months is to just pick the lock and roll out."

"I don't have a lot to work with here. You just make sure you play your part."

"I will."

Sam deposited Frank at the end of the hall. The glass door leading out into the regular ward faced them. On the other side, she could see the less problematic residents moving around freely, chatting, watching television, a few even participating in a chair aerobics class. That side looked almost like a fifty-five plus apartment. The people there were able to come and go on their own, unlike Frank's ward, where they were kept almost behind bars.

"I'll meet you in the parking lot," she said, patting him on the shoulder.

She walked back towards the nurses' station. Two orderlies sat behind the desk. One filling out a logbook, the other watching a camera feed that rotated through different views of the facility.

"Hi," Sam said. "I'm wondering if I could get a list of the medications my grandfather is on."

"Which one is yours?"

"Uh, Malone," she said.

"He's got family?" the mousy woman said. "Somehow I can't picture any woman ever shacking up with him, let alone having his kid."

"Hey," Sam said, not liking the tone. "That's my family, okay?"

"Okay, okay. He's just been a bit of a handful here."

The woman pulled out another binder and started flipping through pages, looking for Frank's information. Sam saw the image on camera flip past him in his chair, working at the lock. The orderly leaned up, interested.

"Hey," Sam said to him. "I saw this woman sitting in the TV room and she'd taken off her dress. She was—"

"Help!"

A woman in a wheelchair started screaming in the middle of the hall, waving a tray above her head. "Help! Help!"

"It's Mrs. Halsey again," the man said and stood up to rush over to her.

On screen, Sam saw Frank still working on the lock before the image shifted again.

"Here you go." The mousy woman passed Sam a list of medications written on a spreadsheet. It was almost a full page, with rows and columns showing each day's dose checked off.

"All this? What do all these do?"

"Help! Help!"

Sam saw the man trying to get the tray away from the old woman. She smacked him in the side of the head.

"Well," the woman said. "This one here is for dementia, this one for incontinence, this one for—"

The image on the screen cycled, showing Frank pushing open the door. He did it! Sam leaned over and flicked off the monitor while the other orderly was distracted with the list in the binder.

"He really needs all this stuff?"

"Absolutely. Dr. Hans' orders. Without these, he'd be so much more of a headache. Maybe even a danger to the other residents."

"Help!" Mrs. Halsey said, smacking the man again.

Another orderly ran in and the two of them worked on subduing the frantic woman.

"Like her?"

"Worse," the mousy orderly said.

"Well, glad to hear he's being taken care of. I'll be back soon to visit."

Sam turned and walked down the hall, leaving the orderlies behind. She tried not to move too fast as she took the turn to the exit hall. She saw Frank sliding his wheelchair into the common area. Nobody seemed to notice.

She arrived at the door, turned the knob, suddenly realized that she had to be buzzed out. She banged on the door once. Frank turned, realized his mistake, and stood up out of his chair.

"Shit," Sam said.

Frank turned around, went back to his chair. He was leaving her.

"Hey!" Sam said, hitting the glass again.

Frank was leaving her here. What the hell was wrong with him? How was she going to get out if he—

A hand closed on her shoulder.

"Excuse me," the mousy woman said behind her.

She turned around, unsure if she was going to have to fight her way out or not.

"Yeah?"

"We have to buzz you out. There's a code. It's for the residents' safety."

"Right. I, uh… this is my first time here."

The woman typed in a code to a small control panel recessed into the wall. The door buzzed and clicked. She pushed it open and motioned for Sam to leave, smiling the whole time.

"Great, thanks. See you again soon."

"I'm sure you will."

Sam, trying to stay calm, moved through the common area, looking for Frank. Would he have gone outside on his own? The front desk was manned with another orderly. No sign of an abandoned wheelchair. People came and went, some heading to the desk, some towards rooms.

"Hey, kid, in here."

His voice came from the left. She turned to see him parked in the mailbox alcove. Sitting in his chair, with a coat and hat on.

"There you are."

"What took you so long?"

"Let's just get out of here, okay?"

He stood and they started walking to the front exit. She tried not to look conspicuous, acting like she was just going for a walk, completely normal. They passed through the double doors, hit the fresh winter air.

"Frank, we did it, we—"

"You sure did, babe."

Two men sat on a park bench near the door, waiting. They wore black leather jackets, billowy shirts, a tangle of necklaces, had long flowing hair. Sam slowed as she realized it was Scott. But there were two of him. One flashed a pirate grin at her.

"Trying to run away, eh?"

"Not gonna happen," the other added.

"Not you. Not here," Sam gasped.

"Mr. Malone, you know you don't belong out of the locked

ward."

The Scotts were gone. In their place sat two orderlies in white.

"I'm sorry," Sam said, trying to recover her composure. "I think there's some mistake here, we—"

"Run for it, kid!"

Frank bolted, the two orderlies moving to chase. Sam put her foot out and tripped one, sending him crashing to the frozen concrete. The other was too fast. She looked back inside, saw the desk clerk on the phone. Residents lined up to look at the commotion.

"Shit, some jail break," she said, and ran after Frank.

The old man headed towards the black van. He was almost there when his feet flew out from under him.

Ice.

He wiped out. The orderly slid to a stop, reached down for him. What else could she do? Sam charged, knocked the guy into the van and to the ground.

"Get up," she said to Frank, lifting him by the arm. "My car is this way."

She dragged him, limping, towards her car. She could see more orderlies emerging from the building, saw the other one getting up from the ground. She dug in her pockets for keys, began pressing the unlock button frantically. The horn sounded.

"Come on, Frank, move."

"I'm trying, kid. That ground did a number on my hip."

Almost there. They wouldn't have much time, but she could peel out, leave them in her dust, get Frank somewhere safe.

Then, two figures stepped in front of her car. Huge, built like body builders, arms crossed over their chests. One, a woman, the other a man, each looked like they could break her in half.

"This isn't good."

"Relax, kid, I've taken dumps harder than those two."

Frank threw a punch, slipped on the ice, fell flat to the snow.

Sam slid, spun with a back fist, hit the man right in the temple, but she lost her balance. The woman grabbed her around the waist and lifted her up. She kicked and flailed, but the woman squeezed. She felt her ribs cracking from the pressure. She couldn't break free.

The other orderlies arrived. Six more bodies. One slid a needle into Frank's arm.

"Now, now, Mr. Malone, let's get you back to bed."

A man with round glasses, a severe chin, and cold eyes approached Sam. "And you, ma'am. Abetting a known felon's escape. Perhaps you need some of what he's been given."

He held up a needle.

"No, you can't," Sam said and kicked out.

"Restrain her."

Two orderlies held her firm while the man slid up her coat. She couldn't stop him from injecting her with whatever it was. She began to feel warm, then sleepy. All the fight left her, and she collapsed into the huge woman's grip and darkness overtook her.

CHAPTER THIRTY-FIVE

S am came to in partial darkness. At first, she couldn't understand where she was. The last thing she remembered, she'd been visiting Frank. She lay next to massive white barrels covered with biohazard logos strapped to a pallet. White walls, the room bounced, the faint sounds of traffic. She realized she was in the cargo area of a van. One side was taken up by shelving with small red and blue containers held in place by bungee cords. She was being transported somewhere, but where?

They'd tied her wrists behind her back with another bungee cord. It was tight, but she could pull it enough to get some give. She started squirming, trying to free herself. A partition cut the cargo area off from the rest of the vehicle. She had no idea who was driving, but she could hear the radio playing an old crooner song.

The van stopped. Sam heard muffled conversation from what sounded like two men, then the doors opening and closing. She panicked, trying to free her hands. She pushed herself up against the largest barrel, her pulse quickening as she waited for the cargo doors to open. She'd have to fight with only her legs. What felt like an eternity passed, but the door never opened.

"What's going on?"

She moved to the front, peering through a small gap in the bulkhead wall. She could see a bright red, white, and yellow sign. "Tim Hortons. They stopped for coffee?"

She slid her arms around her legs to the front of her body and started rubbing the bungee cord against the edge of a shelf. Slowly, it began to fray. She didn't know how much time she had before they came back or arrived at their destination.

Two men left the restaurant, approaching the van carrying brown bags and coffees in red cups. She kept rubbing, but stopped when they got in.

"Why is it no matter what I order, they always get it wrong?" the driver asked.

"You seen who they have working there?"

The two men spoke with vague accents, buried beneath attempted assimilation. Sam couldn't place them – maybe Eastern European?

"I order a large double double and every time get something else. Maybe triple double, maybe single triple, maybe single single, it's never right. I don't know why we keep going back."

The other man shoved some kind of pastry in his mouth, speaking while chewing. "Cheap and fast."

"More like shit and wrong."

The ignition fired up. Sam felt the van reversing, heard the faint beeps coming from the back.

"I can only eat this shit so much."

The radio was back, another crooner sang.

"At least it's edible."

"You sure?"

Sam slowly worked on the cords, trying to keep the noise

down. They drove for another ten minutes before the van pulled into an underground parking garage. The bungee cord snapped. She unwrapped it, rubbing the circulation back into her wrists.

The van slowed, turned, began backing up to a loading dock. She moved to the cargo doors, hit the inside latch, carefully pushed them open just a touch as the van came to a stop. The loading dock was empty, but familiar. She'd been here before.

The van had backed up in front of a freight elevator a few feet off the ground, the perfect height to allow the cargo doors to swing open fully. She saw a regular passenger elevator at the other end of the parkade, but it was too far away to make a break for. The guys would see her running.

The van shut off. She hopped to the loading platform and carefully closed the cargo doors. Staying in the centre of the vehicle, she knew she couldn't run on either side, they'd see her in the side mirrors, so she gingerly hopped up onto the roof, and slid forward, towards the front of the van.

Sam saw the two men getting out and pushed herself down as flat as she could. She heard them shutting the doors and walking around to the back of the van. There was no time to linger; she slid over the vehicle, carefully down the front windshield, then dropped to the concrete. She ducked down, saw the two men pulling open the cargo doors. She climbed underneath the van. The undercarriage rubbed against her as she crawled along the concrete slowly, towards the back, trying to see what they were doing.

"Hey, where's the girl?"

"She's not there?"

"You see a drugged girl anywhere?"

"But where could she go? She was tied up!"

"I told you we should have used a zip-tie. Bungee cords don't do shit."

"Then you should have brought one in the truck. It was all we had."

"Next time, make sure we have our kidnapping gear, okay?"

"But where the fuck is she?"

"She must have jumped out when we stopped at Tim's. I told you to use the fucking drive thru."

"They fuck up the orders even worse there! At least inside, we can get them to fix it and—"

"What the hell are we going to tell the doc? He was prepping for her arrival."

One went into the waiting freight elevator and came back with a hand jack. The other dropped a connecting platform in the space between the dock and the van. Together they started to unload the containers, with one pumping the pallet up onto the jack and pulling it into the freight elevator.

"You want to tell him we let her escape, be my guest."

"You kidding? I don't want to be chopped up like those geezers."

"Then I guess we act like we never had her in the first place."

"That's your brilliant plan?"

"You got a better idea?"

With the elevator loaded, one of the men pushed a button to send it down. But to which floor? She had no idea from her angle, didn't dare peer out from under the van to check either. Once it reached wherever they sent it, the two men headed back to the van.

"Let's just go make another pick up and hope this whole thing blows over."

291

"Leave now? We didn't even put the load away."

"Let the others get the shit, we'll be long gone. Then maybe the doc will forget and—"

"He never forgets. This is the worst plan I've ever heard."

"Just get in."

They both re-entered the van and it fired to life. The muffler roared loud in Sam's ears. They pulled away. The exhaust blew in her face, but she stayed prone. The van drove off. They never noticed her, leaving her alone on the cold concrete.

"This looks like the MTS Centre loading dock," she said.

She hopped up on the platform and went to the freight elevator. There were no floor lights or indication of where it had stopped at all.

"Only one way to find out."

She pressed the up button to call it back.

Suddenly, she panicked, wondering if someone would be coming up with it. She pressed up against the edge of the wall, ready to strike. The elevator stopped. Silence. She peered around the corner tentatively. The pallet and containers were still there. Nobody had unloaded them at the bottom. She leaned back and took a deep breath to steel herself for what she was about to do.

You need to go.

She stepped around the corner, but a man stood in front of the pallet. Still as a statue, open collared shirt revealing dozens of chains over torn skin, the pale-skinned wraith of Scott swayed in place.

"You're not there," Sam said. "You can't be."

She looked to her feet and took another deep breath, then looked back up. The ghost of the man was gone. She got in the elevator and hit the illuminated down arrow. The doors slid shut. She was bathed in yellow light as the elevator slowly descended, well below the arena, deep under the city streets.

Eventually it reached bottom. The door opened out to some kind of laboratory facility. Everything was white, white floor, white walls, white lights in the ceiling. People in lab coats walked the aisles. She crouched behind the pallet and watched.

She'd stand out like a sore thumb dressed all in black, covered in dirt and grease from the concrete. She needed a disguise. The only option was a lab coat.

"There's got to be a locker room or a change room or supply closet."

She pumped the hand jack stuck inside the pallet. Maybe she could bluff her way for a bit. The pallet was heavier than she expected. The jack made a lot of noise, the wheels rumbling on the white floors. She saw streaks of black left behind.

A man in a lab coat passed by, heard the noise, and stopped to scrutinize her.

"Oh, hey," she said. "Where is this supposed to go? Nobody told me. It's from Shady Acres and—"

The man just pointed down the hall where he'd come from. She followed his finger and nodded. "Thanks. It's my first—"

He walked away, clearly not giving a shit about her.

She pulled the pallet down the hall, knocking into the sides a few times before she got the hang of the hand jack. She passed doors, all with windows. Most looked into more labs, one into a locker room, another a lunchroom, then, at the end of the hall, she found double doors that had to be the storage room. She pushed inside, dragging the pallet.

Containers with biohazard markers, jars full of cloudy liquid; the room was colder than the rest of the facility so far. She dropped the jack and walked back down the hall to the locker room she'd passed. Peering inside, it looked empty. She ducked in. A line of lab coats on hooks, hair nets and surgical masks in boxes on a table were waiting for her.

"Disguise time."

She decked herself out in full scientist garb, stuffing her hair inside the hairnet. She looked at herself in a mirror.

"Now you look like you belong."

She opened a few lockers until she found a clipboard and pen. She headed back into the hall and started exploring. The place was deserted. Everyone had gone inside one of the huge lab rooms that she passed, but the doors were all key locked. She hadn't seen an ID badge in any of the lockers. From through the small window on the door, she could see a crowd of people inside some kind of surgical operating theatre. They all wore lab coats, hair nets, and safety goggles. There were machines everywhere, but the crowd obscured much of the view.

I have to get inside.

She stood at the double doors, pretending to write on her clipboard for a while, hoping someone else would come. A straggler ran around the hall, dashed towards the door and held out a scan card. It swung open. He entered and Sam scooted inside just as the door was closing.

What is this?

A large circular room with tiled walls, bright lighting, and stainless-steel machinery. A set of sliding doors at the other end of the room. Sam had no idea where they led. There were about ten other people inside all working on machines around a large empty space in the middle. They were preparing for some kind of surgery.

As casually as she could, she pretended to fidget with the dials on a strange silver and blue monitor, listening in to snippets of conversation.

"—an emergency case."

"—on the way down this very second."

"Must be important—"

"—all the way from up top."

A stretcher was wheeled in through the set of sliding doors, its great bulk pushed by two more men in lab coats with faces covered by masks and eyes hidden by goggles. They stopped the stretcher in the centre of the room. Everyone began pushing their machines in close, hooking up sensors and cords to the body on top.

Why was there an underground hospital beneath the MTS Centre?

"Are the components ready?" a man asked.

"Yes," someone answered and carried over a small box with a pillow inside. Sam saw the twinkling of a gemstone.

The man examined the stone. "Flawless. This will do wonderfully." He stared into the stone intently. "One simple operation and you will find new purpose. Then this one can join with the—"

"Can we begin, doctor?"

"Yes, of course," the man said, laughing. "No more distractions."

One of the other technicians pulled the cloth away from the body on the gurney and Sam saw the horrible truth: it was Rick.

CHAPTER THIRTY-SIX

The shrill fire alarm blared through the white hallway, echoing in Sam's skull. The emergency lights flicked on, bathing the entire laboratory complex in a hazy red glow. The sprinkler system sprayed jets of water all around her in sheets, obscuring her vision as she desperately pushed the gurney down hall after endless hall. Where the hell was the way out?

"Hey, you," someone shouted ahead of her.

Sam broke into a run, ramming him square in the stomach with the stretcher.

"Watch it!"

He held on, trying to reach for her over the prone form of Rick, clawing at the air. She suddenly stopped and he flew off, crashing to the floor in a heap.

"What are you—"

On his knees, she smacked him again with the gurney, this time right in the face with the metal corner, knocking him out cold. Rick moaned unintelligibly as he was soaked with water.

"You know, if you'd wake up, this would be so much easier."

She rolled the stretcher around the unconscious man in the lab coat and hurried down another hall. Where were the stairs? Had she known the elevators would lock down, she might not have been so keen to pull the fire alarm in the first place.

It had seemed like a good idea at the time, and she'd seen no other options at hand. The surgeon was going to operate on Rick, implanting a control stone. Laying on the sheet, stripped, lines drawn on his body and forehead, tools were out, scalpels readied. There'd been no time to think, the fire alarm was all she had. No one saw her pull it, and the shrill wail stopped them all in their tracks.

"Is this a drill?" one had asked.

"I doubt it," another replied.

They'd put down their surgical instruments on the central table and started to file out of the lab in an orderly fashion.

"What about him?" one had asked, pointing to Rick as he left.

"He more important than your own skin?" another replied.

Left alone in the room, she knew she only had a short window. She had to get Rick out fast. She'd tried waking him, but he was out, so she just grabbed the stretcher and pushed through the double doors into a hallway maze of sameness. She'd stopped halfway out, turned back and started toppling over the machines, trying to destroy their ability to do whatever it was they were doing in here. Something sparked. Smoke rose from another wreck. Then, a fire broke out.

"Good thing I pulled the alarm then," she'd said and rolled Rick out.

But the escape wasn't as simple as she'd thought it would be. Everything looked the same. She had no idea where she was. The water splattered on her hairnet, the cold stinging her eyes as she desperately looked for the way out.

An exit sign glowed in the distance, a beacon through the streams of water. The hellish red glow made it all seem otherworldly. The door opened. Two men dressed in full black riot gear exited the stairwell. Their faces were hidden behind helmets. They carried assault rifles.

Maybe she could bluff them. She was still in full surgeon get up, so they wouldn't know who she was. She waved. "You there, help me with this patient – we can't leave him here to die."

The men looked at each other and nodded silently. They closed the distance fast. Were they security guards? They carried flashlights, mace and key cards, but held their guns like they knew how to use them. Rent-a-cops weren't allowed to carry weapons in River City. Were they police?

The first man grabbed the other end of the stretcher and Sam thought for a moment that her ruse had worked, but then the other one reached for her, and she immediately knew how wrong she was.

She sprang into action, pulling him forward by his wrist as he reached, flipping him over her outstretched leg, sending him toppling down. She twisted his wrist back against the grain and snapped it in one clean move.

The other man, shocked by her quickness, raised his gun. Sam took hold of the side of the stretcher and flung her leg around, kicking him square in the head. The contact of foot and helmet made a loud *kabong*, but nothing happened.

The man tilted his head as if to say, "Really?"

Sam grabbed the barrel of the gun, trying to pull it away. He was much stronger. The gun turned dangerously towards her. She couldn't match him in power, so she pivoted, trying to keep the line of fire away, then pushed back with all her strength. The gun swung back towards the man, then POW, it went off.

He'd hit his partner. The man slumped down to the ground, leaving a red stain along the wall.

She stepped inside again, bending the man's wrist over against the weak point and bringing the gun towards the man's face. Leverage was all she had. They struggled.

POW, it went off again, shooting upward into the man's head through his throat. The body dropped in a heap. Crimson mulch oozed under the helmet, swirling with the water on the floor into an intricate pattern.

It was all over so fast. Two dead men lay on the floor.

She gasped in air. Her adrenaline was shooting through the roof. She looked at the two bodies, incredulous. She'd killed them. No, it had been accidental, the result of a struggle. That guy had been the one pulling the trigger. But what if they *were* police?

She had to know. She grabbed one of the men's helmets, sliding it off. The corpse on the ground stared at her with eyes locked open in shock. There was something wrong with his eyes. Then it hit her – they didn't match. One was green and one was blue, like they'd come from different bodies. As the water sprayed over them, she rolled him over, noticed the stitch marks near the base of his hairline, telling her the truth. He wasn't human, he was a golem. Brains and blood gushed out of the hole in his head. The top had been blown open, while turning him over unleashed the floodgates.

Bile rose in her stomach. She lifted her face mask, turned to the side and hurled, losing her lunch all over the floor. The vomit floated away on the rising water.

The image of that would be burned into her mind forever.

The stairs waited for them. The stretcher was useless. She slung Rick's arm over her shoulder and kicked open the door. He was too heavy to carry, so she dragged him slowly up one step at a time. Two, three, four, eight flights up, sweating through her clothes, nearly fainting from exhaustion before they finally emerged from the stairwell into another hallway.

"The arena?"

It was quiet. No alarms blared in here. The two complexes must be somehow separated.

"Oh, shit no," a voice said from her left.

She turned to see a Black security guard standing with a cup of coffee in his hands at the end of the hallway – the same man who'd denied her entry all those weeks ago.

"What the hell is going on here?"

Supporting Rick's dead weight, Sam struggled, trying to keep him upright.

"He's been drugged. I've got to get him to a hospital," she said.

The man ran forward, realizing who she was carrying. "Rick? He okay?"

"I don't know," Sam said. "They shot him with something. I need to get him out of here."

"Why are you soaking wet?" the man asked.

"Long story. Just show me where the exit is."

The man hesitated, hands twitching, thinking maybe he'd reach for his walkie-talkie. Sam realized that she was covered in blood, her white lab coat looking like a butcher's apron. Rick moaned and she nearly dropped him. He'd come to partial consciousness, eyes flickering, head swaying.

"Please. He's in bad shape, he needs help."

"Right," the man said. He motioned for them to follow him. "Where's your car?" he asked.

"I left it at the old folks' home," Sam said.

"What?"

"It's another long story. Can you give us a ride somewhere?"

"Ah, shit. I shouldn't get involved here."

He led them through the cavernous building, down a hallway to a side door. He swiped his card and unlocked it, pushing it open to reveal a side street. The cold winter's air quickly chilled her in her wet clothes.

"He'll get pneumonia," she said.

"Ahh, shit again." He took off his security guard jacket and helped Sam slide it over Rick's arms, zipping it up.

"He'll get frostbite on his feet," she said, pointing to his bare feet.

"For fuck's sake, I just bought these shoes." He slid them off and handed them over. They were too big, but they'd do.

"What about pants?" Sam said, pointing to Rick's bare legs.

"I can't give you my pants. This is as much as I can do," he said. "And I shouldn't even be doing this."

The arena was downtown and only a few blocks from her apartment. She'd have to hurry, get Rick home through the snow before they both got sick. He was mostly upright now. She figured she could prop him on her shoulder and lead him in a staggered walk back to her place, as long as he didn't pass out again.

"Okay. Thanks, Isaiah," she said, finally reading his name tag. "You—"

"No fucking names. I ain't never seen either of you."

He pushed them outside and slammed the side door shut. Sam dragged Rick away through the cold night air, putting as much distance between them and the arena as she could, praying that no one spotted them on their way to her place.

CHAPTER THIRTY-SEVEN

"Am I surrounded by idiots? How do you manage to lose the same asset twice?"

"Sir, he was, uh, unexpectedly liberated by the glitch and—"

"The glitch who'd been subdued and was scheduled for her own transition."

"Right, but her apprehension was unexpected and—"

Fritz stood up, finally having had enough of the excuses. He marched towards the nervous looking man in the white coat.

"And she damaged tens of thousands of dollars of equipment, started a fire, killed two slaves and just, what, walked out the side door?"

"We—"

Fritz grabbed the man by the head, jerked it to the side with a large crack, and let the lifeless body fall to the floor of his office. He pulled a pen off his desk, crouched down, and stabbed the corpse until his arm hurt. The golden pen dripped with blood. The white lab coat slowly turned red as fluid leaked out from dozens of holes.

Letting out a satisfied breath, Arthur went back to his desk and sat down. He picked up the phone and dialed a number.

It was picked up on the second ring.

"Send in a team. Retrieve them both. Don't worry about the condition."

He hung up and regarded the body on the floor of his office. The blood began slowly spreading outwards, soaking the floor. He dialed another number.

"Yes, send a harvesting team to my office right away."

He slammed the phone down and tried to chill his anger. Things seemed to be spiralling out of control lately. It was all supposed to be simple. Take the accumulated research, apply it to the team and the fans, then branch out. Their end goal was still in sight, but every roadblock gave the authority more pause. Delays were too costly. He wondered how one simple girl could be doing so much.

He'd enjoy dissecting her to find out.

CHAPTER THIRTY-EIGHT

"Here we go, Mr. Malone. You sit right here and watch *Make Way for Tomorrow* with the rest of the group, okay?"

Frank's tongue felt like it weighed a hundred pounds as Jesus wheeled him into the television room. The movie was already on, ten minutes through, the black and white images flickering on the flat-screen television mounted to the wall. Everyone was here, Ben and Jerry, Mrs. Vann rocking in her seat; dozens of cloudy eyes glued to the pictures. He wondered what they were thinking about. Old times? The movie palaces of their youth? Or were they just trying not to piss themselves?

"There we are, nice and close. You stay." Jesus locked the wheelchair and walked away, leaving Frank with the rest of the gang.

Whatever they'd slipped him had done a number on him. He felt doped up, semi-comatose, like his mind existed somewhere outside of time. He knew everything, all their secrets, but he couldn't move. He could feel the phone Jimmy had given him in his pants pocket. The papers, too. All the evidence on these bastards; enough to break up this crooked game and send them all downtown in cuffs.

They hadn't bothered to search him. He still had it all. But in this state, he was practically helpless. Come bedtime, they'd wheel him to his room and help him get changed into pyjamas. Then, the jig would be up, and everything would be for naught. He had to stash the evidence back in his dresser.

"Juuuuuu—" he slurred, trying to get Jerry's attention. Words wouldn't form. The old man looked at him and shook his head sadly.

He was going to have to do this all by himself. He slid his foot, trying to flick the lock on the tires of his chair. It took a half dozen tries before he had the thing cleared. Manual control now. He would drag himself back.

The others were all too intent on the TV, but Ben saw him struggling to move. Frank held a shaky finger up in front of his mouth. Ben nodded in recognition.

Frank pushed backwards. He didn't have the strength to drag the chair forward. The tires slowly turned as he wheeled his way out of the sitting room in reverse. Everything was the wrong way. He had to orient himself, sneak back to his room without any of the staff seeing.

The halls were quiet. It was almost bedtime. Most of the staff were busy with prep work, thinking that the residents were all comfortably enjoying movie time. It was now or never.

He pushed himself down the hall, towards the nurses' station. It was empty. His head rolled to the right, to see the computer screen gently pulsing with white light. He watched the security camera cycle from angle to angle. The hall, the exit door, another hall, the television room. Nobody was around.

The halls glimmered in the faint light, as the sun slowly set outside. It was so warm. He was so tired. He could fall asleep right here.

No. He wouldn't let himself.

This place… people dying, a doctor hiding something, mysterious clean-up crews. They didn't want anyone to know. Which meant he was going to tell everyone.

Voices, coming this way.

Shit!

He pushed himself into the nearest open room, an empty one waiting for a new resident of the Shady Acres Family. The place had been cleaned out with nothing left to show that anyone had ever even been in here. They work fast.

"…another shipment due. They want more."

Frank saw two men, one in a black suit, face cold as a lizard's skin, the other, Dr. Hans. The doc seemed nervous, somehow subordinate to the dark-haired man.

"But we just sent specimens. Surely they must understand that we can't—"

"Are you telling me you can't provide what's required?" the man asked.

Hans froze, perhaps in terror, it was hard to tell. He swallowed hard and shook his head. "No, no, no, of course not. But there are limits. We don't want to arouse suspicions. Our cover—"

"If the task is too difficult…"

This was gold. He needed to record it. His hand, moving at half speed, fumbled for the phone. He got it out and rubbed his finger along the screen, trying desperately to open that damn camera app.

"I will arrange it. I know just the candidate."

"Good," the man in black said. "Ensure you don't disappoint

the authority again."

Success. With the app open, Frank held the camera up at the two men. His hand was unsteady, his fingers mashing away at the little red circle.

Click.

Too loud. Hans and the man turned in his direction.

"What was that?" the man asked.

"Probably just someone's CPAP."

"It came from that room over there." The man pointed towards where Frank was hiding.

"That room is empty. The former home of your most recent specimen."

"No, it definitely came from in there." He started walking towards Frank.

Oh shit.

He had to hide. He pushed the chair beside the bed, tried to bend over, almost fell out of the chair. No good. He rolled to the coat rack next to the door. No good either. The bathroom. He pushed himself backwards through the door.

"—sure it was coming from in here," the voice of the man carried.

He slid behind the door just as the two men entered the room. His head dangled to the left. He watched them through the crack between the door and the wall.

"There, you see, no one here," Hans said.

"I was sure I heard a noise…"

"A facility like this, there's always something. There are so many devices and televisions and—"

"Perhaps," the man said, looking at the bathroom.

A drop of sweat fell from Frank's brow as he watched the man in black walking towards him. If he looked inside, he'd be sunk. He couldn't hope to fight his way out in this condition.

The man peered in. Frank tried to clench his fists, but they wouldn't close.

The man in the suit looked towards the extra high toilet, the mirror. Who was he? Why was he here?

"Interesting devices," he said.

"It's for residents who have trouble sitting and rising."

Frank lifted the phone, pointed it at the space between the wall and the door. He clicked. The noise was muffled. The man didn't hear a thing.

"I don't know why you bother, considering what's going to happen to them."

"Appearances," Hans said. "We must maintain appearances."

"Of course. But it seems like a waste for lobsters swimming in an aquarium."

Hans laughed. "Lobsters are more aware of their fate."

They walked out, leaving Frank alone in the bathroom. He had one more clue, maybe the most important one yet. A face. Someone who seemed to be in charge. He hoped Jimmy could figure out who that guy was. He backed out into the room, wheeled over to the door, saw the hallway was empty and pushed himself towards his room. He deposited all of his investigation into the dresser drawer.

He made his way back to the TV room.

"I know just the candidate," Hans had said.

Frank had a feeling he knew who he meant. He only hoped this drug wore off before they came for him. Parking himself back in the room near Jerry, he sat down to see how *Make Way for Tomorrow* ended.

CHAPTER THIRTY-NINE

"What in the hell is this?" Erin said as Sam, balancing the still mostly comatose Rick on her shoulder, unlocked the door to the apartment.

"I need your help with him," Sam said.

"What did you do?"

"*They* drugged him. I got him out before they could operate, but he's wet and cold. We need to warm him up fast."

Erin grabbed a fleece blanket from the couch and brought it over. They wrapped Rick in it and brought him to sit down. Sam started rubbing him vigorously over the thick, blue wrapping.

Rick moaned.

"Sam, what the hell? Is he naked under that jacket?"

"Mostly. There's a sheet, a security guard's jacket, and someone else's shoes."

"Why is he only wearing a security guard's jacket and someone else's shoes?"

"It's such a long story, and I'll tell you the whole thing, but right now, we need to help him snap out of it."

"Out of what? What did he take?"

"I'm guessing a sedative, but he didn't take it willingly."

"What the hell kind of party were you at?"

Rick moaned again. His eyes fluttered.

"Hot chocolate, coffee, NeoCitran, anything, please," Sam said.

Reluctantly, Erin went into the kitchen and boiled some water. Sam ran to her room and quickly stripped out of her wet clothes, changing into sweats. She yanked the blanket off her bed and came back to Rick as Erin approached with a steaming mug of hot chocolate.

Sam sat next to Rick and wrapped her own blanket around him. Erin handed her the mug and sat in the chair opposite the couch.

"Rick, Rick," Sam said. "Can you hear me? It's—"

"Debbie?" he moaned.

Sam saw Erin raise an eyebrow at that name.

"No, Sam. You know me. Samantha from John A."

Rick's eyes opened.

"Sam?" He shook with cold. She kept rubbing him, trying to will the warmth back inside. "What am I doing here?" he asked weakly.

"You really don't remember anything?"

"I was in the shower. Surrounded by men. Naked men and—"

"Seriously, what the hell kind of party was this?" Erin asked.

Sam shot her a look to be quiet. She sat back in the chair.

"When I found you," Sam said, "some doctor was about to operate. He had a heartstone. He was going to implant it in you."

"Wait, wait, wait," Erin interrupted. "You pulled him out of a hospital? Sam, did you kidnap him?"

"Maybe. Depending on how you look at it. But I say I was saving him."

"Oh God, I'm not going to be a part of this." Erin stood up to get her coat.

"I," Rick stammered, "remember Dr. Hans injecting me. The protein shake and—"

Erin threw her hands up in the air. "I should be calling the cops – you know that, right?"

"It's a plot," Sam said. "Just like with the bands that shall not be named. To implant a control mechanism into a person's neck. It turns people into golems."

"To think I had a thing for you. I pegged you as just some confused bisexual arts major with a fetish for hockey players, but now I see you're just crazy."

Now Rick's eyebrows raised.

"Erin, last year, the videos, the music that made you, and me... do things, it's all connected here."

"I don't understand all that happened with Factor 5ive, okay, but you just brought home a drugged out, naked Rick Hansen. Remind me who the predator is?"

"You need to know the full story," Sam said. So she spilled it all, from high school to now: Joshua, Duckie, the necromancers' convention, the heartstones, Frank, the assassins, everything. Four and a half years that she still wasn't sure she believed had happened.

"You expect me to believe all of that?" Erin looked ready to leave.

"She's not lying," Rick said. He pushed himself up to a sitting position. Sam kept rubbing him anyway. "I was there, for some of it. It was... weird."

"Remember the boyfriend I told you about," Sam said, "the one I dumped Rick for? He was a golem. They aren't supposed to live very long. He fell apart in my hands. He'd been made in a lab by some kind of mad scientist. Turns out there's a whole corporation taking that process to another level now. Simon Karlsson was just one branch of it. The Jets are another."

"So call the police," Erin said. "Tell them the whole thing. If this is true, there has to be all kinds of evidence, right? They can bust into this lab and arrest the whole gang."

Rick took a sip of the hot chocolate. "That might be the simplest answer. There's no way they could just hide all that stuff, right? If the stones are implanted in the neck, they should show up on, like, an x-ray or something. Hell, you could just cut one out for them."

"This has all been happening right under our noses," Sam said. "Who knows for how long?"

Erin picked up the landline and held it out to Sam. "If you're so confident, call the cops. Prove it to me."

Sam looked to Rick who nodded in agreement.

"Okay, fine." Sam took the phone and dialed 9-1-1. It picked up on the second ring.

"Yes, Miss Abraham?"

"I want to report a— wait, you did you say Miss Abraham?"

"You have Rick Hansen. He doesn't belong to you—"

Sam hung up.

"What?" Rick asked.

"They knew."

"Knew what?" Erin asked.

"Everything."

Sam ran over to the window. In the distance, she saw a black van turn the corner up her street. A pit opened in her stomach.

"Get dressed, we have to leave."

"What?" Erin asked.

"They're here."

"Who are?"

"The ones that are after him, and me, too, I guess."

"I don't have any clothes," Rick said.

"You'll have to wear something of mine. Hurry. We don't have much time."

"Sam, this is crazy," Erin said, coming to join her at the window. Sam pointed to the van.

"My car's at the old folks' home. Can you drive us there? You don't have to be involved with this, it's us they're after."

"Why's your car—"

Sam grabbed her by the shoulders, realized just how much this had to be overwhelming her. "No time now. Just get what you need. We're leaving." She hugged her, trying to impress upon her just how sorry she was, how much she cared, how everything had gone off the deep end. Erin didn't return the gesture.

"I promise you when this is over, we'll have that talk and figure out the whole us thing." Sam let go and ran to her room. Rick was pulling on a pair of sweatpants that were baggy on her, but left nothing to the imagination on him.

"I'm not wearing any of your underwear, Sam."

"A bridge too far, eh?"

Then they were at the door, pulling on jackets. Rick took one of Sam's, with a furry hood. He pulled a toque over his drying hair to complete the look and they were out. Through the window, Sam saw the van parked outside. The side panels opened and men in black got out.

"The back way," she said, locking the apartment door.

They ran down the hall, descended two flights of stairs to

the main floor, and were out in the back parking lot just as the men forced their way in through the lobby entrance.

Erin fired up the car and they pulled away. Sam saw two men in black standing guard at the apartment entrance.

"Take the back lane," she said, and Erin drove up two blocks of lane before turning onto an actual street.

CHAPTER FORTY

The collected officers of the precinct sat in the conference room in rows, holding coffee cups and donuts, chatting amongst themselves, wondering why this meeting had been called. Jimmy leaned back in his chair and looked over at Veronica. "Any idea what this is about?"

"No clue. But they'd only do this for something big."

The chief walked into the room and the noise died down. He moved to the front and switched on a projector, then hooked it up to his laptop. An image of a smiling man with long dark hair came onto the white wall behind him.

"Henderson, the lights please."

An officer at the door dimmed the room's lights. The chief cleared his throat.

"Okay, I won't take too much of your time, but this is a grade A, top priority situation. Can anyone tell me who this man is?"

"Your son?" someone asked, and a few chuckles made their way around.

"Very funny, Hopkins, no. I'd have thought there were more sports fans here. This is—"

"Rick Hansen," Jimmy shouted out.

"Right, Hooper," the chief said, pointing to him. "He plays for the River City Jets, in case some of you have your heads in the sand."

"He's good, too," a voice called out.

"Yeah, but that's not why we're here. We're here because he's missing."

Murmurs echoed in the room. Jimmy turned to Veronica who mouthed 'missing' in confusion at him.

"I should say missing, presumed kidnapped."

The murmurs rose to chatter. The chief held his hands up to quiet the room. The man acted and dressed like a middle manager, but had turned the precinct from a rowdy boys club, to a model of the modern force. Everyone gave him their full attention as the image on the wall switched to a school photo of a girl with her hair brushed over one eye. Jimmy knew right away who it was – the girl they'd seen way too much of lately.

"This is his presumed kidnapper," the chief said. "Her name is Samantha Mary Abraham, current occupation student, current address suite twenty-two dash ninety-three Edmonton. She's presumed to be dangerously unstable."

"You mean a head case, sir?"

"That's the word I've been given."

"What's her story? She some kind of puck bunny?"

The chief held his hand up to silence them. "A safe assumption. All we know is what we've been told by Hansen's fiancée and the team. This Samantha Abraham seems to have been harbouring a dangerous obsession with Rick. She's been stalking him and—"

"Why didn't they get a restraining order, sir?" Veronica asked.

"I was told they didn't think she was anything more than a— what did you call it, Janzen, a puck bunny?"

"A girl who likes to fuck hockey players."

A few people laughed but the chief quieted them down.

"Also known as an obsessed fan. They didn't think she was a threat, but clearly, they were wrong. I want all eyes to keep a watch out for any signs of either one of them, Hansen or Abraham. The Jets don't want this getting out, especially with all the negative press surrounding the death of that Downie kid. So, discretion, people. We're hoping she makes some ransom demands or shows her face in public. She'll make a mistake. If she's as mentally deranged as we're being told, it's only a matter of time. We just have to pray that she doesn't hurt Hansen. The last thing this city needs is two dead hockey players. Take copies of their pictures and get out there and find them. You are dismissed."

Jimmy and Veronica stood up to join the queue taking copies of the pictures of Rick and Samantha. With the paper in hand, they returned to their desks. Veronica sat scrutinizing the school photo of the girl who, despite what they'd just been told, looked completely normal. "She look like a mentally deranged, dangerously obsessed, uh, puck bunny to you?"

"She did come here looking for him."

"I know. But she seemed sincere, not unhinged."

"She probably was. But you heard the chief."

"I know. But something just doesn't add up here. She's five seven-ish, he's six two. She's what, a hundred thirty, hundred forty pounds? He's got to be two hundred or more. How the heck is she kidnapping someone so much bigger than her? Let alone a pro hockey player who's used to scrapping and fighting for a living."

"Maybe she has a gun?"

"She look like the kind of girl who knows how to use a firearm? Let alone own one?"

"She could have stolen it."

"I know you're right, Jimmy," Veronica said. "But I'm not sold on this. I don't know why, it's just a—"

"A hunch. I know. You've had more than a few. But don't forget she was at the Shark Club that night, too, trying to get close to Hansen."

Veronica folded the paper up and slid it into her jacket pocket. "Maybe I'm off base here. Maybe someone pulls her over for speeding and this turns out to be all just a sicko stalker fan situation. Certainly lines up that way."

"Or maybe your hunch is right and there's more going on here than we thought."

"Hooper, Tockett," the chief called out. "In my office."

They shared a glance and stood up to walk down the aisle of desks through the frosted glass door with the chief's name stencilled on the outside.

"Sir?"

"I understand you two have dealt with this Samantha Abraham before."

"Yes, sir. A few times."

"Good, then I'm putting you two in charge of this kidnapping. Talk to George, he took the initial calls, then get out there and find Hansen. And hurry. There's no telling what this psycho girl might do to him."

"Sure thing, sir," Jimmy said.

"One question," Veronica asked.

"Yeah?"

"How credible was the initial call? That Hansen was kidnapped?"

"What do you mean, how credible was it? It came from the man's fiancée. Then again from the team. Talk to George if you need to. Just go. We don't need another corpse on TMZ."

CHAPTER FORTY-ONE

The ping from a text woke Sam from a deep sleep. She and Rick were in the backseat of her car, wrapped in a fleece blanket, parked in one of the out of the way lots deep in Assiniboine Park. A thin snowfall obscured the front window. She dug out her phone and swiped it open. Her breath fogged as she saw a note from Erin. "Two cops just came to Av's place asking about you. Said you kidnapped Rick. What am I supposed to believe?"

Rick stirred. "What time is it?"

"Early," Sam said.

"I feel like shit."

"Probably from whatever drug they slipped you."

"No, I think it's from sleeping in your car." He rotated his neck awkwardly in circles and rubbed his shoulder.

"Sorry it's not a million-dollar condo."

She scrolled through similar messages from Avital, Everett, and Marlon. Looks like the cops had been doing their homework.

"I know, I know. I just…" Rick stammered. "I guess I should thank you for not giving up on me, trying to warn me. If you hadn't, I'd be… whatever those things are. Would I still be me? Or just some vegetable?"

"I think you'd be you until they wanted you to be what they wanted."

Rick stretched, rotating his neck around again, cracking it a few times.

"What are we going to do, Sam? Where are we going to go? We can't just stay in your car all the time."

"Especially not now that the cops think I kidnapped you." She flipped her phone around to show him the messages from Erin.

"That's easy. I'll just call them and clear the whole thing up."

"That won't stop Arthur Fritz and the Jets. That will be up to us, I think."

"Us? What can we do?"

"I really don't know. I don't know where to turn, who to call for help, or how to stop a hockey team. My dad's in Vancouver, my mom hates me, my friends don't want to talk to me, Frank's locked up in a rest home, the cops are after me, an evil corporation wants to mind fuck us... it's all too much."

"This is the kind of thing you need a coach for. Someone who's been there and has all the answers. Life's so much simpler with—"

"Rick, that's it."

"You've got a coach?"

"Sort of. The only person left I can turn to for help. Although I don't know what he can do, maybe he'll have some ideas."

"Who's this?"

"Master Park."

* * *

"Miss Abraham," Master Park said as she and Rick entered the dojang to the sound of the door chime. "Nice to see you, but you're twenty minutes late for class."

Then he spotted Rick with her, wearing what were clearly not his clothes. His right eyebrow raised in confusion.

"Can we talk in your office, Master Park?"

He nodded silently and waved them past the students in the middle of kicking drills. Rick started to walk in, but Sam stopped him.

"Shoes off," she said as she took off her own.

He followed suit and they proceeded past the curious looks of Jan and the others before joining Master Park in the trophy-filled office. He shut the door behind them and motioned for them to take a seat.

"What seems to be the problem, Miss Abraham?"

"This is Rick Hansen."

"I thought that might be you," Park said and offered his hand to shake. "You've been looking great out there this year. It was quite a shock to hear about your teammate, Jaxxon Downie. Are you interested in taking a class?"

"I—"

"I don't know how else to say this, Master Park, but they think I kidnapped Rick here," Sam said, cutting him off. "The police, I mean."

"Did she?" he asked Rick. "Kidnap you?"

"No way," he said. "She's helping me."

"Then assuming you're not suffering from Stockholm syndrome, I'm not sure what this has to do with me or why you're telling me this."

"I didn't know where else to go. To hide, I guess."

"Why do you need to hide?"

"We have to sort this all out."

"What's to sort out? Just have Rick here phone the police and tell them what's going on."

"Sir," Rick said, leaning forward, "it's not quite that simple. You see, uh, how do I put this in a way that makes sense? Someone's after me, Sam, too, and I think they've set this up to seem like a kidnapping to get us both."

"I'm confused," Master Park said.

Through the Venetian blinds that looked out onto the busy boulevard, Sam saw a police car drive past. It slowed, then turned around and came back, pulling into the parking lot.

"Oh my God," she said. "They're here. The cops."

Park stood up and looked out the window, seeing the same cruiser take a spot and pull to a stop. Two officers got out, looking at the building as if they were confirming that it was exactly where they were headed.

"Miss Abraham, is there something you're not telling me here?"

"Not exactly, we just… can you hide us? At least until we can figure out what we're going to do."

"I will go and talk to the police, but if I get a story that I don't like, I'm not going to obstruct their work."

He left the office. Sam quickly closed the door behind him.

"Shit," she said. "There's no other way out of here. We're trapped."

"Maybe he'll cover for us," Rick said.

"Maybe," Sam said, peering out the window of the office, watching Park greet the two cops she knew as Hooper and Tockett. He seemed to be listening intently to what they were

324

saying, nodding, shaking his head, nodding again, then finally, waving for them to follow him to the office.

"Fuck," Sam said, "he's selling us out."

Rick slumped over defeated into his chair. "That's it then, I guess."

Park knocked on the door, pushed it open and let the two cops enter the room ahead of him.

"Now I think we need to have an open discussion here," he said. "Everyone seems to have different stories."

"Samantha Abraham," Veronica said, "you are under arrest for the kidnapping of Rick Hansen and—"

"She didn't kidnap me," Rick said. "This is all a mistake."

"What?" Jimmy asked.

"She saved me," Rick said.

"From who?"

"Them," he said, pointing back to the inside of the dojang.

The bell rang as two men, both in suits and dark glasses, entered the facility. The class stopped, watching them as they stamped right over the mats with their wet shoes.

"Hey," Mr. Brown said, running over to stop them. "You're supposed to take off your shoes first and—"

The man swung with a back fist, knocking the stocky older man to the floor. They ignored him, heading straight to the office. The younger Brown ran to check on his dad. The two men reached the doorway as Park stepped forward to head them off. Detectives Hooper and Tockett backed him up.

"Give us Hansen and the girl. There will be no negotiations," the lead man said.

"Now just a minute," Master Park said. "You can't just walk in here and—"

The second man snapped his fingers. On cue men in

black combat fatigues smashed in through the front window. Hoods obscured their faces. They carried small clubs and began swinging at the shelves, knocking off trophies and framed photographs of Park with celebrities like Chuck Norris and Arnold Schwarzenegger. In a flash they were trashing the place.

"Why didn't they just come in through the door?" Sam asked.

The second man snapped his fingers again and the men formed a line behind them.

"Final warning."

"River City Police," Jimmy said. "You will stand down. This is a matter for the authorities, not whoever you are."

The hapkido class had all stopped in shock, staring at the strange sight of what seemed like a rival gang attacking them. It had to feel like something out of a movie, but nobody knew what to do.

"Gentlemen." Master Park held his hands out, trying to diffuse the tense situation. "There's no need for violence, we can—"

"There will be no negotiation," the first man in black repeated.

Without warning, his men rushed forward to attack.

In a split second, Park had hit three of them, stopping them in their tracks. Another tried to grab him by the collar. He rolled backward, taking their momentum over his shoulder.

"He can't take all of them," Sam said and pushed through into the gym.

Then it was chaos as the students rushed forward to help as well.

Steven twirled a staff with a chopping blow, Jan ran forward with a tackle, the younger Brown grabbed a man in a choke, holding fast as he took elbows to the gut. The older Brown rose up and tried to restrain the flailing arms.

"Hey, hey, hey," Jimmy said.

"Everyone, enough!" Veronica shouted.

But the men ignored her. One spun and before she could even react, knocked her in the side of the head with a kick.

"Whoa, none of that," Jimmy said and went for his taser.

There were more students than attackers, but the fight was messy and everyone took shots, quickly sporting black eyes, bloody noses, and bruised ribs. Sam did her best to help. One of the men in black leapt at her; she thrust forward, hitting him in the face, but he had fifty pounds on her and they crashed down to the floor in a pile. She squirmed underneath him, but his heavily muscled body pressed her flat. Suddenly the weight was lifted as Rick grabbed him around the waist and pulled him backward. The man swung his elbow back, hitting Rick in the head, staggering him.

Then Jimmy tasered the guy. He danced to the crackling of electricity before collapsing. Jimmy yanked off the obscuring hood to reveal the face of a dead-eyed behemoth with two side mohawks.

"That's the guy from Shady Acres," Sam said. "He grabbed me and Frank and—"

"I saw him at the lodge, too," Rick said.

"He's one of the missing wrestlers," Veronica added.

With the rest of the goons struggling against the student's restraints, the only fight left was Master Park and the two men in suits. Sam had never seen him fight for real. She knew he had skills; he was a seventh-degree black belt after all, but in action, he was something else entirely; a blur of

327

feinting, kicking, screaming, punching, leaping, and twirling.

"This is what you train in, Sam?" Rick said, rubbing the side of his head.

"Yeah, but I'm not that good."

Veronica aimed and fired her taser, hitting the man on the left. He spasmed and crashed back into the wall, knocking over a photo of Master Park with Sammo Hung. Seeing his backup incapacitated, the final man feinted towards Park, then turned and hopped out of the broken window.

"Hey, stop!" Jimmy shouted and ran after him.

"Nobody go anywhere," Veronica said to the room. She threw Master Park a set of handcuffs. He caught them in midair.

"Keep that one restrained. Find whatever you can for the others. We'll be right back. Everyone better be here," she said, looking to Sam and Rick. "I mean everyone."

"Don't worry, officer," Park said. "They will be."

* * *

Jimmy sprinted down the side lane after the fleeing suspect. The man in the suit had a head start, looked to be in better shape, and probably hadn't just eaten an entire footlong hotdog before coming here.

"Be careful, Jimmy," he heard Veronica shout behind him.

"Cut him off," he called over his shoulder, waving for her to take an alternate route.

A foot chase of a suspect. He hadn't had to do this in what felt like ages. Working with Veronica had seen much less action than he'd ever lived with Frank. He wondered if he'd gotten soft from all the regular, normal, boring police work and was paying the price in how badly the weirdo in the suit was outdistancing him.

"Stop, police," Jimmy shouted.

The man said nothing back, simply leapt up on to a dumpster in order to more easily get over a fence at the end of the lane.

Jimmy, already sweating, saw the trouble before he even got to the dumpster.

"Not all of us know parkour, buddy." He awkwardly climbed on top of the dumpster. He leapt to the top of the fence, threw a leg over, felt his pants get caught, and as he threw the other one over to fall down, knew instantly that the crotch of his thin dress pants were ripped to the skin.

"Dammit, stop!" he shouted again.

* * *

The restrained men refused to stop fighting. No matter how much the guys held on, they'd manage to free an arm, an elbow, a foot; swing out with a short blow, and hit someone. It would only be a matter of time before they were able to free themselves completely and do some real damage again.

Master Park locked the handcuffs on the man in the suit who'd recovered enough from the taser shot to try to resist. Park jerked his arms back at an awkward angle and forced him down flat.

"Sam, what do you want to do here?" Rick asked. "If we're going to run, this is the time."

She watched the struggle, knew there was more here than met the eye. She grabbed a hood from the man pinned under the thick-bodied Andy, pulled it off, and was met with the face of another huge brute with dead eyes.

"They're in a golem trance," she said.

"What?" Jan asked as he desperately attempted to restrain one of the men.

Sam walked over to the other man in the suit and patted him down. She felt a bulge under his shirt. She ripped it open to reveal a chain with a purple amethyst set into a locket.

"What are you doing?" Rick asked.

Sam jerked the chain free, snapping it in one pull. Holding fast to the smooth surface, she concentrated on the men and mentally told them to give up. They all went limp, to the surprise of everyone.

"Tie them up," she said. "They won't put up any more struggle."

* * *

The man in the suit was nearly at the end of the alley, where he'd be able to merge into the neighbourhood, quickly get lost in the maze of houses, back lanes, parks, river walks, tree houses and playgrounds. Instead, he stopped, turned around, and crossed his arms over his chest with a cocksure grin.

Something was up, but Jimmy had to get this guy. Whoever he was, whoever he was working for, whatever the connection to the kidnapping, they were in the dark without the answers he could provide.

"Police," he said again, panting now.

The man put an arm on the side of the brick-walled alley and checked an imaginary watch, as if he was bored of waiting for Jimmy to catch up. A few meters away, another man stepped around the corner of the alley, dressed in the same black gear as the others back in the martial arts academy. Face hidden behind a hood, he was built, about two hundred and fifty pounds, with arms that didn't fully straighten. He seemed bloated from obvious steroid use.

"Now, listen," Jimmy warned, "both of you stand down."

But before Jimmy even knew what was going on, the man in the black gear leapt forward, brandishing a metal bar. The taser abandoned back at the gym, Jimmy grabbed for his sidearm, but was too slow. He was hit twice, one high, the other low. His arm went numb from the first just above the elbow, the other shattered his knee.

He toppled over, screaming, watching his gun bounce to the pavement a few meters away.

"Stop," he cried, but they weren't about to listen.

More blows rained down, breaking ribs, bombarding him with pain. He tried to turtle up, but it did little to alleviate the impact from the iron.

"Hands up, against the wall."

Veronica's voice; hard, authoritative. He couldn't see what she was doing, but he assumed she had her gun out and was doing what he should have in the first place. They must not be complying, but Jimmy couldn't move his head to check for sure.

"Last warning," she repeated. "Hands up. Against the wall. You are both under arrest for assaulting an officer, resisting arrest, vandalism, and—"

BLAM. She must have fired a warning shot.

"You, step away from the downed officer, up against the wall."

He could feel the tension from the standoff even if he couldn't see it. Finally, after what felt like ages, another gunshot.

His vision spun as the pain was nearly unbearable now. He couldn't feel his toes. A hand gently touched his shoulder, rolling him over carefully. He stared up into the face of his partner and girlfriend. Her long dark hair was pulled back conservatively and glistened with sweat. Her slightly downturned mouth showed concern. The worry was clear in her warm brown eyes.

"Jimmy?"

"I'm okay, babe," he coughed.

Blood trickled down his chin. Partners in more ways than one, trying to make this relationship work both at work and at home, it had all been going so well until this. This was exactly what they'd both feared might happen. He could tell his injuries were bad from how little she was saying.

"Jimmy, Jimmy, can you hear me?"

He tried to answer, but the words slurred out. His body was revolting against consciousness. The sky above was spinning. It was just one of those things, a risk they'd both signed up for, finally coming to pass.

"I'm sorry," he said as things started to go black.

"Jimmy." She shook him gently to keep him awake. "Hold on, Jimmy. I'm getting you to a hospital. Just hold on."

* * *

The room was a mess; the elder Brown limped to the bench and swung his leg up gingerly. Andy, Steven, Jan, Rick, even Master Park were nursing minor injuries. The five men were tied with rope to the church pews. They weren't struggling anymore.

Sam stared at the gemstone. All of the attackers had their hoods pulled back, each man showing the telltale scars of recent surgery at the base of their hairlines.

"Can anyone explain just what in the hell happened?" Jan asked.

"I believe Miss Abraham may have some answers," Master Park said.

"Those two cops ever coming back?" Andy asked.

"I certainly hope so. I'd like to press more than a few charges," Park said.

"We can't wait," Sam said. "I'm sorry, but if they're willing to come here and do this, then nothing and nowhere is safe for us."

"Sam." Rick put an arm on her shoulder.

She stuffed the gem into her pocket. "Master Park, I am so sorry this happened. Give those two cops my cellphone number. Tell them to call when they come back. I'll answer all their questions. We'll turn ourselves in later, I promise, but right now, I've got to try to stop this insanity."

"Sam, you can't do it alone," Rick said.

"I can't ask anyone to help," she said, looking into Rick's concerned eyes. "This isn't anyone's fight but mine."

"No, it's mine, too," Rick said. "I'm coming."

She thought about arguing but, looking around the room at all of her injured hapkido friends, seeing Master Park's gym trashed, knowing what had happened to Frank, she relented.

"This could get messy."

"It already has."

"Samantha," Master Park said. "I have no idea what in the world you've gotten involved in, but please don't do anything stupid. Let the police handle it."

"I wish I could," she said. "Maybe I can trust those two, I don't know."

"Sam, I'll come," Jan said, stepping forward.

"Sorry," Sam said. "My car's only big enough for two."

Nobody else seemed likely to volunteer, so Sam and Rick headed through the chaos to the door to collect their shoes before heading outside. Nobody tried to stop them. She could hear a siren in the distance as they got into her car.

"So? Where are we going?"

"Back where this started," Sam said. "The arena. There was an elevator that led right into the heart of the whole operation."

"Where?"

"In the parking garage."

"You can't just drive in there, it's key locked. You'll need a pass."

"Don't you have one?"

"Sure."

"Okay, then we're golden."

"It's at home. With Debbie."

CHAPTER FORTY-TWO

Wandering the halls, the familiar feel of Big Bertha in hand. The magnum he'd used for decades, cleaned, stripped and oiled, ready to shoot. He'd end this tonight. Everyone was asleep. All the poor old men and women who were just waiting to die, never knowing that they were about to be farmed for their component parts. He'd save them all.

Jesus rounded the corner, brandishing a longshoreman's hook, dripping blood. He brought it up to his too-long tongue that hung to his neck and licked the gleaming blade clean.

Frank fired. Took the man's head off in a clean blast, spraying his brains all over the white walls.

Ginny shrieked, carrying a giant hypodermic needle above her head. The thing was three feet long with a sparkling tip, A-I-D-S written on the side in bright bold letters. She threw it like a dart. Frank ducked, saw it embedded into the wall behind him. Another needle appeared above her. He fired, blasting her down the hall thirty feet, leaving a line of blood like a road marker, twining the white floor.

They came for him in waves, their white clothes matching the white of the floors and walls, but they weren't white for very long. Each shot knocked another one down in a crimson bath.

Behind him, a slaughterhouse, in front, Nurse Ironhide's door. He kicked it open with one blow, just like in the old days.

"Alright, Ironhide, the jig is up."

The woman was frozen in place, hands dipped into the body of Sanchez, slowly pulling out his entrails. Her hair was pulled back tightly in a bun. She shoved intestines in her mouth, began sucking them back like spaghetti. She looked at Frank with disdain as she ate.

"I know all about what you're doing in here," Frank said. "You can't fool the fool. And I'm the biggest fool there is."

Slurping, blood smeared over her face, her lips pulled back in a sick grin. Her teeth: sharp, pointed, inhuman.

"Time to bust up your little show."

BLAM.

Her face split down the middle. A tiny fountain of blood shot up as the lizard-like tongue danced in the spray.

One more to go. Back to the halls. Every resident stood in their doors now, applauding him, cheering him along.

"Get 'em, Frankie!" Ben and Jerry shouted.

"Give 'em what for," Oscar said.

"Help!" Mrs. Halsey screamed and high-fived him.

"That's what I'm doing," Frank said.

Dr. Hans, in a laboratory, injected someone with another one of those huge needles. This one said DEATH in black.

"Time to pay the piper, doc," he said.

Frank pulled the trigger, was met with only a click. Hans grinned. The needle seemed to absorb into his hands – they both became extensions of it, pointed, filled with a yellow solution.

"Just a little dose, Malone," Hans said.

Frank kicked the man in the balls as hard as he could. His eyes bugged out in shock. Frank chopped him on the back of the neck, sending him down to the ground in a heap. Holding him down with his foot, he slowly reloaded, watching the squirming man try desperately to rise with his giant needle hands. When he'd filled the chambers with bullets, he aimed at the prone man's head.

"Your medical license is hereby revoked."

The blast coated his face with gore. Hans had burst like a zit and Frank felt chunks of brain matter dripping off his cheek.

"Oh, Frank, you did it," a woman's voice said.

There, all around him, were a dozen of the best women he'd ever known. Southside Annie, as young as she'd been the first time he'd met her; Jessica, dressed in combat fatigues. Brutal Suzy, sniper rifle slung over her shoulder; Betty from Lakeshore, smirking in a long coat, Miss Kitty, tentacled baby in her arms. The old gang: Derek, Fuller, Russ Marvin, Stone, Hunglo, Colonel Parker, Blankface, Everyone was cheering his awe-inspiring victory.

"You did it, Frank." Betty ran up to wrap her arms around him. "You stopped them." She started licking the blood off his face like a dog.

"I sure did," he said proudly. "Now let's blow this place and get shitfaced."

Everyone in the room applauded. Jimmy slapped him on the back. He was hoisted up on their shoulders, paraded around Shady Acres like a conquering hero.

* * *

An EKG monitor hooked up to the man on the reclining bed under a blue blanket beeped. He was still alive. The bed, the machines, a dresser with a single photograph on top caught her eye. She picked it up. It was of a group of people posing in an office; a white-haired man in the centre sat in front of a cake with a scowl on his leathery face. A banner behind the group said, "Happy Retirement!"

Police. She spotted the old man, the shorn one that had come to visit, a dozen others that all looked so relieved to be celebrating. She looked at the man in the bed, mouth obscured by a respirator. Tubes hung from his wrist, dripping IV fluid into his veins. His stark white hair was cut short, his skin was pale and leathery, slowly losing its colour. The eyes were closed as he slept. The drugs were doing their work.

The man's breathing slowed, the beeps on the EKG monitor lowered in frequency. He gradually began to deflate into himself. A raspy noise croaked through the breathing mask. The heart rate finally stopped.

Her crisp white uniform crackled as she checked the machines then checked his pulse. Satisfied he was dead, she covered his head with the blanket. Then she opened up the top drawer of the nightstand and began fishing through his things.

Papers, a cellphone, the charging cord, nothing much. Then she found a wallet, pulled out a handful of twenties and pocketed them. An old, tarnished police badge was clipped on the wallet. She pulled it off and tossed it in the trash can with a loud twang. She then took the retirement photo and threw it in, too.

Nurse Ironhide picked up the clipboard at the end of the bed and wrote in it with a black pen. "Time of death, who gives a shit? Next of kin, nobody. Those present?" She looked around the room. "No one. Last wishes? How about feed him to the pigs?" She put the clipboard back into the holder at the end of the bed and walked out of the room

* * *

"So?" Dr. Hans asked Nurse Ironhide as she exited Malone's room.

"It's done."

He motioned to the orderlies, who darted into the room like vultures.

"He'll provide much," he said.

"At least he'll finally do something useful."

The residents began stirring. He saw a few come to their doors to watch as the orderlies pushed the bed carrying the prone body of Mr. Malone out of the room. The authority would be pleased. The man had become a nuisance. But he was just another pest to be swatted away.

He gently touched the body of the old man on the bed as it was pushed past; another life devoted to the greater good, to be recycled and given new purpose. The other residents watched silently, a few saluting the old man as he was pushed past.

"Frank?" Ben asked.

"He's gone," Jerry said.

"Sad," another muttered before turning back to bed.

Only the woman in the wheelchair moved. She pulled herself forward, reaching out, touching the old man's clammy hand.

"Help," Mrs. Halsey said softly as he was dragged away

339

silently, never to be seen again.

Hans saw the scared looks on those who stayed to watch. He knew they all knew that they were next.

CHAPTER FORTY-THREE

Sam and Rick were on edge as they entered the lobby of the glitzy high rise condo building. Everything was quiet, the place was deserted. There'd been no obvious police presence outside, so they just walked in. The door man recognized Rick and let him through without his scan card.

"Hi, Mr. Hansen," he said. "How're things?"

"Not too bad, Hank," Rick said. "Just here to pick up a few things."

They rode the elevator in silence, watching the lights change, expecting the car to suddenly stop at any moment, but it didn't. Sam cleared her throat awkwardly.

"So this is how the one percenters live?"

"You've been here before."

"That doesn't mean I'm still not intimidated by how expensive it all is."

"Debbie picked it out."

"Why her Rick?" Sam asked. "Yeah she's drop-dead gorgeous and all, but she's-"

"You've always hated her."

"Uh yeah, she made my life miserable in high school."

"And now we're grown up. She changed. Or at least I thought she had until she sold me out. Was it all a lie?"

Sam gently put her hand on his arm. "There's only one way to know for sure."

The elevator pinged and they walked down the hall. Standing at his door, Rick hesitated and looked to Sam.

"Let's hope she's home." He knocked.

Sam stepped backwards, away from the peephole's line of sight. After a few moments, the locks unlatched, the door opened, and Debbie leapt out, wrapping Rick in a huge hug.

"Oh, Rick, I was so worried."

He looked over her head at Sam and tried to shrug.

"Where were you? Everyone's looking for you. There's practice today and—"

That was when she noticed that something was off, looked to her left and saw Sam.

"You."

"Me," Sam said.

"Rick, what is—"

Sam lunged forward, grabbed Debbie's arms, twisted and linked them behind her back and pushed her inside the apartment. Rick, shocked at the quickness of the move, followed and carefully shut the door behind them.

"Rick, what is going on? Why is Spot Check—"

Sam levered the arms, sending shooting pain through Debbie's shoulders, bending her over. Using her free hand, she brushed Debbie's hair away from her neck and saw a faint scar at the base of her hairline.

"She's one of them, Rick. She's absolutely a part of this."

"What the hell is she talking about, honey? Why are you—"

Sam wrenched her hard again. Debbie cried out in pain.

"Get what we need and get me something sharp."

"Sam," Rick said haltingly.

342

"Hurry. Being here isn't safe. She's not safe."

Rick nodded and ran down the hall of the condo. Sam kept hold of Debbie, forcing her over to the huge leather sectional. She pressed her hard down onto the couch arm, keeping pressure on her shoulders.

"I don't know what you think you're doing, Spot Check, but it won't work. You—"

"Shut up," Sam said, torquing the arm. "I'm here to help him."

"He doesn't want your help. He has me and—"

"Fuck you, Debbie."

"Sam?"

They turned to see Rick, changed into his own clothes and wearing his own jacket, standing with a pair of scissors and a pass card in hand. He seemed taken aback at what Sam was doing to Debbie.

"Those'll do," Sam said, waving for him to bring them over. Rick tentatively stepped forward.

"Come on, do you want to help me free her or not?"

"What are you—"

Sam snatched the scissors and pressed Debbie down with her knee. She squirmed, but had nowhere to go.

"Rick, please, don't let her do this. She's crazy!"

"Sam…"

"If you can't handle this, then look away." Sam lowered the scissors towards Debbie's scar. "This is going to get messy."

* * *

"Jesus Christ, Sam," Rick said as they rode the elevator down to the parking garage. "I can't believe you just did that."

Rick leaned on one of his old sticks he'd taken out of the closet while Sam clutched a bloody blue stone in her hand. She slid it into her jacket pocket. "She should be okay now. I think."

"Did that thing, that stone, change her?"

"I don't know how the process works, but that's what allows them to control someone not created in the lab. I call them heartstones, but that might not be their official name."

"Do all my teammates have one?"

"No clue. All the ones that were acting weird in the shower probably do."

"Jonesy, Petr, Patrick, Teddy, Dave, Igor..."

She let him work through it all on his own, wondering what it was they were going to walk into. Was this a smart idea? And why had it all fallen on her? If they stopped Arthur Fritz, would that be enough to finally end the nightmare?

Her cellphone rang. She dug it out, saw 'VERONICA TOCKETT' listed on the caller ID.

"Who is it?" Rick asked.

"The cops," Sam said and clicked 'answer.'

* * *

"Am I talking to Samantha Abraham?" Veronica asked. Holding the cellphone against her ear, she exited the hospital and started walking to the cruiser parked in the lot.

"Yes, it's me," the voice on the other end said.

"This is Detective Tockett."

"I know."

"Then you also know that I asked you to stay put at that dojo."

344

"It's dojang in Korean."

"I don't give a shit," she said. "You are in a lot of trouble. Just tell me where you are, and I'll come get you. Then we can go to the precinct and sort all of this out."

"I can't do that," Sam said. "Not right now."

"Miss Abraham—"

"Look, detective, I promise you that I'll turn myself in, but Rick and I have to go and settle something first."

"Is he with you? Put him on the phone for a minute."

Veronica reached her car, put her hand on the roof as she heard shuffling on the phone.

"It's Rick here," a new voice said.

"Rick, this is Detective Tockett. I want you to tell me where you are."

"I'm sorry. I can't right now."

"Rick, you don't have to do what that girl says, you can—"

"She's got something important to do and I'm trying to help her," Rick said. "None of this is going to make sense to you, so I'm not even going to try to explain it. Just understand I'm here of my own free will. Sam didn't kidnap me. She saved me from… well, we'll tell you all about it later. Here's Sam back."

More shuffling. Veronica heard what sounded like the ping of an elevator, the hollowness of an underground parkade. There were hundreds of them downtown, so that clue was useless.

"Samantha, whatever you think you two are about to do, you are not qualified, nor are you—"

"We might just be the only ones who are. Now listen to me. I'll text you where we are. But I need one hour to try to handle things my way. You can be the cavalry to come in and do clean up. Hell, we might need you to save our asses. But that hour is important."

"You don't get to make demands here. My partner is in a critical condition. Things have gotten way out of hand and—"

"One hour. Then you'll know everything. But I need you to do something for me, Detective Tockett."

"Excuse me? This isn't a negotiation."

"Get Frank out of Shady Acres. He's in real danger there. Maybe more than any of us realize. Get him out, send me a pic, and then I'll tell you where we are."

"Malone? He's in Shady Acres because he's dangerously senile and—"

"That's all a lie. But there's no time to elaborate. Just save him, then maybe you can come and save us."

The phone clicked off. Veronica listened to the dial tone for a moment, considering whether or not she should call her back. Looking over at the hospital, where Jimmy lay battered and beaten, possibly even fighting for his life, she tried to understand what was going on. Missing wrestlers in riot gear attacking a marital arts school, men in suits demanding Rick and Sam, a potentially fake kidnapping, a demand for an hour to sort things out, and now a request to save an old man in a care home. This was all so crazy, just like one of Jimmy's stories of his time with Frank.

"I can't believe I'm even entertaining the idea of listening to her."

She dialed into the precinct, asked for the chief. She was put through right away.

"Detective Tockett, I trust you have some good news regarding this kidnapping case?"

"I'm working on that, sir. I wanted to know about those men we busted trashing the martial arts gym. Did we get anything from them? Why they—"

"I'm not sure who you're referring to, Tockett," the chief said.

"What? The guys who took down Jimmy, I mean Detective Hooper, the ones at Tae—"

"You sound like you've been working too hard, Tockett. Maybe letting the stress of seeing your boyfriend being hurt affect your judgement."

Veronica blanched. They hadn't officially told anyone at the precinct about their relationship. They were still debating going to HR when this had all started to spiral out of control on them. But here the chief was confirming that he knew all along.

"Just find Abraham and Hansen. If she won't come willingly, then do what you have to. But ensure his safety. The team has a lot riding on that young man."

Veronica hung up, shell-shocked. The chief had just insinuated that she should kill a suspect, talked about the Jets as if their will was more important than the rule of law. But what was even crazier was that he had tried to gaslight her about the crew she'd helped bust. Was there some kind of cover up going on? Was Samantha right?

She climbed into the driver's seat and buckled her seatbelt. Idling for a moment, she considered her next move. She tapped Shady Acres into the onboard GPS and pulled out of the parking lot.

* * *

Sam and Rick got in his brand new, dark blue Porsche. He slid the hockey stick in the backseat of the sleek model that still had that new car smell.

"Hey, this is nice," she said.

"I've barely had the chance to use it. There's only a thousand kilometres on it."

"I'll bet it cost at least five times what my car did."

"Debbie thought it was a good idea."

"She really took over your life. Did she pick out your socks too?"

"You don't get it Sam. I was, I am, I *still* am, in love with her. We were good together. She was making me a better person. She was-"

"Using you. For them."

"I can't believe that. Not the whole time."

"You need to consider the possibility."

"She's going to have one hell of scar from that amateur surgery you just performed on her."

"She'll be okay, Rick," Sam said. "Back to the supreme bitch she was before. Instead of a supreme bitch under someone's control."

He looked at her, tried to forget the image of Sam slicing into Debbie's neck with scissors, her hands reaching into the cut to fish out a stone, then, gore dripping all over the couch, acting like it was all no big deal. Who was this girl? She'd changed so much since high school.

"I'm telling you she wasn't like that anymore," he said softly. He knew he'd have to get Debbie to a hospital later. The gash was deep. They'd put a Band-Aid and some peroxide on it, but he had no idea how clean those scissors were.

"That could have been a part of the transformation."

"Or maybe you just can't face the thought that people can change."

Rick wondered just when Debbie had been turned. Had her newfound care and attentiveness all been a lie?

"Rick, this is all so much bigger than just Debbie," Sam said. "We're going to stop it. But are you sure you're ready?"

"I don't know. I have no idea what we're walking into and—"

"You've got your stick and I've got my training. Let's hope that's enough." Sam leaned forward and gave him a kiss on the cheek. "What do they always say? For luck?"

"Sam…" Doubts crept into his head. He wondered if they *should* have just turned themselves in to that Detective Tockett.

"We've come this far. We can't let them win now. I promised her one hour. So let's go use it."

Still unsure about the whole thing, Rick turned the key, firing up the eight-cylinder engine. He let it rumble for a moment before pulling out.

* * *

"Sir, we've received word that the glitch is on her way here."

"Let her come."

"Let her?"

"Absolutely. We'll show her the scope of our operation, make her realize the extent of what she's up against, then simply absorb her and the boy."

"Are you sure it's wise to let her inside? She's proven to be resourceful so far."

"What can she do trapped in the nexus of all that we've

built? She'll be ours to take."

"But if she were to find some way to—"

"To what? Destroy something bigger than any single spoke of the wheel? Our lives are meaningless when balanced against what the authority has planned."

"I'm not so sure the team members would agree with that."

"They are even less important than the two of us. Now go and continue your work with renewed vigour. I have to prepare for our visitor."

Arthur Fritz smiled, content that all their troubles would soon be at an end.

CHAPTER FORTY-FOUR

They pulled into the loading dock without incident. Rick had scanned his card, the garage door had opened, and that had been that. He drove the car up to the elevator Sam had pointed out.

"There. That's where I went down to the lab."

Parking the car, they got out and climbed up on to the platform.

"So we just press the button and go down?" Rick asked.

"Unless they've locked us out."

She pressed the DOWN arrow. They waited in near silence, the only sound that of the faint hum of climate control, like a Gregorian chant from the abyss. Then, the house of the elevator rising. Sam tensed up, ready for someone to rush out. The doors opened. The waiting cube sat empty and motionless as they pondered what to do.

"That's it?" Rick said. "No goons, no riot squad, no men in lab coats."

"Doesn't look that way."

"This feels like a trap, Sam."

She took out her phone, showing a timer of forty-five minutes before she was supposed to text Veronica.

"We don't have that much time. I'll pre-type the text, then

all I have to do is hit send and we're golden."

"Assuming there's a signal down there."

She tapped away a note to Veronica, telling her where they were and how to get there. She put the phone away. "It's not the middle of the bush, it's smack in the centre of River City. Whatever kind of secret lair they have, they'd need internet. You can't do anything without it these days."

She stepped into the elevator. Rick hesitated, looking at his hockey stick with a frown. "I kind of wish we had a better weapon."

"You've been using those things your whole life – just imagine you're on the ice and crosscheck a motherfucker."

He snorted. "Sure. It'll be just that simple." He stepped onto the elevator.

Sam pressed the DOWN button.

* * *

The elevator opened into the underground complex. White floors and walls, with blazing florescent lights above nearly as bright as the sun.

"What in the world is this place?" Rick asked.

"Where I found you," Sam said.

"It felt like we went way, way below street level."

"Now you know what's under the MTS Centre."

"I just figured it was Zamboni parking."

The halls were empty, but the rooms were a beehive of activity. One seemed like a full-fledged telemarketing office with row after row of cubicles. Any noise of keyboards clacking, phones ringing, and voices chattering was muted by the door. Sam tried pulling on the handle, but it was locked like the others.

"There's scan cards down here," she said.

"Maybe mine works?"

Rick tried his player pass, but the console near the door simply honked and flashed a red light back.

"Guess not."

In another room they saw a laboratory, with men and women in white lab coats working with strange machines, test tubes, and charts projected on the wall.

"Locked again," Sam said, trying that door.

Another room looked to be a lunchroom: four long tables parallel to each other, a sink, microwave, and refrigerator at the end. Only one man was inside, digging in the fridge, pulling out an old takeout container of Chinese food, and taking it to a table.

"Holy shit," Rick said, "it's Igor."

He wore a black cap and Jets hoodie, and as they watched, he pulled open the top of the box, and started picking out pieces of shrimp with his fingers.

"What the hell is he doing down here?"

"Looks like he's eating lunch," Rick said.

Igor moved methodically, eyes unblinking, face a mask of stone, eating like a robot.

"Something look off about him?" Sam asked.

Rick pounded on the glass to get his attention, but the man didn't show any sign of having heard the noise.

"I think he's one of them," she said.

"They got Igor, too?"

"Just another reason to stop this," Sam said.

The walked to the next room, seeing a man giving a presentation to a large crowd. The lights were dimmed, but on screen was game footage.

"Hey," Rick said. "That's Coach Chapman."

He recognized the Soviet Red Army game film from the lodge, realized that those inside must be his teammates.

He pulled on the door. It was locked, but when he tried his scan card, the tiny light on the console turned green and the latch released. Sam put a hand on his arm.

"Rick, they're not normal."

"They're still my teammates."

"Hansen," Coach Chapman said, pausing in his talk and looking to the open door. "Glad to see you could make it. You're late for practice."

"Sorry, Coach," Rick said.

"Extra laps later, you understand."

"Coach, I—"

"Wait," the man said. "Looks to me like you're not ready for this session yet. Go down the hall, take a right, then another right. Last door. They'll get you fixed up and good to go."

A dozen heads turned to stare at him. Petr, Patrick, Jonesy, Dave, all coldly watching him, with no life in their eyes. For a moment, he thought they were going to get up and come after him, but everyone simply remained motionless, staring.

"Don't make them wait, Hansen," Coach Chapman said. "Show some team spirit."

Rick let the door close. When the lock re-latched, all heads pivoted back to the screen in unison and Coach Chapman continued the talk.

"That was fucking creepy," Sam said.

"A little. I wonder what's down the hall?"

"Only one way to find out."

Walking down the too-bright corridor, they passed an

operating room. A doctor was working on someone obscured by a sheet. He dug into a container and came up with what looked like a kidney, bent down and seemed to be inserting it into whoever it was laying there.

"Organ transplanting?"

"Frank said they were stealing them from the old people in the home."

"This is getting crazier by the minute."

Sam checked her timer. Less than thirty minutes to go. Her phone still showed a signal.

The doctor in the lab looked up, saw them at the door and pointed to his left, as if they should keep going down the hall. Blood dripped from his hands. The others in the room stopped and stared at her.

"Looks like we're supposed to go that way," Sam said.

"This place is creeping me the fuck out."

In the next room, two Jets in full gear were skating on a conveyor belt, hooked up to straps and harnesses that slowed them down as they kicked out with long strides. Monitors on the wall measured their pace. Both were moving impossibly hard.

"More training," Rick said.

"Shouldn't you be used to it?"

The next room contained a wall of jars. The door was locked, but it was eerily similar to the one in Karlsson's facility.

"Brains," Sam said, pointing. "But I don't know why they need so many."

Then they found a freezer door. The small window allowed them to look in to see rows of bodies on stretchers, under sheets. It was hard to tell just how many were inside.

"Corpses?" Rick asked.

"Or new golems."

Every door they came to was something new. Strange naked men, completely hairless and devoid of any skin blemishes, being measured and prodded by interested lab technicians, others in combat gear working on stripping and rebuilding assault rifles, women being filmed by men, a team cataloguing loose body parts, a room of gems being carefully cut, animals in cages, empty offices, then, finally, they came to what seemed like the end of the complex: an ornate set of wooden double doors, glossy and spotless.

"This is it," Rick said. "I guess we go inside?"

"Just get ready to crosscheck a motherfucker."

CHAPTER FORTY-FIVE

"Hansen, Miss Abraham, how nice of you to finally show up."

The double doors opened into a massive board room, with a single long table in the centre. Twenty-five empty chairs were neatly lined up in front of carefully positioned pen sets, pads of paper, and banker's lamps. But it was the man who stood at the head of the table that drew Sam's eyes. He was a ghost: Arthur Fritz. Now that she could see him in person, it was even more obvious that he was the spitting image of Simon Karlsson. They shared the same angular features, the same borderline skeletal face with jutting cheekbones, the same regal posture and same large, thoughtful eyes. The only difference being the hair. Instead of light blond hair brushed back from his forehead, Arthur's was jet black hair combed in a side part.

The room was dominated by a huge screen, currently dim, that took up almost the entire wall behind Fritz. A projector, set into the ceiling above, hummed faintly. The room was large enough to fit another fifty people apart from those who would be sitting in the chairs, but it was only the three of them present.

"I would like to congratulate you on how much of a

nuisance you've managed to be to us, Samantha," Fritz said. "We knew about what you had done to Simon, of course. You thought you were so clever in shutting off the security cameras."

He pressed a small hand remote and the screen behind him came alive, showing black and white footage of Sam speaking to Karlsson, naked hairless men entering the room, then Simon brandishing a stone. The playback continued: Sam elbowing Simon in the face, shattering his nose, then taking the stone. From there, it descended into a slaughterhouse as the naked men tore apart Simon and each other, all while Sam held the stone grimly. When it was done, she was soaked in blood. Her image on screen looked up into the camera and the image froze.

"Jesus, Sam," Rick said in awe.

"You don't know what he did," she said. "He—"

"Do you mean this?" Fritz pressed his remote again and the screen flickered, changing to a grainy cellphone video showing a woman on her knees with two men on either side of her. The mole, her face, and so much more were on display as the video she'd tried to forget played in massive scale.

"What is that?" Rick said, squinting.

"Just another piece of the puzzle," Fritz answered. "A woman who lets her base urges overwhelm her. A confused girl with blood on her hands. A—"

"Cut the crap, Fritz," Sam said. "I know what you're doing here."

"Do you?"

"The stones, the bodies, the organs, the surgeries, the brainwashing, everything."

"Oh, you haven't seen everything," he said, grinning.

The image behind him changed again, to show one of the laboratories. A crew in white lab coats and full-face masks opened up some kind of valve on a windowed chamber. Red goop drained out, through a grate inset into a small platform below. When it was all gone, they pulled open the window, and helped out a liquid-covered, hairless creature. It stepped out slowly, down to the platform, then to the floor. A naked woman. One of the lab workers brought over a huge white towel to clean her off. The face looked up to the camera. Her nose looked familiar, slightly pronounced but still symmetrical to the face. Without hair, it took Sam a minute to realize who she was looking at. It was—

"A clone?"

"Not exactly," Fritz said. "This is more of a carefully constructed facsimile. You'll notice it's not perfect. It lacks some of your more pronounced features."

Sam brushed her hair back from her mole, refusing to give Fritz the pleasure of thinking he'd gotten to her.

"How did you do it?"

"Securing your image was easy. You have been quite busy, after all."

The screen changed again, this time to show a broadcast of an NHL game as seen from the scoreboard in the arena. The kiss cam, flashing through couples sitting together who'd then kiss to applause. It settled on Sam, sitting next to Erin. They both wore Jets jerseys, scarves, toques, held beers in hand. When they saw each other on screen, they cheered and moved in, sloppily kissing each other to thunderous applause.

"Holy shit, Sam," Rick said.

"I don't remember that at all."

"You did see fit to drink a lot of beer that night. Many

nights, in fact."

The screen began splitting into more insets, each showing more game footage, more kiss cams, more examples of Sam and Erin kissing. Upper bowl, lower bowl, near the benches. Six different times, each kiss getting rapturous applause.

"You two became quite popular to the arena audience."

She saw men holding up their phones, recording her and Erin as they kissed, nodding enthusiastically as they were witness to two young, attractive girls making out. One held up a sign reading 'I came for the lipstick lesbians' before it was pulled down by a security guard.

"You did that," Sam said.

"I didn't have to. You did it of your... well, maybe not free will, but let's say your unlocked inhibitions."

"I didn't know what was happening. I was under some kind of control."

"You and everyone else at the game. Some simply call it being a fan."

That's when it finally hit her, they hadn't used a song like they had with Factor 5ive and Radiant Cyanide – it had been something else entirely that had subdued her.

"The beer. You drugged the fucking beer."

"Oh, it's much more subtle than that, Samantha. Our control is a mixture of the complex interplay between the beer, the music, and the movement of the players on the ice. Players like our next superstar here, Mr. Hansen."

Rick tensed his hands on his hockey stick. "I don't belong to you or—"

"Oh, but you do," Fritz said. "To the entire team. The city. The country itself."

Behind them, the boardroom doors opened. The Jets came

in, dressed in their jerseys, carrying their own sticks, moving in two perfectly symmetrical rows, Jonesy in the lead, Patrick Linseman behind him. The two rows diverged, five men moving behind Fritz, five behind Sam and Rick, another five on each side of the boardroom table.

Rick held his stick up defensively, unsure as to what they were going to do, but none of them made any move to attack. Igor stood near Fritz, along with Dave, Petr, Teddy, and Jonesy, while Patrick Linseman, Gordo, Alexsandre, Maurice, and Henrik were between the way out and Sam and Rick.

"There, everyone together," Fritz said. "Like a true team."

He played with a golden crystal, set into a chain dangling from his neck, pulled partway out of his shirt, rolling it over his fingers.

"That's how he's controlling them," Sam whispered to Rick. "If we get it away from him, I can—"

"You can do nothing, Miss Abraham," Fritz said. "There will be no repeat of what happened at Karlsson's facility."

Rick glanced at his stone-faced teammates. They were outnumbered twenty to two. A look of defeat fell over him. "I'm not so sure we can do much of anything here, Sam."

* * *

Veronica pulled up to the parking lot of Shady Acres, still not quite sure what she was doing there. She looked at her phone, but there was no message from Samantha. The hour she'd asked for was almost up.

The care home seemed innocuous enough. A low, brown-roofed building with a sprawling parking lot, mostly filled with the cars of the people that worked here. A few scattered trees, a park bench at the front entrance, rectangular windows... the place certainly didn't seem like anything sinister was going on within. And yet, it looked a little too normal. Like it just might be a front. She wondered if this was her cop intuition at work or just letting the wild claims of a potentially criminal girl get to her. A strange black van parked near the entrance did seem odd, though.

"Frank's convinced there's something shady going on there," Jimmy had said.

"Shady? At Shady Acres?" she'd snorted, dismissing the old man out of hand.

They'd been laying in bed. She'd been twirling his chest hairs around with her fingers, one of those post-coital moments that felt so right with Jimmy. But he would always find a way to bring up work.

"I gave him my phone," he'd said.

"You what?"

"It's probably nothing. But it gave him, I don't know, hope? Something to strive for? He'll go around and take a few pictures, they'll confiscate it, call me, and I'll just pretend I dropped it. Or hell, maybe he uncovers the big plot he's after and this is one last case for him to solve."

"Jimmy, he's senile. And a murderer."

"He was my partner, Ronnie," he'd said.

Now, here she was, walking up to the front entrance, feeling an oblique sense of dread in the pit of her stomach. She passed through the doors and stopped at the front desk. A man in a white lab coat was talking to the clerk.

"Excuse me," Veronica said. "I'm here to see a resident. In the locked ward."

"Oh?" the clerk said. "Who is this?"

"Detective Tockett. Here for Frank Malone."

"Oh dear, I'm afraid that is most impossible," the man in the lab coat said. He had a severe face and wore rounded glasses. Was he a doctor?

She took out her badge and showed it to them. "This says it isn't."

The man clasped his hands together. "Perhaps I was not clear enough – you see, you cannot visit with Mr. Malone because he has sadly passed on."

"What?" Veronica felt a pit grow in her stomach. Not because she grieved for Frank, but because this was a massive red flag. "When? How? Why?"

"It happened overnight sadly. A stroke. As to your final question, you must ask your maker that."

* * *

Fritz stared into the gemstone and pressed the button on the remote with his other hand. The screen behind him flashed to life with footage of the Jets playing.

"Now, Mr. Hansen, kindly join your team."

"You don't control me, Arthur," Rick said. "I'm not one of those… golems."

"Of course you are. You've been one for your whole life. From the time you could walk, your parents put you in skates, signed you up for little league, pushed you into the best training camps. You played a game, lived the life, not even knowing why. You excelled, of course, were given the carrot of a professional career to chase. And you did it all blindly."

"No, I did it because I love playing."

"There is no you, Hansen. You're a cog. There is only

363

hockey. The interplay of ice, stick, rubber, and man that has no meaning, It's nothing more than a thin veneer upon which to hang the dreams and aspirations of your kind, provide an opiate for the rest. It's an industry that absorbs, churns, and spits out. Do you even know why anyone plays this so-called great Canadian game? Chasing after a tiny puck on ice? Tradition? A national identity?" He snorted derisively. "What if I told you it was going to be the instrument of all your downfalls?"

"I'd say you're losing me here, Arthur. Hockey isn't even the most popular sport worldwide. How could—"

"You're not thinking about the big picture."

As he talked, Sam dug out her phone and swiped it. She hit send on the text message to Veronica, telling her where they were.

"We're going to transition every team, control the players and the fans, even subvert nations. But hockey is simply the first step, we'll expand to all sports. Entire rosters of players who don't complain, hold out for more money, demand to be traded. Agents, player's associations, the media; dominoes. And the fans? Docile, self-absorbed, lost in spectacle. Our technology will subliminally make anyone do whatever we want. Consume, spend, drink, live debauched lives, expose themselves, even kill. A global population distracted and subservient."

The screen showed a visual representation of his unhinged speech. Spokes on a giant wheel, spreading outwards to envelop the entire world. It was all so impossible, so vast.

"You cannot stop us," Fritz said. "You don't even know who we are."

He dug into his collar, played with something under his

shirt, then began to peel back his skin, ripping it off in rubbery strips, exposing a white and blue skull-contoured musculature beneath. The face wasn't human. His eyes fell out, revealing that they'd been shells the entire time. Below were glowing yellow orbs, with black around the edges.

"What are you?" Sam said in awe.

"The authority. And now that you know the truth, you will become one with us."

"Not a chance."

"Then you will die."

* * *

From everything that Jimmy had told her, Veronica had always assumed that his old partner would outlive them all. She'd dug into his files a little – the guy was a legend in River City. He'd handled so many redacted and classified cases that she wondered sometimes if he wasn't a myth, or at least partially indestructible. But now Frank Malone was dead, felled by a simple stroke. It made sense, he always sounded high strung.

"Can I see him, doc?" she asked. "I'd like to pay my respects."

"Perhaps you would rather remember him as he was. It can be traumatic to see one in the death state."

She figured she could at least get Jimmy's phone back, if not get a sense of whether or not the death was as natural as they were claiming. Jimmy might never forgive her if she didn't at least look into the possibility.

"Show me."

"Certainly," the man said curtly. He seemed like he was hiding something, but he led Veronica to the door into the locked ward and tapped a code in. When the lock light turned green, he pushed open the door for her.

A few residents were watching television, while some moved through the halls like zombies. The doctor led Veronica to a bedroom in the next hall. There was a body on the bed with a sheet covering the head.

"Here you are. But please hurry. The body is due for... uh, services shortly."

He left her alone in the room. Veronica pulled the sheet down and sure enough, there was the body of Frank Malone laying there with the life gone from his face. He seemed calm and peaceful at last.

In the trash bin next to the bed, she spotted a police badge. She dug it out. It was the old style, from the seventies, tarnished, but still clearly spelling RCPD. Frank's clothes hung in the closet, never to be worn again. She pulled open the drawer, found a stack of papers, scraps with nearly illegible writing all over them. Underneath, shoved into a pair of yellowed and frayed underwear, was Jimmy's cellphone. Looking back to the door, she saw nobody watching, so she gathered up all the papers and tucked the phone into her jacket pocket.

"I hope you got some evidence we can use, Frank," she said softly. "I'm sorry I couldn't have made it here sooner, but I promise you, Jimmy and I won't rest until we figure out what really happened."

Loaded with Frank's research, she looked around the room one more time, trying to see if anything popped out as suspicious. Her phone beeped with a text. She dug it out and saw a paragraph from Samantha, telling her they were deep below the MTS Centre in a secret lab, with instructions on how to get inside.

"Seriously?" she said. "You expect me to believe that shit? Why did I trust you?"

She headed to the door.

"Did you accomplish what you wished, detective, saying your final goodbye?" the man in the lab coat asked.

"We'll see, doc, we'll see."

* * *

Sam dug out her phone again, this time dialing Detective Tockett.

"No one can save you now," Fritz said. "Certainly not the police."

The Jets sprang to life. Rick turned to the approaching Patrick Linseman. "Stay back, Patty." The man ignored him. Rick crosschecked him in the chest, pushing him back into Gordo. Maurice lunged for Sam and she batted aside his hands, coming up with a double thrust into his chin, knocking his head upwards. She grabbed his jersey collar, turned into him, threw him over her shoulder, just as Alexsandre grabbed her by the hair.

Holding his stick high, Rick pushed Patrick back again. Henrik was coming from the other side. He tried to use the stick as a warning, swinging it out threateningly.

"Rick," Sam said desperately. He saw Alexsandre dragging her backward by the hair, as she kicked and fought but couldn't turn to face him.

Rick was no fighter and Dave wasn't going to take care of him this time. He had to do this himself. He charged for Alexsandre, ready to crosscheck him in the face when he saw

Fritz, holding the stone, watching so intently that he didn't realize that Igor behind him hadn't moved. Igor swung his goalie stick like a bat, swatting Fritz's hand, knocking the gem clear.

Fritz spun in shock with his hand dangling open. "What?"

Igor reared back and slammed his stick forward, right into Fritz's monstrous face, knocking his front teeth down his throat. The man bent over backwards on the table, bleeding a gusher from his mangled visage.

"I crosschecked motherfucker!" Igor shouted.

The team momentarily froze. Sam took the opportunity to spin out of Alexsandre's grip, wrenching into his wrist, tripping him. Freeing her hand, she lunged for the stone, diving across the table, sliding along the smooth surface. Fritz slowly rose, saw what she was doing and leapt for the stone, too.

But he was too slow. She had the gem! He grabbed her leg. She kicked him in the space where a human nose would have been. One, twice, four times before he finally let go when her boot shattered the strange carapace-like mouth. He meekly released her, falling to his knees on the carpet, dripping green blood in a wave out of his mouth and nose hole.

Sam, holding the stone, felt the whispers in the back of her mind.

Kill.

Kill him.

The dark energy inside the gem thirsted for blood. The voices demanded action. She sent out mental signals to the team. They all moved together, circling Fritz.

"Babushka, are you okay?" Igor asked her, stepping up beside her, confused as to why she was standing there with her eyes closed, holding a yellow jewel. "Why is my team wanting to hurt you?"

"Igor," Rick said, "how are you down here and not one of them?"

"What are you meaning? I am with my team."

"But the stone didn't work on you. Didn't they change you?"

"I am not sure what you are referring to, Mister Rick. But this place has much excellent food in the cafeteria. I am always coming here for lunch when I am hungry."

"Wait, what?"

But any more questions faded away when he saw what Sam was getting the team to do. They grabbed Fritz by the arms and legs, as if they were going to draw and quarter him. The man dangled in the air, held aloft by entranced Jets. But there were more than just the Jets in the room. Behind them, bathed in shadows that didn't exist, were the mangled, ghastly images of Factor 5ive, Scott, Tommy, and the rest of Radiant Cyanide. They regarded her with blank looks from eyeless husks of faces.

Kill.

"Sam, what are you doing?"

"I'm ending this," she said. "And him."

"Don't." He held his hand out. "Stop and think about it. Fritz is more valuable alive. Just look at him. The world is going to want to see what he is. There's been enough killing. I saw the footage – you killed his twin – and what did that accomplish? Let the police handle this one. You called Detective Tockett. She'll be here soon."

Holding the stone, looking at the already battered form of Arthur Fritz, Sam considered his words. The stone cried out for blood. Scott grinned, the members of Factor 5ive stepping towards her.

Kill.

They'll rip him apart. Do it! Scott's voice rumbled in her mind.

"He's just a cog in the wheel," Rick said. "You heard him. This thing is so much bigger."

"If you knock out a spoke, eventually the wheel gets too fucked up to roll," Sam said.

Kill.

The four Jets holding Fritz began to pull on his limbs. His face grimaced in pain. His body strained against their enhanced strength. Factor 5ive surrounded her. Wisps of shadow leaked from their forms towards her, moving along the floor, nearly touching her boots.

"Babushka, listen to Mister Rick. This will not solve anything. Let your Canadian laws judge him."

Sam paused, thinking about what they were saying. The footage of the bloodbath with Karlsson ran through her mind. She'd been lost in the moment there. She'd maybe even let the dark whispers of the stone overwhelm her. She'd never thought twice about doing it, and yet, killing him had accomplished little. She looked into the dead face of Scott's wraith, saw a reflection of the darkness that had threatened to overtake her. Maybe there was a better way.

"Sam…" Rick said.

"Babushka."

Kill. Kill. Kill him.

You don't have any power over me, not anymore.

She spun and threw the stone as hard as she could at the wall. It shattered into a thousand shards of yellow crystal, twinkling like tiny suns as they fell to the carpet. The spirits of the dead vanished. The Jets all seemed to snap out of their trance in unison. They looked around the room, wondering where the hell they were. Fritz fell to the floor.

"Hansen?" Jonesy said, confused. "What's going on?"

"Special practice," Rick said. "But it's over now."

"Mr. Fritz?" Patrick Linseman said, rushing over to the bloody prone man. He screamed as he turned him over and saw the truth. "What happened to his face?"

"Is it some kind of mask?" Petr asked.

"The police will be here in a few minutes," Rick said. "How about we go and run some laps while we wait?"

"But… Hansen?" Jonesy said.

"Trust me here, guys, this is between them. Let's go."

Confused, the team allowed themselves to be led out of the room. Some looked back, horrified at the bizarre face of Arthur Fritz. Igor put his hand on Sam's shoulder. "You are making the right decision, I think."

"I sure hope so, Igor," Sam said, staring at the mangled face of the monster that was Arthur Fritz.

He started laughing hysterically. "You should have listened to the stone."

Sam grabbed Igor's stick and swung as hard as she could against the kneeling man's head, knocking him out with a clean blow.

"Babushka, that was almost killing blow." Igor bent and checked the man's pulse. Sam wondered if whatever Fritz was would even have a pulse. The monster moaned.

"Key word almost," Sam said.

CHAPTER FORTY-SIX

The noises that came through the phone were a confused mix of voices, crashing sounds, and finally, a frantic pleading before it was cut off. Intrigued, Veronica turned towards the arena, parked in the same back alley she and Jimmy had used the day they'd gone to his favourite hotdog cart, and pressed the call button on the back door they'd seen the security guard opening. It took a few minutes, but eventually, someone showed up, tapped the code in on the other side, and pushed open the door.

"Officer? Something wrong?" It was the same Black man who'd been talking to Samantha, his name tag reading Isaiah.

"Maybe, maybe not," Veronica said. "I got a call from inside and I think I should check it out."

"From inside? I'm on duty here and I don't know anything about it."

"I've got directions, I'll show you."

"Uhhh."

"I'm not asking," she said, flashing her badge.

He reluctantly let her inside.

"Which way to the loading dock?"

* * *

A text came in from Veronica, telling her that she was coming. Sam, sitting in the head chair, watched the bloody form of Arthur Fritz taped to another chair, wondering if this was the right call.

"Second thoughts, Samantha?" he said. His voice was slurred from the missing teeth. "Finally facing the truth that you haven't stopped anything."

"We freed the team, that's a start."

He smirked, then felt around with his tongue inside his mouth. He spat out another bloody tooth onto the desk. Despite his appearance, the teeth still looked human.

"The authority won't stop. They'll never let you go," he said. "They'll destroy you, your life, your city, your country, everything. You have no idea what they're planning."

"You should be planning what you're going to do in prison," she said. "Or maybe the government will dissect you."

"Prison? What crime will they convict me of? What will they find here?"

"Find? There's a whole fucking mad scientist facility. And your goddamn butt ugly face! You just can't cover that up."

He grinned his toothless grin. "Can't we?"

Rick pushed open the boardroom doors in a panic. "Sam, you'd better come quick. Something's going on out here."

"What?"

Fritz just started laughing.

"Igor," Sam said. "Watch him. If he so much as sneezes, give 'em another whack with your stick."

Igor moved from his chair. He brandished his stick menacingly towards Fritz. "I will crosscheck this motherfucker again for you, babushka."

Leaving the boardroom, Sam found complete chaos in the

underground facility. All around her, people were fleeing in droves – lab technicians, suits, confused men and women – taking whatever they could with them: papers, containers, laptops.

"Hey, stop," Sam shouted, but of course no one did.

"See?" Rick said. "Rats leaving a sinking ship. By the time the cops get here, there won't be anything to find."

"They can't just walk away from this."

She ran down the hall, to the clone birthing room they'd seen. A lab technician was helping the Sam doppelganger get back into the glass-doored chamber, holding her hand as she stepped up to the entrance passively.

"There we go," she said. "Nice and easy."

"You're not taking her anywhere," Sam said.

"Didn't you hear the word?" the technician responded. "Full facility cleanout. You should be working on moving your station and—"

"She's my proof." Sam grabbed the clone's arm, trying to pull her back out.

"Hey, she's my team's creation," the woman said. "You're not stealing our credit." She pushed on the clone's back, trying to shove her inside.

"Let go," Sam said. "I'm taking her."

"No, I'm disposing of her."

"No, I'm saving her."

"Say," the woman said. "You know you kind of look like her. Are you from team C? Oh shit, you're theirs! And you already have hair. Wow, how did they get so many blemishes on your skin?" The woman let go of the clone and brushed Sam's hair away from her eye.

"Fuck off," Sam said, pushing her hand away.

"You look just like the schematics. I had no idea there were more teams working on you. Shit, here I thought we were going to get that bonus."

"I'm not a fucking clone," Sam said. "I'm the real me."

The woman tried to pull Sam's shirt up, but she blocked her.

"Come on, I just want to see how their stitch work went. I wonder what organ source they used."

"Is that what they were doing with the old dead people?"

"What do you care?" the woman said. "You're only going to be using them for a few years, tops."

"A few years? Is that the lifecycle of a clone?"

"It would be, if we weren't doing a full blanket erasure and disposal."

"Then why—"

"Look, you can save us both a lot of work if you just climb inside with this one."

"No way."

The clone Sam slid free of her grip. The woman slammed the door shut behind her before Sam could stop her. Locked inside the chamber, the naked copy of Sam sat down obediently, waiting for whatever was coming next.

"Stop," Sam said, slamming on the door. "Rick, help me open this."

Rick tried to pull on the handle, but it was locked tight. The lab technician pressed a series of buttons on the console below the strange chamber and a spray began shooting out of a nozzle on the inside. It slowly filled the chamber with a brown liquid, coating the naked Sam copy until she was totally submerged.

"You're going to drown her," Sam said.

The woman snorted. "Not exactly."

The liquid started eating away at the clone, dissolving her flesh. She imploded in front of them, her component parts drifting into a red slurry. Then the chamber drained, like a washing machine, the combined goop flowing through a pipe inset into the floor. In a flash, the whole thing was empty, with no sign of there ever having been a Sam copy before.

"Okay, your turn," the woman said. "Strip and get in." She pulled open the door and motioned for Sam to get to work.

"Fuck you." Sam grabbed the woman by the collar and tried to shove her inside the chamber. "Let's see how you like it."

"Hey! You're supposed to listen to me."

"Sam," Rick said. "We talked about this. Let the police handle it."

"There won't be anything left for them to handle if they don't hurry up."

* * *

Igor balanced his stick on his finger, working on finding the perfect point at which it stayed even and didn't tip.

"Is strange world, eh, Mister Team Owner?"

Arthur Fritz, taped to the chair, ignored him.

The screen on the wall flashed to life. Surprised, the stick fell from Igor's hands. He turned to see a silhouette of a person against a dark blue background.

"Fritz," a deep-throated voice said.

The man looked up, his face betraying no emotion.

"Your arrogance at your own position has cost the authority much.," the voice continued.

Now Fritz moved, the carapace where his eyebrow would

be raising. "I fail to see how," he coughed out with his slurred voice. "The girl can't do a thing or—"

"You should have stopped her when you had the chance, then you exposed your true self. Now, we have to execute a full facility transfer and move everything we've built."

"But the team and—"

"Your research won't be wasted, we can assure you of that. We've already started using it elsewhere."

"Then I fail to see the problem."

"Which is why we have no further use for you."

Igor watched as the shadowed form disappeared. The screen began strobing, flashing through a thousand colour variations, morphing into patterns that assaulted his eyes. A horrible sound sliced through the air, rippling out of the speakers in waves. Igor covered his ears.

He barely heard Fritz scream. The man frantically tried to escape his tape prison, kicking at the chair, pushing away from the table, but he was trapped. Smoke rippled from his head, his skin began to dissolve, chunks of him fell away, his muscles were exposed, his yellow eyes burst into water puddles. His flesh fell away in waves, melting into a paste, forming a puddle of goo on the base of the chair and floor. The stench was awful, like sulphur and week-old fish. Igor had to force himself to hold his leftover Chinese food in.

When the noise stopped and the images faded away, the room was empty. Igor rose, grabbed his stick and poked at the goo on the ground. Fritz's clothes, in a green blood-soaked pile, were all that was left of him. He gingerly lifted the shirt with the end of his stick.

The door pushed open, and Sam, Rick, and a policewoman came barging in.

"What the hell did you do, Igor?" Sam asked, wide-mouthed.

"Not me, babushka. I am thinking someone did not want Mr. Fritz to go to jail."

The policewoman, looking at the mess, took out a notepad from her coat pocket. "Okay, now we're going to have to start from the top here. Just what in the fuck happened?"

CHAPTER FORTY-SEVEN

Propped up with a pillow behind him, Jimmy picked at a bowl of mush with a plastic spoon as a television mutely played a re-run of *The Simpsons.* His leg, heavily bandaged after surgery rested on another pillow. He needed a shave, his face was criss-crossed with stitches, dark circles had formed around his eyes. The harsh hospital lighting made him look older than he was. Veronica sat on the edge of the bed and rested a hand on his shoulder.

"I'm sorry," she said. "I was too late. They told me he'd died of a stroke and—"

"Did you actually see the body?" he asked.

"Yeah, I did. It was him. Laying there, ready to be—"

"Did you check for a pulse?"

"Jimmy, I—"

"Trust me on this one Ronnie, that old man is harder to kill than you think."

She squeezed his shoulder and smiled, not having the heart to argue with him. He was probably still under the effects of the pain killers from his knee surgery. There was no point in shattering his illusions right now. He'd learn the truth in time.

"They told me you should be back on your feet in no time,"

she said.

"Six months of rehab isn't no time," he said curtly, dropping the spoon in disgust.

"You can stay with us. The kids would love to have you around and I can help you with your exercises."

"What am I supposed to do? Watch soap operas and gain twenty pounds?"

"Enjoy the disability payments. Read some books. Take up knitting. Jimmy, it's not forever. The force will be waiting for you when you're ready."

Jimmy pushed the plate away. "I almost had them, Ronnie. But I slipped up. Now I'm fucking useless."

She leaned in and kissed him on the forehead. "Not to us."

* * *

Sitting around a table in a coffee shop downtown, Sam stirred the foam in her latte. Rick chewed on a Danish and scrolled through game results on his phone. Igor pulled out a sandwich in a bag from his coat's inside pocket. Rick saw a few women in the corner whispering to each other and pointing at him, chuckling when he looked over. Even in this little out of the way place, they still knew who he was.

The door chime sounded as someone entered. He looked up to see Detective Tockett coming in, her coat pulled high to try to keep out the cold winter air. She came directly to the table, taking the empty seat.

"So?" Sam said, looking up.

"I have good news and bad news."

"Let me guess," Sam said. "Nothing's going to happen."

"The chief has buried everything. I don't know if he was

paid off or—"

"Or if he's one of them, too," Sam said.

"Jesus, you think there's more of them?" Rick asked.

"Who knows? We still don't even know what *they* are."

"Very ugly is for sure," Igor said.

"Yeah."

"At least the kidnapping case is gone, and you've been cleared, but there's still a file on you. They might be watching your movements."

"Oh, great. So, what do I do?"

"You might want to consider going on a trip, changing your hair, at least laying low for a while. Maybe take a semester off if you can."

"Put my whole life on hold, sure, that's no big deal. I still need to fix things with my friends and the girl who I was dating while mind-fucked."

"Sam, she's right," Rick said, putting his hand on hers. "You heard what Fritz said. There's something bigger out there and they know who you are and what you've done. They could use your friends as a way to get to you."

"They know about you, too, Rick," Sam said curtly. "What are you supposed to do?"

"I think that Rick is famous enough that he should go back to the team. Igor, too," Veronica said.

"Go back?"

"No," Rick said. "She's right again, Sam. The two of us, Igor and I, we know what to watch for now, who to watch out for. Who's better equipped than us to safeguard the guys and see if any other teams are... infected?"

Igor, seeing a couple leave a table on the other side of the shop, ran over and swiped their leftover newspaper. He

381

rushed back to the table, grinning. "Free, free press!" he said proudly.

"Rick and Igor go back into the hornet's nest, I have to change my name and disappear," Sam said curtly. "What exactly is the good news here?"

"I'm getting to that," Veronica said. "I'm not sure who I can trust either, okay? The force may be more compromised than I know. But at least – and this is the good news, by the way – Jimmy, err, Detective Hooper is going to be okay. He's got a long road of rehab on his knee, but he'll be back to normal eventually. They've given me a new partner for now. I don't know about him just yet, so we need to keep conversations between us four only. For now."

"Okay, so you're saying it's just the group of us and your crippled partner against whatever this authority is. And that the police, members of the Jets and who knows who else might be involved."

"Yeah, pretty much."

"That is bad news," Igor said.

"Don't forget, they could be disguised as anyone, wearing fake faces, presenting as human when they're anything but," Rick added.

"Then who exactly can we trust?" Sam asked.

Everyone at the table looked at each other, unsure of the answer to Sam's question.

TO BE CONTINUED

in

River City Hell Book Three:
THE CANDIDATE

About the Author

Author, filmmaker, martial artist, collector, gamer, dad; Winnipeg based I.D. Russell has been crafting a shared universe of books and films for the past decade and a half. Beginning with the feature films *The Killing Death* and *Cybernetic Showdown* and continuing with the *High School Hell* and *Revengist* book series, his crazy comedy/horror/action stories have found an international audience. *Sudden Death* is the second book in the *River City Hell* Series and the latest project expanding the world of River City Police Officer Frank Malone and University student Samantha Abraham. The next five books in the series have been written, so plenty more is on the way!

Check out *The Killing Death* and *Cybernetic Showdown* now streaming on Amazon Prime, Tubi, Vimeo, and Gumroad. Visit the YouTube pages *Ringo Jones Productions* and *Jeremy Sockman Movie Reviews* for additional content or click to www.ringojones.com to stay up to date on all upcoming work!

Follow on Facebook, Twitter, Instagram, and YouTube!

You can connect with me on:

- http://ringojones.com
- https://twitter.com/IDRussellAuthor
- https://www.facebook.com/IDRUSSELLAUTHOR
- https://www.instagram.com/idrussellauthor
- https://www.patreon.com/ringojones

Subscribe to my newsletter:

- http://ringojones.com

Also by I.D. Russell

The story of Frank and Samantha expands in:

Rock 'N' Roll Nightmare: River City Hell Book 1
High School Hell was just the beginning...

Samantha Abraham graduated, her best friend and golem boyfriend didn't. Hoping to put their deaths behind her, she's off to River City University for a fresh start. Great friends, fun parties; life in the big city was everything she'd hoped. Until she meets Scott, the mysterious, tortured lead singer of the rock band Radiant Cyanide. Their music doesn't just make the crowd go wild, it might be making them go insane...

Suddenly her dream life is turning into a Rock 'N Roll NIGHTMARE

Heart of Stone (High School Hell Book 1)

It's bad enough being the most unpopular girl in school, but when a strange new exchange student shows up, Samantha Abraham discovers she may be in love with a golem.

It was love at first sight for Sam when Joshua, the dark and mysterious foreign student from Eastern Europe, walked in to class. He's dreamy, great at hockey, and she's landed the chance to be his tutor. But the more time she spends with him, the more he seems to harbour a sinister secret. It's starting to look like he's a criminal, but he might also be a monster . . .

With the help of her over-zealous, secretly- crushing BFF Duckie, and with the popular girl bullies nipping at her heels, Sam must go up against a bunch of weird science, and a hellish high school social life, before she has a remote chance of a first kiss . . . or of surviving the Halloween dance.

Heart of Clay (High School Hell Book 2)

Samantha Abraham has the power to magically control her boyfriend's every action, but now someone wants that power—and wants him dead.

After the fallout from Heart of Stone, Sam has learned the truth: that her boyfriend, Joshua, was created in a lab by a mysterious scientist known only as The Professor. A magical ruby gives her the power to control him by thought. It seems like the perfect relationship, until a gauntlet of assassins show up in River City with murder on their minds.

On a quest for the truth that takes her to Toronto and into the den of her enemies, can Sam, Duckie, and hockey-hunk Rick save Joshua's life before it all goes to hell?

Heart of Flesh (High School Hell Book 3)

Samantha Abraham lost everything when she lost Joshua—but the fight for the ruby, and what it means, isn't over yet.

Sam is back in River City and the events of Heart of Clay have left her raw. If deranged necromancers were bad, you'd think Debbie and her slugs would be small potatoes, but Sam's life has gone straight back to hell in her senior year. Even with her high level hapkido skills, and a budding relationship with hockey hunk Rick Hansen, nothing seems to fill the gaping hole that Joshua and Duckie's disappearances have left . . .

But just as suddenly as he vanished, Joshua reappears with grave tidings, and Sam must decide what lengths she'll go to prevent her life—and her boyfriend's body—from falling apart.

The Killing Death

He was ready to retire but then a madman started leaving victims in pieces. Can this aging cop solve one last crime before a killer finishes his deranged pizza?

When an unhinged pizzeria owner stumbles on an ancient Egyptian ritual, he begins a spree of brutal killings that leave a city in shock. It's up to veteran detective Frank Malone and his rookie partner to piece together the clues and catch the murderer. One problem, this isn't just a simple case of catch the bad guy, it could resurrect long dead spirits of evil.

With Egyptian magic, action, gore, and an insane ending you won't believe, this comedy/horror book is a wild good time!

Under Blood Lake

Somewhere in the darkness below the surface of Lake Winnipeg, the Deep Ones are waiting.

He thought it was just a simple weekend trip to put his brother's affairs in order and lay him to rest, but when River City's toughest cop shows up in the sleepy harbour town of Lakeshore, he unwittingly steps right into a community suffering under an ancient curse. Someone is pulling the strings and suddenly he's got bigger fish to fry. Off duty, without a weapon and under orders to stay on vacation, can Frank survive when he faces up to creatures more inhuman than real?

Cursed Words

Some stories should be left unwritten…

Fifty years ago the Van Lundgren estate was the sight of unspeakable acts of evil. The truth has been long buried and forgotten. Now, the house is re-opening as a bed and breakfast and twelve souls show up for the weekend. But some crimes transcend time and when a raging thunderstorm traps them inside, the guests start dropping one by one. Soon the survivors are going to learn that some horrors can never truly be locked away.

Trapped in a nightmare, there's only one truth…

Sticks and Stones may break your bones but Cursed Words can KILL YOU!

Demon in the Sack
Game Over?

The streaming life isn't for everyone. Spending your time hanging out, eating pizza, and playing as many video games as your eyes can handle takes hard work and dedication. But when one third of the popular *Three Gamers* show decides to start looking for love outside of blinking screens and six button controllers, he finds out that while there might be someone for everyone, he's just become the target of a creature not-quite-human.

This one's not after his fame or money, but his SOUL!

Drug Wars Part 1: Lethal Dosage

Yellow Sunshine. More addictive than opium, more potent than cocaine, more dangerous than heroin. It ruins lives, destroys communities, and threatens the very country itself. It will take the River City police force everything they have to fight the scourge from street to bloody street.

Someone's dealing the worst drug the city has ever seen. THE REVENGIST is on the case with a brand new partner and a list of broken lives he's going to avenge. But to find the source of the poison, they'll have to go so far undercover that they might never make it out alive.

Drug Wars Part 2: Blood Money

MechaMountie. The secret CSIS project in cybernetics set to revolutionize the world of law enforcement. Stronger than ten gorillas with a brain faster than twenty IBM computers, the robot is laying down the law in a city under siege!

After the death of Eddie Camponelli, River City is in chaos. Rival gangs are shooting up the streets, attempting to gain control of the drug trade. The police are powerless until the government sends in their top secret weapon.

Now THE REVENGIST is in for the fight of his life to prove that no robot can do his job better than he can. He's going to show that he's still got it, even if it kills him!

Drug Wars Part 3: Iron Curtain

Ninja. The silent assassins. Using ancient martial arts techniques passed down through the secret orders of hired killers, they stalk by night and murder without a trace. Now they've come to River City and it's not to sightsee!

He might have killed the world's biggest drug supplier in Carlos Mendoza, but that only made the real bad guys mad. Now they're after him with everything they've got. In an all out battle for the future of Canada that spans the globe, THE REVENGIST is in a fight for more than just his life!

The explosive finale to the Drug Wars trilogy!

Go-Team # 1: Bitter Rivals / African Assault

The old Go-Team is gone, long live the All-New Go-Team. Led by Jessica "Doll-face" Dawes; they're sent in to infiltrate a tiny African nation in the throes of a bloody civil war. Their mission: to try to preserve the peace in the face of a brutal warlord.

But are the supreme sniper Brutal-Suzy and the kung fu assassin Hunglo enough to take on the American's better equipped, highly public, no-so-secret commando team: Uncle Sam Squad?

It's a battle between Bitter Rivals for the right to save Baangolo in an African Assault full of action, suspense, and… spring break?